KT-523-648

IDLE HANDS

TOM FLETCHER

The Factory Trilogy Book 2

Jo Fletcher
BOOKS

First published in Great Britain in 2017
This edition published in 2018 by

Jo Fletcher Books
an imprint of Quercus Editions Ltd
Carmelite House
50 Victoria Embankment
London EC4Y 0DZ

An Hachette UK company

Copyright © 2017 Tom Fletcher
Illustrations © 2017 Beth Ward

The moral right of Tom Fletcher to be
identified as the author of this work has been
asserted in accordance with the Copyright,
Designs and Patents Act, 1988.

All rights reserved. No part of this publication
may be reproduced or transmitted in any form
or by any means, electronic or mechanical,
including photocopy, recording, or any
information storage and retrieval system,
without permission in writing from the publisher.

A CIP catalogue record for this book is available
from the British Library

PB ISBN 978-1-84866-259-9
EB ISBN 978-1-84866-814-0

This book is a work of fiction. Names, characters,
businesses, organizations, places and events are
either the product of the author's imagination
or used fictitiously. Any resemblance to
actual persons, living or dead, events or
locales is entirely coincidental.

10 9 8 7 6 5 4 3 2 1

Typeset by Jouve (UK), Milton Keynes
Printed and bound in Great Britain by Clays Ltd, Elcograf S.p.A.

For Arlo

Prologue

The claw that held the pen juddered across the scroll. The scroll spooled from the desk, filled with words of black ink. Maybe they would be read, and maybe they wouldn't. The claw continued regardless. It was made of metal and protruded from the desk. In more lucid moments the man behind the desk wondered how the claw worked, how it knew what to write, what machines drove its motion. But he did not have many lucid moments.

The scroll piled up on the black and white tiled floor. The white tiles reflected the orange-pink light of the dying day. The man behind the desk stood at the floor-to-ceiling window and looked through the glass at the inhumanly scaled ruins standing vast and sharp and black against the molten sky. He rested his forehead against the smooth, cool surface. His skin burned and his mind was full of fiery visions: shapes of bone and flame forming and breaking and re-forming in his head. Patterns in spilled blood came unbidden to his mind's eye, and saliva flooded his mouth. The lust for blood was growing stronger.

After the episode passed, after his hands had stopped their twisting, after the shaking had ceased, he returned to the desk and cast his eyes over the scroll. The reports from the Sump and Swamp were still coming in. The levels were approaching tipping point. Already citizens and prisoners of the Lowest Levels had been warped and broken by the seething magics that were accumulating. And of course the warping and breaking had been happening in the Discard for decades. But soon the containments would give way, the Sump would be unleashed into the Swamp, and that which had been buried would return to the world.

The man turned to a parchment thick with spidery scrawls that he'd written with his own hand: blood stocks, from the Library. He looked at the figures without reading them. He didn't need to read them; he knew them backwards already. There was not enough blood. Even though he'd increased the Bleeding frequencies, there was not enough blood. And there would not be time for enough Bleedings to deliver it.

'Troemius,' he whispered. His throat hurt.

A tall, masked Arbitrator stepped silently forward from the corner of the room.

'More blood,' the man behind the desk said. 'For the Library. Discard blood. Constant harvesting now. We don't have long before . . .' He paused. 'Speak to Larissium. She will advise on how much more blood is required to initiate proceedings.'

Troemius nodded, and moved wordlessly away across the tiles.

The man behind the desk watched him go. He could feel another episode coming on. His mind was spinning away from him and his head was starting to hurt. The horns that had long ago sprouted from his skull were heavy; he bowed his head and closed his eyes.

PART ONE

SUMP

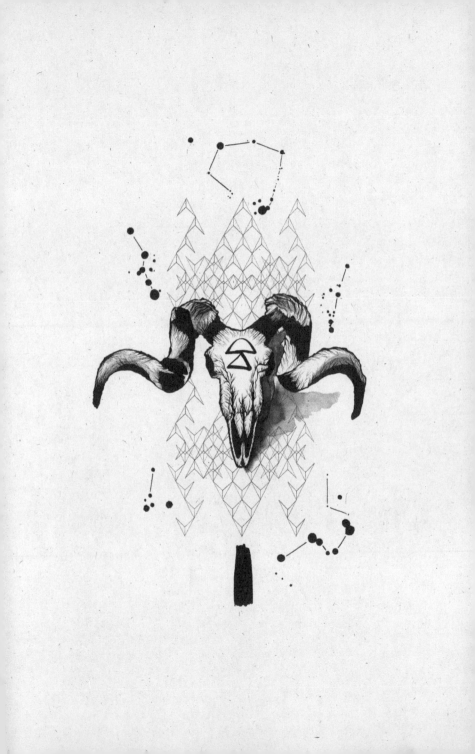

I

Spider Season

The hangover closed in before the night was out. It was rotten and quiet and totally malevolent: an undead beast with venom on its claws, lurking just beyond the edge of vision.

Alan focused on the task at hand: Walk. Walk. Let the hangover come. Carry on regardless. His mouth was dry, his skin sweaty. The rainy season was nearly upon them and the air was close. Small black flies swarmed up from stagnant pools and buzzed angrily around the blooming flowers that grew from cracks in the grey stone ground. The insects must have all hatched over the past day or two, spilling from their soft eggs, breaking free in the rank heat. If rainy season was coming soon, then spider season would be coming sooner. Spider season: when you couldn't take a step without finding the trailing thread of a baby spider wrapped around your face. As a child he'd believed that all spiders floated down out of the sky, come from the stars, maybe dropped by the

Dragons that sped sparkling through the bright night skies of his long-ago youth. What he'd give to be that child again, with the life he'd had before the Arbitrators came with their knives and fire and burned it to the ground. He laughed and cried as he remembered how little he used to know, and how happy he used to be. He wasn't crying for himself though, not any more. *Billy. Billy. Billy.* His son should be free to look up at those skies, free from curfews and Stationing. Free from being bled dry, from being hollowed out, from being scraped clean. That's what the Pyramidders were: they were all husks, all wrung out and used up – and for what? For *what*? They were used up and ground down into dust for nothing but the service of that great stone god they lived in.

And of course, there was the other thing. Billy wasn't just imprisoned in a way of life that *he* hadn't chosen; he was sick, infected by a parasite that even now was working its way through his body. What did Idle Hands look like? What *was* it? Some kind of fungus, he knew that much. Eyes McAlkie, Alan's old friend and mentor, had stabbed Billy, his son, just a boy, with a blade that had been covered in something sticky and black: a medium for the demon that would corrupt Billy's brain and turn him into a different kind of husk, a violent, rapacious host body.

Get a fucking move on. Walk. Walk fast. Let the headache worsen. Let the vomit come. Time now was for nothing but this. Alan was retracing the route he'd taken not all that long ago, although it felt like deep history. He walked a shiningly smooth path built into a concrete cliff face. To his right, the cliff fell away into a ravine. To his left, great statues looked down from over the top of a dark grey wall, their ancient features eroded into twisted expressions. In the distance, he could see a thin arc of stone shining by the starlight: the bridge spanning the ravine.

Last time he'd come this way he hadn't been on foot, and he hadn't been alone; he and his companions had been mounted on motorcycles. Churr had been there, the erstwhile toad-sweat harvester who was now building her own trade empire out of the ruins of Dok. There had been Spider the tattooist, dear old Spider, who had been killed by the Clawbaby. Eyes, Alan's saviour, mentor, oldest friend and betrayer, had been killed by Alan himself. And there was the Mapmaker, Bloody Nora. Alan had last seen her fighting the Clawbaby, but he had to believe – he *had* to believe – that she was still alive, because without Nora, his attempt on the Pyramid would be futile. He'd still try it, but he was in no doubt that if he traversed the horrors of the Sump and braved the security of the Pyramid alone, then he would die. And he didn't want to die, and certainly not before getting to Marion and Billy and warning them of the parasite that was slowly drifting through his son's blood. And he probably couldn't leave it at that; for all the harm the Pyramid had done, there were good people living inside it, people like Marion and Billy. If he was too late to stop the spread of Idle Hands at source, he'd have to warn the inhabitants. But Management . . . what about Management? Management mandated the Bleeding; they mandated the taxes and raids, the partnering and the regimented coupling and the Discarding of babies conceived outside of the correct astronomical windows. Alan spat, but his mouth was dry and nothing came out. He would get to Billy and Marion, and then he would find Management and kill them. He'd crossed that line now: he'd *killed* — and he hadn't only killed, he'd killed his best friend. If he could do that, then surely he could kill some callous, bloody-handed robe easily enough.

But all this was moot if Nora was dead. And if she was, then that meant the Clawbaby was probably still alive, and Dok – Churr's new empire – would be nothing more than yet another lifeless ruin, of the kind Gleam was already full of.

It hurt his eyes to open them fully. A dull ache was growing in the back of his skull. His stomach was a translucent sac stuffed full of filth, wobbling around inside him. If he moved his head even slightly the world tipped wildly, so he kept his head down and his woozy sight trained on the path ahead: the path that led to the bridge. The bridge that crossed to the Oversight. The Oversight that would take him to Mother Margo. Mother Margo, who watched over the bikers' fuel supply and was thus better placed than most to gather and disseminate information. And if she couldn't help — well then, he'd just have to walk all the way to Dok and deal with whatever he found there. Or die. He took a swig from the old Dog Moon bottle he was clutching in white-knuckled fingers, though it didn't contain whisky, not any more. Swallowing the water was difficult — his throat felt all stuck together and it made him want to vomit, but he managed to hold the liquid down. If spider season was on the way, then he was in for an uncomfortably hot few days, as exposed as this area was. And so it was important to drink the water, though he'd've preferred whisky. But that wouldn't be a good idea.

Besides, he didn't have any left.

The inhuman scale of Gleam meant things were even further away than they looked, but as his perception of distance flexed and warped, so did his perception of time. The placing of one foot in front of another required no conscious thought, no exercise of mind, and he passed into a kind of waking unconsciousness. The hangover endured. Tall sprigs of lavender thrust up from between cracks in the stone. Alan ate one of the rat pasties he'd bought in Market Top before setting off. It was a chore; the pastry was stale now, and the filling past its best already, and his stomach was not feeling good. But he needed the sustenance.

He fell down when he came to the bridge and went forward on hands and knees, not trusting to his sense of balance. The air was still and so humid it felt wet, though the sun had not yet risen. This was where Eyes had fallen, and Alan had pulled him back up. He remembered Eyes' entreaties to let him die – he should have. *He should have.* And then Eyes wouldn't have infected Billy with Idle Hands. And Eyes was dead anyway, so he might as well have died on the bridge. Nothing else would be any different, except Billy would not be sick. Maybe Billy didn't even know he was sick yet. The first symptom of Idle Hands was loss of control of the fingers; they would start moving of their own accord. What would Billy make of that? What would any six-year-old make of that? Alan imagined his son looking wide-eyed at his own wriggling fingers, terrified, tears spilling down his face. He'd shout for his mother, and Marion would come running, and she too would be terrified. How long would it take for that first symptom to manifest itself – a week? A month? Alan found himself gasping for breath as he pictured the scene. He stared down at the surface of the bridge between his hands, paralysed. Gleam stretched out endlessly all around him: a pre-dawn mess of concrete and marble and wood and rust and glass and chitin and moss and bone and swamp in every direction. It was frozen and brittle, on the verge of shattering completely. The edge of the bridge called to him: he could end it all, right now. But only for himself. Everybody else would have to carry on living with the chaos he'd wrought.

He pushed away the picture of Marion and Billy and

his breath came back. He gulped, and swallowed air down. He flexed his fingers: he could move his hands again. He breathed out, deeply, and felt as if Gleam too exhaled with him.

He had to keep these thoughts at a distance if he was going to do any good at all. That was something whisky helped with, and he wished again that he had something stronger than water in his Dog Moon bottle as he started crawling across the bridge, moving slowly and carefully. He felt like a slug or a snail, leaving behind a trail of sweat. He could hear the calling of birds, and at the apex of the span he stopped a while and watched them wheeling and diving far below.

He got back to his feet.

He walked and walked. The dawn was met by a chorus of broken corvid voices and more melodious songs from small, bright-bodied birds that flitted across the plant-cracked stone of the Oversight. Alan pressed on as the sun rose until his soles were sore and his legs were burning. He was perspiring heavily in the fierce heat, and the red of his skin deepened as noon approached. Snapper bounced against his back with each step, its strap chafing through the thick, rough fabric of his sweat-stained shirt. Good old Snapper. At least he still had Snapper. He'd give the guitar a tune when he stopped. *I don't have time to stop*. He swung the guitar round and tapped its body, listened carefully to the sound it made. The air felt thick. Rodents scurried and hopped from his path. It wasn't that long since he'd last come this way, but the grasses and shrubs had grown monstrously in that time. The constant buzzing of insects gnawed on the edges of his consciousness. Occasionally beetles arose from the plants, deeply *whirring* like tiny machines. He walked and walked. He picked at plants that he recognised and ate their leaves and buds. And he bore on as the sun sank, its light coloured now by the swirling striped moons, Satis and Corval, that had come to dominate the sky in the late day.

As the sun met the horizon, Alan squinted; what was that low block silhouetted against the sunset? Not Mother Margo's oil store; it wasn't the right direction for that. And as he watched, he saw there were two or three of these things, and they were moving. Probably a caravan, maybe traders. He sighed. He was *so* hungry. He was rationing the horrible pasties, and eating grass and grubs was not exactly hitting the spot. He didn't have much water left either. But he couldn't head for the caravan; he couldn't deviate from his path, not for a caravan that he probably would never catch up with anyway. He was headed to Mother Margo's and then Dok to find Nora. And then on into the Pyramid, to deliver Billy the anti-dote he required. And then back *out* of the Pyramid, *alive*. Though to be honest, he wasn't sure how likely that last step was.

As he walked and as the landscape grew dull around him, his feet got heavier and heavier, and his water bottle lighter, and as his pace slowed, his thinking grew wilder. Fantasies and horrors whirled through his brain.

When he got to the Pyramid he would heal Billy and Billy and Marion would help him escape, and escape with him. Marion would still love him. Marion would hate him, but Billy would show her that her hate was merely anger, and then she would love him. Marion would hate him and attack him, *kill* him. Marion would kill him before he healed Billy. Billy would hate him. Or he'd give Billy the Green's Benedictions, but they wouldn't work. They'd make Billy worse. Or he'd get there and Billy would already be a mindless animal, eyes blood-shot, fungal horns sprouting from his sweet little skull. Or he'd get there and Billy would be fine, the parasite would have failed, or was never there in the first place. Panic unwarranted. And they'd all escape together.

There was another thread to the fantasies, though; they didn't simply consist of healing and escape. There was bloodshed, too.

Alan would get there and save the day and Billy would be healed and Marion would love him and they'd escape, but not together. Billy and Marion would escape, but Alan would stay behind. He had work to do before join-ing his family in the Discard. Alan would stay behind and take his revenge. He'd wreak bloody havoc on the Pyra-mid, on the Arbitrators. He'd find the Commander who killed his parents, who stalked his nightmares and his memories, and he'd kill him. He'd find Tromo, who'd held Billy hostage and blackmailed him into this whole mess in the first place, and kill him. He'd find the Arbitrators who'd tortured and broken Eyes, who'd forced hatred deep into his heart, and he'd kill them. And he'd kill whoever was responsible for the Bleedings, for the fear, for the Discard raids. He'd work his way right up to the top and kill the Chief Architect. He'd tear the Pyramid down, he'd blow it up. And then he'd return to the Discard. Except it wouldn't be the Discard any more – there would be no Pyramid left for the Discard to be an alternative to. It would all simply be Gleam.

But first: save Billy. Billy was the reason he kept putting one foot in front of the other.

And to do that – Mother Margo's, Dok, Nora, Pyramid. Margo's, Dok, Nora, Pyramid. Margo's, Dok, Nora, Pyramid.

The caravan wasn't the only sign of human life Alan encountered as the days rolled by. He found scorched black patches on the stone, a couple of broken abandoned butterfly nets, and on one occasion a still, straight plume of cook-fire smoke visible against the starry sky. He didn't bother with fire; he had nothing to cook. He finished his rat pasties, chewed on leaves and roots and swallowed fat grubs whole, grimacing. And he tried to keep walking. Sometimes he had to stop, but if he could walk, then he did.

There were no streams or even puddles on the Oversight, and now he'd swallowed every last drop from his water bottle. And he was still sweating copiously. His stomach and head hurt, but this wasn't like the hangover; this felt different. His eyes itched, and he was struggling to swallow. There were little succulents with fat round leaves nestled in cracks in the ground, but the moisture they contained smelled acrid; he thought he remembered being told they were safe, but he wasn't sure and so decided against them. A fine rescue mission this would turn out to be: Wild Alan, fool of fools, good at nothing but drinking, dying for want of a drink. And probably never to be found. Maybe never even to be missed.

The Oversight stretched out before him. The sky was bright blue, and clear. Beetles trundled along beside him, many black and shiny, a few bright and spotted. Out of habit he kept his eyes peeled for the highly iridescent sheen that marked out bugs, whose dead bodies were used for currency, but he'd never seen one alive, and neither had anybody he knew. Maggie the Red had once told him that there were none left living, but surely she couldn't know that for sure, not really. He did see a yellow-and-orange striped beetle just bigger than his fist – he'd never seen one that large before, not this high up.

The skin of his face and hands came up in great puffy blisters under the hot sun. His once-white shirt was now stained yellow and brown with sweat and old blood and Green knew what, and it clung damply to his flesh. He longed to take it off, but he knew better than that.

He couldn't recall when he'd last shaved; he just knew his beard itched maddeningly.

In the end he ran the risk and ate the succulents. Safe or not, there was liquid harboured within those fleshy leaves; it was viscous and sticky and it tasted foul.

He felt as if time were speeding up: the sun's arc was moving faster and faster until each day was over in a matter of minutes. The moons danced a complicated dance, Satis and Corval crisscrossing each other's paths across light skies and dark. Alan could hear the music they moved to, the playing of distant strings, as the days and nights flickered by. He began to realise that not only had his hangover not dissipated but his headache was growing worse, and he was now dogged by constant nausea. The great flat expanse of the Oversight sometimes felt soft beneath his feet, sometimes unstable, as if it were tilting beneath his weight and might at any point tip to the vertical, dropping him. He could hear voices, hoarse, unkind voices, whispering into his ears — he did not understand the language but the tone was bitter and scornful. Sometimes he thought he saw hunched figures hiding in the long grass; they had nasty faces and he tried not to look at them, but he sensed they were all around him; he could feel the warm breath on his face.

He didn't know how many days he'd been awake, but he didn't want to go to sleep for fear of what these figures would do to him. But even before setting out to find Mother Margo, peaceful slumber had been difficult. As his mind let go of waking thought, it invariably filled up with images of bloodshed, offal and violently distressing scenarios usually featuring Marion and Billy. The deep, dark semi-coma of extreme drunkenness was the closest thing to rest that Alan had experienced in years, but it had been a long time since he'd drunk himself into that blissful stupor.

He felt something on his hands, and when he peered down, he found them draped in trailing threads of spider-silk. The air was full of it, strands falling like strange rain, and spiders floated towards him, legs wriggling – but they were larger than they were supposed to be. Or maybe they were just very close, hanging right in front of his eyes. Soon they were all over him, and all over the Oversight, busy at their work, and it wasn't long before he was wearing a ragged, insubstantial shroud, and every-where he could see was dressed in webs. Heat emanated from everything.

He saw not just baby spiders but his old friend Spider, riding alongside him on a gigantic motorbike, beard and long hair swept backwards by the motion, red shirt ruf-fled in the wind, and yet somehow he was travelling no faster than Alan's slow trudge. He looked happy – he had been very happy on the bike. His eyes were smiling and his fingers were laden with gold rings and the gold bled into the colour of the bike, which reflected the brief fire of the sunset. Then the sky was dark blue, and so was the bike, and Spider sped up. Alan called after him, but Spider did not look back. The motorcycle accelerated, going faster and faster, until it was streaking away towards the horizon as the stars wheeled dizzily around and the firmament changed colour again and again, and then Spider was gone once more.

The next thing Alan knew, he was crawling on all fours: one hand, then one knee, then the other hand, then the other knee. His palms were bleeding and coated in shreds of spiderweb. He could feel the Oversight shaking, strange old energies vibrating through the stonework of Gleam, almost as if vast machines had started powering up inside the ancient tower of which the Oversight was just the top. The voices in his ears were growing in volume, merging into a long, low roar. Consciousness came and went. He knew he had to eat, and kept trying to feed himself, but each time he rediscovered that his hands were empty.

2

Skeffington Lutwidge
and the Carcase

The rumbling roar had been the last thing to leave him, and it was the first thing to come back. At first he was aware of nothing but that thunder, then he felt cool air on his skin. *Cool air.* That was unusual enough to prod his brain into action. He realised that he must be waking up.

The sound was that of engines: he was strapped onto the back of a motorbike, surrounded by the fire, fumes and lanterns of what looked like a hundred other bikes, and all of them were racing through a black night. He immediately saw — and was relieved to find — that the days and nights were no longer only seconds long; the darkness was steady. The smells of oil and leather filled his nostrils. There was a large, rotund figure sitting in front of him; it was wearing a tight black vest with a face on the back, partly obscured by the biker's thick, greasy plait. As Alan's eyes adjusted, the image resolved itself into the long face of a goat, slot-eyes gazing coldly out, long horns curving into vicious points.

Alan's hands were cuffed, and with a jolt of horror, he realised that Snapper was no longer on his back. He looked the goat in the eyes. Well. Nothing else for it.

He leaned forward, caught that greasy, matted rope of hair between his teeth and wrenched his head backwards, hard. The biker leaped in his seat and howled, so loudly that Alan thought he could hear the shriek over the sound of all of the engines around them. The bike wobbled, then swerved, peeling off from the pack as the biker tried to regain control of it, and as the rest of the hot, buzzing swarm moved on, suddenly reduced by speed to a mass of giant fireflies, they were alone on the Oversight. The biker twisted slowly in his seat and backhanded Alan across the face, a lazy movement, but still Alan felt metal studs break the skin and blood burst from his nose. If it hadn't been for his being cuffed to the bike, he would have been thrown off the machine.

The biker didn't stop the bike.

Alan's handcuffs were threaded through a metal ring to the right of the seat. He raised his left leg and with some difficulty managed to manoeuvre himself so that he was sitting side-saddle, facing the right. The air rushed past, flattening his hair across his eyes. His face hurt. His captor didn't appear to have noticed him changing position. His arms were across his body, secured on his left. He took a deep breath, twisted, and placed his feet flat against the side of the bike on either side of the loop. *Now* his captor turned to look — and Alan headbutted him directly on the nose, *hard*.

The biker's head snapped backwards and he let go of the handlebars with his right hand to hold his nose. The biker hung there, leaning backwards out from the bike, eyes furious and panicked over the held nose. Had Alan hit him hard enough to really throw him? Or was he just going to right himself? For a moment Alan wasn't sure which way it was going to go; the biker was maybe gathering strength for a counter-attack — but his eyes widened and he slipped slowly further and further from his seat until he was falling. He kept hold of the handlebar though.

The biker landed heavily on his back and the bike went over onto its side, wheels screeching as they tried to maintain purchase on the stone. Alan found himself almost on all fours on top of the bucking vehicle, his feet still planted against the side of the machine, his hands bound to it via the cuffs — but only for a moment, and then he was catapulted heels over head to land on top of the biker. His boot connected with something soft and there was another shout. The bike's wheels bounced against the ground and gained momentary traction, dragging Alan immediately away again. It spun around in circles, throwing Alan about like a wet rag. He was dimly aware of the biker getting up, but couldn't focus on much other than the bike. He yanked with all his might at the loop that he was cuffed to, but his might wasn't all that much. His wrists, elbows and shoulders felt like they were at breaking point. The loop was just a thin metal thing, probably for clipping luggage to. He tried to smack it with the cuffs themselves, ignoring the pain as the cuffs transferred the pressure of the impact directly to the soft skin of his wrists: it hurt like hell, but it did make a dent. He tried it again, kneeling on the side of the hot bike as it juddered. He was about to try a third time but he was tossed forward and hit his face. A meaty hand swiped at him, but missed, thanks to the motion of the bike. Alan got back to his knees and with the third smack, the loop snapped and broke. Freeing himself, he reached for the handlebars – if he could just get this damned thing upright, he could – *just imagine how fast he could go, how quickly he could get there, if*— He tried to lift it and mount it at the same time, but it was heavy, and he still had his cuffs on. *If only*—

The biker grabbed him from behind, pulled him from the bike as easily as if he were a child's doll and threw him to the ground. He jumped onto Alan's back, knees first, and knocked all of the breath from his body, then he grabbed Alan by the hair and lifted his face from the stone.

'Mess up me bike, would yer?' he hissed into Alan's ear. His breath carried the sharp scent of wasproot; a bitter tuber that lent a weird, manic energy when chewed. 'Mess up me nose? Count yer lucky stars Skeffy wants yer alive, otherwise I'd pulp yer and leave yer here to rot.'

'My guitar,' Alan said, hoarsely, spraying blood as he spoke. 'Where's my guitar?'

'Skeffy's got it. It's safe, as long as yer behave.'

Alan decided against asking who Skeffy was yet. 'Water, then,' he said. 'I want some water. I *need* it.'

After a moment, the biker passed Alan a hard, hairy wineskin. Alan put the wineskin to his mouth, tipped it back and drank greedily. The water was warm and tasted old, but it was still an effort to stop himself from guzzling it all. 'Thank you,' he said, between gulps. His mouth didn't feel quite like it was coated in slug-slime any more. 'I mean it,' he added. He went to drink some more, but the biker snatched the wineskin back again. 'Who are you?' Alan asked. 'Why do you want me at all?'

'Name's Byron. I'm with the Goatherds, Oversight Chapter. As for the why, well the boss wants what the boss wants. You know bosses.' Byron was hauling him back to the bike by the hair. The fight had apparently taken nothing out of him, while Alan felt like he'd been through the wringer. 'Got to truss you up like a Green-damned goat now. Can't have yer trying to run again.' The biker clicked open a pannier and pulled out a bundle of straps. He waved it in front of Alan's face. 'Look what yer get for being an arsehole.'

'Look, I don't want to fight. You're stronger than me, you'll just win. But I have to get where I'm going quickly. I can't – I haven't got *time* to go with you—'

'Tough. You don't have a choice, Alan.'

'How do you know my name?'

'Whole bleeding territory'll know your name 'fore long.'

'But—'

'Time to shut the fuck up now, Mister.' Byron hit Alan again and his vision swam. The biker started trussing him up and he did not feel able to fight back. He was a giant of a man, smelling of leather and grease. His smoked-glass goggles looked tiny on his large face, giving the impression of black holes where his eyes should have been. Alan felt like something small and breakable, perched on the bike behind him. He was pale for a Discarder, but bikers often were. They used the wide tunnels, corridors and channels of the original structure to get around, which meant travelling the lower levels, unlike other Discard denizens. The speed of their vehicles was an effective protection against the dangers that deterred others from making those journeys on foot.

And so it was in the company of Byron that Alan finally reached his initial destination, which was the gigantic fuel tank on top of which Mother Margo lived in a flimsy wooden hut. Upon their arrival, some of the Goatherds turned their engines off and started building fires, while others took off again to race about or spin their machines, their whoops and cries and laughter carrying through the night and communicating the sort of unqualified happiness that Alan had not experienced for too long.

Byron untied Alan from the bike, but left his hands bound. 'I need to take you to Skeffy,' he announced.

'Who is this Skeffy?' Alan asked. 'Your leader, right?'

'Yes, but leader of all the Goatherds, not just the Oversight Chapter.'

'King of the Goatherds,' Alan said, stretching as best he could. His legs felt weak, his stomach sensitive, and an ache still throbbed in his head. 'I'd better prepare myself. Why are you called the Goatherds, anyway?'

'Why d'you think? We look after the goats.'

'What does that mean?'

Byron looked at Alan as if he was stupid.

'You're not talking about actual goats,' Alan said.

'I am,' Byron said. 'Actual, real living goats.'

'Where are they, then? I haven't seen any.'

Byron shrugged. 'Discard's a big place. We've got droves and droves of 'em roaming around the courtyards.'

As they spoke, Byron led Alan towards the shadow of the fuel tank, passing between burgeoning fires, cooling-down motorcycles and bikers rummaging around in boxes and saddlebags for food and drink. Some were already sitting down and playing cards. Most ignored him, but a couple gave him curious looks.

Then, in the distance, another swarm of lanterns became visible. 'More Goatherds?' Alan asked.

Byron looked. 'Yeah, all the chapters are gathering.'

'What's the occasion?'

'Don't know yet. Skeffy called the meet, and when

everybody's here he'll tell us. Something's happening, though, no doubt about that.'

'Is this a rare thing?'

'I've never known it happen before, not since I became a biker. And others who've been bikers much longer than me have never known it happen before either.'

'When did you become a biker, then? How do you even become a biker?'

'They picked me up, didn't they? When I was starving in the dust. I was thirteen and I'd just been Discarded out the Pyramid and I didn't stand a chance. They just happened by, and they picked me up. And that was that.'

'You're a Pyramidder? You *were* a Pyramidder?'

'I was, but I'm not any more, and I'm glad of it. Anyway, look: we're here now.'

Alan glanced towards where Byron was indicating and was immediately transfixed by a gigantic trike, quite the most magnificent machine he'd ever seen. It had tyres three times the width of most of the others, with the front wheel extending way out ahead, long low forks gleaming in the firelight. The chassis was bulked out with curved panels and shields of polished brass. A myriad mirrors bristled from its handlebars, between which was mounted a majestically horned goat skull. The vehicle didn't have a saddle so much as a recessed seat, like a leather nest sunk into the frame. Furs and silks draped the metalwork.

'This is the Carcase,' Byron said proudly, clarifying, 'Skeffington Lutwidge's trike and throne, his pride and joy.'

'It's very nice,' Alan said, still staring. The Carcase radiated heat and, just as tangibly, a kind of coiled-up, ready-to-pounce power. 'He just leaves it lying around like this?'

'He does,' came a husky voice from behind them. Byron and Alan spun around. Byron bowed. Alan did so too, a moment later.

Skeffington Lutwidge stood a good head taller than Alan, and was more broadly built. His face was lean, his skin dark brown, his short stubble white. Unlike most of the other bikers he wore a leather jacket with long sleeves, buttoned up despite the heat, and white linen trousers. On his head was a round leather cap with the same sort of goggles Mother Margo wore – as had Loon the Maker, Alan recollected, back at the House of a Thousand Hollows, to protect her eyes when she was working over the cauldron. Skeffington's hands were ungloved, and he had an identical gold ring on each middle finger. The faded tattoos on the backs of his hands were partially obscured by the cuffs of his jacket.

Snapper was strapped to his back.

Skeffington lifted the goggles, revealing cold blue eyes. 'I trust my fellow Goatherds with both my life and my Carcase,' he said. 'Do you think I am mistaken to do so?'

'No,' Alan said, then took a deep breath and corrected himself. 'I mean, I don't know, do I? I don't know the Goatherds very well. But you *do* know them, so if you trust them, then fine. Now, I need my guit—'

'I found the Carcase deep, deep down,' Skeffington said, suddenly stepping over to the trike and placing a hand on the curved metal of the fuel tank. 'Out in Forge Country. Deep, deep down, all greened and rusted by the encroaching swamp. It was lapping at her wheels. And on top of her was a length of heavy chain, fallen from a great height. She was ancient and broken and nearly sunk, but I found her and I dragged her through the slanted hallways all by myself. Forge Country is an evil place – everything is coated in poisonous black ash, and the swamp is full of thick oils, and strange-coloured flames erupt from it, and foul vapours make the air difficult to breathe. Everything is made out of once-molten metal that has solidified into shapes from the worst of your nightmares, and it is haunted by the swamp-twisted creatures that flee the Pilgrims' defences around Dok.' He walked around the Carcase and then lifted his gaze to meet Alan's. 'Or perhaps I should say *fled*.' He smiled thinly. His eyes remained icy. 'They flee no longer, of course, because the defences are no longer there.'

'Are – are they not?' Alan asked.

'They are not, Wild Alan. But of course, you know that.'

'How do you know my name?'

'You are a wanted man. It is lucky for those of us who might wish to claim the bounty on your head that you have decorated your skin so distinctively.'

'Wanted by who?'

'The Lady Redcapper, for one – she believes you stole from her. And refugees from Dok desire revenge for the destruction of the Sanctuary and their sacred Terrarium. And of course, there is the Pyramid: there are more Arbitrators abroad in the Discard than ever before, and during those brief moments when they're not brutalising Discarders with their fists and their feet and their swords, they repeat, "Wild Alan. Wild Alan. Wild Alan." Though their reasons for desiring you are not well known.'

'So you were all out here looking for me?'

Skeffington laughed at that. 'No! Do not flatter yourself. You were a lucky find. Or maybe a gift from Old Green himself.'

Alan snapped. 'Look. I have been walking for days. I *cannot* be delayed. I'm exhausted. I'm a mess. And I need my guitar back. If you're going to kill me, kill me. If you're going to hand me over, just fucking . . . knock me out and do it. If you're not going to do either of those things then give me back my instrument. I have *not* got the energy for any long, drawn-out, wait-and-see snakeshit. Let's just get it over with.'

Skeffington surveyed him coolly. 'Well, then,' he said, at length. 'You and I had best go on up the ladder to consult with Mother Margo.'

Skeffington beckoned Byron, who hurried forward and sliced through Alan's bonds. Then he gestured towards the hulking great fuel tank protruding from the surface of the Oversight like the tip of a giant obelisk thrust up from beneath, or a vast metal artefact that had fallen from the heavens, punctured the ground here and become stuck. Corval, hanging in the sky behind it, turned it into a sharp black silhouette.

'After you,' Skeffington said.

Mother Margo was peering down from the edge of the tank, blunderbuss in her hands, muttering. 'Excitement . . . a lot of excitement for this time of night. If I slept it would have woken me.' Then, as Alan reached the top of the ladder, 'Who's this then? Who's this idiot?'

'It's me – Alan,' Alan said, flinching from the dented funnel of the gun levelled at his head. 'We've met before.'

'Have we? I don't remember.'

'I sang for you.'

Mother Margo mouthed words, her eyes invisible behind her goggles, and her sharp teeth, unevenly spaced, flashed in the firelight. Eventually she said, 'You sang for me and my baby. Baby Beetle. That was you, wasn't it? Yeah, you were okay. You were okay. You didn't hurt us none. You're a good one. You and Skeffy Lutwidge, you're good folks. Not many of us left.' She burst into a peal of laughter.

At first, Alan was touched and he smiled. So not *everybody* thought him a destructive waste of skin after all. But the warmth didn't last long; within moments he wanted to correct her: *I maybe didn't hurt you, but I've hurt plenty of others, or caused them to be hurt.* He didn't, though; he kept his mouth shut and let her believe what she believed. There was nothing in it for him, but perhaps there was for her.

'Yes,' he said, 'Baby Beetle. That was me. I'll play it again for you if you like – if Mr Lutwidge here would be so kind as to return my guitar.'

'You can have your guitar,' Skeffington said, sliding his arm through the strap, 'and you can call me Skeffington. I am Mr Lutwidge to nobody.' He carefully handed Snapper to Alan – almost reverently, in fact.

Alan took the guitar and immediately felt more peaceful. 'Thank you,' he said. He ran his fingers across the strings and Snapper quietly spoke. Instinctively, unthinkingly, Alan started tuning it.

'Your guitar is to you what the Carcase is to me,' Skeffington said. 'I can see that. I would not keep her from you.'

'You're right,' Alan said, adjusting the strap, 'except Snapper isn't a "she".'

'A he, then?' Skeffington said. 'I have picked up many Pyramidders exiled from the Pyramid for the non-crime of loving another of the same sex – picked them up out of that deathly dust. Young Byron down there was amongst them. I did not mean to presume that you are not such a man. I apologise.'

'No,' Alan said, 'no, Snapper's not a "he", either. Snapper's just . . . *Snapper*. Not neither, and not both.' He looked over the instrument. 'Though if Snapper is to me what the Carcase is to you, you might think me negligent in my care.'

'It is as if you know Snapper to be a companion, and yet still treat it like a tool.'

'Yes,' Alan agreed.

'I imagine you treat any human companions in much the same way.'

'I do not.'

Skeffington surveyed him impassively. 'Well,' he said, 'I am not interested in whether my assessment is true or not. I am merely relating it to you. Enough of this.' He turned to Mother Margo and bowed low. 'Our Mother,' he said, 'Keeper of the Rock. How goes it with you? Have you blown the heads from the bodies of any attackers of late? Has your blunderbuss served you well?'

'Oh,' laughed Margo, 'just a few! If when their heads pop up there's a knife 'twixt their teeth, that's it. I don't give them a chance, no, I don't. Just point it at them and *fire! fire!* Let the rodents finish them, once they're down there bleeding on the ground. Let the rodents drag them off.' She grinned. 'And they all have knives 'twixt their teeth these days, they do. Oh yes they do. Everybody's worried about something.'

'And how are you otherwise?'

'You know I like this season, Skeffy. The heat, I like the heat. It relaxes me, it does. You know how cold I get – my little love, she makes me awful cold sometimes, she does.' Mother Margo patted the side of her long wax jacket, where, Alan knew, she kept the small coffin of her baby daughter. 'And the spiders'll be good eating when they're a bit fatter, make a nice change from snail. I get sick of snail, I do. And the grasses are getting big and juicy too. Oh yes, times are good for old Mother Margo. These are the best of times for me.' She paused to pick her teeth. 'You'll be wanting news, Skeffy, eh?'

'Only if there is any.'

'You know all about this'n here, I take it?' She waved a dirty gnarled hand at Alan.

'I do indeed.'

'What?' Alan asked. 'What do you mean? What do you—?'

Skeffington held up a hand. 'Please, Mother,' he said, 'continue.'

'Other bikers have told me that the surviving Pilgrims have settled up topside. They've sent some back down to Dok to assess the damage and they're waiting for reports. But they're not happy, and they're not coping with the heat – they don't love it, not like old Mother Margo does. They're nearly swampies. And they're telling tales about some beast: a great black shadow, with glowing green eyes and razor-blade fingers. It came with laddo here' – she pointed at Alan – 'and laid waste before being driven off into the swamp, leaving laddo and his mates to loot and pillage to their hearts' content. And the Sadist has recalled all her thugs, and we can all guess at what *she's* up to. I press the odd wolf who rides for her when they stop by for the fuel, but they keep their lips tight. She knows how to rule her people, that one does. What one of them did tell me, though – and you'll like this, Skeffy – is, there's been a collapse! A great dome to the east – and what came out from underneath it? Old Green himself, they're saying! A gigantic croc with six legs and a working brain. Not like one of those specimens some trickster's stitched together. Anyways, it thrashed off into the swamp, if you can believe it!'

'Old Green I don't believe,' Skeffington said; 'that sounds like elaboration. But the collapse? That is verifiable, and if true, it is very worrying.'

'I've never known of a collapse before,' Alan said.

'Nor me. Nor anyone,' Skeffington said. 'That Gleam does not collapse is one of the fundamentals.'

'Unless it wasn't a collapse,' Alan said.

'It weren't!' Margo said. 'It was Old Green!' And then she was laughing again. 'Other news – aye, there was a bit. This one's bandit friend has put out a call to arms.'

'My bandit friend?' Alan asked.

'The one you helped conquer Dok,' Skeffington said.

'I didn't help her!' Alan protested. 'I didn't want her to do what she did! And anyway, it wasn't us; it was the Clawbaby. Churr just . . . took advantage of what the thing had done.' *Before it was driven off into the swamp.* So it was still alive. Alan shuddered. Though it sounded as if Nora was, too. Fear and hope tussled in his roiling belly.

'We should tell him,' Mother Margo said to Skeffington,

and when he nodded, she withdrew a tightly rolled scroll from inside her coat. 'Found this on a would-be fuel thief,' she said, and tossed it to Alan.

Alan unrolled the document. He could just about read it in the light of the dawn. Across the top in capitals were the words:

WANTED: DEAD OR ALIVE

Below that was a picture – of him, he realised, not very well drawn, but enough. The artist had paid particular attention to his tattoos, and done a good job of them at least. Below the picture it read:

REWARD: 1000 BUGS

The poster was marked with Daunt's mushroom symbol.

'A thousand bugs?' Alan said. 'I'd turn myself in if I could.'

'You're making light of a pretty bleak situation,' Skeffington commented. 'I could do a lot with a thousand bugs myself.'

'You don't intend to hand me over to Daunt,' Alan said. 'I'm vulnerable right now, but I'm not stupid. If that was your intention, you'd have left me tied up down there.'

'What I want to make clear is this: whether it was you or your bandit friend – or indeed, this "Clawbaby" – who was responsible for what happened to the Pilgrims, Daunt is holding you responsible, and she is doing a good job of *making* you responsible in the eyes of the Discard. Since news got out about your ruinous jaunt, she has put two and two together. You went to Dok and destroyed it for the Benedictions: hence, it was you who stole the Benedictions from her in the first place. And of course you've laid waste to her supply chain. She is not happy, Alan, and she is preparing to act. She intends to punish you and to take back what was hers, and more than that, even. She intends to seize the source itself and manage the entire production of the mushrooms, as well as the distribution.'

'She'll need the Pilgrims.'

'I'm sure she'll have them. Who would you ally yourself with, if you were a Pilgrim? Your established trading partner, or the handful of angry, disrespectful freaks who desecrated your holy place? The Pilgrims and Daunt have common enemies: you, your bandit friend and . . . the Mapmaker.' Skeffington fell silent and gazed at Alan.

'So what?' Alan snapped. 'What? What do you want?'

'I want the Mapmaker. You must deliver her to me, or I will deliver you to Daunt.'

' "Deliver her to you"? What do you mean? I'm going to find her because I need her help. If she can't help me, if I have to betray her to you, you may as well give me to Daunt and let her kill me. Without Nora I'll die anyway.'

'What I mean, Alan, is that you either persuade or mislead your Mapmaker friend into meeting with me.'

Alan laughed. 'And then what? You think she'll help you if she doesn't want to? She won't be captured and bound by you, not like I've been. Why do you even want her anyway?'

'Originally I approached the Mapmaker Council, but they would not speak to me – they do not *help* anybody; they appear to regard helping as a kind of servitude. Their representative told me that they have their own Work, and the Work of others does not concern them. What I want is to lead my Goatherds to safety. I want to leave, and I would like a Mapmaker to help.'

'What do you mean, *leave*?' Alan asked. 'Leave what?'

'Gleam,' Skeffington said. 'Leave Gleam. Its time is coming to an end. You can read the signs if you know how.'

'There's nothing beyond it,' Alan said.

'How do you know?'

'Nobody's ever found the end of it.'

'How do you know?'

'Well,' Alan said, discomfited, 'you can't expect Nora just to help you, even if I get her to you.'

'I will hold you responsible if she is not cooperative. You persuade her, or you render her powerless. How you do it is up to you, but if you don't, I will hand-deliver you to the Lady Redcapper herself.'

A bridge to cross when he came to it. 'The sooner I get

to Dok, the sooner I can get you what you want. Give me a bike.'

'Never. You will abscond with it.'

'Assign me one of your people. Somebody who won't let me steal it.'

Byron stepped forward. 'Me,' he said. 'I'll do it.'

'No!' Alan said, 'not that oaf — I didn't mean *him*. Why do you want to do it, anyway? You hate me.'

'I've got me reasons.'

'I burst your nose, I dented your bike. I nearly had you.'

'You were nowhere bloody near. And like I said, I've got me reasons.'

'But—'

'*Quiet* now,' Skeffington hissed, grabbing Alan's jaw with a whip-fast hand. His grip was cold, it was hard, it was iron. 'Stop *fighting*, for the love of Gleam. Know when you're beaten.' He looked at Byron from beneath his heavy lids. Skeffington was grinding his teeth, Alan realised. 'Very well,' he said, eventually. 'Byron. You will be Alan's captor. Together you will find the Mapmaker, and quickly. Then you will bring her to me. Understood?'

Alan nodded wordlessly as Byron replied, 'Yes, sir.'

Skeffington let go of Alan's jaw. 'Good,' he said.

'Can I speak?' Alan asked, warily.

Skeffington sighed. 'Go on,' he said.

'Earlier,' Alan said, 'you said Churr has put out a call to arms?'

'Churr? The bandit? She can see the truth of it,' Skeffington said. 'The truth that I can see.'

'And me!' Mother Margo exclaimed. 'I can see it too,
I can.'

'And what truth is that?'

'Well,' Mother Margo said. 'Well. Hellfire. Just wait,
damn it. I got something stuck, right good.' She stuck
her finger into her mouth. 'Hang on.' The moment
stretched interminably. Then she spat, and out shot a
fragment of snail shell. 'At last,' she said, grinning. Her
teeth were red. 'The truth of it! There's a war coming.
And it'll be bloody.' She cackled.

'A war? I mean, Daunt'll retaliate, but—'

'Daunt's wealth matters out here, Alan,' Skeffington
said. 'She doesn't lead a gang. She runs an empire. This
isn't just rival traders fighting over a patch. Everybody has
a stake, one way or another. It's going to escalate.' He put
a hand on Alan's shoulder. 'And I think that you might
just be on the wrong side.'

The Discard Operations Commander held up her hand, and the troop came to a standstill. They could see the canal now, shining like a bright ribbon in the moonlight. Smoke rose from numerous narrowboat chimneys. A couple of lively orange fires burned on the shore. Voices and laughter drifted through the still night air, and fireflies floated above the surface of the water. The thousand voices of insects, toads and night-birds filled the shadows. The Commander herself was no stranger to the sounds of animal life, but thanks to the urgency of the mission some of these Arbitrators had never been outside the Pyramid before. Yet they all stood statue-still, despite any discomfort with their surroundings. They wore mesh masks and on their backs carried cylindrical metal tanks to which great glass syringes were attached by snaking tubes. They looked like automata carrying their own fuel, just waiting to be wound up and set off. Behind them were the slave cages.

The Commander raised her helmet. The night air was cool on her face. 'These river people have been sourcing explosive minerals from the far reaches of the Discard wilds,' she announced to her unit, 'and then delivering them to known dissidents in the central regions.' She kept her voice quiet but clear. 'We take them out, we greatly diminish the Discard's ability to mount a penetrative attack on the Pyramid. And once we've eliminated the threat and secured the area, we cage the survivors and exsanguinate the dead. Only then do we gather the other goods: cloth, food, captives, herbalist supplies, any suspicious minerals. They also harvest algae that we can use for poultices and ointments. We'll take those too. And then we burn the boats. Understood?'

Nods.

'Blood for the black stone!' she whispered.

'Blood for the stone heart!' they intoned.

She lowered her mask, turned back to the view of the canal, raised her arm, and gave the signal.

The troop moved out. After a moment or two, the laughter from the canal-side fires stopped, and then the shouting began. The Commander ran with her people, crouched down low. More shouting. People were emerging from the boats and crowding on the shore. As the Commander closed in, she saw a rangy, long-haired man step forward. His hair and beard were almost white. He held up his hands. 'Stop,' he said. 'We want no trouble. We will not resist. You want our trade goods? Our gems, our algae? You can have them. Consider it a tithe. Please, take what you want, but do us no harm.'

All of the Arbitrators stopped, except one. But the one who didn't barrelled into the old man and sapped him; the man collapsed, and a child screamed. 'We want you, though,' the Arbitrator snarled. Simultaneously the child appeared: a young girl, slipping *from between the legs of the river people, lifting the knife from the Arbitrator's hip, plunging it up between the leather armour plates and into his gut. The Arbitrator fell, and the crowd surged forwards.*

It was true what they said about Discarders, the Commander reflected. They were savages, even the children. Each and every one of them could be a threat. 'Clean kills!' she yelled. 'Try not to spill!' And even though the Arbitrators were striking out with saps and sword hilts, the air tasted of blood.

3

Byron of the Pyramid

Skeffington bade Alan and Byron get a few hours of good solid slumber and Alan tried, but he didn't sleep so much as endure nightmares. The horrors in his head lasted for hours, days, weeks — but he would wake from them and find that only minutes had passed since his last shocked coming-to. And those waking moments were unpleasant too: just as haunted, just as panicked. He'd sit up with a start, hands reaching for Snapper, and remember that he'd been bound once more. Snapper lay on the ground next to him, tied to his wrist by a short length of hairy rope. Alan gazed at the guitar to calm himself. The need for rest became a mountainous beast that loomed over him, making his heart beat faster and faster, pushing sleep itself further away, minutes warping into sweaty, sweltering hours.

By the time Byron was ready to go, Alan felt pretty dreadful, but once the air was rushing past the bike, their clothes trailing threads of spidersilk, he felt better than he had in weeks. The cold rushing air was magnificent. It was as if their speed was somehow a source of energy. The ride brought back childhood memories of bathing in a waterfall: something Alan hadn't thought about in years.

They tore through the long grasses of the Oversight, the dawn sky yellow and blue at the horizon, gauzy clouds smeared across it like smoke. They made their way right to the edge and, for a while, rode alongside it. Visibility was good; Alan could see rooftop villages waking up in the distance, travellers on criss-cross bridges far below, clerics throwing open the windows of Domes of the Toads near and far. Bells rang across the gulfs between buildings, birds called and dogs howled. Lanterns were snuffed out and fires extinguished as the sunlight filtered its way down between the various structures, through the coats and mounds of ivy and around the ancient statues and the rusted machines. From this vantage point, Alan could see it all; when you were down there in the midst of it all, you couldn't see half as much of the life unfolding all around you. Down there in the midst of it, Gleam could feel very quiet.

Byron steered the bike towards the edge and dropped down onto a staircase that hugged the wall of the building below the Oversight. Alan's heart rose into his throat. The steps were long and shallow and worn, so they didn't pose much of an obstacle to the bike, but the speed, nearness to the edge and constant slight bumping made Alan nervous.

The staircase followed the curve of the wall until, after what felt like an eternity, it peeled away from the building and became a bridge over a dark ravine to a large, ornate balcony that protruded from a thin white tower. The balcony was half-buried beneath a pile of deep green leaves – some kind of creeper that coated the stone and trailed far below it. Byron brought the bike to a halt, turned off the engine and lifted his goggles from his eyes. The sudden silence was eerie. The tower stood in the middle of the ravine, connected by more bridges to the taller, darker buildings surrounding it. Alan looked over the edge of the balcony. Far below was a pale band, though he couldn't work out if it was a path or a river. Arches and bridges cut through the air above and below them.

'What's happening?' Alan asked, his voice sounding strange in the silence. Byron didn't reply, but dismounted and then proceeded to stretch. 'Why have we stopped?'

'We're taking a detour. Need some supplies. But it means going low for a bit. There's a trading post down here, but it's a hole. Not good people. We need to be ready. So we're having a rest and a bite to eat. Can yer fight?'

'I . . . A bit. With my hands untied, that is.'

Byron eyed Alan balefully. 'Well, all being well, yer won't have to. Now, we've got some goat jerky, we've got some goat's cheese, we've got some old bread. What makes it good, though, are *these*.' He thrust his hand into the creeper leaves and plucked out a bunch of bright red berries. 'Mash them up with the cheese.'

'We stopped here for the berries?'

'Had to stop somewhere. Take yer pleasure where yer can, that's what I say. Gleam's full of it if yer know where to look.' Byron took some waxed paper bundles from a pannier, handed a couple to Alan, unfolded his own and began to eat. 'Quick,' he said. 'Taking pleasure where yer can doesn't mean dawdling. What yer doin', anyway? What d'you need this Nora's help for?'

Though Alan had been reluctant to stop, his mouth watered at the prospect of bread and cheese and his hands shook slightly as he unfolded the packaging. He resisted the urge to just shove it all into his mouth, and slowly placed the cheese on the bread, the berries on the cheese. He raised the food to his lips and closed his eyes. Sharp fruit, strong cheese and tough bread: it was the finest meal Alan had eaten in a long time. The pleasure was invigorating; he felt almost as if the flavours were coursing through his body. He shivered. And he didn't know if it was the hunger or tiredness or some kind of sun-sickness, but he found himself talking, words spilling out between mouthfuls.

'My son,' he said. 'My son, my Billy – he's sick because of me. I need to get into the Pyramid to help him, to give him the antidote.' He took another bite and chewed. 'I'm from the Pyramid – I mean, not originally, but I grew up there. And I need to go in through the Sump – through

Dok. Nora can help me. Maybe she can help me. I left her at Dok. She might be dead. If she's dead, that's because of me too. I don't want her to be dead. I don't want it. I . . .' He trailed off.

Byron put a hand on Alan's shoulder. 'Trading post not far from here,' he said, mouth full. 'We'll be stopping at it, but it's not a safe place. Yer not to get off the bike, yer not to make a fuss. Got it?'

Alan just nodded.

'Your son. We need to get there quick, right? If he's sick?'

'Yeah.'

'I'll pick up something to help me go. Listen.' He squeezed Alan's shoulder. 'We'll get there. And we'll get there fast. Don't worry.'

From the balcony, they took a different bridge and descended via a series of courtyards, shallow staircases and on a couple of occasions the side of a blackened and burnt tower that had tilted to rest against the side of the Oversight. Now that they were lower, the temperature was dropping. Byron lifted his neckscarf and secured it around the lower half of his face.

They passed other people on their way: mostly Transients on foot; dour, tough-looking wiry types, armed to the teeth and staring suspiciously from wide toad-sweat eyes.

Before long they came to a dark underspace, a great shadowy network of uneven and irregularly shaped brick caverns connected by open archways of different sizes. Flickering torches were ensconced on the walls and the air felt oily and smoky. There was traffic down here and the hallways were busy with Transients, traders and mangy scavenger dogs. The torches didn't give out much light. Byron slowed right down, just pushing the bike along with one foot. It wasn't too hot in the dark; the men and women wore layers – jerkins and leggings, shawls, capes, cloaks, leather gloves, and everything patched, everything covered with stitched-on pockets. They carried great bags around on their backs and sat behind open rolls of tools, blades, dried herbs, stoppered clay bottles, eyeglasses, metal charms, crystals, posies, animal parts, coloured glass and more. Music drifted through the marketplace, or at least an attempt at music – maybe it was just a drunk pawing away at a broken-down old piano. Alan looked at all the people and wondered about that WANTED poster. Any one of them could've seen it; all of them could do with the bugs. He kept his face down-turned, grateful for the poor light.

Byron stopped the bike by a table piled high with swatches of bright, if grimy, fabric. Scarves, Alan realised. A big-nosed little man peered out from behind the mountains of colour. Wordlessly, Byron slapped a couple of small bugs down on the table in front of the man and picked up a couple of red scarves. The man pursed his lips, nodded and took the bugs.

'Thank you, sir,' Byron said. Then he turned to Alan

and started tying them around Alan's head. 'These're fer you. Put one round yer nose and mouth; use the other like a hat. You don't want ter be recognised by this next lot.' Before Alan could reply, he'd kicked the bike back into motion.

Byron also bought knives, oil, ground coffee, packets of dried fruit, sage, bay, rosemary, a large paper bag of small dark tubers, and some spices Alan wasn't familiar with. Everything was secreted into panniers, pockets and canisters before they moved more deeply into the labyrinth, the bike quietly puttering as Byron walked it along. Alan became totally disorientated as tunnels branched from tunnels, rooms opened out from rooms, archways opened onto archways, laughter and that drunken piano music floating through the space. Figures ghosted through the stuttering shadows and people lay moaning and insensible against the walls. Red light spilled out from one chamber, writhing bodies just glimpsed within. If the people leaning against the walls or standing in alcoves in these corridors were traders, their wares were not on display. Alan could feel his blood quickening.

'What are we here for?' he hissed. 'All the good stuff was back there, where we came in. You bought everything we need already – that was some good stuff you got. Coffee! Haven't had coffee in a long, long—'

'Quiet!' Byron snapped. 'Keep yer face well covered and yer mouth well shut.'

And then the passage opened out into a larger space

and Alan understood. The walls were hung with runners bearing Daunt's mushroom symbol. The room was well lit by lanterns. Wiry women stood either side of the entrance, Daunt's mark tattooed into their foreheads, barbed spears in their hands and wickedly sharp curved swords on their hips. They gazed impassively at Byron and Alan, but made no move to stop them. There were more enforcers inside, pacing warily around the display cabinets and bookcases full of vials, bottles, parchments, loose leaves, mushrooms and powders, bowls, jars, while merchants, also Daunt's, extolled the virtues of their products to all customers present.

Was Byron turning Alan in? Alan couldn't accuse him of it without revealing who he was – but no, Byron had just ensured his face was covered. Alan kept his mouth shut as he'd been told, listened to the blood thunder in his ears, and sweated. He felt as if every eye in the place was on him. There was a good cross-section of Daunt's people here: merchants, goons, gatherers, rogues – but nobody he recognised, no Bittewood. This was probably just one of her many little central Discard dens. Still, it was too heavily defended for him to escape if he was spotted.

Byron caught the attention of a big, soft-looking bald man who smiled obsequiously as he approached.

'How can I help you today?' he asked, his voice syrupy.

Just then, Alan noticed a copy of the WANTED poster pinned to the wall, and when he looked carefully around:

yep, his face was plastered all over the place. He could barely breathe. Byron lowered his mask.

'A hand of wasproot,' he replied. 'And a half of dried dream-meat, too. Oh, and some of that nice red moss from out Rainbow River way.'

The bald man nodded. 'Very well, sir,' he said. 'Coming right up.'

Alan watched the bald man busy himself at one of the cabinets. He moved so *slowly*. Alan gritted his teeth. If anybody recognised him . . . *Come on,* he urged the bald man, *come on, come on, come on . . .*

Then the man was back and handing over the little packets, and Byron was paying up, and the man was giving a tiny bow, and Byron was walking the bike out of there, and the discordant *plink-plonking* of that damned pianist was echoing around, and the WANTED poster was visible everywhere Alan looked, and Alan's heart was in his mouth, and they were passing back out between the sentries, and they were back out in the corridor, and they'd done it.

As soon as we're out of here, Alan resolved, *I am going to kill this brain-dead biker, take the bike and be done with this whole rotten deal.*

Except as soon as they were back outside and alone again, Byron acted first. 'Just hedging me bets,' he said, after cutting the engine. 'Needed to pick up me bits, and I just thought – well, if I'd've left yer behind anywhere you'd have ballsed it up, or run off – no, don't deny it. Or some chump else'd've recognised yer. If anybody's going to collect on that bounty, it's gonna be me. And I'm not gonna get caught in any crossfire, understand?'

'Not really.' Alan didn't bother to keep the venom from his voice.

'If Daunt's people see you with me, I'm gonna claim I was taking you to 'em. I'm not gonna risk being seen together unless I can make that claim.'

'But you didn't have to stop there at all.'

'You want to get to where we're going quickly, right? Then I need me wasproot – keeps me going. There'll be no sleeping now.'

They stayed low, biking through the network of gantries, bridges and balconies that was woven between the towers. The towers started to take on the aspect of gigantic ancient trees; they were cracked and mossy, with weird irregular bridges and turrets branching off. Byron would stop the bike for a moment here and there and, without dismounting, pull down clumps of moss or tear chunks of rotten wood from doorways or windows. Up above, between the tops of the towers, Alan could see Corval rise and night began to fall. Not long after, they stopped for food in the lee of a great wall that was obscured entirely by thick vine. At least Alan assumed that there was a wall in there somewhere. He sat, his hands still bound, and watched Byron build a small fire of vine, moss, broken-up window-frames from the last tower they rode past, and a few lumps of charcoal from one of his many bags.

'I could help, you know,' he said.

'Aye,' Byron said, 'I know. But would yer? Or would yer try to push me over the edge into the deep?'

'I'm not a killer.'

'You're an angry man, Alan. I can see that anyway. And you're even angrier that I took you right down into the croc's mouth. But I want yer to know, I could've turned you in, claimed the bounty, gone back to Skeffy and told him you'd escaped – told him you'd tried to kill me. Or I could've just taken the bugs and rode off into the sunset. I'd'a been a rich man. I wanted to show yer how easy it would be. And I wanted yer to see me refuse that opportunity. I want yer to trust me, Alan.'

'Unbind my hands and I might.'

'Can I trust *you*, though? That's what I'm gettin' at. When you're so angry with me.' He started heating up a pot of beans and soft old tomatoes disgorged from another saddlebag and sprinkled in some of the herbs he'd bought from the trading post. 'We'll eat the old food first.'

Alan didn't reply. Byron shrugged and stared at the pan, watching as the fruit broke down and began to bubble. He got out the wasproot, broke off a finger and shaved away the yellow skin. The scent was sharp enough to reach Alan over the fire. 'Wasproot is best when it's chewed,' Byron said. 'Tastes like shite but it sure as hell sharpens yer. Need to char it, though. And if we're going to have a fire, well, may as well cook on it. After this, no more fires – no more camps. After this, we go straight to Dok. We'll be there within three days. Now, those herbs I put in the pot, they were bay and basil. If I could do magic, my first spell'd be to make tomatoes and basil grow on the same vine. And the bay's good for warmth and depth on cold nights. Tonight's gonna be a cold one down here. You can smell it, right? Not the wasproot – I mean the pot. The food.'

Alan could indeed smell the food. It had been a while since their bread and cheese, and the scent of the tomatoes and herbs awoke a fresh hunger. First the bread and cheese, and now this – Byron was spoiling him. He remembered sitting by the stove in Eyes' kitchen, the dried herbs hanging from the ceiling; he remembered Maggie's chilli back at the House of a Thousand Hollows. He'd forgotten the restorative and emotional power of food. All these long days of eating mushrooms, snails and moss had dulled his senses. Parts of his brain were waking back up. Above, the stretches of sky he could see were full and vivid. The great mass of stars to the south – Green's Eye – hung in a faint purple cloud. The vine whispered in the cool evening breeze. Crickets chirruped and fireflies emerged, dancing in the darkness between towers.

'I'm even angrier than you think,' Alan said suddenly, 'but you can trust me. You're my companion. Please, unbind my hands.'

'You know,' Byron said, as he came over to Alan and

conjured a key from somewhere about his person, 'I'm from the Pyramid too.'

'I remember you saying. How old were you when you . . .?'

'I was Discarded at thirteen.' Byron unlocked Alan's cuffs. Alan closed his eyes with relief as the biker lifted the shackles from his wrists. 'Now let's eat.' Byron spooned the stew out into a couple of tin dishes. 'I was thirteen when my da kicked me out,' he said. 'Old enough for it all to be pretty solid up here.' He tapped the side of his head. 'What about you?'

'Well, I was born in the Discard, but my parents . . . well, something happened to them. I'm not going to go into it.' Alan tasted the stew. 'Good food,' he said. 'Very good. And an Arbitrator took me back into the Pyramid. I was raised by the Teachers, then I began my Stationing – I was in Administration – and assigned a wife, as she was assigned to me. Poor woman. Marion, her name was . . . *is*. We had – *have* – a child, a boy called Billy. Marion and Billy are still in there, but I had to leave. I angered the Arbitrators, and that endangered my family, so I dropped down a chute.'

'Ha! Yeah, I was dropped down a chute by me da, after a good beatin'. He was a quiet man; always quiet and kind. Until he caught me and another lad kissing behind one of the plaza statues. I was on me way home from school, and me and this boy – it was kind of playing – well, it weren't playing, it were *more* than playing. I knew the law, like, but it never felt like we'd gone far enough to *break* the law. It weren't innocent, but it all felt — right, somehow. It's not like me dad got the wrong idea, is what I'm trying to say, but we weren't doing anything wrong. Not compared to — I mean—'

'It's all right,' Alan said, 'you don't have to justify it to me. But I know that in the Pyramid . . .'

'Yeah. But I don't think I'd been as scared or as careful as I should've been. I just thought — well, if me parents found out, they'd understand, tell me off maybe, but keep it quiet. I didn't know then it was so weird, so bad. But when he caught us, me da, straight away I knew it was really bad. I knew it was way worse than I'd thought. Me da, he — you know how pale Pyramidders are anyway — he just froze and went see-through, almost. He stared at me, and none of us moved. It felt like for ever. Then he grabbed me by the hair and just pulled me away. He dragged me down the corridor — I remember, he was moving too quickly for me to find me feet and his robes were all billowing out, he was going so fast. I wondered — I remember wondering — I thought, maybe it weren't me da after all, just another Astronomer that looked like him. I mean, I'd always thought if we got caught there'd be some anger, but not like *that*. He hurt me so much — and people stopped and stared but he didn't care, and that weren't like him at all. He was always so reserved. In the end we were alone somewhere, not somewhere I'd ever been before. I remember a big brass — what are they called? Those machines with the moons that go round—?'

'An orrery.'

'Yeah, one of them. And he smacked me across the face. I wasn't yet fourteen. It were like he'd been replaced or possessed. He smacked me the other way and then he held me down and started punching me. He was saying – I couldn't hear a lot of it, but I did hear some, that if the Arbitrators found out they'd Discard me anyway. He kept saying things like, "Freaks are no good for bleeding and they are no good for breeding!" so I guess I was useless to the Alchemists and the Astronomers. He was pointing at the orrery and saying "Clockwork! Clockwork! No room for dead cogs!" It was like he'd gone mad. I think he *had* gone mad.'

'What did he do in Astronomy?'

Byron chuckled grimly. 'He was one of the Datemakers.'

Alan allowed himself a smile too. The Datemakers assigned husbands to wives and *vice versa*, and drew up the calendars that dictated when individual couples had to attempt conception – those dates were dictated by the moons and the stars and anything else that the Astronomers knew was up there – they had vast arrays of telescopes and other, stranger devices which they used to observe the skies as they spun, and the factors they integrated into their calculations were myriad. The intention was to create the right *kinds* of babies – babies with the physicality and character to fill the Stationing roles that the Astronomers predicted the Pyramid would require by the time the newborns came of age.

'I was in bits. There was blood everywhere and he was punching me all over. *All over*. And he was kicking me too, until he wore himself out, I think, because he ended up lying next to me. Neither of us could breathe for sobbing. I tried to crawl away, but he caught me and started beating me again.'

Byron wiped his eyes. After a moment, his voice choked, he said, 'Next thing I knew, I was lying in the Discard dust, coughing up all kinds of shit. He'd knocked me out and cast me out. That was how Skeffy found me: broken up and Discarded.'

'I'm sorry,' Alan said, after a moment. 'That's rough. Your own father.'

'Yeah. Well, what was really hard was that it wasn't like him. If he'd always been a thug or a madman, then – I don't know, I don't think it would've hurt so much. If he'd been an unkind man. But – well. Like I say, I was thirteen. For a long time I thought there must have been something really, *really* wrong with me, to have pushed him over the edge like that, a patient, quiet man like him. What hurt besides the violence, besides the Discarding, was the sense of – well, not betrayal, but something else. Reversal, maybe. Undoing. And you know what they tell you about the Discard in the Pyramid: I was so scared, I thought I was going to die. I was sure of it. That was his intention, I suppose. Me own da's intention was for me to die. As soon as I came to I was looking out for snakes and crocodiles and horned men.'

'And how have you found it, out here?'

'Hard. No doubt it's hard. There's more weather. There're more knives in the night. But as a biker, you've got people who'll watch yer back. Yeah, it's hard, but it's not half as hard as they'd have you believe in the Pyramid.'

'More dick, too.'

'Yeah.' Byron grinned. 'It's got that going for it. Nearly makes up for all the fucking goatmeat.'

'Be grateful for what you've got. Most of us non-bikers have to make do with snail.'

'Yeah, well. That's your problem.'

'So how do you become a biker? Can anybody join? Do you just decide? Or is there an initiation?'

'Invite only,' Byron said, then, hastily, 'invite from a chapter chief only. I couldn't invite you. Then there's a kind of initiation – you have to go through all the bleedin' stages. Eventually the chapter votes on yer full membership. I'm not a full member yet. You can see from my patches.' He twisted awkwardly and pointed. 'See? I've got the GH for Goatherd, and a skull, but the skull doesn't have the big horns, so that means I'm a Prospect.' Byron looked at Snapper. 'They'd have you, I bet,' he continued. 'I don't think there's a single guitarist in the whole chapter, nor a good singer. You should hear them at night, all whiskied up. Sound like a bunch of toads.'

'I'd love to join,' Alan said. 'You've no idea. But I've got commitments, and for once I'm trying to honour them.'

'You want to talk about it?'

'No, I don't even want to think about it. I'm trying to act without thinking.'

Byron laughed, and then fell silent. 'D'you partake, then?' he asked after a moment.

'In what?'

'Dick.'

'Have done, in the past.' Alan felt himself blush, and Byron too suddenly looked bashful. Alan watched him as he devoted himself to his food.

The silence lengthened. Alan tuned Snapper and began to play. Byron put down his empty bowl, closed his eyes and listened. Ever since the rumble of the bike had stopped the place had been peaceful, but the sparse, melodic music spoke of a much greater peace, a peace of another kind. Alan's quickened heartbeat slowed, and the awkwardness passed. The implications remained, however, hanging tantalisingly in the air.

'What was that?' Byron asked, after Alan stopped playing.

'I call it "Trees and Moss".'

''s beautiful.'

'Thank you.'

Byron looked at him. 'Are you a faithful man?' he asked. He unrolled a couple of smokes, took some of the red Rainbow River moss from a hidden pocket and sprinkled it into the open papers.

Alan thought about the question and then slowly shook his head. 'No,' he said. 'By no means.' He reached over the fire to take the roll-up that Byron proffered.

'Would it be unfaithful of you to be with me tonight?'

Alan lit up and inhaled. 'I don't know,' he said. 'Yes, in that I love another. But no, in that she does not want me any more. Anyway. Are there degrees of unfaithfulness? Surely a vow can only really be broken once.' He inhaled, exhaled, shook his head. 'Byron, I have fucked up many times, and quite badly, and I do so more and more, despite trying not to. So if I'm going to keep fucking up, then – well, it might as well be in a manner of my choosing.' He reached out and took Byron's hand.

They shuffled closer to each other around the fire. Byron leaned in and Alan kissed him. Byron's mouth was hot and smoky, his tongue delicate.

But then Byron broke away. 'Skullfrog,' he hissed, looking at something behind Alan.

Alan turned around. 'What?' he said. Then he saw it: a face, almost human, peering over the lip of the path. The eyes and mouth were little more than dark saggy holes, the flesh swollen and white. It shouldn't have been possible for anybody – or any*thing* – to stand where this thing was.

Then the head suddenly rose up and Alan and Byron scrabbled backwards towards the vine. A mass of soft white tendrils floated silently up around the face and a thick, suckered tentacle slapped onto the path surface. Then the thing was moving quickly; a host of tentacles appeared from below and gripped the stone and it hauled itself up from the underside of the path onto the top.

Even once it was wholly visible, Alan couldn't work out what it was. A mass of white, stippled flesh with five or six tentacles and innumerable tendrils, with that horrible head located close to the central body. It was humanoid in a sense, although it seemed to be crawling around on its belly. The creature wasn't making any noise except for the quiet rustle made by its slithering. Before Alan could react, one of those thinner protuberances had lashed out and wrapped itself around his ankle.

He screamed – the contact burned – but he was already unthinkingly grabbing it with his hands, trying to pull himself free; the same fiery pain lanced through his fingers and hands and he screamed again.

Byron kicked the fire at the creature and the embers sizzled deep into it. It writhed silently, but still didn't let Alan go. It lashed at Byron, but the stingers weren't able to find purchase on his leathers. He slashed and cut with his long knife as the thing groped for his throat. Tendrils continued to wriggle around on the ground after they'd been severed.

'Byron,' Alan shouted, 'my knives!'

Byron had his back against the bike, but couldn't turn to retrieve Alan's weapons without making himself vulnerable.

Alan braced himself and grabbed at his own fleshy leash once more. The stinging pain was eye-watering, but he didn't let go this time; he pulled it and stretched it, willing it to snap — until it did! He looked at the detached, worm-like appendage he held and quivered with both revulsion and delight. The delight was short-lived, however; within seconds, countless more of the appendages were squirming around his body.

The pain shot through his whole being and he fell to the ground. And before he could even think about standing up, the beast threw him over the edge of the abyss.

Alan dangled upside down, staring into the drop. The *shock* of the pain had dissipated, but the pain itself throbbed. The thin white tendrils that held him jerked as Byron fought the creature, making him dance like a puppet.

Below was darkness bounded by tall towers and vast curved walls, punctuated by the faint relief of the kind of pale stone bridge they'd traversed on their journey. But not much moonlight got down here, and Alan couldn't see very far into the depths. He twisted his neck to look up. Byron had forced the creature back to the edge. 'No,' Alan whispered, 'no, no, no—' He gathered all the breath he could, and yelled, 'Byron! Byron, *I'm still here!*'

He didn't know if Byron had heard or not. He started grabbing the tendrils by the bunch and pulled himself upright. His legs were bound together. The tendrils were like nettles, covered in fine crystalline hairs that pierced the skin and hurt much more than they looked capable of, and brambles, with vicious hook-like thorns. But Alan found that the hairs and thorns all lay one way; he could take hold of the tendrils carefully and avoid most of the pain. The wall itself was smooth, offering no purchase. He could hear the sounds of the fight up above and prayed to Green that he'd reach the ledge before Byron dispatched the creature. He shouted again, and kept shouting, 'I'm here! I'm still here!' He climbed slowly up the swinging, twitching skin strings, trying to ignore the sickening motion, just methodically placing hand over hand – until he looked up, to see how far he had left to ascend.

And then he stopped.

A pale lump clung to the wall up above, near the lip of the path. Its shape was hard to make out, but what had drawn Alan's eye was what looked like a cloud of pink sparks dancing in the air nearby. He squinted.

The pink moonlight was picking out the tips of its tendril mass as they swayed beyond the shadows. It was another one of these creatures. And then as soon as he'd noticed that one, Alan noticed another further along, and then a third, just below that. He looked down, and sure enough, there were more down below him. He looked out and around and saw that they were attached to the other walls and towers too. None of them were moving as fast as the one that had attacked them; they were creeping, subtly rippling their soft bodies across the flat surfaces.

Alan swore and redoubled his efforts. He could hear Byron grunting, and then yelling triumphantly, 'Take *that,* yer bleedin' maggot!'

The twitching and thrashing stopped, and then Byron was hanging over the edge, reaching down, gathering up the dangling tendrils with his gloved hands, pulling Alan up.

'We've got to go,' Alan said. 'There are more – *look.*'

Byron's eyes widened as he took in the scene beyond the edge. 'Back to the bike,' he said, '*now.*' He scooped up the wasproot as he passed by the remains of the fire and shoved a handful in his mouth.

Alan scrambled to his feet and followed. Byron spoke through his full mouth. 'Don't stop t'look, but that damned thing's got *human* bones.' He mounted the bike. 'They don't normally come up this high. We can't stop again.'

Alan gathered up the pot and their packs, swung Snapper onto his back and climbed on board, hurriedly securing the gear as Byron revved up. He checked that his knife was to hand – it was still in his belt. He looked at the mess Byron had made of their attacker. Dark brown blood oozed from the white rubbery flesh, and a human skull gazed lifelessly out from the hacked-up ruins. 'Agreed,' he said. 'Straight on, now. And skullfrogs? What the fuck are they? Why are they coming up?'

'Somethin's changin',' Byron said. 'Come on, let's get.'
And then they were away.

Alan relived the fight over and over as they sped through
the Discard. They were low, now, and they didn't see
many travellers, but there were people living at every
level in Gleam. And they'd be encountering those creatures for the first time too. Skeffington had said that
creatures were coming back to Dok now that the Pilgrims had been driven out, but these things had left the
Swamp completely to ascend to the surface levels. Like
the snail, Alan realised: the gargantuan snail that had
risen the night he met Churr. This was part of a pattern
that went back to before his expedition to Dok.

Skullfrogs, Byron had called them.

Alan could smell the wasproot that Byron was chewing; he could still taste their kiss.

They found themselves riding in between mossy hil-
locks, the moss white with spidersilk. Deep funnel webs
disappeared into holes in the landscape. There was nothing between them and the sky now, so the white of the
spidersilk glowed pink, purple and orange in the moonlight. The path twisted and turned between the hills. The
landscape felt eerie to Alan; too soft, too natural. He
couldn't work out how or why this place had been *built.*
They drank water from wineskins and chewed dried fruit
and strips of tough goatmeat as they rode.

There was a spindly tower in the distance. They

approached as dawn broke and Alan saw that it was the grey ruin of a mill that sprouted from the hillside like a blade from skin. It was full, not of old machinery, but bones. Glass-fronted cabinets lined the walls of the ground floor, inside which were bones, sorted by type and neatly stacked. Byron stopped the bike here, dismounted, and refuelled it from one of several canisters stored beneath the seat. Alan stared at the bones and a cold, nameless dread stirred in his gut. Beyond the mill, they found a village of small tents occupied by tiny people – Alan thought at first that they were children, which was disconcerting, because outside of the Safe Houses, the Discard was generally empty of children. But then he caught sight of one of their faces by the light of a morning cookfire and saw that it was old and sad and wizened. And the nose was large and bulbous, and there were no whites of the eyes; the woman's eyes were solid black, from lid to lid.

Alan beat Byron on the shoulder. 'Stop,' he shouted, unsure whether or not Byron could hear him. 'Stop!' He hit Byron again.

Byron brought the bike to just on the other side of the village. 'What?' he asked, irritably.

'We need to warn them, about the . . . about the skullfrogs.'

'No we don't. Don't need to warn *them* about anythin', do we?'

'Them in particular? What do you mean? Why not?'

Byron looked confused for a moment, and then

laughed. 'You really don't know fuck all about the Discard, huh? They're Gnomes. Y'know. *Maintenance.*'

Alan looked at him. 'No,' he said. 'I don't know.'

'Bein' honest, I don't know an awful lot about them meself. What I do know, though, is they're not only of our world. They've got one foot here, one foot somewhere else. They can't or don't communicate with us, and they don't need to fear the things we fear. And we shouldn't linger near them.'

'What do you mean about maintenance though?'

'Some of the older bikers say that certain features are maintained: that's how they put it. *Certain features are maintained.* But seriously now, we've got to move.' Byron spat a wad of wasproot out, shoved in another one and took off once again.

The words *certain features are maintained* were familiar to Alan; he cast his mind back. It was Nora who'd uttered them, back in Glasstown, of a tap that dispensed clean water.

Nora. He hoped to hell he'd see her again.

The new day found them tearing along the straight edge of a marble canal. The water had long since stopped flowing and now stood still, but it was not quite stagnant; it was alive with lilies and dragonflies, and, as the early-morning mist rose, they passed a long low raft with a half-barrel home on it being punted along. The punter was a large woman with tangled black grey hair so long that it dragged in the water. There were sunken craft in the canal, too: ghostly shells with empty windows that put Alan in mind of strangely shaped skulls.

Soon they were surrounded by large buildings of corrugated iron sheets, many of which had come loose, leaving great holes in the sides of the structures, through which cylindrical silos and complex networks of pipes could be seen. Although no two buildings in Gleam were exactly alike, it did repeat itself; Alan had been somewhere like this before. Long chutes and sloping conveyors crisscrossed the empty space between the buildings and arches dangling copper pipes bridged the gap over the canal. There was a sulphurous smell in the air and the metal of the buildings was discoloured in strange ways. There were still lilies in the water, but the pads were black now, and they bore no flowers. Pale things moved beneath them. Rats as large as dogs scurried away from the path of the bike, swerving back into the shadows of the rusted silos. Byron decided to stop, and they dismounted. 'Need to move me legs,' he said. 'They're dead. And I can show you how to prepare a rat. If you're going to survive in the Discard – and if you're going to be responsible for anybody else out here – there's shit you need to learn.'

'I know how to survive in the Discard!'

'You bleedin' don't. Any old body can see that. You've spent too long in the House of a Thousand Hollows. The Houses aren't the Pyramid, for sure, but they're not quite the Discard proper either.'

Alan scowled, but Byron was right. Once all this was done — if it was ever done — he would need to adapt to a new way of life.

They waited until another rodent made an appearance, and then Alan got it with a knife. He was pleased to see that he was still accurate with a blade — and then almost immediately he felt sickened as the vision of Spider being skewered by the Clawbaby returned forcefully to his mind. He struggled to pull the knife back out again, scared to see the blood that would follow. The rat's fur was alive with fleas and the rat itself was still alive, squealing and twisting away from the blade. Alan managed to withdraw the knife, then drove it into the rat's back and it fell silent.

'I can't envisage ever wanting to eat this bag of shit,' he said out loud, not looking at Byron.

'Yeah, well. Nobody eats rat because they want to.' He handed Alan a leather roll. 'Let's make this quick.'

4

The Army of the Unwell

Rats, the occasional cat, steam, stone, bones, stagnant waters . . . the roar of the engine . . . hermits, tribes and wanderers: here was life, lived precariously. The rat was ribboned, dried, eaten. Flowers on stems twisted greenly from piles of red rust; skies so deep blue as to be hallucinatory had wisps of white cloud and huge white birds with ugly voices. The red glass lens that roofed Glasstown bulged upwards over to the east; it would be hot beneath it at this time of year. If Alan lived in Glasstown he too would be mad. He'd been glad Byron knew of another route, but then, there was madness to be found everywhere. They saw a pack of wild dogs with foamy mouths racing along the other side of the canal; Alan could hear their frenzied yapping even over the sound of the bike. One of them carried a small arm between its jaws. *A doll's arm. It's just a doll's arm, bloodied by the dog's own diseased mouth.*

Alan caught the scent of smoke on the breeze. It was

pleasant at first, reminiscent of food, drinks and stories around the fire, but as it began to haze the air and catch in his throat it brought back memories of something else: the night the Pyramid came for Modest Mills. The haze grew thicker and thicker as they followed the side of the canal and then, as they passed the old ruin of a lock and house, the source came into view.

Plumes of dark smoke rose lazily from the blackened, sinking wrecks of narrowboats. The canal was wider here and the boats were packed in along the side. Byron slowed down and stopped. Alan jumped off the bike and ran to the edge of the path where one of the wrecks was butting up against the stone. 'Hello?' he shouted. 'Anyone in there? Hello?' But there was no answer.

Some of the boats were still attached to mooring posts on the shore by chains that had rusted solid; that and the burnt remains of wooden structures on the shore suggested to Alan a sort of permanent settlement. He looked out over the water. There had been a lot of boats here. The charred wooden struts and ribs and the ash and the smell and the smoke: he'd seen this before. He listened for the screams and crying that had accompanied the destruction he'd experienced at Modest Mills, but there were no human voices here, just birds squawking and dogs whining.

Dogs. Alan's heart sank. He'd known really that it hadn't been a doll's arm that animal had had in its mouth. 'Hello?' he said again, but his voice was quiet now. He looked again at the boats, harder this time. He looked through the broken windows and the splintered doors. He looked into the water between the boats. He looked again at the wooden huts on the shore. And now he saw them everywhere. And once he'd seen the bodies, he could smell them.

Somebody grabbed him by the shoulder and he spun round, fist clenched. He punched Byron square on the jaw before he'd seen who it was. Byron staggered backwards. Alan opened his mouth to apologise, but anger spilled out of it instead. 'What the fuck are you doing, creeping around?' he was shouting. He couldn't control his voice. 'Get away from me! Get the fuck away! Don't *ever* touch me again!' He wiped spit from his chin and turned back to the water.

'I'm sorry,' Byron said, having retreated. 'I know you lived through this. I'm here for you, if . . . if you want to talk.'

'Fuck off.' Alan heard himself as if he were a bystander. His whole body was shaking. He reached down and punched through the burnt wooden side of the boat closest to him as if it was paper. Inside there was the dead body of an old man. 'We build a pyre,' he shouted. He grabbed the old man's body under the arms and tried to pull him out. The body's head lolled to one side and Alan saw something on its throat that he first thought was a great spider. He leaned down to brush it away and then realised what it truly was. He dropped the body, falling backwards.

The corpse had a circular puncture wound in its neck, ringed by bruising. Alan stared at it. These Discarders had been Bled.

They fished them out and gathered them up: men, women and children, all ages. Alan shivered and cried for hours, a prisoner in his own head, locked into a corner of his mind and helpless to intervene as his thoughts spun away into darker and darker places. Neither Alan nor Byron spoke until the pyre was lit.

'The Pyramid?' Alan asked. 'At first I just assumed, y'know, because it brought back everything from Modest Mills, and it *was* the Pyramid that sacked Modest Mills. But the Pyramid had a reason to do that, and—'

'Whoah,' Byron interrupted, holding up a hand. 'Whoah! What kind of damn reason could there be?'

'No, I mean – I mean—' Alan clutched at his shirt. 'It was in retaliation. I fired something at the Pyramid first. I was just a kid, I didn't mean to do it, I didn't know what I was doing, I let loose this thing – this bomb – and it hit the Pyramid, and—'

'No.' Byron shook his head. 'The Pyramid don't need a reason.' His voice was soft. 'Maybe that was their justification on that occasion. But they do this. You've spent most of yer Discard life in the House of a Thousand Hollows, so yer won't have seen it, but they do this. We bikers see it. We sometimes find the mess they leave behind. They do it to remind the Discard who's boss. Or they do it when the Discard has something they need. There are some things they can't grow or make; cotton is one. They come out here for that. Some animals they come for. If people don't hand over what they want, they wind up dead. They call it taxes. But it's just a show of . . . not strength. *Ruthlessness*.' He shook his head. 'This Bleedin', though . . . that's new to me.'

'Eyes used to talk about the taxes. And the raids. I didn't really . . . I didn't really listen.'

'Eyes?'

Alan looked at the ground. 'Long story.'

'These folk here,' Byron continued, 'I traded with them sometimes. They sold good algae, good polished gems – from some rapids a long way upriver, brought down on barges – and the best leeches. The Pyramid must've come calling, and when they didn't just roll over . . . look. What happened at Modest Mills, that was bleedin' awful. Of course it was. You'll never get over it. But try not to blame yerself. The Pyramid's vicious. You think it's vicious, but it's even worse than you think. You didn't cause what happened. Just like nobody here caused it.'

'There aren't as many bodies as you'd think,' Alan said, suddenly. 'Given how many boats there are, I mean. You think some of them got away?'

'No,' Byron murmured.

Alan closed his eyes. That was something else Eyes had told him, something else that he'd pushed away. 'Kidnapped,' he said.

'Yeah,' Byron confirmed. They watched the flames

take hold. The clothes of the dead had been sodden with canal water and they started to steam. 'They take slaves.'

'I never saw any slaves when I was in there.'

'Me neither. Reckon they're for the high-ups. Don't rightly know. But I've watched 'em, I've watched 'em return to the Pyramid after their raiding. Seen the Discarders all tied up in cages.'

Alan stared into the fire. He made himself watch for a while, then he turned back to the bike. 'We've got to go now,' he said.

They passed through yards full of carts and ancient wheeled machines deteriorating into heaps of component parts, those parts themselves slowly disintegrating. Thick cables once neatly coiled were springing loose from huge wooden wheels that had rotted away; others sagged between buildings; in the middle of one distant stretch hung a small carriage, the cable on either side suspended from tall, crumbling spires. Other yards looked as if they had perhaps been set aside for the accumulation of waste, for they were full of mounds of scrap metal, broken bricks, unidentifiable wooden things, frayed, faded textiles. Some of these heaps had paths worn into them, leading into dark holes; they reminded Alan of the badger setts his father had shown him in the woods around Modest Mills when he was a little boy, before the massacre.

Byron followed the canal-side path as it widened and split off from the waterway, becoming a road, crossing others. Alan felt as if the landscape was familiar, though he was sure he hadn't been here before. There were more scrapyards, different canals, other creaking, looming sheds of metal and stone towers and vast brick cubes of tiny rooms, as well as regions reclaimed by plant life. Gleam repeated itself, variations on a succession of templates, or perhaps more accurately, the same process occurring in lots of different places, at different times, and always slightly differently, although the shape of the original structure was very difficult to discern, beneath the accumulations of hundreds of years of further building. Byron chewed wasproot and they drank mint tea from a flask, ate cheese, bread, dried ratmeat, moss and pink slug mash. 'The pink slugs're a pick-me-up,' Byron said. Alan remembered Nora preparing the same manky dish once; it tasted foul, but he knew it worked.

Byron finally stopped in a small room in an airy structure made of stone. He dismounted and started fiddling about with an arrangement of brass cogs standing proud from one of the walls. 'What's that?' Alan asked, climbing off and stretching. Their passage had disturbed the dust. Looking back the way they'd come, Alan could see clouds of motes twinkling in the hard-edged beams of sunlight let in through the numerous small skylights. There was broken glass on the floor, and the remains of wooden doors rested in piles either side of a series of archways. There was a great sense of peace, as if nobody had been in here for a long, long time.

'Your Mapmaker didn't know about it?' Byron asked.
'Know about what?'

Suddenly the floor fell away and Alan's stomach floated up and nearly out of his mouth. He reached out with his hands to grab something – *anything* – but there was nothing there for him to cling to, as everything was falling with him, and he was too short of breath to scream, and then—

—the falling stopped, though his stomach – and everything else – carried on towards the now-solid floor. Alan fell over, feeling not as if he'd lost his balance but as if a great weight had been applied to his shoulders.

'What the fuck was that?' he managed after a moment or two more gasping for breath, then, 'Byron, why are you laughing?'

'It's a lift,' Byron said. 'Don't look like one, but it is.'

'A lift? What? Oh, like – like in the House of a Thousand Hollows? There was a platform that you could use to get into and out of Loon's workshop – it went up and down . . . but it was operated by all these levers and pulleys, and you could see all of the ropes and wheels and—'

The lift dropped again. Alan closed his eyes as Byron laughed.

There were no day-and-night cycles when Alan and Byron got deep underground. They rode through a gulley into an extravagant residence: mirrored walls, now tarnished, and black and white tiled floors that stretched throughout each storey. There were no windows. The place was a labyrinth of large rooms connected by arch-ways of irregular sizes and spacing. Alan swung a lantern upwards and saw that the ceilings were painted with scenes of a battle between a gigantic toad and a crocodile, with hordes of tiny humans clashing with each other around the animals. Many more were lying dead on the ground. The noise of the engine was echoing so loudly and combined with the flashing lights that were reflect-ing back from the tarnished mirrors and the generally disorientating architecture, they lost their way. Byron called a stop to find their bearings, getting off the bike and walking back to the previous room to check that they hadn't missed a doorway.

'We're looking for a long table,' he shouted back to Alan, 'snapped completely in the middle. A big pile of bird bones. No door.'

'There's nothing in here but a bad smell,' Alan replied, pacing the walls. Now the bike's engine had stopped they could hear their voices bouncing back off the walls, and something dripping – *lots* of dripping. With the bike's lights off, they couldn't see anything until Byron handed out torches and cranked them until wavering lights shone out. Alan moved through into the next room and slipped and something beneath his feet, something brown, streaked across the tiles. As he followed the trail the smell became stronger. It wasn't just the smell of death; it was danker than that, and sourer.

Then, in the darkness beyond the lamplight, something

exhaled, long and breathy, and Alan's guts roiled. He waved the torch and glimpsed lank grey hair and strange grey eyes, a pale, scarred face, slimy lips opening into a smile. He tried to step backwards but skidded and landed on his torch, breaking it.

'*Bittewood!*' he yelled, scrambling to his feet. 'Byron, Daunt's here! *Run!* Back to the bike!'

He was already running as his memory flooded his mouth with the foul taste of Bittewood's fingers. He could hear the man chasing him, but dared not look to see how close behind he was. He spat, trying to clear the imagined taste. There was a person, or maybe people, running down some stairway somewhere; he could hear the sound of their feet landing on the steps. He caught sight of Byron's light and ran towards it, but too late he saw his own shadowy reflection, indistinct and wide-mouthed, hurtling towards him, a pale ghoul in pursuit, and realised that it was only a reflection of Byron's light that he had seen. He collided with the glass at full pelt and pain riddled him, pure and sharp. He felt flattened. Somewhere in some small part of his brain he remembered throwing rotten fruit from an upstairs window as a child and delighting in the way it burst open upon hitting the ground.

Then rough hands were gathering him up. He felt like he'd spent his whole life being hurt and then rescued — but these hands were not rescuing him; they were slapping and punching and probing his body. There was a low snigger, and he doubled over as a boot kicked him, first in the ribs and then the stomach. He rolled to one side, groaning, in the stinking dark. There were no lights – had he been unconscious? No, it was just dark. Byron's torch had gone out – maybe Daunt herself had got hold of Byron, poor bastard. Shards of mirror jabbed his skin.

'My lady's gonna want a word,' Bittewood said, gripping Alan's face with clammy fingers. 'She's been looking for you. Got a song in you for her, eh?' Then he shoved Alan over and knelt on his back. 'Sure as fuck ain't got no fight in you, anyway.' Alan wriggled, trying to think of something to say, then Bittewood slashed his back and he shrieked as hot blood ran down his sides. 'I could've shouted for her myself,' Bittewood said, 'but y'know, you're the one with a voice.' He slashed again, and Alan cried out again. 'You're not sounding too good,' Bittewood said. 'I wouldn't give you a bed, not for that noise.' He cut Alan again. 'She'll be here soon,' he said, 'and I'll stop cutting, and things will get worse.'

As the knife came down once more, there was a sudden noise that boomed around the tiled halls like the angry growl of the crocodile that Alan had once fought in the swamp – that's what he thought it was: the crocodile come back, for his sins. But no, of course it was the motorbike. Waves of sound crashed back and forth, the floor shook and Bittewood jumped off his back, looking around for the source. Alan crawled away, though he didn't know where to, the wounds on his back stinging like hell. He clambered to his feet and could see Byron's speeding lantern reflected again in some of the mirrors. One was real, but he didn't know which – and evidently Bittewood didn't either, for he came for Alan once again. But this time Alan drew a blade instead of running and stood, hunched, one hand holding his bruised stomach, long knife in the other. Bittewood remained just out of reach, prowling around, grinning. He said something, but Alan couldn't hear what over the sound of the engine getting closer.

It was approaching from behind Bittewood, Alan realised, and just in time, Bittewood turned and ducked. Byron's swinging, knuckle-dustered fist scraped the top of his head and Bittewood staggered away, clutching at the wound. Byron brought the bike to a halt and Alan tried to climb on, but the biker had to help, more or less dragging him up onto the pillion. Alan's whole body was burning. He sensed rather than felt hands clutching at him as Byron took off again and turned his head a little, but he couldn't see their pursuers in the dark. The bike careened through archways, slid around corners and roared down wide corridors, a rain of black and white tiles clattering in their wake. Alan didn't know the way out and he was quite sure that Byron didn't know, either. Then through an archway on their left, he glimpsed light. He grabbed Byron's shoulder, leaned forward painfully and shouted in his ear, 'That left!'

Byron hit the brakes and swung the bike round, and the headlamp, lighting the way they'd just come, revealed figures, led by Bittewood, who was obviously not badly hurt, chasing them down the corridor. Byron pointed the bike at their hunters and raced back down the corridor – then, just before ploughing into them, he took a sharp turn towards the source of dim light that Alan had noticed coming through one of these many archways. As they sped towards it, getting nearer, it looked like a large, open double door – or maybe like some kind of big . . . *window*—

Alan's fingers dug into Byron's shoulders. Beyond the opening, the chequered tiled floor extended, so it wasn't a window, but then there was a rail, and—

The bike carried Byron and Alan out of the black interior into a sickly green light and they were briefly able to take in their surroundings. The archway led out onto a narrow railed balcony, beyond which was nothing. Byron was turning the bike round, or trying to, but they were going too fast; the rear end smashed through the rotten rail and the bike flew out into the nothingness. Alan glanced round to see they had emerged from a great house, one of many looking like giant limpets on the side of a great brick cliff.

Below them – *far* below them – was the pale green surface of the swamp. Cold air whipped past Alan's ears and nose as the bike plummeted. He twisted around again, looking down over his shoulder – the bike was falling backwards. His back, wet with blood, felt icy. The sludge below looked slick and smooth from up here. He wasn't aware of any sound; just the sensation of descent, and the stinking, glowing swamp rising to meet them. *Let there be no machines beneath us,* he thought, over and over, like a mantra. Slowly, *slowly,* the bike tipped further back, until it was upside down, while a rat in a wheel ran around and around where his stomach should have been. Even if there were nothing solid in the swamp, landing on their heads would mean death. The bike's rotation continued around until it was pointing straight down. Alan stared at the slime as they hit it, the front wheel splitting the pale green expanse, which exploded into shining globules and waves . . . and then they had passed into it and all was a cold darkness.

Things brushed slimily against Alan; strange plants or creatures, suspended debris, wood and bones . . . he didn't know what. Byron was in front of him still, and he could feel the bike pulling away from between their legs, the weight of it plunging it deeper. He grabbed Byron around the waist and kicked off the bike, pushing it further away, but also, he hoped, propelling them up and up, towards the surface. The swamp wasn't water; it was thicker than that, and difficult to swim in, like trying to move through cold, oily soup.

And suddenly Byron was conscious and kicking too, and at last they broke the surface, gasping. Alan tried not to think about the open wounds on his back, the filth that had no doubt found its way inside. Black and brown swirls muddied the swaying green, and this close, he could see glowing sparks flickering and dying in the swamp's disturbance. The accreted cliff with its wartish houses bordered one side, the enormous trunks of gigantic trees reared up on the other – this wasn't the gutwood, though; these trees were huge and straight, and only branched far above.

Alan's back stung. He cast about for a shoreline they could make for, but nowhere looked inviting.

'Fucking hell,' Byron said, and then, 'Cold.' He was shivering.

Alan realised they both were. 'Swim,' he managed. 'We need to swim.'

'Where to?'

'Doesn't matter. Come on.'

'Not the route I meant to take.'

'No.'

As Alan bobbed through the muck, his eyes were drawn to something green flashing from halfway up one of the vast trees. Then the swamp roiled and in trying to keep his head above water he lost sight of it. He splashed to a halt and turned himself around. There it was again: two green lights, visible in the shadows between the trees further back. Two green lights, shining from the gloom. As he stared, he narrowed his eyes until he thought he could make out a black shape clinging to the tree trunk, a dark shapeless form. It was staring back. And then came the scream, a baby's wailing cry.

'What's that?' Byron said, spitting out swamp water.

Alan watched in frozen horror as the Clawbaby detached itself from the tree trunk and dropped like a stone. He didn't see it hit the swamp, but he heard the faint splash. It echoed around inside his skull.

'Alan? What was it?' Byron repeated, looking around.

'That was the Clawbaby,' Alan panted, breathless with panic. 'We're well and truly fucked. Where can we go? Where can we *go*? No. *Fuck*. Let's just swim in the other direction.'

'But that's back towards the cliff,' Byron pointed out, his teeth chattering.

'Doesn't matter,' Alan said grimly. 'We head towards that thing, we're dead.' He struck out for the far shore, but the swamp was still peculiarly active and as they tried to swim, it became even more turbulent.

'These waves and bubbles,' Alan said suddenly, 'we're not making them.' But surely the Clawbaby couldn't have reached them yet? After a few moments he said softly, 'Byron, there are *things* in here with us.'

Pale forms of various size and shape breached the surface and sank again.

'What now?' he moaned. 'What have we disturbed?'

As if summoned by his words, a bulge appeared before them, grew and then split, pushing something grey and smooth upwards out of the sludge. The viscous liquids coating it started slipping away and Alan saw it was a large, hairless head, as large as Byron, but just a head. The eyes were protected by thick, transparent lids. Though a gigantic spherical head, the female face was strangely beautiful. She gazed down at the two men, and though Alan became slowly aware of other things crowding around them – people like toads, human heads on serpentine necks, a humanoid shape made of something like wax, with no face at all – still he couldn't tear his gaze from the giant woman. Her head rose higher out of the swamp; there was no neck supporting it but a hand. Alan frowned. Then the woman opened her large mouth wide, lassoed Byron with a long forked tongue and ate him. Byron started to scream just as her mouth closed on him.

'Hang on,' Alan started, but then she ate him too.

All Alan later remembered of being eaten was lying on a hillside the like of which he'd never known, watching clouds pass by overhead. The emerald grasslands rolled away into the distance, unbroken by buildings or ruins or Pyramids. Small yellow flowers dotted the ground. He didn't get up or move around; he felt at once sleepy, well rested and relaxed, with no desire to explore or otherwise exert himself. A cool breeze carried a clean green scent. He could hear distant voices that sounded vaguely familiar – his parents, maybe.

But that was later, and in retrospect. The first thing he was really aware of was a face coming into focus above him, and a pain screaming in his back. At first he thought the face was the one which had risen from the swamp, but no, it was different, smaller – and familiar. *Churr*. He was lying on a wooden table with a blanket beneath his head in a cold room with moisture dribbling down the moss-clad stone walls.

Churr smiled down at him. 'Alan,' she said. 'Alan. How goes it, sweet spunk-fungus?'

'The Clawbaby,' Alan said, trying to sit up, 'is it here? It was in the swamp – has it followed us? Is this Dok? And Nora? Is Nora here?'

'There have been no sightings of the Clawbaby,' Churr said. 'It might well have tried, but my people have brought you to me by a torturous and – to those of other natures – occasionally impossible route. And yes, this is Dok. My people brought you to me, and I am here, in Dok, where I remained after you fled. And Nora – yes, she is here too.'

'Green's teeth,' Alan said, almost laughing with relief. 'Thank the Builders! But Churr, what . . . what brought me here, to you?'

'You met some of my people,' Churr said. 'Daunt has her people, and now I have mine.'

'The Afflicted?'

'That's what the Pilgrims called them, which is not entirely fair, in my opinion. They might have been driven by the magic twisting within them to descend into the depths. Some of them might be in pain. And I will still help them, if I can. But I won't treat them all as sufferers, looking for healing or salvation. Many of them don't feel like victims at all.' She paused. 'Many more don't feel *anything*.'

'You're using them.'

'I've offered them what the Pilgrims never did and what Daunt won't: gainful employment. They help me here and now; they become part of my trading company. Once we've seen Daunt off we'll establish ourselves as production *and* distribution, and together we'll grow further and more quickly than Daunt, even.'

'I don't know where to start,' Alan said, sitting up, then he corrected himself. 'Wait – I do know where to start. Or, rather, let me ask again: what exactly was that thing that picked us up out there? And where's Byron?'

'Your friend is in another cell. And as for that *thing*, she's a *person*, Alan.'

'Come on—'

She sighed. 'I guess I of all people shouldn't expect you to accord a woman due respect.'

'What's her name, then?'

'Dunno – she never speaks. We all call her Head-in-Hands. She seems to have limitless interior capacity. She'll eat anything, and regurgitate it later, whole, unharmed. She doesn't have a mouth; it's a portal. She'd be great for transporting goods, if she could leave the swamp.'

'You're unbelievable.'

'What do you remember from being inside her?'

'Nothing.'

'You will. You haven't been in her stomach, as such;

when she swallows you, you go somewhere else — everybody goes somewhere different. Where inanimate objects go, we have no idea, but it's remarkable. The people down here, Alan; the magic — its reputation as a hellhole was entirely undeserved.'

'Maybe it was just supposed to be a deterrent? To stop people coming here? Anyway, it's lovely to catch up, Churr, really it is, but I need to see Nora.'

Churr's mocking smile vanished. 'My Nora,' she whispered, 'is here, but I found her nearly dead — and because of you. Did you honestly think you were going to be leaving this bed, Alan? Think again! You're here so I can take my long and bloody revenge on your worthless, scrawny body — and in case you were wondering, that is something else that I can be better at than Daunt: *sadism*.'

'Churr, I'm sorry. I really am.'

'Do not apologise, Alan,' came another voice, from the doorway. 'You did the right thing.'

Alan slid from the gurney to see Nora limping through the cell door and into the room. 'Fucking hell,' he said, hobbling forward to embrace her. 'Nora. Thank fuck. Nora, you're a fucking star. I didn't want to leave you behind, but it was thanks to you we got away. And you're still here. How badly are you hurt?'

'Well,' Nora said, frowning slightly, 'let us come back to that. How about you? You are still alive too! So you were successful?'

'Well,' Alan said, his throat tightening. 'Well.' He

thought about how to say it. 'In a way, yes we were. But in another way we were not.'

'Eyes is not here,' Nora said.

'No,' Alan said.

Nora was looking at him – staring at him. 'Where is Eyes, Alan?'

'He's dead,' Alan said.

'I'm sorry. What happened?'

'It was at the Pyramid – at the handover. I . . . don't want to talk about it.'

'The Arbitrators.' Churr stated it as a fact, not a question, and Alan did not correct her.

5

Sumpwards

Dok was buzzing with activity. A large man wearing a long, shapeless shift reached up and placed his palms flat against the wall. Tiny versions of himself clambered up from under the neckline of his shift, ran easily up his arms and climbed onto the wall, wedging their little feet and hands into the cracks between the stones. They sawed at the stems of mushrooms with miniature hacksaws and passed them backwards to more of them who kept appearing from inside the sleeves. Byron stared, open-mouthed.

'That's Gorge,' Churr said. 'He keeps birthing these homunculi – I won't go into how; it's awful to see. I think it's causing him damage, both physically and spiritually, but he won't stop.'

Other Afflicted were also helping to harvest the crop. Some were arranging wooden gurneys against the wall, and yet more were building new ones.

But Alan could see plenty who could not help, even if

they'd wanted to: men, women and the occasional child with bodies simply disrupted by rifts or extra fleshy appendages or glass globes, or with weird insects and creatures erupting out of some inner place. Some were just lying on the floor, moaning. Some bore little resemblance to actual human people. In one wooden bed was a pile of heads, all fused together; some were blinking, a few were crying. In another bed was a short, fat snake, and it took Alan several moments to realise that the colours of its scales formed a pattern of human faces. For all of the reconstruction going on around him, there were obviously still a lot of people in Dok who needed care and attention.

'I've been told that the Pilgrims kept the Afflicted animals away from Dok,' Alan murmured, 'and without their efforts, those animals will come back.'

'There have been sightings of strange creatures,' Churr agreed, 'but the corruption seems to affect humans and animals differently. The animals might end up physically different, but that's all – some of the people end up . . . well, *impossible*. But not the animals: the animals can turn into something stronger, or bigger – like that snail, remember? – or they end up in pain and more aggressive. Or they're warped in ways that they simply can't survive.'

'The skullfrogs,' Byron said. 'Are there skullfrogs here?'

'What are skullfrogs?' Churr asked.

'Monsters,' Byron said. 'You're a ba— You're a transient, right? You'll have seen them. White things with tentacles instead of arms and legs, lots of stingin' whips growing out of their backs. Bikers call 'em skullfrogs, because they're like the little skullfrogs you get in the reservoirs way out east.'

'I know what you mean,' Churr said. 'Nope, none here. They're rare, though. Only ever seen one or two, even when I journeyed deep.'

'They were massin', and they were high – high for skullfrogs, anyway,' Byron said. 'We cut one up on the way down. Thing had a human skeleton. What does that mean?'

'I'd always assumed they were Swamp-spawned. Just . . . y'know.' Churr shrugged. 'A Swamp species. Never thought about them much. Maybe they're Swamp-dwellers who get warped beyond the usual? Or dead bodies that get taken over by something else, like Idle Hands or like . . . how the Hermits strap on those empty snail shells. I mean, the Swamp makes monsters. We all know that.'

They came to the ruins of the Giving Beast, which was lying in the centre of the ground floor of the circular tower. It looked like a huge giant slug now, with its canopy pitted and sweating, its fringe turning to slime. The soft, rotting skin had split open in places and the ribs and struts of its interior were protruding through like broken bones.

'We removed the remains of the Terrarium from inside,' Churr explained, 'and we're still in the process of moving the beds from the gills of the Beast to the cells – we'll be keeping the internal walls clear for the mushrooms to grow. We're also going to bring in dead wood so there'll be more surface area for the fungi.'

'You're just leaving the Sanctuary there to rot?'

'No, of course not,' Churr said airily. 'We're going to slice it up and dry it out, for food. They said it would be blasphemy, but everybody needs to eat.'

'Who said?'

'The few remaining Pilgrims – I've got them locked up. They say they mean us no harm, but if I was in their position I'd be looking for revenge first chance I got.'

'Hell,' Alan said, 'you're going to be a popular mushroom queen.'

'You can't be friends with everyone.' She sounded pragmatic. Then she asked, 'Is your back hurting?'

'It's hurting really fucking badly, since you ask—'

'Poor thing,' Churr said. Then she slapped him hard across the shoulders, and laughed.

Alan winced, paling, and struggled to remain upright. 'You monster,' he hissed. 'It's going to get infected – my back's going to go all green and soft and rotten and slide right off. I know it.'

'Yeah, probably.'

'Get yerself a good wash,' Byron said. 'I 'ad a snakebite went bad a couple of years back. No venom, just dirt. In

me armpit too. Yer might think a wash is more trouble
than it's worth, but—'

'Thank you, Byron! Think I've heard enough. But
Churr; listen, what did you do with the bodies?'

'Gave them to Green.'

'You just dumped them in the swamp? By the Builders, Churr! I don't know which of us is more despicable—'

'No, we didn't just *dump* them! We gave them to
Green – that's what they call it here. It's a ceremony. We
did it properly – we did it the way they do it down here.
We wrapped them, and—'

'All of them?'

Churr rolled her eyes. 'Yes, well, as many as we could
before we ran out of the bark they use. So, no, in fact.
But we *tried*, damn it! And it was a lot of work, what
with Nora hurt and . . . and the state the dead were in.
We did well. We're *doing* well. Anyway, an old Pilgrim
lady consecrated the bodies, and then we pushed them
out into the swamp on big rafts – you know, from where
Daunt kept her snails – trailing chum to draw the
crocodiles.'

'Oh, yeah, very nice. That's just how I'd like to pass into
the Great Beyond: chewed up by a fucking croc. Through
a stinking reptile's mouth. And out of its arsehole too, presumably. Right this way to everlasting peace.'

'There'll be no peace for you, Alan.'

'Spider? Spider too? I wanted to pay my respects.'

'Yes, Spider too. I'm sorry. There are no crypts down

here; they don't do it like that. And of course, there's no earth we could have buried him in.'

'Bloody hell.' Alan blinked. 'Bloody hell.'

In the canteen, Alan, Churr, Nora and Byron ate slices of swanmeat fried in nut oil, and great wedges of roasted mushroom. Byron quickly wolfed down his helping and went for more.

'Seems like a dull sort,' Churr said, in his absence. 'Something going on between you?'

'No. Not much. But he's not dull.'

Churr nodded. Alan braced himself for some kind of barb, but it didn't come. Churr was squeezing Nora's hand in her own.

'So what comes next?' Churr asked upon Byron's return. 'What exactly brought you here, Alan?'

'I've got to get into the Pyramid,' Alan said, taking Snapper from his back and idly picking at the strings. 'And . . . I'm going in through the Sump.'

'You're fucking not,' Churr blurted. 'The Sump is . . . well, we don't know, do we? Ippil told us it's where the corruption comes from. Why the Swamp warps things. Because the Pyramid dumps all its shit in there.' Ippil was the Pilgrim who had welcomed Alan and his companions on their first visit to Dok, when they'd journeyed there to acquire the Green's Benedictions that Alan had been blackmailed into trafficking. 'You know the Pilgrims wouldn't allow the Seal to be opened. It was because they were scared of what might escape from the Sump. That's where the Horned came from, remember?'

'The what?' Byron asked.

'People whose whole bodies had been taken over by this kind of fungus. They called it Idle Hands. It works its way through them, changing them, their brains, their bones . . . and then it grows out of their heads as *horns*.'

'Nice,' Byron said, putting down his forkful of mushroom. 'Nice.'

'Yes, yes,' Alan said. 'I remember. When the time comes, just – open the Seal, and then immediately close it again. Snappy. That's the way we're going in, Churr. No risk to you, is there? If you're quick.'

'What about the Horned?' Byron asked. 'If them Horned came from down there, there must've been people down there in the first place. Might still be down there, is what I'm sayin'.'

'Might be,' Alan conceded.

'And what about spores? All fungi have spores, right?'

'We don't know much, but what we do know suggests the parasite spreads through blood, not air; it grows inside the body. That's why it urges its hosts towards violence. That's one reason why it's so dangerous.'

'But why? Why take the risk at all?' Churr laughed. 'You're telling me you came all this way to go through the Sump into the Pyramid? You're mad.'

'Billy is sick and I need to get him something that will make him better.'

'Doesn't the Pyramid have physics?'

'Yeah, but . . . look.' Alan thumped Snapper with the flat of his hand, lifted the instrument from round his neck and placed it on the table. 'Billy was wounded with a knife that carried Idle Hands in some kind of ichor. Probably blood-based, now I think about it. I've got Green's Benedictions, they'll cure him. They *should* cure him. They don't have them in the Pyramid; we know this, because Tromo, the Arbitrator, blackmailed me to provide them. And so I'm going in there, whether you come with me or not, whether you like it or not, to deliver what he needs.'

Churr frowned. 'Who would hurt Billy?' Her voice was softer than Alan expected.

Alan shook his head. 'I can't . . . I can't say.'

'What do you mean?' Churr's eyes flashed. 'Billy is your *son*. Who are you protect—?'

'So who were the Benedictions for, then?' Nora interrupted, gently taking hold of Churr's arm. 'Did Tromo have Idle Hands?'

'No,' Alan replied, grateful for the intervention. He hadn't told Nora what Eyes had done to Billy, or what he had done to Eyes, but she might have worked it out. Or she might just have been trying to ease his apparent discomfort. Either way, he jumped at the change of direction. 'The Benedictions were generally traded as an intoxicant. They're powerfully – some would say transcendentally – hallucinogenic; they're reputed to grant foresight or visions of the distant past.' He picked Snapper up from the table and reached inside for the small packet of Benedictions he'd secured there. He opened the packet and laid it flat on the table. The mushrooms had been dried, and looked like little more than a small pile of spindly twigs, green with lichen. 'But they're also addictive. Well, maybe not the mushrooms, but the *experiences*. Tromo was an addict, plain and simple. He was hooked. The Benedictions are a cure, but they're dangerous things in their own right.' He paused. 'For Billy's sake, it's a good job there are no more.' He stared at the mushrooms in front of him a moment longer, and then hastily wrapped them back up.

'And you, Byron?' Churr asked. 'You off on this suicide mission?'

'Yep.'

'Are you?' Alan said. 'I thought you were just—' He looked at Nora to try and gauge her thoughts. 'I thought your duty was done. Lutwidge only told you to escort me here.'

'Maybe. But I'm still comin' with.'

'Why? Why do you want to come?'

'Why do I have to *want* somethin'?'

'Everybody *always* wants something. It's the only reason anybody ever does anything in this damn place.'

'Yeah, well. Thought I might drop in on my old folks, see how they're doin'.'

'You can't hold us up, or draw attention to us.'

'Once we're in, I don't even need to stay with yer. I can find me mum and dad, talk to them and then Discard meself.'

'Well, no, no splitting up. What if your parents lose it, and raise the alarm? No. Not happening.'

'I'll be coming, too,' Nora said.

'No!' Churr sounded genuinely anguished now. 'Nora, please—'

'I have to go,' Nora said. 'I know it now.'

'You owe that prick *nothing*,' Churr growled.

'I'm not going for him. I have my own reasons. But we can help each other.'

'Well, my plan is this,' Alan said. 'I've got to get in, and get these Benedictions to Billy. Then I'm going to . . .' He trailed off. He closed his eyes and saw the Bleeding Chairs. He saw the burning mills, he saw the burning boats, he saw the burning bodies. He saw the Arbitrators dragging Eyes through the mud. He saw his own blood spattering the clean stone floors of the Pyramid plaza he used to sing in, brought forth by an Arbitrator's fist. He imagined the terror felt by the kidnapped. 'We've got to bring them down,' he said, quietly. 'Eyes was right.'

'And how?' Churr glanced around the group, an incredulous smile on her face.

'If you can take on Daunt, then I can take on the fucking Pyramid,' Alan snarled. 'I don't need you to believe in me.'

'You do need a plan, though,' Nora cautioned. 'Churr's

question is a good one, and you should think of an answer.'

'We go in. We have to disguise ourselves; we'll need robes. We'll need to steal them. We get to Marion's quarters, we give Billy the Benedictions. Then – and I'm not asking anybody to come with me – I ascend. I find the Management, and kill them.'

Churr burst out laughing. 'That's not a plan! That's an *intention*. How the hell would you get close to Management? I mean, I know I don't know the Pyramid, but I'm guessing there'd be Arbitrators between you and them.'

'I don't know yet, okay? And I haven't got time to work it out. Billy needs us *now*. One thing we can arrange, though: what happens to Billy after he's got the antidote, and what happens to Marion?'

'If we've got that far,' Byron said, 'we can assume we haven't been caught, right? So we can just leave again.'

'I don't want to leave them there.'

'What they want is more important,' Nora said.

Alan ran his fingers through his hair, pulling out gritty strands of some kind of swampweed. 'Yeah, you're right. You're right. But we need a contingency, in case they have to escape. If they have to come down the chutes, who meets them?'

A pause. Then, 'Churr,' Nora said.

'I don't know about that,' Alan said.

'Why not?' Churr asked. 'Don't you trust me?'

'No. That is my reservation exactly, as you well know.'

'Churr will not hurt them, or let them be hurt,' Nora said. 'Will you, Churr?'

'No – don't worry. They've done me no wrong at all and I will not let harm close to them. Though I myself will probably not make the journey. I will use my people.'

'Then choose your people wisely,' Alan said. 'And make sure they know where the House of a Thousand Hollows is; they're to take Marion and Billy straight there. No delaying, no diversions, no adventures. Maggie the Red will take them in.'

'Understood.'

'We'll need to send a message to the Goatherds – Skeffington Lutwidge is helping us in return for . . . in return for some help from you, Nora. So let's make it worth our while.'

'*My* help?' Nora frowned. 'Soon I will tire of being everybody's pet renegade Mapmaker, Alan. I am not a bargaining chip.'

'I know that!' Alan said indignantly. 'And you're quite right, we need to make sure everybody else knows that too. But . . . let's wait until after they've helped us before we educate them.' He sighed. 'There's one more thing I need to tell you before we get ready and go. I told Churr, I saw the Clawbaby just before Head-in-Hands picked us up. It's still out there. So how the hell did you survive, Nora? You didn't kill it, but you're still here.'

'As you have seen, I did not destroy it,' Nora said. 'Its body is not a proper body. Beneath that dusty cloak it is all just hard flesh; like a tree is all wood, no soft spots to pierce, no veins to open, no organs to rupture. How it works, I cannot say. The baby was closed up inside it and I couldn't get at it, even though its head had been removed and it could not see me. In truth the thing bested me, despite its blindness; in trying to penetrate it I kept showing it where I was, and it cut me and threw me around a bit. But it wanted *you*, Alan. It was furious at having to waste its time on *a little scrap* like me. Those were its words: *A little scrap*. Anyway, it threw me across the place and I hit the stalk of the Giving Beast, hard, and I fell to the ground, hard, but I landed in a big pile of mush – Pilgrims, cut up really bad – so I quickly pulled a load of gore over me and stuffed some into my mouth – brains and teeth and such – and played dead. So it looked as if all of that filth had come out of me, you know. I held my breath and closed my eyes and rolled my eyes right back, in case it came after me, but it did not. It could have run me through to be sure I was gone, but it did not, because it wanted *you*, Alan. It wanted you and only you. So it just left in pursuit of you.'

'Thank you, Nora,' Alan said. 'I'm sorry you got hurt for my sake.'

'That's all right – but that's not the end. Once it left, I got up and snuck after it – quiet as a dead leaf on the water; that's what the Mapmaker tutors used to say. It screamed, you know its baby scream, but the screaming came from its severed head, back at the ruins of the

Giving Beast. Its body blundered into the swamp and sank right down, but it kept on going. It left a muddy path through the green.'

'Well, at least it won't be able to follow us where we're going next.'

'I don't want you to go, Nora,' Churr said. 'Alan, I don't even want you to go – this is suicide.'

'We won't get in any other way,' Alan said. 'There are too many Arbitrators, even for Nora.'

'And I would rather not let it be known that I am a Mapmaker,' Nora said. 'There is a peace treaty between the Pyramid and the Mapmakers, and I am about to violate it by trespassing upon their property. I am not prepared for us to fight our way in so we must enter secretly, and then remain undiscovered.'

'Once inside, we should be able to lie low,' Alan said. 'And the less violence, the better – I don't want to be responsible for any more killing.'

'Apart from whatever is in the Sump,' Nora added. 'We will have to do some killing in there.'

'Not killing of humans, though,' Alan qualified.

'Will the corruption affect you?' Churr asked Nora quietly. 'The Swamp affected us all badly last time, and the Giving Beast healed us. But now . . . sometimes I can feel the Swamp reaching out, the corruption eating into our minds. And you, going in there, disappearing into the depths of it . . .'

'We will have to be quick.'

'Perhaps there's still some power in the body of the Beast,' Alan said. 'Maybe we should load up on what's left of it.' He speared another piece of swan with his fork. 'Before we do, Churr, you said there are some Pilgrims still here?'

'Yeah.'

'I'll have to speak with them.'

'I'll take you to their cells.'

'Thank you.' He pulled some more filth from his hair, then sniffed at his shirt. 'Might have that wash first, though.'

The remaining Pilgrims were living in some of the same rooms that had been theirs before their world had been turned inside out, except that Churr had them all corralled into one corridor and locked the doors from the outside.

Churr let Alan into the corridor alone. He felt like a new man, having washed in rainwater fed down to Dok through a system of runnels and pipes. He wore clean dry clothes; not the shirt and dark trousers he was accustomed to, but a pale grey tunic, grey leggings and a brown jerkin. The fabric was thick and rough, but it was clean and dry.

Some of the cage doors had sheets hung up on the inside and murmuring voices could be heard behind the make-shift curtains: chanting, mantras, conversations between adjacent cells. Alan stopped at a cell that didn't have anything obscuring the scene within and saw an elderly woman kneeling before a glass bowl in which some kind of luminescent fungus was growing. Her eyes were closed and her lips moved silently. She wore a pale robe, stained with blood around the hem, and her hair was bound in a long grey plait. Alan didn't interrupt her prayer but waited patiently.

When she finished, she rose slowly from her knees.

'Excuse me,' Alan said.

'Goodness,' the woman said, putting a hand to her throat and turning around. 'You gave me a shock.'

'I'm sorry. I was hoping to speak with you.'

'You can speak with me.' She sat down on the edge of her hard wooden bed. 'Do I know you?'

'No,' he said firmly.

'My memory was getting worse anyway, but since the Sanctuary fell . . .' The woman smiled. 'I think it kept us young.'

Alan opened his mouth to apologise, but then closed it again; she probably wouldn't appreciate his apology. And it would hold them up – he didn't have time for that. As it was, she didn't know who he was and he resolved to keep it that way. 'I wanted to find somebody,' he started, 'who understood Green's Benedictions, and how they were used.'

'There are no Benedictions left,' the woman said. 'The Terrarium was destroyed by vandals and the remaining Benedictions were taken.'

'So I hear – but I intend to get them back, because I've also heard rumours' – Alan leaned in and lowered his voice to a whisper – 'that horned men have been seen again. And if that's the case, it's now, more than ever, that those Green's Benedictions are required.'

'I told them not to sell to the Redcapper. I *told* them. Especially the Benedictions. Green save us, the Benedictions were *sacred*. The *Terrarium* was sacred. And it's all gone now, of course. All ruined.' The woman was playing with her plait, twisting it between thin-skinned hands. 'Horned men?' she repeated suddenly.

'Yes.'

'Idle Hands? Oh Green! Old Green, save us.' She got up from the bed and started pacing up and down the small cell.

'You remember it, then? Idle Hands?'

'I am not *that* old,' she snorted. 'I remember the stories my grandparents told, though.'

'So what did they have to do with the Benedictions? Did your grandparents tell you that? Do you need to prepare them? Do you need to administer them in any particular way?'

'They must be dried and then ingested – that knowledge was passed on.' She paused in her pacing for a moment and said, 'Of course, the Benedictions can't reverse any damage done; all they can do is halt the spread of Idle Hands itself: kill the fungus, and kill the host's urge to propagate it.'

'And what of the side-effects?'

But before the woman could answer, somebody shouted from across the passage, '*You!*'

'Yes?' Alan said, turning around.

'I know you – yes, yes, I do! I know those tattoos! You're the bastard – yes, you are! It's *you!*'

'Weddle,' Alan sighed. Weddle's interfering had made things difficult for them last time.

'Indeed! Yes!'

Weddle had had another go at shaving his head, but he'd missed most of the tufts and given himself plenty of new cuts in the process. 'You! Yes, you—! You did it! You're one of the bastards! You're the boss bastard—!'

'You're one of the desecrators?' the woman demanded, suddenly standing at the cell door, gripping the bars. Alan hesitated, and that gave her all of the confirmation she needed. She spat a large gobbet of saliva into his face.

He wiped himself and slipped away as the rattling of cage doors spread and intensified and voices started shouting '*Vandal!*', '*Thief!*', '*Sacrilege!*' and '*Monster!*' The cries echoed around his head long after he'd left the Pilgrims behind.

Alan played cards with the Afflicted at the Seal while he waited for Nora and Byron. He recognised Gorge, but not the other players; Gorge introduced them as Nasha, Darrity and Helena. Nasha was quick to laugh, a young bright girl with cheekbones protruding through the skin of her face, one arm, and patches of what looked like bark growing over her skin. She seemed to play without thinking, and won round after round. Darrity was a big man, his head, face and arms covered in thick hair and his jaw twisted in such a way that he found it difficult to speak. His eyes had a faint glow to them; it wasn't that they were bright, but they left an afterimage burned across Alan's vision. And Helena's whole form was indistinct; when Alan looked at her she seemed solid, but when he looked away he had the sense of her flesh breaking the bounds of her form, somehow; the sense of seething movement. Helena was older, and wore her grey hair in a mohawk.

'Your turn, Darrity,' Nasha said, placing one of her cards face down in front of her. The game was called The Crocodile, and was one of bluffing; Alan had thought it overly simple at first, but he had been wrong. Darrity looked at his hand, at the stack in front of him and back at his hand. 'I played a toad,' Nasha told him. 'Trust me. It was a toad. Come on.'

Darrity shook his head and placed a card on his own stack. Gorge laughed a low laugh and put a card down too.

Alan looked at all the cards on the table. 'I'm gonna challenge,' he said. 'I'm gonna flip four.'

Helena pursed her lips and shook her head. Nasha said, 'Five. I can do five. Come on, Darrity. Six? You going six?'

Darrity shook his great head. Gorge raised a hand.

'Six,' he rumbled, and the other smaller Gorges spectating all gasped. 'I can do six.'

Alan shook his head. Where were Byron and Nora? He'd have to go and find them after this round. 'Do it, Gorge,' he said. 'You're a braver man than me.'

Gorge, smiling, flipped the uppermost card from his stack. A toad. The cards were square, beautifully illustrated by an artist named Harn whose affliction had grown fatal; one morning she had been found dead on a swamp jetty, glass globes having burst from her stomach. The illustrations were stylised, blocky black renderings of toads and crocodiles surrounded by bright patterns of snakes, birds and swamp flowers. Gorge flipped the next: another toad. If he managed to reveal six toads and not a single croc, he'd have won the round. If he turned over a croc, then he'd lose a card – each player started with four – and everybody would take their stack back and start the round again. Gorge flipped his last card. Another toad. Now he had to move onto somebody else's stack.

'Nasha,' he said, 'you were going five. Must've known your own stack's clean. Let me see the top one.'

Nasha, laughing, flipped the card to reveal a crocodile. Harn's crocodile wasn't just any old crocodile: it was Old Green, the six-legged crocodile god.

Gorge threw his hand of cards to the table, grinning. 'Damn you, Nasha!'

Nasha danced a little in her seat. Alan couldn't take his eyes off the crocodile card. *Old Green*. But Nasha gathered up her cards, including Old Green, and the spell was broken.

Alan stood up abruptly. 'Thanks for the game, but you'll have to count me out now,' he said. 'I need to find out where my reprobate friends are at. We should have left already.'

'We're waiting too,' said Helena. 'Churr assigned us to help you lift the Seal. She said she'd meet us here as well.'

'After all this, let's play again.'

'We will,' Gorge said. 'We will.'

Byron was back in the canteen. 'Don't know when we'll be eatin' again,' he said, somewhat sheepishly, when Alan caught up with him. 'And this swamp swan's bleedin' beautiful.' He waved a hunk of meat at Alan. 'Y'should get some yerself.'

'I would, but . . . I could never eat much before a gig. Feels a bit like that, y'know? But more so. Stomach like a walnut. After that food before, I'm stuffed. I'm looking for Nora – have you seen her? Or Churr? It's time for us to go I think.'

'All right, all right. Just let me—'

'No, finish your food. Take pleasure while you can, right? And I haven't found the others yet. We'll come back here and get you once I've found them.'

'Sure I saw Churr heading back to her chambers. In that direction, at least.'

'Great, thanks. And where are they?'

'Where we woke up.'

'I thought they were cells of some kind?'

Byron shook his head, mouth full. 'That's where Churr sleeps, man.'

Making his way back through the corridors, Alan wondered if he'd got Churr wrong. He wasn't sure which he'd rather believe: that Churr was a callous opportunist who'd do anything to get what she wanted, or that she was deep-down decent but putting up a cruel front. He knew which would stand a better chance, and it wasn't the latter.

He walked past empty cells, some with signs of inhabit-ation, but many without. None of them looked that homely or comfortable. He could hear movement in a corridor up ahead; these quarters were a bit of a maze. But what part of Gleam wasn't?

Alan turned a corner to see Churr pinning Nora up against the wall, Nora's legs wrapped around Churr's waist, Churr's mouth on Nora's, her hands – Alan's own hand was halfway to his knife before his brain caught up with his eyes.

'Shit,' he said, and quailed before the two fierce glares that were turned upon him. 'Sorry. Sorry!' He reversed back around the corner and then hurried away.

He'd just wait for them back at the Seal, then.

Churr rounded up a team of some of the biggest Afflicted she could find and met Alan, Nora and Byron at the remains of the Giving Beast. Churr was not alone in carrying coils of rope over her shoulders.

'We're going to hoist it up,' she announced. 'It's shrivelled away to almost nothing of its former glory, so what's left will be rotten and light.'

We're going to hoist it. Alan looked at its remains – *its corpse?* He really didn't know what to call it. *We're going to hoist it.* Lift it away from the sealed plug that led down to the Sump, the place where it had finally settled after who knows how many years, decades or centuries roaming Gleam, followed by the Pilgrims' ancestors, travelling from each location to the next.

The Afflicted got to work straight away, slinging the ropes through hooks hanging from the beams crisscrossing the central space of the tower. Alan watched them for a moment before joining in to help. For all Churr spoke of paying them respect, of honouring their self-determination by employing them, of not seeing them as victims alone, she was definitely *using* them. Last time they'd all come down here, the Afflicted had spoken to him. Yes, they'd been . . . well, *afflicted* – they'd obviously been in pain, scared – but they'd been alert, conversational. This time, it was almost as if they'd had something removed – their spirit.

Or perhaps the clever ones aren't as willing to be exploited so she's given them to Green.

The Giving Beast was brown and slimy. Much of what had been its canopy almost liquefied at first contact with the ropes and simply sluiced away across the ground. The ropes did manage to snag on the ribs and the stem, though, and they tautened as Alan and the others pulled on them. Nora stood further back; Churr had insisted her injury prevented her from helping. More and more of the Beast was sliced off by the ropes, and as the larger pieces fell splattering to the ground, they threw maggots everywhere. Alan looked down and shook his leg to displace the wriggling grubs from his foot just as one of the hooks pinged from its beam above, shooting through the air and narrowly missing Nora's head, showering sparks as it hit the ground. The Beast's remains might not be heavy, but the trunk was firmly rooted in place and Alan began to fear it might snap the ropes.

Churr gave the call, Alan and the Afflicted strained at the ropes and as they all pulled, another hook came loose and Churr fell backwards, knocking her elbows on the hard ground, and then there was a grinding sound and something shifted, ever so slightly, and then the Giving Beast's trunk wobbled a little and came loose, and there was much more of that *grinding*, and the trunk slowly rose from the Seal, or rather, it rose *with* the Seal, a great metal disc, held fast by what looked like a thick, rubbery white mould.

'*Shit*,' Churr said, back on her feet and running over. '*Shit!* Right – Alan, Nora, Byron, fuck off. Go – get down there, do what you have to do. Nora, do your carto down there. We need to get that plug back into place immediately. Darrity, Nasha, you – I've forgotten your name . . . yes, you, *Helena* – knives out. Once these fools have dropped through, we've got to start cutting that mould or that root or whatever it is if we're going to be able to drop the Seal back into place. We need to keep whatever's down there down there. Here.' She took the rope Alan was holding from him. 'Good luck, fucker. And Nora—!'

Nora looked up at her from the edge of the big dark hole beneath the lifted Seal. 'Yes?'

'I love you.'

'I love you too, Churr,' she said.

'Now, go!'

6

The Sump

The Seal fell back into place above them, closing off the light as they dropped the last ten feet or so into the filth. *Yet more filth.* The rope they'd used to climb down splashed into the murk beside them and sank. *Filth everywhere,* Alan thought, taking Snapper from his back and tipping the water out. It couldn't really be called water. *Swamp or blood or filth — it just never ends. Life's a series of dives from shithole to shithole.* He gagged on it and spat it out before trying to wade through it, holding Snapper above his head. There was a base of some kind, some soft, spongy matter. He turned and crawled up the slope, emerged onto the shore — not dry land, you couldn't call it that — and retched. Nora climbed up beside him. Byron heaved himself up, coughing.

'One day I'll stay clean,' Alan said, unidentifiable fluid dripping from his hair and running down his face. 'I'll have a good long wash and just go and sit somewhere for a while — some warm dry rooftop. I'll eat something plain and wholesome and drink nothing but water – no, I'll drink beer. Beer is safer. But I won't drink too much, just enough to ensure a nice, restful state of mind. I'll watch the sun go down and all of the stars come out and I'll drift off and I'll sleep for *hours*.'

'You can't sleep without drinking too much,' Nora said. 'Good sleep and not drinking too much – the two are incompatible for you. Just one of your many dilemmas. Now look at this extraordinary place. Come on, man, get up.'

Alan got to his feet. The wounds on his back were stinging, but they felt better for being cleaned. His body was stiff. He'd never been fat but these days he was positively wiry – wiry and tense. He could hear something dripping and trickling, and he could smell earth.

They stood on a shoreline of damp mulch at the edge of a large, square room that looked as if it might be part of the original structure. There were more heaps of the mulch protruding out of the liquid and banked up against the other walls. Everything was illuminated by large, flat mushrooms that glowed with a bright light as well as luminous slime that coated the walls and hung as small globules in the liquid lapping at their feet. Alan could see two exits from the room, facing each other: large openings that nearly reached the ceiling and through which he could see similar rooms.

'Here,' Nora said, pulling something from one of the pouches she wore around her waist. 'Eat.' She thrust whatever it was up into Alan's face and he recoiled. 'Flesh of the Giving Beast,' she said.

'Oh.' Alan took it gingerly; it felt like an internal organ, dank and heavy in his hand. 'Could do with a knife and fork.'

'Shut up and eat it.'

'I'm regrettin' this already,' Byron said as Nora handed him his portion.

Alan forced himself to take a bite of the rotting mushroom and it burst in his mouth, filling it with sour mush and flooding his sinuses with an acrid stench. It took everything he had not to immediately throw it back up.

'By the Builders,' he said, after he'd eventually swallowed it, 'that's fucking foul.'

'Seconded.' Byron was gagging, his hands on his knees.

'You eat what you've got to eat,' Nora said. She was already on her third bite, chewing methodically. 'It's all we've got against the corruption.'

'And it might not even work.'

'I think it will: it helped people against the effects of the corruption when it was alive and magic doesn't just disappear in death. The swamp certainly hasn't affected me like it was doing before we reached Dok, even though the Giving Beast is dead.'

'If you say so.' Alan took another bite. 'Bloody hell,' he said, grimacing. Chewing, he asked, 'So the swamp madness that took you – it hasn't come back?'

'I can feel tendrils,' Nora said. 'The swamp is full of sick magic that hurts the spirit of Gleam, which means that it hurts me – any Mapmaker would be similarly affected. The Giving Beast is an antidote against it. When it was alive, its spores filled the air and our lungs and our blood, and its power flooded my body that way. Now it is dead, the only way for it to work on us is if we eat it – but in eating it, we destroy it, of course. And that which is not eaten will soon rot to nothing, so once the Giving Beast is gone, the swamp will once again reach out and grip me, if I am here for it to grip. In short, I will have to stay away from it.'

Once they'd finished the noisome chunks, Alan pulled something from his own bag. 'To wash it down with,' he said, waggling a bottle of Dog Moon at Nora. 'They had a few in the stores there. You can say *that* for the Pilgrims, no high-faluting taste in whisky, thank Green.'

'We destroyed their Terrarium and killed their Giving Beast and led the Clawbaby there to massacre them – and now you steal from their supplies? And what do you steal? A bottle of whisky!'

'*Please*,' Alan said. 'I stole three.' He uncorked the bottle in his hand and drank deeply. 'Just in time. If I'd waited a moment later to burn that taste out of my mouth I'd have brought the whole lot back up again.'

Nora took the bottle from him and took a swig. 'Yes,' she said. 'It was most unpleasant. I cannot disagree.'

'Which way do we go?'

'I think we should head towards the source of the corruption.'

'Naturally – but which way is that?'

'This close to the corruption, I cannot use my gems and cartos as I usually would, but I can at least use them to indicate its direction. The spirit of Gleam is still here – it is sick, but it is here, and it can speak to me still.'

'We need to head towards the Pyramid.'

'Yes, yes, yes, very good. Now let me be.'

Alan and Byron watched as Nora conducted her carto. It began with deep breathing and a kind of impossible stillness: she stood, hands together at her front, head back, before progressing into a series of arm movements, a few quick steps forwards, her feet sinking into the mulch, her body twisting, leg now up as if to kick, a jump and crouch . . . and so it went on, every move grace-ful and controlled.

'What's this, then?' Byron asked.

'The carto. She explained it to me once as a "winding-in"; she's winding in the spirit of Gleam from the surrounding area and kind of reading it. Normally it would leave her with a good picture of the nearby terrain and enable her to plan her journey. But it's more than that: it's a form of communion with the spirit. Not that the spirit exists just to help Mapmakers in their travels; it's a two-way thing, somehow. But I can't pretend to understand it.' Alan put his hand on Byron's shoulder. 'I appreciate you being here, truth be told. Nora scares me sometimes. Not because of her magic, but because of her . . . *capability.*'

'That right?' Byron asked, smiling wryly. 'That why yer glad I'm here? What about that kiss? Mean anythin' to yer?'

Alan folded his arms. 'Not now,' he said. Abruptly he turned and walked down the slope and into the shallows. He decided on calling it 'swamp'. It maybe wasn't *the* Swamp, but it was born of the Swamp and probably consisted of the same stuff. Those small blue-glowing globules broke up, rejoined, bobbed around in his wake. Byron could *fuck off*. The luminescent slime seemed to remain distinct from whatever it floated in, like oil on water. Now his eyes had adjusted, the slime gave off more than enough light to see by. Well, no; that wasn't it; everything was coated in the stuff to a greater or lesser extent, and so it was all visible against the darkness, though it didn't penetrate the darkness as such. He waded through the swamp towards one of the exits and felt his heartbeat increasing as he approached it and saw more and more of what lay beyond.

The swamp receded into the distance, broken by islands of the mulch and by strange, blocky formations. There was a distant ceiling, far higher than that which they'd just dropped through, also streaked with the glowing slime; at a faraway point, the ceiling met the surface of the swamp: two blue-glowing planes converging. The effect was disorientating. It stretched into forever in front and to either side. Would Marion care that he'd slept with other people, the two most recent of whom she was probably about to meet? Or would she just not give a fuck? Which was worse? Would Byron and Churr keep their mouths shut?

Did he have a right to hope they would?

Despite a small warning voice in the back of his head, Alan gravitated towards one of the smaller, closer blocky formations. He saw that it was a heap of cuboid objects and reached out and touched one. Now his hand was also coated in the blue slime. The thing was made out of something soft and fibrous: wood. Old rotting wood. It was a crate; this island was a small pile of crates. Some were gigantic piles of crates; some were teetering towers. And the mulch . . . that must have been wood that had given up the ghost and had broken down, so nothing too nasty, then.

Ripples radiated out from Alan as he moved, some coming back towards him. They were just bouncing back from the various islands, of course, but still. He watched the illuminated slimy liquids move around his waist, turned and dashed back into the smaller room as quickly as the swamp would allow.

When he returned, Nora was spinning: the end of the carto, the motion that would wind the spirit of Gleam back into her consciousness, like thread being wound around a bobbin. Or like that parasitic worm Alan had once watched Loon the Maker remove from a child in the

House; Loon had wrapped one end of it around a thin stick and slowly twisted it, drawing the worm from beneath the child's skin. You had to do it that way, Loon had explained, keeping the speed and tension completely constant – give the worm any reason to recoil and it would snap itself and the part left inside would die and fester, becoming potentially far more dangerous than the living worm would ever have been.

There weren't many children in the Discard. Discarders tried not to have children, partly because pregnancy and delivery were so dangerous and partly because many of those children who did survive delivery never lived to see adulthood. Of course the death of a child brought an intense grief, and that intense grief often brought yet more death with it. There were more children in the House than anywhere else in the Discard, as far as Alan knew; one of the reasons for Maggie's ruthlessness in defending the House was that it was, in her words, 'something of an incubator'. But even considering the House, the Discard's population would carry on declining, growing emptier and yet emptier. The emptiness would start spreading: rooms emptying out, buildings emptying out, leaving the old warm stones behind, the stones that Alan had started to believe remained stacked one on top of the other only through some kind of enchantment: a magic that protected the buildings but not the people. And what kind of magic was that?

Nora stopped spinning and a faint hum that hadn't registered on Alan's consciousness before faded away.

'Now,' Nora said, 'just let me meditate on what the spirit has shown me.' And she promptly collapsed into a cross-legged sitting position.

'Fine,' Alan said. 'Whatever.'

Of course, the plan had been to get all of this done back up top, before the Seal was broken, but they hadn't been expecting the Giving Beast stalk to pull the Seal up with it. Perhaps they should have been expecting that, but as with so much else, they were dealing with unknowns. What they *had* all agreed on was that once the Seal had been broken, it was imperative to get into the Sump so Churr's people could get the Seal back in place as quickly as possible, before anything could escape. Nothing could be allowed out, not even spores or vapours, at least as far as that kind of thing could be prevented or controlled. The exchange of atmospheres had to be kept to an absolute minimum.

Byron gestured silently to the swamp. There were still ripples moving across the surface – arcs passing through the exit Alan had explored and expanding into the room where he now waited with Nora for the spirit to give her a sense of direction. Alan watched them, waited for them to slow and to stop.

Nora reached out to Alan when she'd finished meditating; surprised, he grabbed her hand and helped her stand.

'The spirit is almost unrecognisable,' she said, her voice wavering. 'It does not communicate like it should.' She bent over and spat, one hand on her stomach, then straightened up again. 'I'm okay,' she said in reply to Alan's unspoken question. 'I feel like something has squashed my head, but I am okay.'

'What did it say?' Byron asked.

'It doesn't speak. It isn't an entity like you or me, or a ghost or a fairy thing. It is an energy; it is something to be read, almost. Imagine a map: the map is there, whether you read it or not, yes?'

'Yeah,' Alan said, uncertainly.

'The spirit is there, whether you pay attention to it or not. But if you do try to commune, then it . . . communicates something to you – like a map, when you read it. The spirit is like . . . *meaning*.' She tutted in exasperation. 'I am not explaining it well. It is a case of being *aware*, feeling the shapes of Gleam all around you, like a bat with its voice, almost. No, that is not right. I don't know.' She waved a hand. 'I don't know. Anyway, here it is all wrong, and even if I could explain it, none of what I'd be saying would be true down here. Here it is . . . fucked up.'

'Could I learn to commune with the spirit?' Alan asked.

'You? No. You are too dense and self-obsessed.'

'Okay then,' Alan said, ignoring Byron's snort of laughter, 'thanks. I guess. So, do you know which way we need to go?'

'We're going that way,' Nora said, pointing through into the cavernous space that Alan had already tentatively explored.

'Sure?'

'Yes.'

'Really sure?'

'Yes. I cannot read the shape of Gleam; I cannot see which twists and turns we need to follow, which doors we need to go through, which staircases to ascend. I cannot see as much as I normally can see. But I can feel the spirit – the soul – groaning out, and the . . . *distress* . . . comes from that way. That is as much as I know. Why?'

'I think there are things moving out there. See these ripples?' Alan gestured at the motion in the swamp. 'I thought they were from me; I thought they'd stop. But they haven't. They keep coming. They're small, and few and far between, but they're there.'

'I was expecting life, and a lot of it. It is quieter than I thought it would be. This is not too bad. We should be thankful.'

'I think we've got a long way to go, though.'

As Alan led Nora and Byron through the archway they gasped at the expanse that lay beyond. Quickly, Nora gathered herself. 'Now. Let's go.'

They kept close to the wall. A bank of mulch just beneath the surface made it easier for them to move more quickly and quietly than if they'd had to wade through the waist-deep swamp. They made fewer waves that way, too. They started to see rounded islands and more of the blocky heaps protruding from the swamp, as well as stunted trees with soft, pale tendrils that dropped down into the liquid, and, inevitably, gigantic gnarly fungi, their large flat caps stippled with dark spots, the colour impossible to ascertain by the weird luminous light. As they progressed, they came across more and more of these piles of boxes, and they were growing in size.

Nora halted. She held up her hand against Alan's chest, as if to keep him quiet. 'Stop,' she said. 'Can you hear a buzzing sound?'

'No.' Then, after a moment, 'Oh – wait. Yeah.' It was quiet, but growing louder, getting closer.

'Come on,' Nora said, 'let's keep going.'

'What if it hears us?'

'It will have heard us anyway,' she pointed out, and it did indeed soon became apparent that it didn't matter whether they carried on or not, for the buzzing grew louder and louder, and then—

—the sound passed right by their faces, the creature making itself completely invisible in the semi-darkness. It faded away into the distance.

Alan shuddered and swiped at his cheeks, his nose, his hair. 'Goddamn it,' he said. 'A fucking bee or something?'

'No bees where there are no flowers,' Byron said. 'Probably a big nasty fly.'

'I desperately want to get out of here. Are we still going the right way?'

'Soon we will have to head across the cavern, but it looks like there are more and more box islands the way we need to go; we could use them to stay above the swamp. I think Alan's right: there are things in the swamp – living things, I mean. I mean *animals*. I think if there are living things down here, bigger than insects, then that will be where they are. Beneath the surface. That must be why we haven't seen anything.'

As if in response, a squat dark form suddenly erupted from the swamp some thirty feet away from them and hauled itself up until it was crouching on top of one of the crates. Before Alan could determine what it was, it let loose an enormous croak that tore the silence in two, echoing around the vast chamber from all directions. The great toad shifted around, its fat limbs slapping on the wood, blue slime dripping from it, and seemed to stare at Alan and Nora.

'Fuck me,' Byron said.

The toad croaked again: a long, abrasive sound. Then out came its tongue; Alan felt like it was licking its lips, and although its mouth wasn't really visible, he felt as if it was *grinning* at him.

'We keep going,' Nora said. 'Come on. *We keep going.*'

'Yeah, definitely,' Alan said. 'Let's run.'

They broke into a sprint, but it wasn't long until Alan got a stitch. 'Green damn it,' he said, panting, but it was only then that he realised how much further behind Byron was. The biker wasn't really used to using his legs.

'We need to strike out,' Nora said, once Byron had caught up, his breath ragged. 'We need to cross this channel – it's fifty feet across, maybe – and steer clear of the trees. I don't trust them – and then look, there are so many crates over there that we can just stay on top of them.'

Alan set out, striding towards the nearest box island.

They were halfway across, the swamp up to their hips, when something started moving in front of them – another toad, maybe? Whatever it was, it was broad-backed and pale beneath the slime, and for one horrible moment, Alan thought it was a crocodile.

It reared up at them, emerging almost completely from the water, but Alan still couldn't tell what it was: something with segments, with lots of thick little legs wriggling beneath it, something with twitching antennae.

Nora plunged her long knife into its underbelly before it had a chance to do anything and the thing squealed wildly as she waggled the knife around. 'Just another critter,' she said. 'Things are bigger down here is all. That toad must have been a little baby. Now go – *run*. Quick.'

'I think you've dealt with it, Nora,' Alan pointed out, but she was shaking her head and pointing.

'It's not *that* I'm worried about. The trees. Look.'

Alan turned to look at the trees. They were shuffling slowly forward, and there was one in front that actually looked a bit like – a bit like a person. It was raising its head.

A face warped, rippled and then set: gaping holes where once the mouth and nose had been, blank bulges instead of eyes, skin hardened into something like papery bark. They weren't branches, but long, twisted protuberances that grew from the chest, stomach, shoulders and head. The soft, hanging tendrils broke and slipped away as the Horned moved – they'd just been viscous ropes of some sick fluid.

The millipede was trying to get away from the Horned, but the wound Nora had given it was debilitating and its progress was negated by its body spasming and thrashing from side to side, knocking it, shuddering, backwards. It chattered piercingly, drawing the attention of Green knew what else.

'We've got to get up out of this,' Alan said quietly, and he lurched into the space between the beast and the Horned, which – *who?* – were still a little too far away to reach him. Byron followed his lead, but wading through this thigh-deep muck was painfully, heart-stoppingly slow and the Horned were moving more quickly than them, coming in from the left; the millipede thing writhing to the right. Nora was on the other side of it, Alan thought. Hoped. He tried to run, but the resistance of the semi-fluid swamp-water pressed back, waves buffeting him, pushing him ever so slightly towards the advancing Horned. They had been so far away, but that was no longer the case, not now. For a moment he paused and watched one of them moving; its skin broke as it walked, sending spores puffing out. Its antlerish horns were not solid; they swayed slightly as it moved. Its ragged parody of a face still appeared to bear expression: it looked *malicious*.

Alan redoubled his efforts to move, his feet dragging through silt, mulch, slime . . . *filth*. Never-ending filth. By the Builders, he was so sick of it.

A hand appeared in front of him: Nora had already reached the boxes. She was standing on top of the first, leaning down and holding out a hand to him. He tried to gain purchase against the side of the crate, but his boot slipped on the rotten wood. He could hear something approaching from behind. The millipede was screaming even louder. He got a knee up on the edge of it and pulled himself up.

The crate bowed beneath their combined weight, then cracked . . . then it broke.

Nora was already leaping through the air, but Alan fell straight into the box, which was full of swamp, and what felt like glass bottles that crunched as he flailed around. He hauled himself out and clambered up onto the next one, Byron by his side and Nora helping him once more, and this next one bore them.

Only then did he turn around.

Some of the Horned were closing in on the millipede, but others were gazing desolately at the broken box, various of their arms or branches or extra limbs, whatever they were, feeling around the wooden edges.

The three of them sped away across the boxes, keeping to the edges and the corners of the crates where the wood was strongest. Other sounds came from the darkness across the water, and there was something moving up ahead: something hunched, human. *Horned*. It was running much more quickly than the tree-specimens in the swamp, and as it closed on them it became obvious that it wasn't as far gone as the others. It bore only two long, curved horns, protruding from the top of its head, no other extraneous limbs. It had more control over its body too, and its skin was not yet dead and ripped.

It loped towards Alan, Byron and Nora, knuckles low, mouth hanging open and oozing. Nora, in front, swerved, and it followed her, turning its back on Alan. Alan grabbed his knife, secured his grip and drove the blade deep into the back of the thing's neck. Byron, at Alan's frantic gestures, carried straight on past, not even stopping to look. Gurgling, it fell to its knees; it reached behind with wasted arms and clawed at itself. Dark blood trickled slowly out. Its reactions were muted, as if it wasn't feeling much pain, and Alan wondered if he'd cut into a human body or if some kind of thick fungal tendril had superseded the vertebrae and veins and cords of a spine. What made the thing move? What kept it going? A functional body was what attracted Idle Hands in the first place; it must occupy and *use* the host, as opposed to completely taking it over. Those Horned tree-things, back by the millipede – perhaps the fungus had grown too much in them, clogged their passages, solidified inside their organs and rendered them useless.

The Horned Man prostrate before him was not as far gone, so Alan's knife had done some damage. It looked like the thing was unable to get back up again – but it was obviously not paralysed; it was as if each leg – each limb, each individual digit – had become its own animal, wriggling and squirming independently. The man – it had been a man, Alan was pretty sure of it – kept pushing himself up on his fists, only for a twitch or spasm to undo him again and send him crashing back down. The overall human locomotive system had been broken by the blade; now all that was left was muscles being pulled and prodded by some other power.

Alan crouched down behind him and cut the Horned Man's throat – but not much came out, and it still kept on moving. Panicking, he stamped on its neck until he heard a *crunch*. There was momentary stillness – then suddenly the head started jerking about in a way that should *not* have been possible. The mouth was snapping and one of the horns punctured a wooden box, which broke it off; Alan hurriedly backed away as a small cloud of spores escaped.

Where were this Horned Man's parents? Did they know what had become of their son? Would Billy's jaw one day move like that? Would somebody one day stamp on Billy's neck, and do so easily, without compunction?

'Leave it, idiot!' Nora shouted. 'It cannot follow now – *come*!'

Alan tore his attention from the Horned Man and gazed vacantly at Nora for a moment. She was a phantasm: her cloak was smeared with blue-glowing streaks. She beckoned. At his feet, the Horned Man reached out.

Horror lent him energy, and Alan ran.

The Sump shifted into unreality. Whether it was something in the air or the flesh of the Giving Beast working its magic on him, or maybe just exhaustion and shock, but the sights and sounds flattened out: a world behind glass. He felt like he could move through it without engaging with anything, as if he was only a spirit himself. It was an illusion, of course; his boots were getting sodden, his ankles bloody, his legs raw, his stomach tight and aching. But he felt everything at one remove.

He saw things moving in the swamp: great fleshy masses without faces; grubs like babies. He saw bones; small bones – a tiny skull was pushed to the surface by something beneath it. And Horned Men and Women were now stalking them. They were approaching a veritable mountain of the crates, many smashed open or crushed beneath others; revealing more glass bottles, or small metal canisters or mechanical contraptions, or rusting cogs and wheels. Beyond the box mountain was the far wall, in which there was a huge aperture. Judging by the contours, it was the bottom of a chute, Alan thought, then he realised that there were similar openings all the way along, with mounds of indeterminate matter piled up in front of them.

The first mound they got to was an enormous heap of rusty metal tins from which a burning, acrid smell emanated. The next was just a great heap of rust. The next, mulch, but they spotted a few semi-intact planks of wood still surviving. They found long conveyor belts, too many to count, running the length of the vast space, a little proud of the surface of the water, but Alan felt as if he was remembering a dream, with only certain details standing out as important. Brainless hunks of meat wobbled and sloshed around in the water, and moans filled the air. It was as if all of these organic objects had been lying dormant until Nora, Byron and Alan had disturbed the calm. They weren't creatures, as such – they were *bits of* creatures, or had once been creatures. They were just objects made of flesh that were not animated the usual way but by Idle Hands, Alan suspected, or perhaps by something else, maybe even the magic that was corrupting the spirit of Gleam.

Amongst the muck and ruin they found glass bottles with metal shavings inside, gelatinous masses, metal tubes, ball-bearings, wax-sealed jars of grey powder, small machines packaged individually, a sudden writhing nest of fat white foot-long worms, something like a too-large human hand, crawling along on its own, unmarked cans, something like a vast bulbous stomach with a whimpering face stretched across it. And all the while, more humanoid figures registered on Alan's consciousness: the

Horned, awakened, were scratching their way inwards from the peripheries of perception.

They passed more piles of indeterminate waste, but none of them wanted to stop to investigate. In the distance was a mountain that put the initial crate heap behind them to shame. This was a terrain of peaks, mounds, towers, piles, heaps; accumulation, accretion: a colossal backing-up – there was too much of everything, and all of it rotting: the passing of time manifested as waste.

A rumbling noise started building, and then a scraping sound came too. Alan's senses were twisted almost inside out and he thought at first that something was rasping at the insides of his skull – and then there was a cascade of darkness as *things* started pouring out of one of the chute apertures, the sound enveloping the great chamber as the stuff all came rushing down, temporarily obscuring the blue glow and piling on top of the heap already there. There were sounds of shifting and squelching as the new arrivals settled.

Then there was nothing but the horrible noises that had been there before.

'So all of this stuff is still coming,' Nora said. Her voice sounded distant. 'Where is it coming from?'

'The Pyramid,' Alan replied. His voice sounded quiet too. 'And if it came from the Pyramid, then we could take that route back up into the Pyramid.'

'Do we know? Do we know for sure?' Nora's face was a pale shape, floating; everything else shimmered and wavered.

'For sure? No.'

'And the chutes will be steep and smooth, Alan. We could get swept back down again. There will be a better way. The spirit, the fracture in the spirit . . . we have not reached it yet. We need to go further.'

'I'm with the Mapmaker,' Byron said. 'Don't want to climb up too soon and have to come back down again.'

'The Horned . . .' Alan's protestation wavered. Fighting with a Mapmaker about which way to go was foolishness.

'Yes,' Nora said, 'the Horned are here. But still, we must continue.'

Alan was beginning to feel tired. The surreal sense of flight, of speedy, blurred motion, was fading and his legs were beginning to hurt. And the Horned were closer behind than they had been, and he could see more of them in front now. They might be slow – he guessed that the longer someone had been a host to Idle Hands, the more sluggish they became, and there can't have been much in the way of fresh meat down here for a long time – but more and more were coming after them.

Then he saw that the Horned weren't necessarily making directly for them. Many had suddenly switched direction, turning towards the pile at the end of the chute, and others had just begun rising up out of the surrounding water as if in response to the recent commotion.

The sound.

Alan suddenly realised these far-gone Horned couldn't see.

There was a mountain ahead of them, but this one didn't appear to be made of boxes, like the others. It was taller, more central to the space, and more steep-sided. All the blue-limned conveyor belts emerged from its base, radiating out in all directions. Above it, the coating of slime on the ceiling picked out the shape of a circle – a great circle on the ceiling above the mountain, against which the tip of the mountain was pressed.

'Here,' Nora whispered. And before Alan or Byron could say anything, she burst into a sprint, racing ahead of them at a speed Alan could never hope to match. As was her wont, she made barely a sound – Nora always moved as silently as a cat.

Byron was about to take off after her, but Alan grabbed him before he got too far. '*Quiet,*' he said. 'They're drawn by noise.'

Byron looked around and nodded, and the two of them went after Nora more slowly. Alan could hardly stand their slow speed; the Horned were all around now, and close. The fact that they had slowed in their pursuit, confused by the near-quiet of their prey's flight, was little consolation. They passed the Horned almost at arm's length; Alan stared at them, trying to move as fast as he could without breaking the silence. He stared at their human faces, the rags they wore, the protuberances that sprouted from their heads like antlers or spikes or root vegetables, the forking branches of trees, or monstrous combinations of all, the balls of fungus that bulged from eye sockets, the wet sheen of their flesh, all only part-lit in the dim blue.

When they reached it, they found the mountain to be made of small machines, bones, rotten organics, broken glass and other, stranger things that could not be identified: jet-black orbs, softly glowing stones, screes of susurrating grit that seemed to move of their own accord, flowing uphill as much as down. Byron skirted the lower slope, looking for an easier way up, but Alan impatiently ploughed straight ahead, digging foot- and hand-holds into the mass. A pale white light emanated from one of the holes he made and he reached for it unthinkingly. His fingers curled around something, a metal object, and when he pulled it out he found an egg, an ovoid, split down the middle, with a glass tube inside which was glowing with that luminous white light. It felt warm in his hands. On the side of the glass tube was a tiny dark strip and Alan brought it close, squinting in the darkness, already knowing what it was but not quite believing it . . . . But the interior of the metal shell was reflecting enough light back at the dark strip, a little plaque attached to the glass tube, for him to be able to read the words engraved into it.

WHO DO YOU HATE?

Alan opened his mouth and then snapped it shut again as his brain tripped over itself, trying to suppress names even before they properly surfaced. His head was suddenly full of voices, each trying to shout louder than the last. He closed his eyes, forced the metal egg shut and sank to his knees – but when he put out his hands to catch his balance, he found dozens more of the metal eggs all around him. He couldn't answer the question – he couldn't *let* himself – but nor could he distract himself with the names of people he did not hate, or loved, not even in his own mind; that might be all that the spell required. He imagined himself screaming; a long, loud, throat-shredding roar, and he made it louder and louder, trying to occupy his thoughts with its volume. He imagined it drowning out everything else, overwhelming the chaos of names and not-names.

Then pain blossomed and his head rocked back at a sharp slap across the cheek that made a sound like slate cracking. The echoes of the scream sounded mad – he hadn't intended to actually let it out, but he had.

'Alan, stop being such a damned fool,' Nora hissed. Alan hadn't even known she was close by. 'Stop this nonsense and get up. They are really coming for us now – they are on our very tails.'

The thing was not in his hands any more; he'd dropped it amongst the others. He didn't answer Nora, or stop to think; he just obeyed. He clambered back to his feet, trying not to touch any of the eggs, and ploughed ahead, until he came to a stretch of swords and knives and crossbows and arrows, then more bottles and jars. He picked up a sword – heavier than it looked – and swung it experimentally. The blade sheared from the hilt. He picked up another. He swung this one and it remained intact, but his satisfaction was short-lived; the hilt started to wriggle in his hand. He dropped it with a yelp and hurried on. The other weapons crunched and crumbled as he stepped on them.

Further on up, Alan heard somebody crying beneath his feet and he paused for a moment and dug down, only to unearth a wooden cube that was sobbing uncontrollably. Maybe it would distract the Horned. He threw it as far as he could, and was both gratified and distressed when it landed with a piercing shriek of pain. He found a small ring of metal – it looked as if it had melted and then re-solidified – which framed a view across some slate rooftops. A light breeze came through it as Alan peered into it. There were thousands of small, squashy things that went un-investigated.

Alan felt a hand on his ankle and when he turned, expecting Byron, he saw a Horned woman, pretty far gone – and behind her was another, and behind her, a horde of the Horned. The lower slopes of the mountain were thick with them.

'Oh fuck,' he said, kicking furiously, 'oh fuck. *Fuck*.'

'This is what you get for screaming like a stabbed croc,'

Nora said. 'You are a hopeless case.' She swept up a small metal blade from the mountain and buried it in the Horned Woman's face, pushing her backwards as she did so, and the woman let go of Alan to try and remove it.

Nora pushed him, and Alan ran, though his legs were burning now. The mere act of heaving his own body up the hill was taking all his strength. He'd lost sight of Byron; he had to hope that his screaming had drawn their pursuers away from the slower man.

'The plan is this,' Nora said, and even she was panting a little, 'we will get to the top – as close to the top as we can get – and you will find a place to stand, a place you can defend. You will make some use of that guitar you carry everywhere on your back: you will make some noise. You will draw the Horned to you.'

Alan waited for her to finish.

'And then what?' he asked, eventually, when it became clear she wasn't going to add anything more.

'You will fight them off.' She sounded pragmatic. 'If you are standing in the right place then you will only have to face them one at a time.'

'What about you? What about Byron?'

'Byron is still on his way up. He is not here, and so I cannot assign him a task. His job is just to survive. As for me – I will be trying to open the way.'

'What way?'

'This is the corruption, Alan. This is it: the fracture. This mountain and what feeds it is the source of the broken magic, the wound in Gleam's spirit. It is mystical power twisted and gone rancid. It is also the working connection between the Pyramid and the Discard – up there, where the mountain presses against the ceiling. That is our way in, but it is closed.'

The Horned did not appear to tire, but their presence was incentive enough for Alan and Nora to keep their own speed up. The distance between pursued and pursuers remained constant for the last long slog up the slope: the Horned were never more than about twenty feet behind, a tide of gurgles and rasping breath lapping at their heels. Alan had been casting about for the right place and finally he found a nook, an alcove near the top formed by a large, shapeless blob of something translucent held up by drifts of stinking plant matter. He slipped Snapper from his back, turned and wedged himself in, grimacing at the smell. Nora climbed past him and disappeared from view.

The Horned were massing before him. At first glance they looked like a forest of large, many-fingered hands thrust up out of the mountain of mysterious objects, but that impression was swiftly shattered by their forward motion. He strummed Snapper, hesitantly at first, but when that provoked no real reaction, more loudly, and he was both relieved and revolted to see the horns sway and twist towards him as the Horned traced the sound. He pressed backwards against the heap. It was cold up there, but sweat was trickling down the back of his neck.

He wasn't playing Snapper – he hadn't even tuned it, not in so long, and the air here was so damp – but the ugly, discordant rhythm as he kept striking the strings was doing the job. His fingers were stiff and hurting, so anything more was probably beyond him anyway. He watched as the Horned responded to the racket, forming into a wedge shape, the thin end pointed directly at him. He couldn't hear Nora or Byron, which was good, which was *right* – but despite that being the plan, he wished he *could* hear them; he felt lonely and the mass of infected inhumanity advancing towards him only made him feel lonelier.

His hands were clammy and slick now, and slipping across the strings. The front-runner, a quick mover with short curved horns, would be with him soon. It was climbing almost like a normal human. Its arms were long and ridged, either with taut tendons or something else growing beneath the skin. It was already nearly within reaching distance of his feet, but it wasn't moaning; instead, it growled loudly, like a croc. And then it was at him.

Alan pointed Snapper's head at the Horned's open mouth and, just as its gnarled hand was closing on his leg, rammed the guitar down. He felt the strings tighten as the tuning keys twisted against his attacker's jawbone. The Horned's fingers closed hard on nothing as the impact pushed it away. Alan yanked Snapper back and a spray of teeth came with it. The Horned tipped backwards, howling as it clutched at a mouth that in the bad light looked too wide.

But like in all the good old songs, two more rose up to take its place as it fell, and like the previous Horned, these, the pack leaders, were fresh, still more human, less fungus, and they were agile, clambering over each other to get at him. Snapper caught the first in the throat and sent the body flying across the heads of those below it. He hooked the second behind the knee with Snapper's neck and, as it went down, stamped hard on its head. The Horned's bones were soft.

Alan retreated, wriggling backwards into the heap of Green-knew-what so that they had to come at him one at a time, and he took out each one as it drew near, driving Snapper into the giving tissue, ripping holes in their dry, slightly fuzzy skin, pushing them back off the guitar with his heavy boots, until it became a rhythmic, unconscious movement. His arms were getting tired and his thoughts were drifting, but he was starting to enjoy himself. It was a bit like performing, after all. Somewhere in the back of his mind he was picturing a conveyor belt bringing these beings up the mountain towards him; he imagined a great machine built for death, carrying one hapless vessel after another towards the killing mechanism, which was him.

He punched Snapper through another throat. He wasn't a machine, though; he couldn't just keep going and going. Snapper was feeling heavier with each new attack, and it was getting harder to push the Horned back; more were climbing up all the time, pressing in, pushing the wounded ones backwards – and he was only wounding them, not killing them dead, despite the purpose of the machine. Alan suddenly remembered his father telling him all about mushrooms: you could pick them and they'd grow back because the ground *remembered* them. Stamping on them didn't kill them; picking them and eating them didn't kill them – they were like spirits. And now the Horned were coming back too, in pieces, their bodies crawling around without heads, and the heads groaning where they lay.

He lifted his boot to the latest fucker's chest and pushed, but instead of Snapper coming loose from inside the stomach of the Horned, Snapper came loose from his sweaty hands.

'No!' he screamed, following it, rushing forwards. It was buried up to its neck in the Horned's body and Alan grabbed it and yanked with all his strength to free it – but in that moment he was exposed, and the hand of yet another Horned caught hold of his yellowed shirt sleeve and pulled. He glimpsed a world of twitching bodies and slithering parts, all limned in blue luminescence, everything visible moving and moaning, kind of alive and kind of not, like oiled gears interlocking inside the dark workings of something that didn't need light. Then from out of the mass loomed a face, attached to the neck and shoulder of the arm that held him, and he let go of

Snapper, swung his knife from his waist and sliced it right through that crumbly neck. It caught on the spine and the face froze, and in that dim, hellish moment, Alan realised that the face was Billy's. The hand on his sleeve let go. Snapper floated away from him. Alan reached out with his left hand and grabbed it by the strings. They dug into his fingers. Alan held Snapper there, and Snapper held Billy. Alan stared into his son's face. His son was stretching out to him with those awful hands, but couldn't reach. Alan couldn't bring himself to let go. Then another blade came flashing and Billy's head went spinning through the air. Snapper's head came loose from his stomach. Light was spilling down from above: the sun was coming up and it illuminated a pile of Horned – and Nora, working her bloody magic on those still standing. Alan gazed down at the carpet of twisted, furred bodies that he himself had dispatched and by this new light he saw that they *all* had Billy's face. He stumbled backwards into his alcove as his knees gave out. He clutched his own knife in his hand and watched Nora kill.

PART TWO

PYRAMID

Daunt closed her eyes as the masseurs' hands moved from her calves and then further up, further. She parted her knees ever so slightly and lifted the hem of her green skirt as one of the men relaxed his grip and let his strong fingers trace delicate lines across her tingling skin. Her senses were on fire; moonfruit tea made sure of it. She sighed and pressed herself backwards into the furs on which she reclined. Her chambers were a nest; a warm, red nest of furs and skins and silks, like the warm, red chamber of the skull, and she, Daunt, luxuriating at the very nerve centre. Pleasure shivered through her body and she reached out and grabbed the hard shoulder of one of her masseurs. He responded wisely, sliding his hand up her thigh, and she gasped quietly, just a little, just enough to tell him yes, and then the other masseur followed suit, and she dug her fingernails in to the skin of that shoulder, heard a pained grunt, laughed a little . . .

'Stop,' she said, sitting up suddenly. The masseurs — the two men served as her protectors as well as her lovers — removed their hands from her body immediately and sprang to their feet. They grabbed their weapons from the wall, vicious barbed daggers, good for gutting. Not that Daunt wanted entrails spilled in here; the stink was invariably awful.

After a moment, she relaxed. 'It's just Bittewood,' she declared. 'I can smell him. Carry on.'

The masseurs were back on their knees by the time Bittewood knocked. 'Enter!' Daunt shouted. 'I trust you've brought me that rotten thief to liven up my night a little. I've got so many ideas . . .'

The way Bittewood coughed was not encouraging. Daunt's green eyes snapped open and she was up and across the room in a heartbeat, thumb pressed just deeply enough into Bittewood's throat, which she could barely reach. 'Where is he?' she hissed. She felt her men rise up behind her.

Bittewood gulped, his bloodshot blue eyes darting around the room. His face was livid with spots, and his grey skin filthy with dried grime. 'My Lady,' he croaked, 'my Queen. The little fucker . . . I had him. I was beating him good. But this biker fucker came along.'

Daunt screamed and clawed bloody streaks across his chest. 'Yes?' she screeched. 'Yes? This "biker fucker" came along, and . . . and what? Because if that's the end of the story it sounds very much like the Hollowboy got *away, and if you're back, then presumably you lost the trail. Tell me I'm wrong, Bittewood.'*

'He got away from me. But he's proper fucking dead. I'm sorry I didn't bring him still wriggling, desperate for the knife.' Bittewood licked his lips. 'But he's dead. Not what you wanted but not all bad.'

Daunt considered. 'How did he die?' she asked. 'Was it painful?'

Bittewood grinned. 'We chased them into the Swamp. They went an' woke up a band of freaks. Swamp magic freaks. There was this big one. A giant head carried by . . . by a big fucking hand. Head ate Songbird and the biker fucker, then disappeared.'

'He was eaten alive?'

'Swallowed right on down.'

'Bloody?'

'Didn't see no blood.'

Daunt paced. 'I asked for him alive, though.'

'Yes, Queen.'

'Men,' Daunt said. 'One of you make this sorry wretch unconscious. The other, go and fetch a tanner, and then stand watch outside. I want no more interruptions tonight. Bittewood, we are going to flay you. Alive.'

Bittewood had hit the floor almost before Daunt had finished speaking. The door opened and closed as one of her men left. Daunt stared down at Bittewood. 'You know how I like a little violence,' she breathed to her remaining masseur. 'It heightens everything, just a little.

But Bittewood . . . no. He is too ugly. Please restrain him and leave him outside the room, and then return to me immediately.'

Would that I could eat a man alive, she thought, as she reclined amongst the furs. What a wonderful way to kill that would be. The taste of the flesh, the fear, the pain. But even with Alan gone, there was plenty of killing to look forward to. Her people were gathering. Soon they would descend upon Dok and take it from that upstart Bandit.

And was he gone? Bittewood had not been blessed with a great brain; he was not connecting the dots between that Bandit bitch and the Swamp freaks. The search for Wild Alan would continue, and he would be punished for his deceitful ways. But Bittewood was not the man for that job, not any more.

She smiled lazily as her masseur returned. She watched him dip his hands in the small basin of oil and drip it onto her bare legs. She closed her eyes and let her body respond to the touching. Yes. She thought of all the blood that would soon flow, and her skin tingled. Yes.

7

Machine Rooms

An intricate array of thick, wide discs of beaten metal slid towards each other across the great round space and silently interleaved, and the sounds of the Sump — the moaning and the almost insectile hum of thousands of weird things rustling against each other — were immediately and completely silenced. Alan, lying on his back on one side of the floordoor, exhaled.

When the door had opened the light had flooded through, together with a shower of unidentifiable objects, all raining down from the space above, tumbling down the slopes of the mountain and crashing into the Horned horde. Strange things came down right in front of Alan: filigree metal orbs, a couple of large bloody eyeballs, misshapen glass bottles, clouds of dust and glittering powder, spatters of foul-smelling liquid, a tusked skull, from the eye sockets of which came the sounds of a terrible storm, blank and immobile figurines that smashed like pots, a shower of arrowheads that wriggled around of their own accord, burrowing into the mountain almost as quickly as Alan registered their presence. And then an Arbitrator fell through – no, two Arbitrators, three Arbitrators. Their broken bodies landed heavily, their screams barely registering in the chaos. They were each holding a long pole. Then, a moment later, Nora dropped down across the mouth of Alan's little alcove. Her eyes gleamed and her arms glistened.

'Now. *Come.*'

Alan made a last desperate, pained scramble up to the top of the heap, his legs feeling leaden, agonising. Reaching the top, seeing that bright circle into the Pyramid, needing to jump that last tiny distance, his legs started buckling at the thought. He got a grip on himself, straightened his back and gathered his strength, and then—

—they'd done it. Of course they had. Of course they had. They always did. They always would.

He looked around for the others. Nora was sitting beside him, muttering and crying. She was hunched up, her arms wrapped around herself, curled around her broken rib. Byron was there too, but he looked relatively unscathed. It looked like the Horned had all come for Alan, summoned by Snapper's sound, and left Byron alone. Alan was glad that he'd been able to save the biker some trouble, after all the help Byron had given him.

Alan reached out and put a hand on Nora's shoulder.

She backhanded him across the face, hard, and stalked away. Alan was knocked sprawling, not only by the blow but by the violence in her eyes. Stunned into silence, he watched her go.

The room they were in was not really that bright; it just appeared so compared with the darkness of the Sump. It was lit by a globe suspended far, far above, and between the floor on which Alan was lying and the ceiling-mounted globe there was a horrendously complex system of machines. Silhouetted against the distant glow there were ropes, pulleys, junctions, shining metal wheels, carefully aligned conveyor belts, apparatus that held delicate glass tubes and bottles, lenses, funnels . . . Alan rolled over so that he was looking at the floor, which was wet with blood-trails leading to the now-closed floordoor. So Nora had killed the Arbitrators here and thrown them over. That made sense. They must have been tasked with guarding the Pyramid against Sump life: just prod back down anything that might try to get up. But that meant that there would be a shift-change at some point. Their entry into the Pyramid would not go unnoticed.

He stood up.

'What was that about?' Byron asked, cleaning his knives.

'Not sure yet,' Alan replied, holding his tender face.

Byron put his knives away and got to his feet. A wide conveyor belt was squeaking away, depositing nothing on top of the floordoor, and it was fed by many tributary conveyors, also currently empty – but presumably that wasn't always the case; that must have been where all that stuff had come from when the floordoor opened, building up the whole mountain over time. Maybe that was also part of the Arbitrators' job: opening the floordoor to discard whatever was on top of it. The conveyor belts weren't the only things moving, Alan realised; much of the machine was shifting, filling the room with rattles and creaks. It didn't look much like the Pyramid Alan knew; it was altogether darker and dirtier. The floor was covered in grit and powder of some sort, and the air tasted stale.

He picked Snapper up and crept through the shadows, looking for Nora. They had to leave before the replacement Arbitrators arrived. He didn't want to fight with her – he hoped that she wouldn't still be angry. What had caused the anger, he wasn't exactly sure.

Something clanged above and as he looked up he caught a glimpse of a small hole in the ceiling closing. There was an object – no, multiple objects – clattering their way down through the system. He saw a sequence of conveyor belts passing these things on, one swinging around to the next, until eventually the objects in question made their way down to the largest conveyor, the one that ended at the floordoor, and were dropped unceremoniously on top of the sliding metal panels with an almighty racket of metal on metal. Alan darted back to see what they were: a clutch of dull metal ovoids, egg-shaped . . . He drew back his hand. He knew exactly what they were and he wasn't going to touch them, let alone open any of them up. Not this time.

'Byron,' he said, 'these are the . . . these are the things. I told you what I did at Modest Mills, how I let something loose.'

Byron went to pick one up, and then stopped himself. 'Better not,' he murmured.

Nora coalesced from the shadows on the other side of the floordoor. She had her hood up and Alan couldn't see her face.

'Are we ready to go?' Alan asked.

Nora nodded, and then crouched down to scoop up some of the metal cylinders.

'Don't,' Alan said urgently, 'they're dangerous—'

But she completely ignored him and packed three of them away into her backpack.

'What's wrong?' Alan asked. 'Have I done something?'

Nora thought about it for a moment and then briefly shook her head. 'I should not have let you see me in pain. It is shameful and embarrassing. But that is my mistake and not yours.'

'There's no bleedin' shame in pain, Nora,' Byron said. 'A body doesn't choose to feel it.'

Nora inclined her head. 'But letting you both know that I am physically impaired, letting you know that injury has consequences for a Mapmaker . . .' She let out a small laugh like a cough. 'It is against our teachings.'

'Well, don't worry,' Alan said. 'We won't tell anybody.

Come on. Let's get out of here before the Sump-watch shift-change.'

Nora nodded.

'Good. Come on, then. Let's go.' Alan set off, and Byron turned to follow him.

'Alan,' Nora said.

'Yes?'

'That's the wrong way. Follow me.'

The corridors were white stone, but cracked and badly lit; though glow-globes were mounted at regular intervals, at this depth they apparently didn't emit as much light as those up nearer the top. The air was thick and orange and there was dust underfoot. There were many, many rooms opening off the corridor that looked just like the one they'd left, except that the machines had collapsed. There were more they couldn't get into because the products that should have been evicted through floor-doors had not been; instead, they'd filled the rooms and were spilling out into the corridor. The only sounds to be heard were those from the room they'd left behind.

'There are great stairwells,' Alan said, 'and as far as I know, these are the only ways you can get from one floor to the next. But they don't offer much in the way of cover. We're going to need disguises.'

'We need to kill Pyramidders for their robes,' Nora said.

'We could just . . . take their robes, maybe,' Alan suggested.

'Won't they tell people what's happened to them?' Byron asked.

'We'll knock them out.'

Nora looked at him. 'And what about when they come to?'

'We could tie them up after we knock them out.'

Nora sighed. 'I don't know, Alan.'

'I do not like killing.'

'No,' Nora said.

'It makes me sick.'

'You were killing plenty of Horned,' Byron pointed out.

'Well, but they're not real people.' He'd said the words before realising their implications. He shook his head. He wanted Nora to say something. The conversation had to move forward, but his own brain was stuck on the Horned, and Billy being Horned, and how easy the Horned were to kill, how unlike people . . .

'We could knock them out and tie them up and secure them somewhere down here,' Nora said after a minute or two.

'Yes!' Alan leaped at Nora's words and clung to them. 'Yes, we could do that.'

'It's a compromise that I'm willing to make in order to indicate to you my respect for your feelings.'

'Well . . . thank you.'

'You're welcome. I'm not convinced of its logic. But we'll do it your way.'

'So. We need to find somebody – not Arbitrators; we need plain robes. Administrative, ideally.'

'Judging by the state of these passages, people do not frequent them.'

'No. We'll need to go higher.'

'Then bring the unconscious bodies back down?'

'. . . yes. And . . .' Alan stopped in the passage. 'What about Snapper? What do I do with Snapper?' He shrugged off the guitar and looked at it. 'Bloody hell,' he whispered. The neck of the instrument was wet with grey sludge, strings of viscera drying between the tuning keys. Alan shuddered. That stuff had been drawn directly from inside the Horned. 'I can't take Snapper with me,' he said.

'Can't take it anywhere, looking like that,' Byron offered.

'Yeah, thanks. No clean water down here to wash it.' He stared at Byron and Nora. 'What do I do?' he asked, helplessly.

'Come on now, Alan,' Nora said. 'You have to leave the guitar down here, in the depths and in the dark. I know it is special to you. But it is just a thing.'

'Okay, yes. Okay. And then afterwards, we'll come back down to get it.'

Nora gazed at him and slowly shook her head. 'No, Alan,' she said. 'If we are still alive, we will be hightailing it out. Not back in.'

'But then – but—'

'And it's a big if, Alan.'

'But then I won't get Snapper back.'

'No.'

Alan stared at the guitar a moment longer. 'Right,' he said. 'Right.' He stopped in the passage and shrugged off the guitar. 'Let's find somewhere now – one of these Machine Rooms.'

'Very well.'

They chose a room that contained a row of large metal stills; it looked like a Discard moonshine distillery, except the metal was not mismatched and patched up. Copper pipes extended from the tops of the stills, bent almost at ninety degrees, and disappeared into the walls. One of the stills had collapsed. Byron stuck his head inside and inhaled. 'Just copper,' he said, wistfully.

'We'll gag them and tie them and stick them in that drum,' Alan said, pointing to the collapsed unit. 'That way they'll be invisible from the door. And I'll hide Snapper under those fallen panels there, see?'

He laid Snapper down on the dusty stone floor, reached inside its body and with no small effort detached a packet of Green's Benedictions from the wooden interior. The little parcels lined the cavity, held fast by the snail-slime that Alan had applied in thick handfuls. It had dried like glue.

'Do the Pyramid robes have pockets?' Nora asked.

'No.'

'Then how will you carry them?'

'I'll be wearing my trousers underneath. I can fit them in.' He stuffed his pockets.

They took a stairwell that was evidently not used by the Arbitrators on their way to and from the functional floor-door. The steps were carpeted with thick dust, meaning they could walk quietly – which was vital, because the stairwells were open all the way up; even this deep they could hear the murmur and footsteps of Pyramidders using the stairs far above. The stairs curved to the left and they kept their backs to the left-hand wall. They moved slowly, Alan in front. The dust meant that they were leaving a trail that they could not obscure, but they planned to have hidden themselves amongst the Pyramidders by the time the Arbitrators supposed to be guarding the floordoor had been missed.

They passed one shut and obviously disused door, a grand, highly decorated affair made of beaten gold: the gateway to its respective floor. Golden pieces had been inlaid in the walls around it, and extensive and detailed symbols including eyes, arrows pointing up and down, vaguely humanoid figures, skulls and skulls with horns depicted – to those who could decipher them – the nature of the Stationing that had gone on here in the past. But the gold and the symbols and the doors were all tarnished, and some of the inlays had come loose and disappeared; they weren't lying on the floor at any rate.

Alan wondered which floor had borne witness to Eyes' torture, and he suppressed a shudder. He wanted to discuss that with his companions but didn't, for fear of how far up the stairwell their voices would travel. They continued upwards and passed another door in a similar state. It had some of the same symbols, but not the skulls; instead there were straight metal lines, chain-links and what looked like swords.

They passed three more such doors and then, silently rounding the corner to what would be the fifth, Alan caught sight of a motionless Arbitrator, standing facing away from Alan, watching the door and the stairs that descended from above. Alan ducked back and put a finger to his lips. Byron nodded in return but Nora, several steps below, rolled her eyes. Alan got his knife out, darted around the corner and clapped a hand over the Arbitrator's mouth and pressed his knife to the Arbitrator's throat. Any nascent resistance was dropped as soon as that cold metal touched skin. As Alan dragged the Arbitrator backwards, he noted with satisfaction that the floor here was swept; this door must mark the first of the inhabited floors. Above this point, the stairwell would be in use.

The Arbitrator was very good and did not kick or bang knuckle-dusters against the walls. Alan was proud to show Nora what he'd done, but she shook her head, undid the helmet clasp beneath the Arbitrator's chin and took off the helmet, revealing a very young man's face. She smacked the top of the Arbitrator's head with the hilt of her own knife, instantly knocking him out, then shot Alan a furious look and gestured down at the body. 'Knock the next ones out straight away,' she hissed. 'Don't give them a chance to make a sound. Don't bring them to me to do. I'm not some . . . some kind of *sleep fairy*.'

Alan picked up the body, which was lighter than he'd feared; the boy was skinny underneath the uniform. He followed Nora down the stairs.

In the shadow of the doorway of the floor below, Nora very quietly communicated the next steps to Alan and Byron. 'You put on his clothes – they won't fit Byron – wait in his position for more plainly robed Pyramidders to come through the door or down the stairs and then *knock them out*. Immediately. No hands over mouths, no tricky knife stuff – don't give them even the tiniest chance to shout out. Wait for singletons, knock them out, pass them back to me. Byron, you stay down here, behind me, a whole turn of the stairs behind me. Do you both understand?'

Alan nodded as he continued undressing.

The Arbitrator uniform was ever so slightly too small, and after a while standing in the watch position, Alan started to feel as if the straps that secured the breastplate were restricting his breathing. And the helmet was heavy and tight. The pressure on his skull was beginning to hurt. Standing still was really hard; his body was trying to shut down now that it had finally come to a rest for the first time in days.

How long had he been standing here now? Too long. The purpose of the post was clearly not to guard from below but to prevent Pyramidders from accessing the lower floors from above. However, not only was there no apparent interest in the floors below, there were no apparent Pyramidders either. He shifted his weight from foot to foot, drew the curved sword that hung from his belt, examined the backs of his hands. Any minute now the floordoor shift would change, or the opening of the floordoor would be due and the killings would be discovered and the alarm would be raised and there would be Arbitrators flooding down all the stairwells . . .

The door opened and a Pyramidder stepped through: a middle-aged woman with mid-ranking Alchemical detailing on her robe, not quite plain enough for Alan's purposes. Her greying hair was cut short. She looked at him without really paying attention, nodded at him, and turned to go upstairs. Then she turned back to him. 'Your hands,' she said. 'They're tattooed—'

Alan drew the sword and smacked the flat of it against the side of her head in one smooth motion. As she fell, he froze. The door was still open and there were footsteps echoing through from the corridor beyond. He rushed forward, closed it and then turned to deal with the unconscious Alchemist. She was not tall enough for her robe to fit Alan, but it would do for Nora. He lifted the body – again, not heavy – and took it round the corner for Nora to deal with.

Then he returned to his post. Had he made any noise? He probably had. He definitely had. But had it sounded out of place? He was suddenly sweaty. There had been no shouting, no screaming . . .

This is how it would be, he realised; the whole time they were in here, they were on the verge of getting discovered. At least once robed he could walk normally, move amongst the other Pyramidders, without being called upon to do something. He'd have to keep the hood up and his hands hidden. Would that in itself draw attention? The footsteps in the corridor continued on past the door and Alan breathed out. He could hear Nora removing the Alchemist's robe around the corner, behind him. Then there was the sound of somebody coming down the stairs from above. Alan crossed his arms and hid his hands in his armpits. If the approaching person had a robe that would fit him, well, then he'd take them out – but if they didn't, or if they were an Arbitrator, then he'd have to let them pass.

An Arbitrator. Alan's blood ran cold. *Did they all know each other?* he wondered, then quickly answered himself: *No, of course not; there are too many of them for that*. But did they know the ones they worked with, those they worked opposite? He cursed himself for not paying more attention when he lived here. The Arbitrator descended towards him and Alan resisted the urge to go for his sword. Would they be expected to speak to each other? The Arbitrator came to a halt directly in front of him and made eye contact – was he to be replaced? Would the new Arbitrator recognise that he was not the one who'd been Stationed here before? He opened his mouth to speak, to say something innocuous, disingenuous, something slick, but nothing came.

The other Arbitrator's head inclined, very slightly, and Alan returned the gesture. The other Arbitrator opened the door and passed through, then closed the door—

—which opened almost immediately afterwards, revealing an Administrator. Perfect. He was quite big, and red-faced. High-ranking, judging by his robes. He was carrying a book and a couple of scrolls. Alan waited for the heavy door to close itself behind him, and then acted; the sword came out, the hilt came down and the man – already on his way upstairs without so much as a nod of the head – collapsed. Alan grabbed him and pulled him round the corner.

Nora was fully robed, to all appearances just a Pyramidder. The Alchemist's body had gone – already spirited away to the stillroom hiding place. 'This one's for Byron,' Alan hissed. 'Just one more.'

Alan stood and waited. And waited. Time stretched. The distant murmurings of activity softened into a *shh-shh-shushing*. His eyelids were heavy and his eyes sore. His head was pounding and felt too big for his neck. Now he had nothing else to distract him, the wounds on his back had flared into burning pain. His knees wanted to give way – in fact, his whole being wanted nothing more than to sink into the floor. He felt as if he were on the verge of passing out. His vision hazed and came back, hazed and came back. Where were these Green-damned Pyramidders? If he had to wait much longer, he wouldn't be able to act when they did show up. He blinked, and blinked again. Maybe he could leave his eyes closed for a moment. Just a moment. If anybody came down the stairs or through the door, he'd hear them. He closed his eyes.

He jerked his head up, smacking his head into the wall behind him. Even through the helmet the blow shook his skull and he staggered forward, clenching his teeth to stop himself shouting out. The pain in his head was *unreal*. He longed to be able to decapitate himself, just for a break.

Voices! That's what had woken him: a couple of Pyramidders, coming down the stairs. It wasn't ideal, but maybe he could take two. He couldn't see them yet.

But before he did, he was joined by Byron, who positioned himself by the door as if he'd just come through it. He pulled back his sleeves to show Alan a sap hidden in his hand, and Alan grinned.

Alan was quickly back in Pyramid robes once more.

8

Robes

They left the four Pyramidders behind in the old still-room, all unconscious and trussed up with their own undergarments.

Not long after hitting the stairs, Alan's legs began to hurt again. It was a long way up, and at some point they'd have to duck out of this stairwell and make their way across one of the floors to get to another stairwell – because of the shape of the complex there were more stairwells on the lower storeys than on the higher, and few of them went all the way to the top. He'd never been down to these levels before – in the Pyramid, you had set paths: you went from your quarters to your various Stations, from your Station to the canteen and back, from your Station to one of the pools, to the Bleeding Chambers, to the Conception Chambers . . . you wouldn't do it in that order, but the point was that you fell into routines, into runnels that led you from one familiar location to the next. And you did not leave them again. That happened in the Discard too, but in the Discard you created your own patterns; they weren't created for you by Astronomers. And in the Pyramid, if you abandoned your patterns, there would be consequences.

Still, the dangers of nonconformity were for actual Pyramidders who failed to adhere to the rules: those who failed to show up in the right place at the right time. They were not really at risk of that – Arbitrators might pass them in the corridors, but there was no reason for them to be stopped and questioned, not unless they *looked* out of place. It's not as if they had appointments to keep or Managers to appease.

'What floor do Marion and Billy live on, then?' Nora asked.

'Fifth-Tier Workers, South-East Straits. Fifth-Tier is . . .' He had to stop and count. 'It's the ninth floor – but we count down from the top, not up from the bottom. So from here – um—'

'It's *we* now, is it?' Byron murmured, raising an eyebrow at Alan.

'They. We. They. I don't know – I don't care.'

Byron laughed softly.

'I don't know what floor we're on here,' Alan admitted.

'Aren't the doors numbered in some way?' Nora asked.

'No,' Byron said. 'That'd make it easier to find your way around, which they don't want. Yer told how to get to where yer need to go and that's it. Nobody knows all of it.'

'Not even Management?'

'Probably not even Management.'

They fell silent as a group of Pyramidders passed them on the stairs. At the next landing, Byron pulled Nora to a stop. 'My bleedin' legs,' he said. 'The Sump nearly killed 'em.'

'The Giving Beast flesh was a potent anaesthetic, was it not?' Nora said. 'It becomes especially apparent now that the effects are wearing off.'

'Potent in lots of ways,' Alan said.

'An anaesthetic, a time-thinner, a stimulant and a shield against the swamp-madness. I would be interested to find another of its kind, if there are any.'

'And let's not kill them, if there are,' Alan added.

'Point is,' Byron said, 'I need a little break.'

They kept their hands hidden in their sleeves and their hoods up while they rested in the stairwell, standing by a door as if they had just met and were catching up before going their separate ways.

They were in the minority in keeping their hoods up, but it was not so unusual as to draw attention. After a short breather they continued up the stairs. Alan felt himself relaxing as they encountered more and more Pyramidders without incident. Nora kept her head down. Her pink facial tattoos were the single greatest threat to their passage, but her robe was slightly too big, so her hood hung low and did a good job of covering up the ink.

As they rose through the levels and the décor became

more ornate, Alan started to build up a picture of where they were through the snatches of Discard architecture he glimpsed through occasional open doors. They were near an outer wall of the Pyramid, and so there were balconies and verandahs and other openings out onto the Pyramid slope, though they were all guarded by Arbitrators.

Eventually he tapped Nora discreetly on the shoulder and indicated the door they were passing. 'Here,' he said. They opened it and entered into the network of corridors: a true labyrinth. Alan had forgotten the extent of it, and how difficult it was to navigate should you step out of your usual paths.

Through an open archway the sounds of clicking could be heard over a monotonous voice and the murmuring of other people. They stopped to look and saw Pyramidders inside, standing in rows, heads bowed over tall lecterns. Alan grabbed Nora by the arm. 'Watch,' he whispered. 'We must have reached Administration. This is the kind of thing most Pyramidders do all the time. This is a Station. This is what they do – in shifts. It never ends.'

The walls and floor of the room were bare stone. The light from the globes was dimmed by a haze of smoke rising up to the ceiling from the censers swung by the Administrative Supervisors pacing up and down the central aisle. The Supervisors' robes were decorated with patterns of golden thread around the hems and cuffs. Their robes were thicker, and their hoods longer and more pointed. The Supervisors kept their heads completely clean-shaven, and one — no doubt the most senior Pyramidder in the room — wore a wide metal circlet that was fitted so closely to her skull that it looked like a band of shining skin. She was standing at the far end of the room, speaking into a horn.

As Alan, Nora and Byron listened, she said, '—by the Administrative Stationing Instructions (Revision Seven Hundred and Eighty-Two, Issue Twelve) Chapter Thirty-Three, Section Six Point One, Paragraph Six: Station Eight Thousand and Twenty, The Order of the Black Bones, Revision Eight. The Order of the Black Bones is to be determined by the Administrators of Station Eight Thousand and Nineteen, in accordance with the Pyramid Demand, the Pyramid Desire, the Pyramid Wish. In receiving and fulfilling the Black Bones, the Administrators of Station Eight Thousand and Twenty are fulfilling the very flesh of the Pyramid itself. The Pyramid of Mirrors, the Pyramid of Light, the Sky Tower. The Pyramid of Many Aspects. The Pyramid of a Thousand Pyramids. And as the Black Bones are received and fulfilled, so those who receive and fulfil them shall be elevated in the Pyramid memory. The Deep Walls shall remember you. The Ten Thousand Corridors shall remember you. The Cascades shall remember you. The Calm Pools shall remember you. The memory of you shall travel the Brass Veins and soar above the Staggered Observatories. You will be as a bird accompanying the

Pyramid into the future, into all of the Pyramid futures: the grey futures and the bright futures, the near futures and the far. You will be brightly coloured birds flying alongside our great gleaming ship as it sails deep and leaden waters. Let your hard-working hands receive and fulfil the Black Bones. Let your hands and your mind work in accordance with the Great Pyramid Books, let your eyes seek—'

At each Station the tall wooden lectern had a brass funnel underneath the desk part and two brass tubes that came down from the ceiling. Alan, Nora and Byron watched the Pyramidder closest to the archway as he took a black, palm-sized disc deposited from the left-hand tube, examined it – the discs were embossed or engraved with a pattern of holes – and then searched through a stack of smaller coloured discs on his desktop. He picked up a selection of them and somehow attached them to the black disc, then he dropped the bundle into the funnel at his feet. Then another black disc arrived and he repeated the process. They looked around the chamber and could see every Pyramidder was doing the same thing, again and again and again and again.

A nearby Pyramidder apparently couldn't find the required coloured discs to attach to the black one – after checking and double-checking, she lifted the black disc to the mouth of the right-hand brass tube and trod on a pedal that must have activated some kind of suction device, because the black disc was pulled from the

Pyramidder's hand up into the tube and disappeared from sight.

'What is it, though?' Nora asked. 'What is it for?'

'It's vital to the being of the Pyramid,' Alan whispered. 'Can't you tell? Can't you see its importance? And of course it's to train you to think and behave in a particular way: it teaches you focus, discipline and stamina. Everyone has targets; whatever your Station is, you've got to hit your target. So these Administrators will have to process a particular number of discs. It means you have to concentrate. It's good for you.'

'So nobody knows what the discs are for?'

'We don't know,' Byron said, 'and they probably don't know either. The Supervisors probably don't bleedin' know. The discs will go somewhere else and somebody else will do something else with them, but they won't know what they're for any more than this lot do.'

'Don't they *want* to know?'

Alan answered, 'If you're born and raised in the Pyramid, you don't want to know the specifics, no – the questions don't even occur to you. In a general sense, the answer is simply that this is what Pyramidders are born to do – and this is what differentiates the Pyramid from the Discard; this is what prevents the Pyramid becoming the Discard, or sinking into it. That's reason enough.'

The Senior Supervisor was still speaking into the horn. She was small and wizened, her deep-set eyes surrounded by an intricate network of wrinkles. She stopped to cough, then continued, '—receive the Black Bone and utter your thanks. Breathe deeply of the curling smoke. Seek amongst the tokens before you those required by the Pattern of the Black Bone, and in doing so seek yourself in the Great Pattern of the Pyramid.'

'That's her Station,' Alan whispered, 'reading from one of the Great Pyramid Books. Look at her robes – she's of quite high rank so she's probably got other duties too, maybe checking the Administrators' targets, something like that.'

Nora asked, 'So what's to stop a Pyramidder just doing it wrong? Just sending all the discs away, back up the pipe?'

'There'll be another Station somewhere assessing the outputs of this one. I worked a Station once where I patterned the discs. All of the Stations are interconnected; they all depend on each other for what they do.'

'They must all go towards building *something*, though,' Nora said. 'What about those vile things dropping into the Sump – where do they come from? They must be made by Stations, right?'

'I don't know,' Alan said. 'I guess so.'

'So the Pyramidders don't know they're making anything?'

'No, you just perform your Stationing,' Alan tried to explain. 'You get moved around a bit if you're in Administration, but you never see enough to make out the whole picture. You can hear her in there – it's all ritual; they don't actually tell you what the Black Bones are.'

'Does it matter?' Byron broke in. 'Let's get a move on, shall we? Before someone catches us.'

They passed more Stationing rooms, sorting rooms overflowing with sheaves of paper, records-storage rooms with rows of identical alcoves carved into the walls and thousands of narrow cylinders sealed with wax plugs. There were rooms lined with monstrous abaci strung with countless tiny beads, and others that hung down from the ceiling instead of rising up from the floor. Administrators on tall wheeled ladders pulled themselves around using dangling ropes, continually adjusting the beads and counters and speaking entirely in numbers, without reference to anything even as concrete as the Black Bones. The devices were so complex neither Alan, nor Byron or Nora could understand their purpose. Different incense burned in each room, different passages from the Great Books were recited, the Supervisor robes were all slightly different – but the unquestioning obedience was absolutely consistent.

At last the three of them found themselves in a plaza, a great open space with soaring aqueducts. 'Yes,' Alan said, 'this is right. We're going the right way. We keep going, keep our heads down, it'll be okay. We'll be with Billy in no time.'

They mingled with the other Pyramidders talking in the plaza. Craning their necks, they could see people punting rafts along the waterways. Large metal sculptures suspended in the air made ambient sounds as breezes moved through them. Decorative waterfalls spilled from higher levels, sometimes running through the sculptures themselves, and mechanical birds perched on ledges or sang from hanging cages. Glow-globes within elaborate frames rotated, casting moving panels of warm orange light everywhere. A huge tinted window provided indistinct views out over the Discard, the thick glass accentuating the bright colours of the moons. The sun was setting out there, and the light of it combined with that of the shaded glow-globes lent the plaza a kind of twilight atmosphere.

Byron raised a hand and pointed to the far side of the space. 'My mother,' he breathed.

'Where?' Alan couldn't see anybody who might have been Byron's mother. Any women he could see were too young, or their features were shadowed by their hoods. 'Are you sure?'

'She left through that archway,' Byron said. 'I'm going after her.'

'Wait.'

'You go save your boy; I'm going to go catch up with my folks.'

'No,' Nora said, 'we are all here to do different things, but we do one and then another and then we do the last, and we stick together all the while. If we split up we are each a threat to the others.'

'Nora's right, Byron,' Alan said. 'We need to help each other. And besides, we can't *chase* her. *You* can't chase her.

You'll give us all away.' He didn't voice his other concern; that Byron's sighting had just been wishful thinking. The big man's eyes were looking glazed, his mouth was slack.

And he wasn't listening. He was walking away from them.

'*Byron!*' Nora hissed.

Alan cursed under his breath. They couldn't raise their voices, they couldn't run after him . . . they couldn't draw attention to themselves at all. Maybe they should just let him go.

Nora was evidently following the same train of thought. 'Let him go?' she suggested. 'He is soft and pale enough to pass easily for a Pyramidder. He should attract no attention.'

'Not until he gets to where he's going – then who knows? I mean. The way he's fucked off on his own like this? This is what alarms me. If we were with him, we could control things.'

'You think he'd jeopardise us? Do you not trust him?'

'I did trust him,' Alan said, the nerves in his belly joined by the first faint flames of a fresh anger, 'but that was before he fucking . . . did *this*. Slipped off.'

'If we're going to go after him, we need to go now. Look; he is nearly lost to us.'

'Yeah.' More and more Pyramidders were between them and Byron. 'Let's go.'

They picked up their pace without breaking into a

run – Pyramidders didn't run, generally; if they did, people would stop and gawk; they'd want to know why. Byron was threading his way through the plaza towards a grand archway, through which they could see a dining hall. As they got closer they could make out the large round tables groaning beneath a variety of foodstuffs Alan had forgotten even existed: plates piled high with roasted meats, colourful vegetables prepared in oils and herbs, bowls of fresh, vibrant salads, warm breads, sauces and dips, stews, bakes, curries, grains and pulses, cakes, biscuits and more, with not a single fucking snail to be seen. Nora forgot her discretion and looked all around her, her mouth open. 'This is more than they had at Dok – more than even the Mushroom Queen could provide. This is *impossible*. What are those meats, Alan?'

'Cover your face,' he said urgently. 'Those meats are from farmed creatures that don't even have names' – they hurried through the milling diners – 'born of Alchemy in deep, lightless vats. Delicious, though. They are delicious.'

Byron led them down more corridors, through plazas, into dining halls, along verandahs, but they didn't call after him; they didn't want to raise their voices. There was always somebody else around. He was moving at a fair speed – too fast – and Alan was pretty sure he knew they were after him. There was no sign of his mother, or the woman he thought was his mother.

'It looks like we're approaching a Residential area,' Alan told Nora. 'The North-East Straits, I think.' And sure enough, they were soon strolling past the round brass doors of people's homes. Byron was just ahead of the curve of the corridor, but if Alan hurried a few steps, he could catch a glimpse of him. There were fewer people around now, but every time Alan felt like he could safely run or shout, a stranger would appear.

And then Byron came to a stop outside one of the doors, looked back at Alan and Nora, something mournful in his eyes, and raised his fist to knock.

There was nobody else in front of them. Alan checked behind him; nobody else there either. He ran, jumped and collided with Byron just as Byron's knuckles had been about to connect with the door.

'Where is your mother?' Nora asked. 'Alan, get up off him. Byron, get off the floor. Quickly, before we are seen! Byron – where is your mother? The woman you saw?'

Alan and Byron got to their feet. Alan rearranged his robe to conceal his trousers, but Byron just stood there. Apart from something troubled in his eyes, his expression was blank. Nora grabbed his robe and tugged it back into position. 'Answer my question, biker,' she said.

Byron looked at her, but said nothing.

'This is bad,' Alan said. 'I feel like it's bad.'

'I never saw her,' Byron said. 'Not really.'

'So where are we?' Nora pressed.

'I came home. I just wanted to come home. Alone.'

'Byron,' Alan reached up and put his hands on the biker's shoulders. 'This isn't your home any more.'

'I used to go to the plaza with my parents and we'd play skittles. Punt along the 'ducts. Listen to the metal birds. I loved that plaza. The clean running water. The light. The *food*. I try not to remember it.'

'Byron . . .'

'We were so happy.' Byron's voice was quiet. 'We were one of those families. Just . . . happy. Lucky. Happy. Until I went and bleedin' ruined it.'

'No. You—'

'I want them back,' he said, his voice breaking. He put a hand over his eyes and his shoulders shook. 'I want it all back.' He waved at the door. 'This is where we lived, before I . . . before he . . . before it all happened.'

'Byron,' Alan said, 'you can't go backwards. You can't retrace your steps to a place you used to know and just drop back into your old life. The place has changed, you've changed, the people you knew have changed. You know this. Come on.'

'Your bleedin' need is always greater, isn't it?' Byron sneered suddenly. He glared at Alan, wrested himself free of Alan's grip and hammered on the door. Then he turned and shoved Alan away. 'Leave me be now,' he said.

Alan felt Nora pulling at him from behind and he backed away with her, further down the corridor.

The door rolled back and a young woman stood there, her dark hair tousled on one side and stuck flat to her head on the other. She'd clearly been woken by the knocking. 'H-hello?' she said. 'Am I late? Wh-what's—?'

'Who are you?' Byron asked.

'Iniron Aylus,' the woman said. 'Astronomer.'

'Where's them who lived here before? Barious the Astronomer and Cirium the Alchemist?'

'B-Barious Lis? The High-Tier Senior Datemaker? I didn't know he lived here!'

'He did well for himself, did he? Yeah, him: he lived here. Where is he now? Did he move up a few levels?'

'I always assumed he lived up high, yeah,' the woman said. She stifled a yawn. 'But not any more; he's dead. I thought the news was cascaded down – he died a while back . . .' She paused, working it out, then finished, 'a couple of years ago, I think.'

Byron rocked backwards onto his heels. 'Green damn it,' he said, softly. He wiped at his eyes.

The woman frowned. 'Green?'

Alan and Nora stepped forwards. 'Are you okay?' Alan asked. Byron put a hand out to stop them.

'And Cirium? Cirium Lis? What about her?' Byron's voice wavered, threatening sobs.

'I don't know who she is.' The woman was retreating, closing the door, a wariness on her face now she was properly awake. But Byron jumped after her, grabbed her arm and pulled her out of the room. Her screams pierced the air and Alan ducked, looked over his shoulder to see if they'd yet attracted attention, and when he turned back Byron had a knife at the woman's throat. His face was wet with tears.

'Fucking hell!' Alan exploded. 'What's wrong with you? Let her go!'

'Stay out of this!' Byron shouted, briefly pointing the knife at Alan and Nora. 'You're just passers-by and trust me, that's a good thing for you.' Then he spoke to Iniron. 'Take me to the Arbitrators,' he said, 'or I will kill you.'

'What the fuck are you doing?' Alan demanded, but Byron ignored him.

'Point,' Byron told Iniron. 'Show me which way we've got to go.'

Iniron pointed, and Byron walked her backwards in that direction. Alan checked again, but he and Nora were still the only people around.

Suddenly Nora broke into a run, heading back the way they'd come, away from Byron and his captive. 'Come on!' she shouted back to Alan, 'let's go and get help!'

She reached a junction, led him around a couple more corners and came to a stop. 'Okay,' she said, 'good.'

'What do you mean, "good"? We haven't found any-body yet.'

'We can't help. Byron wants the Arbitrators and she'll take him to the Arbitrators. We send Arbitrators, he gets Arbitrators. Either way, he gets what he wants.'

'But what about her?'

'He doesn't want to hurt her. You heard him. He is offering himself up as a diversion. He told her we were just passers-by. Any signs of a breach, now, and he will be in the frame. She realised that he was a Discarder; you could see it. But we ran off to help, so she will think we're Pyramidders. Now *Byron* is the threat; *Byron* came in from the Discard, *he* knocked out those Pyramidders below. We have much less to be worried about now.'

Alan felt worried, all the same. 'But he'll tell people we were with him—'

'Will he? I don't know. He could have landed us in it right then, but he didn't. I don't think he wants to ruin things for us, Alan. He's doing his own thing, but he's helping us at the same time. It's good that he came with us. Now let's go. Let's do *your* thing.'

'Bloody hell,' Alan said, pacing and clutching at his hair beneath his hood. 'Bloody, bloody hell. How do we know though? What if he has actually flipped? What if he *does* hurt her?'

'Did you use his name when you were talking to him?'

'I don't know. No, I don't think so.'

'Then it can't be connected to us.'

'I don't care about *that,* you fucking – fucking . . .'

Nora tilted her head. 'Fucking what?' she asked, her voice light. 'What am I, Alan?'

'How do you not *care*?' Alan wasn't shouting, but his voice was strained. 'What's *wrong* with you?'

'I do care. Just because I don't show it doesn't mean I don't care.'

'We haven't got time for this. I'm going after them.'

'Alan.'

'I'm going.'

'What about Billy?' Nora called after him.

Alan stopped.

And as they stared at each other, the wild pealing of bells broke out, the sound coming from all around, though the bells were nowhere to be seen. Nora put her hands to her ears. The sound was hard and cold, as hard and as cold as the stone walls to either side, and it echoed down the corridor in waves. Alan's ears rang, the sound doubling up inside his head. Pyramidders were shouting, doors were opening and there was a thunderous noise from the direction that Nora had been urging they head in. Then a detachment of Arbitrators appeared, pounding towards them. The corridor wasn't wide enough for Alan and Nora to get past them without squeezing close enough to risk their robes being snagged.

'Okay,' Nora said urgently, 'we do it your way. Back to Byron and Iniron. Go. *Go.*'

Nora and Alan hurried back towards Iniron's quarters, those Pyramidders who'd left their rooms swept up behind them, as if the Arbitrators were a tide rushing in. They stayed ahead of the mass until they arrived at a great intersection between many corridors. In the centre were two large apertures: a Discard chute and a laundry chute, from which steam rose. Alan slammed to a halt when he saw that Byron was standing next to the Discard chute, Iniron still his captive, his knife still at her throat. The Arbitrators distributed themselves at the entrance to each corridor off the intersection while Pyramidders who had been throwing their laundry down the chute or who'd been carried along by the Arbitrators stood awkwardly, spectators to something they didn't want to see. Iniron was struggling against Byron's arms.

Byron was shouting, 'I want my mother! Cirium! Cirium, the Alchemist! I want my mother! I want my mother! *Take me to my mother!*' His voice was strained. His eyes were red, his cheeks were tearstained, his mouth a jagged hole.

The Arbitrators behind Alan and Nora shouldered them out of the way. One of them was a Commander with silver plumage sprouting from his helmet, a silver-hemmed cape swinging from his shoulders and a silver ring in his nose. His mesh mask hung from the helmet. He was pale even for a Pyramidder; his veins were visible as blue webbing beneath his skin. He raised the crossbow he was holding in his right hand and pointed it at Byron. When he spoke, his voice was sepulchral.

'You,' he said. 'Unhand our Astronomer.'

'He's a Discarder!' yelled Iniron.

'Take me to Cirium Lis, the Alchemist!' Byron shouted. 'Take me to my mother!'

'Cirium Lis,' said the Commander, thoughtfully. 'Her partner, Barious Lis, Discarded their son – you, presumably – for sexual deviancy. But nobody knew at the time; for years, the son's disappearance was a mystery. Everybody thought he must have fallen, or been thrown down a chute in a fight with another boy. It was a tragedy, and Cirium and Barious received much sympathy. Cirium's heart was truly broken. But the truth came out eventually. Another boy had indeed been involved, but they hadn't been fighting – and once the truth *was* out, Barious killed himself. A Senior Astronomer, with all of the responsibility for coupling and procreation that that entails, and his own son came out broken? I too would have wanted to die.'

Byron was frozen, his face a mask.

'And as for Cirium . . . well, she deteriorated quite rapidly after that. She stopped caring, stopped meeting her duties, stopped making her Stations. I think she was Discarded herself, in the end, but I'm not sure. She faded into illness and irrelevance quickly, and publicly. And now – here you are!'

He paused, as if expecting Byron to respond, but Byron just stared.

The Commander continued, 'So you have infiltrated the Pyramid from outside?'

'I want to see my mother,' Byron whispered. 'I want to know – I want to know—'

'You are a madman and a deviant,' the Commander interrupted. He didn't shout, but his voice carried in a way that Byron's didn't. 'And that in itself merited Discarding. But not only that, you *came back in*. Who knows what Discard parasites infest you, what deviant diseases you carry? You came back in to the Pyramid, into *our* Pyramid, you expose us to your filth and your grime and your depraved soul, and you make demands upon *us*?' He gestured to the Arbitrators standing nearest to Byron and ordered, 'Strip him. We will Discard him for his deviancy, and we will Discard him for his infiltration, but we can't Discard him twice, so we'll Discard him naked.'

'No!' Byron shouted, and he shoved Iniron, as if to remind everybody that he still held her hostage.

'You won't kill her, scum. I know by your eyes. Let her go.'

Byron's gaze flicked from the Commander to the Arbitrators bearing crossbows to the knife in his hand to the chute. His chin was trembling. Alan could see that he didn't have a plan, not really. He'd been swept away by his memories, swept back into the runnels of his old life. But those he'd loved were no longer there to meet him. Byron's shoulders sagged and his head dropped and his arm fell from Iniron. The knife clattered to the stone floor.

As Iniron ran away from Byron, Alan braced himself to launch into the Commander from the side. But before he could move, two Arbitrators stepped forward and ripped Byron's robe from him, revealing his Discard attire. They threw the robe down the laundry chute, then they removed his other clothes, each piece following the robe, until Byron was left naked and shivering. He made no attempt to cover himself.

'I thought all Discarders were all starving and scrawny,' the Commander commented, 'but you've got some meat on you.'

Byron didn't say anything.

'You cannot have succeeded alone. Who came with you?'

'Nobody.'

'Nobody? I don't believe you. Where are the others?'

Byron looked around, meeting the eyes of the Pyramidders who had found themselves trapped at the intersection. Alan shifted uncomfortably; he felt like Byron was looking for him and Nora – and then suddenly Byron *was* looking directly at him, meeting his eyes.

Alan froze as the Commander repeated, 'Where are the others?'

But Byron's gaze had already passed on. 'There were no others,' he said.

'Very well,' the Commander said. 'Arbitrators, Discard him.'

Alan breathed out. Byron would be okay in the Discard, even naked. The other Goatherds would be looking out for him – and there were plenty of Transients out there who wore barely any clothes anyway.

'Discard him naked,' the Commander said, 'and because he is lying, Discard him dead.'

The crossbow bolt flew straight and true, but Byron was already rolling over the edge of the Discard chute. Alan saw a flash of red and heard a cry of pain as it struck Byron's shoulder – and then Byron was gone.

The Commander pursed his lips. 'Not ideal,' he said,

'but it will suffice. That's the problem with exile as a catch-all punishment, I suppose. It's difficult to punish a person for multiple crimes.' He smiled as he looked around. 'I think we managed it, though. Now please return to your quarters.' He then bent his head to his nearest companion. 'Instigate a full search: all entrances and exits, doors, balconies, terraces – everywhere.'

'Nora,' Alan said quietly, 'with me.'

'Where—?'

Alan felt as if he were a long way away from his own body, but somehow he compelled his arm to reach up and out, and the sleeve of his robe slowly slipped back, revealing his tattooed hand. Billy's name was dyed into his knuckles, a skull grinned from the back and a snake wound itself around his wrist. Small black teeth and nails filled the gaps in between. His hand moved slowly, so slowly. The Commander stared, momentarily cross-eyed as the hand approached his face. Alan seized hold of the nose ring and ripped it out. The Commander screamed and Alan screamed back as he rushed forwards, his hood coming down, the Commander scrabbling for his sword, and all around was movement and unintelligible shouting, and Alan got his hand around the Commander's neck and the Commander tripped backwards over the lip of the laundry chute and a crossbow bolt whistled through the air past Alan's head, and then another, and Alan was falling forward, the Commander beneath him, into the dark, wet, steaming pit of the laundry chute.

Bolts rattled all around them as they plunged headfirst down the hole.

The chute was smooth and slippery, and the thick steam quickly dampened their clothes and made it impossible to see. Alan kept a firm hold on the Commander's throat as they shot downwards. The plumed helmet fell off and bounced away into nothing, the sound subsumed by the rushing of their bodies. Alan couldn't even look behind to see if Nora was there or not as they fell, twisting, beyond the reach of the light. He could feel the Commander trying to scrabble for his weapons, but they were moving too fast, and the Commander was too scared.

'Not another one,' Alan heard himself say. 'Not another one.'

The chute curve shallowed slightly and the Commander bounced off the wall. Alan realised he could see again in the light coming from below. Suddenly there it was: first a speck and then a widening circle of white, growing ever bigger, until suddenly they fell out of it and Alan caught a glimpse of a grey, churning mass: a huge vat of steaming water. There was a large metal paddle attached to a central pole that was rotating, stirring the water. The Commander's exposed head split on the paddle and everything went red.

He shot past the stuck corpse of the Commander into the tank and discovered the water was scalding hot. He got caught up in the clothes, which stopped him from going deep, but they clung to him as he tried to resurface until he felt like he was surrounded by formless spectres hanging on to his arms and legs, weighing him down. His mother and father were there. Raspy, the Commander who'd led the attack on the Cavern Tavern, was there. There was Spider, there was Eyes, and there was the Clawbaby. They were burning—

He broke the surface and saw the dead Commander hanging over the paddle, his split-open head leaking blood and other fluids into the soup. Bits of skull bobbed around and Alan felt faint. The heat and the blood and the death . . . He scrambled to the side of the vat and clawed his way up. There was a strong smell of lemon and lavender and other herbs he couldn't identify; it smelled good. He couldn't see anything much because of the thick steam, but he could hear shouting, and those damned bells were still pealing away, though they were quieter down here. The shouting wasn't panicked, he realised; it was rhythmic, almost like a working song. He couldn't make out the words, or even tell if there were words. He'd never been down to Laundry before. Was he deep? He must be deep.

A hand appeared from out of the fug: a small hand with chipped green fingernails. Nora. He grabbed it, and with the extra leverage, managed to haul himself over the edge.

Nora pulled him down and clapped a hand over his

mouth. Like him, she was wet through. She whispered into his ear, 'This is a good place to be. With the steam, they don't know we're here. They'll see the Commander in a moment, but if we stay low . . .'

'We need to find our way back up,' Alan whispered in return, brushing wet lavender flowers from his clothes. 'We could use a laundry lift, though.'

'I thought there weren't any lifts?'

'Well, they're not really lifts. They're just bags on hooks, and they tip out of a little hole when they get to the right floor – designed precisely to prevent people getting in and using them.'

'So we need to find the one for the ninth floor.'

'We do. Excuse me, everything's going white. I'm feeling rather . . . light-headed. The heat. It's the heat.' Alan leaned over and quietly retched. 'Green damn it,' he muttered when he'd finished.

'We need to go.'

'I know, I know.'

They rose to a crouch and shuffled around the side of the vat, thankful for the rough texture of the floor, obviously deliberate to avoid the condensation making it impossibly slippery. Indistinct figures stood above them on platforms, thick arms holding long poles with which they pushed and pulled the contents of the swirling vat. They were moving in time with the shouts. As Alan and Nora slipped through an archway into another similar room, a shriek pierced the air, audible even over the bells, and Alan glanced back to see that the steam had momentarily parted to reveal the dead Commander; in that split-second the veils drew closed once more.

They ducked into an alcove stacked high with baskets loaded with fruit and herbs. Beside them, there was a wooden door, heavily varnished and glistening with rivulets of condensation. Alan yanked on the handle, but it didn't open easily – it was edged in leather.

When he did get it open he found a long, dark chamber lined with shelves stacked high with dry, folded robes. Each stack was labelled with an address.

It wasn't just one chamber, though: similar rooms opened up from this one and the more they explored, the more they realised what a warren it was. 'Twenty-first floor,' Alan mumbled, reading the signs above each archway, 'eleventh floor. Eighteenth floor. We need the ninth floor – Fifth-Tier Admin is on the ninth floor.'

'So that's pretty high-ranking, is it?' Nora asked.

'Yeah, it's high-ranking Admin – but Admin is the lowest discipline and there are far more Administrators than there are Alchemists or Astronomers. Speaking of which . . .' Alan took a robe from one of the shelves, shook it out to check the length, and proceeded to change from the wet one. Nora ventured into an adjacent room for privacy, and followed suit. Alan continued talking as they changed. 'That's the way it's meant to be, though; they need more Administrators, so the Astronomers pair people up and assign conception dates in order to create more babies that will grow up to be suited to Administrating. You can move around inside each Discipline, but you can't ever move from one to the other. Your Discipline is largely determined before your birth – before your conception, even – and it's for life.'

'So when the children are told what they are going to be, do they just accept it? Don't they ever say no, not me, I am not going to be one of . . . those?'

'They aren't told – the parents aren't told. We find out when we leave school what Discipline we're going to be allocated to. Up until that point, I guess there's a chance – a very slim chance – that a child can jink from the course set for them by excelling in their studies. So there is that motivation for them to work hard, you know. But most children will work exceptionally hard just to find that they are going to be an Administrator their whole life after all, and by that age, of course, they are terrified of the Discard, so they accept the path.' Alan gripped a shelf and bent over. 'By Green, it's hot down here. I feel really sick.'

'Do you think Byron will survive?'

'Yes,' Alan said, immediately.

'You didn't think about that question before answering it.'

'No. Now let's get a move on. They'll soon hear that the Commander didn't fall down the chute alone. You take that chamber on the right, I'll take this one on the left. We're looking for the ninth floor.'

Not a minute had passed before Nora hissed out. 'Found it. I have got it here. So what? Why were we looking for this room?'

'Each floor has a laundry hatch – just one, judging by what we've seen down here – from which the sacks of clean robes are deposited,' Alan said, hurrying back to Nora's position. 'And these chambers each have a named floor above their entrance. So I'm guessing that each of these chambers is connected somehow to the hatch on the corresponding floor. Hopefully by some sort of lift.' Nora pointed at a hatch at the back of the room. 'Yeah, that's it. Open it up. Let's see how it works.'

The wooden hatch slid upwards to reveal a heavy cloth sack resting on the floor, attached by a pair of rope handles to a vicious-looking metal hook that in turn descended from a lightless shaft.

'Yes!' Alan said. 'Yes, this must be it. So this lift takes the clean clothes up and tips them out. Administrators are assigned to the collection point; it's their Station to sort and distribute clean washing.' He held the neck open. 'Get in.'

'How do we——? Oh, it's on a pulley.'

'Yeah. I'm guessing normally it's operated by somebody down here, but we'll need to pull ourselves up.' Alan climbed in himself. The four pulley ropes were fixed to a bracket screwed to the wall. Alan untied them and passed one to Nora. 'I guess this is so that more than one person can stand at the bottom and raise the sack,' he said. 'They must be heavy when they're full.'

'It will be heavy now, too,' Nora pointed out.

'Yeah, it will, but at least our legs can have a rest,' Alan said, optimistically. He closed the hatch behind them and they were plunged into absolute darkness.

'On three,' Nora said. 'One, two, three, *heave*.'

Alan did not have the strength or energy to speak. This had been a terrible idea. *Terrible*. His lacerated back stung and itched abominably, his arms were on fire, his lungs were on fire and his hands were wet with blood – and yet he could not let go of the rope. He was sure that Nora felt the same, but she was not talking either; he wasn't sure who was making the whimpering noises he could hear, Nora or himself. The agony and exhaustion were mutual, shared. And for all that effort, they were rising at a snail's pace.

'Finally,' said a small voice some while later, and Alan was startled to find that he could see a thin line of light. 'We can get out. This will open onto the correct floor, yes?'

'It said ninth floor at the bottom, so yes, I think so. Yes.' Alan rested his forehead against the taut rope. 'I'll push it open.'

'Go on, then,' Nora said, after a moment.

'I . . . I can't.' Alan willed his fingers to uncurl. 'I can't let go of this bloody rope. I'm trying, but my body's not listening. I'm shaking. My arms are fucked. My body knows that if I let go with one, the other fails.'

'You mean you are scared.'

'Yes, fine. Scared. Thanks, Nora.'

'I am closer anyway,' Nora said. 'Are you ready?'

'Yes.'

The sack suddenly felt heavier and wobbled alarmingly as Nora leaned out. Alan groaned as the rope slipped slightly through his bloody hands and his stomach lurched. He gripped it more tightly, ignoring the deep stinging pain, and brought it to a halt. He didn't look down – there was nothing to see – but despite that, he couldn't help but picture yawning nothingness beneath.

'I can't open it,' Nora said urgently. 'Alan, I can't open it. What are we going to do?'

'Hold the rope – get both hands back on the rope. I can't take the whole weight much longer.'

'I have got both hands on the rope already.'

Alan groaned again.

'We will not survive a fall,' Nora said. 'We are very high now, and there is a great distance below us, straight down, ending in a stone floor. Our bones would—'

'Wait,' Alan said, 'if this sack was full of robes, there would be nobody here to open the hatch from this side.'

'So it must be opened from the other side, you're saying.'

'By the Builders! What a stupid way to die.'

Nora began to whisper to herself: Mapmaker prayers of some description, no doubt, Alan thought. He had nobody to pray to. There must be *something* they could do . . . He thought back to the last time he'd collected clean robes for Marion, Billy and himself: he'd seen stacks of robes slide from the hatch, into the waiting arms of Administrative Assistants, who'd then sorted them. But they hadn't had to do anything to *open* the hatch. He'd watched them break off conversation, turn and face the hatch, and raise their arms – as if something had alerted them.

'We need to go higher,' he announced. 'Pull.'

'I will try,' Nora said.

'If each shaft goes only to one floor, then we must be near the top of this one. There must be some sort of a mechanism for opening the hatch.'

'On the count of three,' Nora said wearily. 'One. Two. Three. *Heave.*'

Alan tried, but his torso had turned to stone.

'Heave,' Nora said again, flatly.

'I'm trying—'

'*Heave!*'

With a colossal effort that dragged some weird animal sound from the depths of his throat and made him feel as if his muscles were going to burst through his skin, they managed to raise the lift maybe half an inch – but that was all it took to start the momentum; they were on the move again, and after just a moment, they found themselves pressed against a ceiling. But it wasn't made of stone; it was made of wood. Nora rapped against it.

'Hollow,' she said. She felt around a bit. 'The pulley rope disappears up through a slot in the middle. There's a gap around the edge. It would move, if we push it. Let's keep pulling. I think if we push – if we push against this, then—'

They pulled on the ropes with the last of their strength and found themselves flattened against the wooden panel.

'This is it,' Alan said. 'If nothing happens right now, my body's going to give up.'

And with that there was a clicking sound above them, light flooded up from below and Alan looked down to see the hatch opening inwards, falling against the opposite wall and bridging the abyss. Without actually intending to, both he and Nora let go of their ropes and the sack fell the short distance to the bridge. They slid down the shallow slope through the hatch, the rope snaking behind them, and landed in a tangle on the cool stone floor of a quiet corridor.

9

Home Again

Alan looked at Nora and wondered if he looked as bloody, as broken down, as sick as she did. Probably more so. But there was no time to rest, much as their bodies required it.

They left red handprints on the sack and on the floor as they got themselves to their feet. 'Wipe your hands on the sack, quickly,' Alan said. 'If we pass anybody with us looking like this they'll know exactly who we are.' He was already wiping the blood and sweat off his own face and hands, wincing as the rough fabric stung his palms. 'We'll stick it back through the hatch.'

But they couldn't work out how to close it up again; they settled for wedging the bag into the gap between the hatch door and the wall of the shaft and walking quickly away. 'These robes are slightly higher-ranking than the first lot,' Alan commented, as they went. 'I didn't realise it down there in Laundry. I wouldn't have chosen them if I had.'

They turned a couple of corners into yet another

corridor with regular round brass doors set into the wall and slowed to a less conspicuous pace. 'So this is it,' Alan said. 'Home. Or what used to be home.'

'What will you tell Marion?' Nora asked.

'I wanted to work it all out back at Dok,' Alan said, 'before we accidentally lifted the Seal with the remains of the Giving Beast. I meant to think about it, properly.' He sighed. 'I'll just tell her the truth: that Billy is sick and we have the cure.'

'Will she trust you?'

'I don't know,' he admitted. 'I mean, there are plenty of reasons why she wouldn't, but . . .' He tailed off, and then said firmly, 'The thing is, I'm *right* about this: Billy needs us – he needs the Benedictions. And everybody else needs him to be well.'

'You're going to have to do some serious convincing, Alan. Just showing up with these funny mushrooms and saying here, eat these, trust me, I am your father . . . after everything, it is a lot to expect of them.'

'But I'm right.'

'I am not disagreeing with you.'

'Nora,' Alan said, 'I'm scared we're too late.'

'We won't know until we arrive.'

'The Pilgrims said it was terrible – virulent, and fast-acting.'

'I know. I know. How long has it been since Eyes stabbed him? You came straight to Dok, yes? With Byron, on his bike?'

'I walked a lot, then the bike. I remember nights flashing by. I— A week? Idle Hands is a parasite, not a virus; it will be in him but it won't have control yet. His brain will still be his own.'

'But it is a *magical* parasite,' Nora pointed out.

'Yes,' Alan sighed. 'Yes, it is. How . . . how fucking stupid.'

Alan knew his way around these corridors as well as he knew the worn carpet between his old room at the House of a Thousand Hollows and the Cavern Tavern. As he passed those round brass doors that rolled back into their wall housings once unlocked he found himself breaking into a run, all his aches and pains be damned. There were windows that let in the pink moonlight on their right. His heart rose in his chest; he could feel it beating. He could see it: the door; that one was his – *theirs*. By the Builders, he could barely breathe. He put his hand on the door. The metal was cool to the touch. He didn't have the key any more, of course; he would have to knock. He swallowed back a cough, or maybe it was a grunt or a sob, he wasn't sure. He loved this woman and she hated him. He could picture the look on her face when she answered the knock to find him standing there: fear, loathing, disgust, maybe. She wouldn't let him in, so they would have to fight again, and Billy would see. It would be just like old times: their lovely little boy watching as they knocked lumps out of each other. He raised his fist, and then let it drop.

'Useless man,' Nora said quietly, pushing him aside. 'Keep out of sight so as not to cause any problems or embarrass yourself. I will knock, and they will let me in. Give me five minutes and then you knock and *I* will let *you* in.'

Before Alan could object she had knocked, a short, hard knock. He stood with his back to the wall to the left of the door, out of sight of anybody answering. He heard the door being unlocked, and the smooth mechanism of its opening, the reassuring sound of its rolling back into the wall.

And then her voice. *Marion's* voice. 'Hello?'

Alan felt the tears roll freely. He and Marion had been assigned to each other according to the stars and skies of their births, as was the Pyramid way, but they, unlike many of their peers, had come to love each other, and they'd loved hard. He'd fucked it up, of course, as was the Alan way, but that wasn't a reflection of their relationship. He cried, and tried not to make a sound.

'Good evening. Marion, is it? Excuse me for the unexpected visit. But I need to come in.'

'I don't think so. No. I don't think I know you.'

'You're right in that you don't know me. I have been running tests on your blood and I have found something that we need to discuss. It is very important that we have this conversation in private.'

A moment's silence, then Nora stepped through the doorway and the great disc rolled back into place.

He'd fucked around in the Discard with many lovers, and Eyes had taken that to mean that his feelings for Marion were shallow or faded. Alan *had* raged against her in his darker moments, that was true, but he had never stopped loving her. He had sought to alleviate his sense of loss in the arms of others; he had looked to distract himself, to replicate those feelings of warmth and safety her embrace had granted him. He'd even embarked upon relationships with women and men in the hope that he'd find something as deep and as powerful as he'd had with Marion.

None of that meant that he didn't love her. It was something else Eyes had been wrong about.

He steeled himself to knock. Had Nora told Marion he was here? Before letting his thoughts deter him any longer, he rapped sharply on the brass.

Nothing happened. He waited, but there was still no movement. He knocked again, and this time there was a slight shift, then the slow roll-back, so agonisingly slow. He expected Nora on the other side, but it was Marion who stood there. He lowered his hood. She stared at him, her eyes rimmed red. Her flyaway blonde hair was bound back in a ponytail. Her white skin was almost translucent. Her mouth was slightly open and her teeth were gritted, her jaw set.

He blinked and shuffled under her penetrating gaze. He had a beard now, and was physically changed in further ways, none good, really. He was inadequate, filthy, stinking, wasted – and on the inside, too. And Marion was clean, and good, and selfless.

She was shaking slightly and he wanted to put his arms around her, but he knew better. After waiting in case she wanted to speak first, he said, 'Marion. May I come in?'

She stepped aside and Alan walked past her and into the rooms that had once been home, and he was struck by how warm and dry and secure it was, how calm and how pleasantly lit, how *safe*. But it hadn't been safe, had it? Not in the end. He heard the door roll closed behind him. Nora was sitting at the table. He looked around for Billy, but couldn't see him. Nora made eye contact and shook her head, very slightly, but Alan wasn't sure what that meant.

'She said you were here.' Marion's voice was low and clear. She was pointing at Nora. 'I didn't believe her.'

'I know—'

'I didn't think you'd be so foolish as to endanger us *again*.'

'You're already in danger. Billy is—'

'Stop.' Nora stood up. 'None of this. Alan, Marion is entirely justified in her anger. Accept that. Do not fight. Explain the purpose of your being here once you have resolved your personal issues. The success of the former depends on the success of the latter, I think.'

'Yes,' Alan said. He took a deep breath. 'Okay. You're right.'

'Of course she's right,' Marion said. 'Sit down. Billy's

not here, which is good for his sake. I don't want him getting any more confused.'

'Where is he?' Alan asked, sitting down. He tried to keep his voice casual.

'None of your business any more. Now.' Marion inhaled deeply. 'You're an exile and a fugitive. And I don't know the first thing about you, lady. My foot are you an Alchemist. You get caught in here, then *I* am complicit – I am your *accomplice*. That is the first and greatest reason for my anger. Surely you understand that, Alan?'

'I do.'

'So you will not be staying.'

'No.'

'And nobody knows you're here.'

'. . . nobody knows *we're* here. They know that the Pyramid has been infiltrated from outside.'

'Then you cannot stay here. You will conclude your business with me, whatever it is, and then immediately leave.'

'Marion, I . . . I'm sorry. I miss you. I love you. I wish I could undo the hurt I've caused you. I want you to know that.'

Marion fiddled with the belt on her robe and then sat down. 'Tell me why you're here.'

'Billy has been infected with a parasite. It's dangerous, but I have the antidote. We need to administer it as quickly as possible.'

'This is the wound in his foot.'

'Yes.'

'The wound McAlkie gave him.'

'That's right, yes.'

'Your *friend* McAlkie.'

'He betrayed me.'

'Isn't that par for the course out there in the Discard? Wake up together in the morning, betray each other in the afternoon, drink each other under the table at moonrise?' Her voice was rising. 'I bet you and he are still friends. You always did put him before us. You always put your family and your past before us. You—'

'I killed him.'

Marion stopped in mid-flow. Alan felt rather than saw Nora's eyes widen.

'He was wrong. And I've been wrong, in so many ways. I was wrong to trust him, to follow him and then to kill him – his death solved nothing. It was meaningless, but now I can think of little else.' He stopped. 'I'm sorry. I didn't come here to talk about Eyes. The important thing is that we get to Billy and make him better. Where is he?'

'He is with the Alchemists. He is in one of the wards. I was about to go and visit him there. They say they're making him better.'

'Do they know what's wrong with him?'

'Remember, Alan,' Nora said, 'Ippil told us Idle Hands came from the Sump, so in all probability, from the Pyramid. They may be more familiar with it here than the

Pilgrims were when it was loosed in the Discard. They may have their own resources.'

'They didn't say what was wrong with him, exactly,' Marion said, 'except that it was an illness caused by the wound.'

'Was he exhibiting any symptoms?'

'No, not beyond the pain of a wound and infection. The wound hasn't healed; it's grown hot and inflamed.'

'Then why is he getting special attention if there aren't any unusual symptoms?'

'Because he was wounded in the Discard, which means he's at higher risk of disease.'

Alan was about to spit, but he suddenly realised that he was indoors and held back, settling for cursing. 'Fucking Pyramid!' Then, 'Have they proposed a cure?'

'They said they'd bring his Bleeding forward instead of waiting till he's of age—'

'And you *let* them?'

'This is the *Pyramid*!' Marion shouted, standing up again. 'What fucking choice do I have? You think you're so fucking strong, standing up for what's right, sacrificing your privileged life for what you believe in – but tell me – tell me *honestly* – should I have refused them? Should I have let them Discard us? Would Billy be okay out there if he's as ill as you say? Is the Discard *good* to the sick? Is it good to the old, or the young? Do you see many babies out there, Alan? Do you see any elders? If we were exiled, how many years would we have left?'

'No, but—'

'You've had a child and he's grown up in here: so what kind of life is out there for Billy? Could he have a family? Could he have children? Would he even grow old enough to try? And what about *afterwards*? What kind of life is in store for you, or for us, once sight starts failing, once bones get brittle, confusion sets in?'

'The Mapmakers die a ceremonial death at fifty years,' Nora said.

'Wh— What?' Alan said.

'For much the same reasons as those outlined by Marion,' she continued. 'You cannot deny that the Discard offers freedom only to the strong. It is a dangerous place for the vulnerable.'

Alan held his hands up. 'I am *not* denying it, okay? I'm not! I'm sorry – but the thought of them Bleeding our little boy – a *child* – starting *now,* taking all his blood, turning him into a washed-out fucking *rag*, draining him of—'

'Might the Bleeding in fact help?' Nora asked.

Alan whipped round to face her. 'Whose side are you on?'

'Draining the blood and any spores it carries from his body could be a good thing. We should administer the Benedictions too, of course. That's what we call the antidote,' she explained to Marion. 'They're mushrooms. And please, there are no *sides*.' She bared her teeth. 'And if there *were* sides, Alan, maybe I would not be on yours.

The parasite needs to spread throughout his body and reach his brain before it can change his behaviour, so if the Alchemists are Bleeding him, they might be buying us some time.'

'How much blood?' Alan asked. 'How would they know which blood to take out? And from which part of his body? Or – or is it a certain amount from various different parts? This is ridiculous. I can't believe we're even talking about it.'

'All of it: they take all of it. And replace it.'

Marion's words were met by silence.

'Are you *mad*?' Alan said.

'She's right,' Nora said.

'But we have the antidote——! We don't need them to do that——!'

'I don't know the first thing about your *mushrooms*,' Marion pointed out, her voice brittle, 'so why should I trust them? And why should *you*? He's my son as much as yours. You're not happy with the thought of the Bleeding; you think I'm happy with the thought of you shoving a load of mysterious fungi down his throat? Besides which, I'm not just thinking of the cure. I'm trying to think like an Alchemist: I'm thinking of the conclusion they'll be coming to, if they haven't already.'

Nora held up her hand to stop Alan replying. 'What is true and certain is that if we do nothing, then he will die,' she said. 'He will become a vessel for the parasite attacking and killing, until he becomes a kind of fungal husk, retaining only a semblance – the barest semblance – of humanity and only the illusion of self-control. My suggestion is that you, Alan, allow the Pyramid to Bleed him, if that's what they're doing, or if that's what they propose. And if they have not already come to that conclusion, Marion, I think you should suggest it. And Marion, you should allow Alan and me to administer the Benedictions. One Pyramid method and one Discard.'

Alan was listening carefully to Nora and when she'd finished, he said, 'Yes, very well. Belt and braces.'

'Is what she said true?' Marion asked, faintly. 'About the parasite?'

'Yes. I'm sorry, Marion. And if Billy succumbs to it, then it will spread throughout the Pyramid, and it will spread quickly.'

'How many Alchemists are there?' Nora asked. 'Do they all know each other?'

'I presume not,' Marion answered, sounding as if her mind was elsewhere. 'There are hundreds of them.'

'So you could wear this robe and they would accept you as one of their own?'

'What—? No – I don't know—'

'How do you all identify each other?' Nora was getting frustrated with Marion's answers. 'Marion, we are trying to save your child. Tell me: how do you identify who is what rank, who has what authority?'

'*Don't*,' Marion said, her eyes narrowed. 'Don't yet speak to me as if you two have convinced me of your righteousness. Any problem here is *your* doing. I am still deciding whether or not I trust you. I will tell you exactly what I want to and no more. And to answer your question, *yes*: when you don't know a person, you go by the insignia on the robe. That's what it comes down to. That's what the insignia is for.'

'Neither Alan nor I can do it. He might be recognised, or somebody might see the tattoos on his hands, and as you can see, I have my own needlestick markings. So it must be you.'

'It must be me to do *what*, exactly?'

'To go to Billy, arrange the Bleeding and give him the mushrooms.'

'No!' Marion cried, 'I'll be discovered – they'll *exile* us!'

'It's potential exile or Billy's certain death,' Alan said gently. 'I'm so sorry it's come to this—'

The look in Marion's eyes as she looked at Alan then was so hateful it made him recoil. 'You're *sorry*,' she said, her voice low. 'Well Alan, I appreciate that.' She turned to Nora. 'I'll do it,' she said. 'Of course I will.'

'We will all go,' Nora said, 'but Alan and I will not engage the Alchemists. I will wear your robe and you will wear the one I am wearing. It is an Alchemist robe, yes?'

'It is,' Marion said, slowly, appraising Nora. 'Of some rank, too.'

'Alan will remain in the one he's got on now.'

'But why?' Marion said. 'Why don't I go alone?'

'Just in case it all goes wrong,' Alan said, after a moment. 'Just in case.' *And just in case you have a change of heart*, he thought.

'Then let us ready ourselves,' Nora said, 'and let's go.'

10

Alchemy

The door to the first of the dedicated Alchemy floors was guarded by two Arbitrators who were deep in conversation. As they stood aside to allow Marion, Alan and Nora through, Alan caught a few words – 'breach' and 'Discard scum' – which made their topic of conversation quite clear. A mid-ranking Alchemist flanked by two Administrators was not, Alan supposed, an unusual sight at this level – and it wasn't as if the Alchemy floors were forbidden to non-Alchemists anyway; Pyramidders were allowed to visit sick relatives, for example, provided they weren't absent from their Stations.

The Alchemy floor was immediately different. Alan had never been there before. Instead of a labyrinth of narrow corridors with many rooms branching off, it was a series of wide-open spaces full of desks and benches piled high with instruments and artefacts. As they hurried past, Alan glimpsed pendulums and bell jars, vials full of what looked like blood, candles burning beneath

glass bulbs, cabinets full of small stones, crystal identifi-
cation charts and much more.

'We're headed for the Recuperation Wards,' Marion
said quietly. 'It's about five minutes' walk.'

Alchemical Officiators were standing on elevated slabs,
reading from books mounted on – and chained to –
lecterns, much like the Senior Administrators had been.
One man with glinting eyeglasses and a long grey topknot
was close enough for them to hear his sonorous, cadenced
voice as he read, '—the blood, as determined by the birth.
The birth, as determined by the conception. The conception, as determined by the stars. The stars, as read
by the Astronomers. The Astronomers, as determined by
the blood. We are the Pyramid, and our blood is Pyramid
blood. We Alchemists are the conduit through which
the blood flows from the people to the Pyramid. We
serve the blood, and so we serve the Pyramid. Take the
blood and—'

'Creepy,' whispered Alan.

'There is so much learning here,' Nora said. There was
admiration in her voice, Alan thought. 'And it is all just
here for the taking.'

'No violence, Nora,' Alan said. 'Please, no violence,
and no theft.'

'That's not what I'm thinking about. I'm thinking
about you – well, not *you*, but you Pyramidders: you can
just come up here and . . . *look*. It is not kept secret.'

'No, you can't really come and look,' Marion

corrected. 'Once I was Stationed on this floor, in the next room, recording measurements, but they wouldn't tell me what I was measuring, or why – I'm not sure the Alchemist in charge even knew herself. It was just a task passed down, like all of the others. It's not just that you can't look, though; it's that you don't know what you're looking at. It's all fragmented, disjointed. And also – there are more Arbitrators here, see?'

She was right; there were Arbitrators posted at every corner of the room, and at every entrance and exit.

'During my Stationing I tried to ask a question of a Senior Alchemical Co-ordinator and an Arbitrator came and stood in between us – she didn't say a word, just blocked me. And the Co-ordinator carried on like she hadn't even seen me.'

'And also,' Alan added, 'I suspect that there's a lot of secret learning and experimenting; it just goes on above us, on those floors ordinary Pyramidders aren't allowed access to. The higher-up floors are off-limits.'

'As are certain rooms on this floor,' Marion agreed.

'What is their function?' Nora asked. 'What is the importance of the Alchemists in the Pyramid?'

'They take the blood,' Alan said, 'but nobody knows what they do with it.'

'They heal the sick,' Marion said. 'They provide food.'

'That doesn't account for the blood, though,' Alan said, 'so they're doing something else as well. Something secret, something sinister.'

'Who manufactures the artefacts piling up beneath the Pyramid? Is that the Alchemists?'

Marion looked at Nora curiously. 'What do you mean?'

'There is a sump beneath the Pyramid, full of . . . output.'

'What kind of output?'

'Objects of unknowable purpose – things that look like they are non-functional, or broken.'

'Waste?'

'No. *Product.*'

'The Sump is full of crates,' Alan tried to explain, 'or what used to be crates, but they look like they've been stacked up deliberately. Waste wouldn't be packaged up like that; it'd just be chucked out. It's as if the Pyramid is producing something intentionally, or at least, once intentionally, but now not.'

'One of those things being Idle Hands,' Nora added. 'Intentionally or not.'

'Why would the Pyramid want to create something so vile?'

'Maybe they were trying to purge the Discard,' Alan said.

'That's ridiculous,' Marion said, 'especially because, as I've said, the Pyramid doesn't produce anything. The Stationings aren't . . . nobody *makes* anything.'

'What are the Stationings for, then?'

'To develop our character. To make us strong and

wise. To manage our thoughts. To teach us discipline and morality. It's not about *producing* – who would we be making things for? The Discard?'

'But you said that nobody knows what other people are doing, so how do you know nobody makes anything?'

'Because there's no *reason* to make anything. I mean, there's no reason to make anything for the *outside*. We make *food*, we make robes, we make the things we need in our daily lives. But there's no output apart from waste.'

'Well, none that they ever tell you about,' Alan said. 'There are definitely processes – you know that – and there's definitely manufacture, even if nobody knows about it. It would be pretty weird if the two things weren't connected.'

They passed through another similar room and then into the Ward, which was filled with row upon row of large padded chairs like those Alan remembered in the Bleeding Chambers. There were large metal frameworks surrounding each chair, each bearing an array of tools and implements. Some of the chairs were curtained off, but many were empty. The walls were white marble veined with grey and blue, very similar to what they'd seen in their journey through the Discard. An Alchemist slipped from behind a desk and approached them. Before he got too close he evidently noticed the markings on Marion's robe and performed a quick double-take. He bowed ever so slightly. 'Greetings,' he said. 'We were not

expecting anybody from the Libraries today. I apologise.
I don't believe we have prepared a tour . . .'

'Please do not be alarmed,' Marion said. 'I have come
at short notice, to visit a particular patient.'

Alan wanted to kick himself. He hadn't realised that
the Alchemist's robe he'd stolen would be high-level
enough to attract attention; he'd wanted it to grant them
access, not get them noticed or require reception parties
or special tours.

'Of course, of course.' The Alchemist – an Assistant
Alchemical Something-or-other, judging by his robe –
nodded furiously. 'I apologise. It's just – with the breach,
with that Discard thug breaking in, we have to be careful.
Which patient? I have the records at the desk over here' –
he gestured – 'all the names, all the bay numbers. Do you
have a name?'

'We do. *I* do. Billy Marious.'

The Assistant flinched. 'Wild Alan's son.'

'That is correct.'

'Billy' wasn't a Pyramid name, which made Billy's lin-
eage clear to all. At the time of Billy's birth, being honest
about his heritage had been a matter of principle for both
of them; now it looked like foolishness of the highest
order. They had been so naïve.

The Assistant Alchemical Something-or-other led
them through the ward. The patients were all hidden in
the curtained-off chairs, and there were no worrying
sounds or foul smells as they passed through. Alan thought

back to the Sanctuary of the Giving Beast: it had been warm and comfortable, but the ailments and afflictions had been terrible and traumatic, and non-containable. He thought about the Sick Rooms in the House of a Thousand Hollows, where medical care basically consisted of Loon force-feeding you experimental medicines and herbal teas and changing the bedsheets every now and again. He'd seen sick people in the Discard Wilds – injured, mad, diseased – with no care, no company and no hope, and nothing to look forward to but more bodily breakdown, more pain and probably an opportunistic bandit attack or two.

'What's this about a breach?' Marion was asking.

'A . . . um . . . well, a Discarder fought his way in through the Sump, stole some robes, disguised himself and then took an Astronomer hostage. Have you not heard? He was demanding to see his mother, if you can believe such a thing. Apparently he'd been a Pyramidder once – he must have been out there for a long time to have forgotten that nobody over eighteen even *has* parents. Anyway, I heard the Arbitrators killed him, and good riddance – but there might be others; he might not have got in alone. It's a disgraceful failure on the part of Arbitration, don't you think? I wouldn't be surprised if there were a few new Discarders in the world before this day is out. Anyway . . . *uh* . . . here we are.'

Then they were standing before a red velvet curtain. The Assistant twitched back the curtain, rattling the brass rings, and revealed Billy lying there, strapped to the chair, eyes closed, wounded foot extended from beneath a sheet that covered him from neck to knee.

'The Supervising Alchemical Physic is making her rounds,' the Assistant said. 'She'll be with him very soon.'

'For the Bleeding, yes?' Marion enquired. Her tone was icy and the Assistant quailed visibly.

'The . . . um . . . Bleeding? I don't believe there's a Bleeding scheduled, good Librarian. I . . . um—'

'Really? I had been informed otherwise. It's the Bleeding that I came for. I've re-arranged my whole day's scheduling for this, and as such, a whole day's scheduling for each of my Subordinates, and one or two of my Superiors. Please do not tell me that I've been misinformed?' Marion was playing the role perfectly.

Sweat was dotting the poor boy's brow and he could barely get his words out. 'No, I . . . uh . . . well . . . I'm sure . . . um—'

'I will have to speak with the Supervisor, whenever she decides to show up,' Marion said.

'She'll be here any minute – any minute – and I'm sure . . . um . . . I'm sure there'll be a Bleeding arranged; I just . . . ah . . . I hadn't . . . I didn't know. Although I must have been informed . . . but I don't . . . um . . . I will gather the requisite . . . um . . . the materials. The bottles, and—'

'You do know why this Bleeding is of particular interest to me, yes? Why I've come all the way down here for this Bleeding? And why that has a bearing on the particular equipment you will need?'

'I – I'm afraid that—'

'We will be draining him entirely.'

The Assistant's face dropped yet further, which Alan hadn't thought possible. He was feeling rather sick himself.

'All of his blood will need bottling. And of course you will need blood to pump back in. So if you didn't know about the Bleeding, then I'm sure you won't have ordered the blood you need from the Library – you haven't, have you? No. So remember: you will need the full five litres. Use the mother's, if it's available.'

The Assistant spluttered, blinked and scurried away, sweat dripping onto the cool stone floor. As soon as he'd disappeared on his mission, Marion hastily drew the curtains around them all.

Alan stared at Billy as his son slept. His face was drawn, dark circles under his eyes, and even beneath the sheet it was clear that he'd lost weight. He looked much younger than his six years. The skin around the stab wound on his foot had started to blister and turn white.

'Why is he strapped down?' Alan asked. He reached out and took Billy's hand.

'They strap all patients down,' Marion said, 'don't you remember? They always have. They strapped me down when I gave birth to him, remember?'

'Yeah, of course – I thought it was wrong then too.'

Alan cleared his throat. 'You make a brilliant Superior, Marion.'

'Well, I do actually have some Subordinates now,' she admitted, 'so I've learned how to speak down.' Then she smiled a little. 'Your face! I'm joking, you idiot! I do have Subordinates, but I'm better to them than any Superiors have ever been to me.'

Before the conversation could continue, the curtains were swept open and the Assistant wheeled a trolley into the bay and began setting up. He fixed needles to one side of the framework around the chair and then tubes to the needles, and then big empty glass bottles to the tubes. Then he bolted something that looked like an accordion to the arm of the chair on the other side and attached even more needles and tubes to that. Everything was threaded through the framework and secured with clamps. 'The blood's on its way,' he said, and then left them alone again.

'Can we set this off?' Nora asked. 'Do you know how?'

Alan looked at Marion, but she bit her lip and shook her head. 'No,' she said. 'If it was just a normal Bleeding, then yes – I've been through it enough times. But this – the pumping blood back in? – no, I don't know how to do that.'

'They have the tools here,' Nora said, 'so they must be able to do it themselves. It's just a question of authorisation.'

Before anyone could respond a young woman appeared

at the gap in the curtain. Her brown hair was cut in a sharp bob, her nose was sharp and her voice was sharp too. 'Excuse me,' she said. 'I'm the Supervising Alchemical Physic currently Stationed here. The Assistant tells me that you're expecting a Bleeding – there *is* a Bleeding, *not* a transfusion, scheduled for tomorrow. I think there must have been—'

'I think there must have been a misunderstanding,' Marion cut the woman off smoothly. 'That poor Assistant seems to be at the middle of quite a few. I have been sent down here to authorise and arrange an immediate Bleeding for this patient.'

'A full transfusion, though? As a Librarian you will know fine well that stocks are limited – I don't see why we should waste them on the son of a known degenerate.'

Alan sensed that Marion was slightly wrong-footed by that and he clenched his hands, wishing he could help but with no idea what to say that might fix it.

The Physic waited for a response, and once she'd decided that there was no response forthcoming, she opened her mouth to speak.

That was when Marion replied. Her voice was cool and calm, as she said, 'Is it not *obvious* to you? The Library wants all of this patient's blood removed from the Pyramid bloodlines: that is the reason. It is not for his *health*; it is so that this boy will be fit to reproduce in accordance with the Pyramid Wish when he is old enough.'

The Physic glanced impassively at Billy, and then

suddenly she smirked and leaned in towards Marion. 'It's not generally their *blood* that men use to conceive a child.'

'Tell me this,' Marion said, stepping right into the Physic's personal space. 'Do you have a *full* understanding of the Alchemist's Blood Magic? Do you have a *full* understanding of the methodology used by the Astronomers to assign partners to each other? Because if you wish to disobey my orders based on your own half-witted assumptions as to their purpose, then you go ahead . . .'

'But you said—'

'I said that they want his blood removed from the Pyramid bloodlines. And that is *precisely* what I meant. As an Alchemist, you *do* know, I sincerely hope, that blood has *magical* qualities? It is those very qualities that are of importance here. We are not talking about the boy's ejaculate – I apologise for being crude, but as it appears that your mind is stuck fast in the gutter, I feel that I need to be explicit. Now, if you value your role, your rank – in fact, your whole damn *life* – here in the Pyramid, I suggest you stop arguing with me and do as I say.'

The Physic said nothing, but her scowl spoke volumes, and it was clear to all three of them that she was deciding whether or not to respond. The moment stretched out. *Will she have to do any double-checking?* Alan wondered. *Will she fabricate some pretext—?*

Instead, she turned to the apparatus and noisily checked what the Assistant had done. 'So we're just waiting for the blood,' she said.

'That is correct.'

'Let me see what I ca—'

'Supervisor! Supervisor!' The panicked voice of the Assistant cut the Physic off in mid-word.

'What now?' the Physic muttered as the young man stumbled into the bay.

'The Arbitrators said – they've sent word – *cascaded!* – it's the breach . . .' He was having real difficulty in getting his words out again. 'They found signs of entry . . . at the lowest levels,' he managed at last. 'There were *footprints*! Senior Advisor Wylun has advised that the likelihood is that – that – *Wild Alan* came up out of the Sump! But they don't know where he is – they think he might be coming for his son!'

'This was the rabid, red-skinned Discard animal that once tainted our halls, yes?' the Physic said. 'So easily identifiable, I should imagine.'

'We had better take precautions,' Marion said. 'Keep this patient unconscious – let's get him out of here and into a more secure location at once. Then proceed with the Bleeding immediately – once Wild Alan finds out what we are doing he'll want to stop it; I have no doubt of that. I understand that his rabid opposition to the Bleedings was one of the motivations for his violence.'

What violence? Alan nearly asked the question out loud.

'You two' – Marion turned to Nora and Alan – 'go directly upstairs to discuss the change of plan. I'll send them the details in a message via the Assistant's desk tube and ensure your clearance. I am making an Executive Decision; make it clear that I am not looking for their authorisation in moving the patient.'

'Very well,' Nora said, nodding, and looked at Alan. 'Clarious, do you have that message cylinder for our Superior?'

'I do . . . not.' Alan tried to change his voice, to smooth out the rough corners, soften up the vowels.

'I believe I gave it to you earlier.' Alan was lost, but Nora continued smoothly, 'It was from the Alchemical Administrative Wing, Cross-Disciplinary – they were trying out their new inks. This message was written in green – quite striking, I thought. I understand it was particularly difficult to acquire and stabilise.'

'*Green* . . .? Oh! Yes, of course.' Alan bowed to Marion. 'My apologies, Superior. Please – here is the message cylinder outlining the proposed changes to the . . . Cataloguing System.' He slipped Marion the packet of Green's Benedictions and after checking that the Physic was still preoccupied with the accordion-like Bleeding machine, he whispered, so quietly that he wasn't even sure Marion heard, 'They're ready. He just needs to chew and swallow them.' He had wanted to discuss this more fully with Marion, to prepare her for any potential side-effects – he didn't know what they might be himself, but at least they would have been able to talk about it all. Too late now; Nora was leading him out through the red velvet curtains. He'd wanted Billy to be awake; he'd wanted to see him, to say hello. He'd wanted Billy to *see him*. They were hurrying now, though not as quickly as he would have liked. They were still surrounded by low-ranking Alchemists so they couldn't give in to the urge to run.

Every room they passed through was abuzz with the news, and more and more Arbitrators were pouring in through the door Alan and Nora were headed for. But nobody stopped them, or even looked at them. Nobody had yet mentioned the beaten Pyramidders they'd left tied up in the stillroom, or the Commander who'd lost his head in Laundry. Perhaps the Arbitrators didn't know yet – or perhaps they did, but they didn't want the intruders to know that they knew that. If they did, they'd doubtless be looking for people wearing stolen robes, not wanting to prompt their quarry into getting changed – good job they already had, Alan thought.

By the time Alan and Nora escaped to the stairwell the sudden influx of people had died down. They hurried down the steps and as soon as they were clear of the last of the Arbitrators, Alan turned to Nora and said bitterly, 'They're all rushing to protect *my* son from *me*.' There was a great pain in his chest at the thought.

'Their primary objective is to capture you, I imagine,' Nora said pragmatically. 'Now, where do we need to go?'

'Back to our quarters – oh, no, wait; we can't go there, can we? They'll go to Marion's first. Shit. Fuck. *Fuck, fuck, fuck*. Not this again. And what about Billy?'

'He's in Marion's hands – he'll be safe with her. She is clearly a very capable woman.'

Alan came to a sudden halt. 'We have to get her out,' he said. 'We have to get them both out, or the Arbitrators will kill them. Once they've worked it all out, they'll get rid of them both.'

'There is, of course, the other matter to attend to,' Nora said.

'What "other matter"? What's that?'

'My own reason for being here.'

'You can't be thinking about staying here any longer than necessary—?'

'When you say "necessary", you mean, "after what you need to do", yes?'

'Well—'

'I have my own "necessary", Alan,' she said firmly.

'Okay, okay.'

'Billy is as safe as he ever was; if they wanted to kill him, they would have done so already. Marion . . . yes, we have to protect her. Though – she was not Stationed, was she?'

'No, she was off-shift.' Alan pushed the next door they came to open and the pair of them slipped into a nondescript corridor.

'And they won't be able to find her until her new Station begins, because she is disguised.'

'It's not like putting somebody else's robe on is foolproof, though.'

'Isn't it? Are other people's robes generally easy to come by?'

'Well, we came by them pretty easily.'

'But for Pyramidders, I mean.'

Alan considered her words. 'Maybe not,' he conceded after a moment. 'They're all terribly scared of being Discarded, so they wouldn't dare do what we did, even if they wanted to. And I can't think that many *would* want to, because they're all conditioned from birth to behave.' He thought about Byron. 'Stepping out of line first requires a great sense of alienation – the feeling that you don't belong and never will be able to belong. And even then it takes great courage.'

'So the robes are a code: it's what Pyramidders use to identify each other. Outside of social circles – are there even any social circles here?' She didn't wait for Alan to answer but went on, 'People don't go by names or faces, do they? I think Marion will be safe, for now at least.'

'Until they know what we've done.'

'Well,' Nora said, 'yes.' She moved into a passageway on her left as a couple of Arbitrators appeared up ahead.

'What if we just Discard her?'

'Marion?'

'Yes.'

'I'm not sure she'd like that.'

'But she would live.'

'You would be taking her away from everything she's ever known – taking her from safety, she might think.'

'She's in more danger here.'

'But will she see it that way quickly enough? And, also' – Nora sighed – 'the danger she *is* in here . . . well, once she does recognise it, which she will, well . . .' She paused and then said quietly, 'She could be forgiven for blaming that on you.'

'I know,' Alan said. 'I know: I've brought this all down on her. I have forced her into this decision. I know this is all my fault.'

'Will it be her decision?'

'*Is* it a decision?'

Nora considered his question. 'Death or exile – an easy choice for us, perhaps, but for a Pyramidder . . .'

'But Billy – she won't leave our son.' He knew that for certain.

'We could take Billy.'

'It feels like a very long time ago, Nora, but you did counsel me against that.'

'It was long enough ago for our circumstances to have changed dramatically,' she pointed out.

They came to one of the great plazas and sat on a stone bench set into a bush that was itself shaped into a hexagonal pyramid: one of several topiary pieces in this plaza, each trimmed and carved into a different shape. Looking around, catching their breath, they could see, as well as the pyramid, a sphere, a cube on its corner and other more elaborately cut bushes.

'So,' Alan said, 'once Billy's undergone the transfusion

and had the Benedictions, we bundle him and Marion out.'

Nora looked at him. 'It has to be Marion's choice.'

'Okay, okay – but she will choose wisely, I know that. And then – and then—'

'And then we remain inside and we find the information I need in order to return to my people.'

'I made a deal with you, Nora, and I will honour it, but let me just say: fucking *hell*, that's a bad idea!'

'I wouldn't be here if you hadn't agreed to help me. And so neither would you.'

'I know, I know, *I know*.'

'So. First: we need to remain close by and wait for Marion.'

'Just wait?'

'Yes.'

'That can't be right – a moment ago everything was so urgent.'

'Think it through, Alan. Think of your *purpose*. Think of Billy and of Marion.'

Alan did, and finally he sighed. 'Yes, okay.' He looked around. 'I know this place,' he said suddenly, and he laughed a little. 'This is where they knocked seven shades of shit out of me the first time.'

'Can we stay here until the Arbitrators have arranged themselves? Will it trouble you?'

'No,' Alan said. 'No. It's as good a place as any to wait.'

Side Effects

By the time Alan and Nora got to their feet and made their way back up to Billy's ward the Arbitrator presence had been visibly heightened. Again and again Alan felt their gaze crawling over the details and insignia on their robes, but nobody troubled them. When they entered the ward, the Assistant glanced up from his desk momentarily, then realised who he'd seen and jumped up out of his seat. 'Administrators,' he said, 'greetings! Please – the Librarian – uh, your Superior – is this way. Please, follow me. The procedure is underway.'

As Alan and Nora followed the Assistant, an Arbitrator came forward from her position at the door to stand over the desk. She stared impassively at them and Alan had to resist the urge to tug at his collar and sleeves. Sweat was trickling down his back. Nora kept her head down and looked completely impassive, but Alan couldn't stop thinking, *What has been cascaded to whom? What is she looking at – or* for? *Any minute now, Arbitrators will start demanding hoods be lowered, sleeves be rolled up . . .*

But the Assistant led them quietly to the back of the room and down a narrow corridor, then round a corner, round another corner, past many, many doors, some closed, some open, and up a short ramp. All was clean and white and cool; the glow-globes imbued the marble walls with its own eerie light. They passed through a room housing a great irregular pale pink crystal set into a metal base that almost filled the space. Alan thought at first that it was making a squeaky breathing sound, but then he realised that it was actually coming from the room next door, and when they squeezed past the rock they found Billy lying in a tiny chamber and the noise was coming from the apparatus that was piercing him, draining him and pumping fresh blood into him. There was a trolley full of glass jars next to the bed. Alan stared at them. The blood inside was fresh and vibrant – he'd never seen blood look like this before. Whenever he'd come across blood it was always splattered, mixed up with other bodily fluids, bits of hair or bone or flesh, coagulating, or already dried up. Some of the jars were nearly empty; in others, the level was rising. The room was small so it should have been fully lit, but there was a darkness here that didn't make sense, especially as when he looked up at the glow-globe, it was bright. Robed figures stood against the back wall. At first Alan thought they were Pilgrims, preparing a body for death, but then he realised that of course they were Marion and the Physic. The accordion thing wheezed and squeaked, blood coursed through glass tubes and brass tubes and catgut and Billy's chest rose and fell with each shallow breath.

'Is it nearly done?' Alan asked.

'Yes,' said the Physic. She looked up at him appraisingly. 'You sound different.'

'I'm . . . out of breath.' Alan spoke in his new voice again and the Physic stared at him.

'Get the Assistant,' Marion said.

Alan looked at her. 'What?' he started, but Nora was already moving. She grabbed the Assistant's arms behind his back and as Alan watched in horror, Marion covered the Physic's mouth with one hand and then stabbed her in the back.

'No!' he said, 'by the Builders, Marion—'

The Physic managed a muffled scream and jerked around, but Marion was holding her tightly as tears flooded down her cheeks. She fixed Alan with a baleful stare. 'It's them or us, isn't it?' she asked. 'It is, isn't it? Thanks to you.'

She was right of course, Alan realised.

'She'd realised – you spoke in your Discard accent,' Marion went on grimly. 'It was over – if I hadn't killed her, she would have told the Arbitrators about us and they would have killed us all.'

'We might now have time to wait until the transfusion

is finished,' Nora said. 'Then, Marion, I think you must take him outside, or you will die. I think they will want to kill even him too, after all of this.' She dropped the Assistant's lifeless body next to the Physic's. 'Of course, the decision is yours.'

'I had already come to the same conclusion,' Marion said heavily. Then she asked, 'But why just us? Will you not be coming with us?'

'We have further business inside the Pyramid,' Nora said.

'We've arranged for somebody to pick you up,' Alan said. He held Billy's hand. 'You will have to take the mushrooms with you, and give them to him once he regains.consciousness. Will you do this?'

'I will,' Marion spoke through gritted teeth, 'because I said I would. But it will be the last thing I do for you, Alan.'

'Of course,' Alan said. 'I understand. When we get out – well, *if* we get out – I will find you and I will introduce you to—'

'You stop right there. Even if you do get out, I *never* want to see you again. And I don't want Billy to ever see you again. You bring nothing but chaos and blood and – and' – she held up her shaking, bloodied hands – '*death*. It's you who has endangered Billy's life and you've made a monster of me and I want nothing more to do with you.'

'No.' Alan swallowed. 'No. I wouldn't expect you to feel any differently.'

'Very fucking magnanimous.'

Nora was watching the jars on the trolley. 'It's nearly done. I propose we—'

The door rattled as somebody tried to open it. A voice was raised on the other side of it, but nobody inside the room could make out what the person was saying. The door was made of beaten brass, like most of the Pyramid doors, but this wasn't one of the circular roll-backs; it was a hinged affair. 'How did they know where we were?' Alan demanded.

'Just by fucking talking to each other,' Marion hissed. 'The ward's been under observation. I knew they'd work it out; I just hoped to buy us a little more time, that's all.'

There was a resounding impact from the other side and the metal buckled towards them. More shouting was followed by another great crash. The third strike broke the lock and took the door off its hinges. Alan caught a glimpse of an Arbitrator holding a heavy-looking dark grey cylinder backing away before two of his companions stepped through the gap and blocked his view. But the two companions were not companions at all; they were Commanders. All the Commanders Alan had so far encountered had worn silver plumage on their helmets, but these feathers were of gold, and they wore no masks. One of them had lines of glimmering stones running down his face from the outside corners of his eyes, and beads implanted into his eyebrows and cheekbones.

Alan stared. He knew that face. Everything but that face diminished into nothing.

The face smiled at him. 'Do you remember me?' it said, quietly, green eyes flashing, voice as clear as fresh rainwater. 'I remember you.' The Commander carried the same knife he'd carried on that night of flame and blood and noise. It was not a remarkable weapon, but it was the first that Alan had ever had pointed at him, and he found that he recognised every single detail: the leather binding, the slight curve of the blade, the nicks in it. For a moment he was seven years old again and he could smell smoke. His parents lay dead on the ground in front of him. The Commander raised the knife. He had not aged at all. His thin face was almost split right open by a wide smile. He pressed the tip of the knife against Alan's throat. 'Should I kill you?' the Commander said. 'I had been thinking perhaps I should have killed the wild man when he was just a child, but actually, after everything, you are just as easy to kill now as when you were a little boy.'

Alan closed his eyes. Nobody could help him. Nora was behind him – and besides, any movement from anybody and the Commander would just sink the knife in his flesh. He almost wanted it. *Almost*.

'You can do what you want with me,' he said, 'but let the others go. Let Billy go – he is an innocent in all this. Let my friends go.'

'Or . . . what?' The Commander laughed. 'You will put up a fight?'

'I'm appealing to your honour.'

'You are *all* guilty,' the Commander said. 'How

typical of "Wild Alan" to think that we have come for him and him alone. You grew up with a fine sense of your own exception, did you not? Wild Alan: the lone Discarder. You see yourself as special because you were unique, but you were only ever unique in the same way that the first bad apple is unique.'

'They can't hurt you if they're Discarded.'

'You have proven otherwise, I think.' The Commander cocked his head. 'According to our law, I could put you all to death right now. Personally, I think I should. I let you go once and I now regret it. These fellow Pyramidders have paid for my poor decision with their lives.' He indicated the dead Assistant and Physic. 'Not to mention the Arbitrators down in the Machine Rooms and the Commander dead in Laundry.' He locked eyes with Alan and smiled again. 'You were an ordinary child when last we met. Since then you have acquired quite the reputation. But in truth, you are an unimpressive man and I believe you should die for your crimes. However, I cannot kill you. In a moment, I am going to remove my knife from your filthy Discard throat. If you even briefly consider that as an opportunity to try to fight, then your blood will flow after all. There are many Arbitrators behind me, and should I fall, then they have their orders. Do you understand?'

Alan nodded.

'And you: aiders and abetters of this Discard scum. Do *you* all understand?'

Alan couldn't see, but Nora and Marion must have nodded as well.

'I have been instructed to take you up-Pyramid,' the Commander said. 'You and the other intruder.'

'We will come with you quietly,' Alan said, 'if you let Marion and Billy go into exile. We will go up-Pyramid past a Discard chute and I see them Discarded — otherwise I will fight you, and you will kill me, and you will have failed in your duty to deliver me to your Superior.'

'Yes,' said the Commander. 'I had anticipated such a negotiation. I do not find it unacceptable. We will go to a Discard chute, and we will go now.'

Marion sat behind Billy, who was wrapped like a corpse, and as the two of them slid down together she held him tightly. Alan hoped against hope that the bikers were already approaching this side of the Pyramid; Billy was in no condition to survive the Discard unaided – and that wasn't taking into account any side-effects from the Benedictions which Marion *would* give him as soon as he came round. She *would* give them to him . . .

Marion didn't say a word; she didn't even look back as she went. Alan had been tempted to try and break free of his captors and jump down after them, but he doubted that he'd have made it – and besides, they'd come out into the Discard for him, and probably kill everyone else just to make the point. After all, they'd done it before.

He settled for silent tears.

They'd probably kill him anyway, of course, once he'd served his purpose, whatever that was.

The Commander stripped both Alan and Nora of their robes, then he slashed Alan's back with the knife, the blade cutting deeply, re-opening the wounds Bittewood had given him. He kicked Alan in the backs of the legs, forcing him to the floor, and then kicked him in the side before hauling him back up again by the hair. Pyramidders in the corridors gawked at him, gasping at both the blood and at his red skin, his beard and his tattoos. Nora didn't fare much better; every now and again the second Commander – who had similar ridged eyebrows and cheekbones to Alan's old acquaintance, but not the skin-crystals – would cuff her across the back of the head, and hard, and before long Alan noted blood seeping through her pale blonde hair. On the third occasion, she went down onto her knees, wincing.

'Who are you taking us to?' Alan managed to ask, between blows. 'Will they want us hurt and bleeding?'

The Commander pursed his lips. 'He will not be concerned for your condition. But the good people of the Pyramid need to see that your sins are not going unpunished.'

And sure enough, the Pyramidders crowded together in the next plaza they passed through, cheered to see the beating. Alan wondered what they'd been told about him.

The stairwells went on interminably, followed by

more anonymous corridors, another busy plaza and another stairwell. Alan's legs burned, sweat ran down his face, blood ran down his back; he was sure he was leaving a trail behind him. He lifted one foot, then the other, a conscious effort, as the steps in front of him telescoped out into an endless staircase.

The Commander pressed the knife against his back once again.

12

Supplier and Demander

Alan didn't take much in during the ascent, other than to be vaguely aware that whenever they crossed a floor, the doors stayed shut. There were fewer Pyramidders scurrying around up here, and more windows. He was dimly conscious of background noise fading away, but it felt like the silence was growing heavier and more oppressive, smothering all sound. The Arbitrators trooping along behind them did not speak. He had expected more: Observatories, Management figures wearing incredibly elaborate robes, general ostentatious luxury; there must be more to these upper levels, places they weren't being shown. Nora limped along beside him. Her hair was matted with blood now. She might have been involved in murder, but at least she had not yet been identified as a Mapmaker.

They stopped at a golden-framed door set in the centre of one side of a short corridor with windows at either end. The walls were white marble with glinting veins of silver; the door was a sizeable, sharp-edged block of rock, the same marble as the walls, inlaid with gold. The Arbitrators came to a halt and Alan came back to himself. He stared at the door. He thought at first he could see a pattern to the designs that spidered their way across the portal, but on closer examination he could find no repetitions. The inlay played with his eyes and he felt faintly nauseated – although that might have been the infection that he was sure he'd contracted from the Swamp, after Bittewood had wounded him.

'We're here,' said the Commander.

A lower-ranked Arbitrator stepped forward, holding something wrapped in rich blue cloth, as others moved Alan and Nora away. She knelt before the door and unwrapped the object, all the while talking quietly, her words co-ordinating with her movements. Each slow peeling-back of the fabric was matched by a susurrating wave of whispers from the whole first rank of the Arbitrator column.

Alan had heard of the Ritualists, but he'd never seen one. It hadn't occurred to him that they might also be Arbitrators, or any of the other established Pyramid divisions. He'd always expected they would somehow look different; that if he did ever meet any, they'd be wearing bright robes and headdresses, or jewellery. The Teachers had described them as 'integral to the Pyramid workings', but he'd dismissed that as the usual Teachery load of hot air. As an adult, he'd occasionally wondered if

'Ritualist' was a generic term that covered almost all Pyramidders – after all, his Stations had felt just like empty ritual – but since he'd been discarded, he'd not given them another thought.

The Ritualist, if that was who she was, continued the unwinding and chanting and as the cloth wrapped around her right fist, the object in her left hand was gradually revealed as a polished sceptre made of dark-coloured wood. Its head was still covered, but the whispering was growing louder, making the marble corridor vibrate, though her voice was low; the ugly, angular words she spoke were unrecognisable. Then the last of the blue cloth was whipped away – and instantaneously, the chanting stopped.

The silence was disorientating.

The head of the sceptre was a great uneven lump of molten-looking metal, many colours swirling together – brass, gold, silver, the rainbow sheens of bad water, running in solid rivulets down the wooden handle. The Ritualist held it over her head, keeping it in position as she slowly stood. Her eyes shone unhealthily through her mask. She placed the metal head of the sceptre against the centre of a spiralling section of the gold inlay.

'By Appointment,' she said, and lifted the sceptre, then planted it firmly back into place. The impact wasn't loud, but Alan detected a faint reverberation, as if a great bell had rung far away. 'By Appointment,' the Ritualist said again, and she repeated the knock. She did it again, a third and final time.

Alan wanted to laugh; of course there was no 'appointment'. They'd just been caught and marched up here.

With a quiet click the stone door opened and swung inwards noiselessly.

The two Commanders dragged Alan and Nora into the room, leaving the Arbitrator column in the corridor. The room was darker than Alan had expected, but he could still see the floor was black and white, the tiles large, glossy and reflective, with points of light shining deep within them. White columns heavily decorated with gold filigree rose up to the slanted ceiling, which was made of panels of tinted glass and some kind of black metal. The tiled floor stretching away from them reminded Alan of the bulbous mansion house Byron had taken him, where Bittewood had caught up with them, except this was clean and unbroken.

Tall robed figures, hoods up, arms buried in deep sleeves, stood in the alcoves spaced regularly around the room. Alan thought at first they must be guards, but he wasn't sure; they could equally well have been statues, they were so completely motionless.

There was only one sound now: the murmur of a distant voice coming from the far end of the room a long way away. Alan couldn't make out what it was saying, but he'd know soon enough, for the Commanders were dragging them towards that distant voice.

Through the glass, Alan could see Satis and Corval.

Their colours were different through the tints, but even so, their presence above him was a comfort. It felt like it had been a long time – too long – since he had been outside. And how long had it been since they'd last slept? That might be the reason for his increasing sense of mental dislocation. It was late; the sun had already set, but the Discard was lit by the moons and it looked glorious to him, so varied and so colourful. In fact, he could see to a remarkable level of detail – it was almost as if the view had been magnified. Then with a start he noticed that was exactly the case: the windows were made of multiple layers of glass which had turned them into a great magnifying unit that focused on different areas as he moved through the room.

He dragged his attention away from the Discard. They were approaching the huge desk which crouched at the far end of the room. It was made of some dark wood similar to the sceptre. The window behind the desk was so layered it almost rippled. The soft, calm voice was definitely coming from behind the desk, but Alan still couldn't see the speaker, who spoke constantly; though the voice wavered sometimes, it did not stop but went on without pause and without end. The desk was a beast with its own presence. Its legs ended in vast clawed feet and two candles burned steadily on top of it, like two eyes looking out. There was an array of telescopes at the window beside the desk.

As they got closer, Alan began to make out the odd word or phrase, though they meant little.

'—disc management . . . Administration . . . beast dem-
onstrations . . . performance reviews . . . half-shipment
. . . Striated Plains . . . half-shipment . . . full-shipment
. . . full-shipment . . . shipment, shipment . . . fourteen
full shipments . . . quality assurance . . . catastrophic
quality failures . . . seventh sub-storey . . . full Station
disconnect . . .'

He could hear another sound now as well: a kind of
clicking, scratching sound.

Ten paces before the desk, the Commanders brought
them to a halt.

'Chief Architect,' said the highest-ranking Commander, 'I beg your pardon for the interruption, but here
I have Wild Alan, as requested.'

The voice stopped, but the clicking continued, only to
be overwhelmed by a terrible screech as a heavy chair was
scraped back.

The Pyramid's Chief Architect rose up from his seat
behind the great desk and became visible.

He moved slowly. He was tall and emaciated. His robe
was pure black – Alan had never seen anything so black –
and beneath it he wore a spotless white shirt and black
trousers not dissimilar to Alan's own, except cleaner and
with no holes. His sunken eyes looked painfully blood-
shot. Like the Commander, his skin was patterned with
crystals. His mouth was downturned. His fingers were
long, and his fingernails too: long, and sharp and clean.

He had an air of precision, scrupulousness, cleanliness, but his face radiated despair.

And from the top of his bald head rose two long, curved horns.

'I do not have long,' he said in that soft, sad voice. 'As you can hear' – he put a hand to his ear – 'the words just keep coming.'

The clicking, scratching sound was quiet, but it carried.

The Chief Architect waved lazily and the Commander took his knife from Alan's throat. Alan's mind came back to life, returning to the battered, bloody and broken cage of his body. He felt a moment's certainty that the Commander would die by his hand.

'Fuck you,' Alan said, quietly. The Commander's fist crashed into the back of his head and he fell forwards. He brought himself back to his knees. 'Fuck you!' he said again, louder. And again, the punch, the white water of pain exploding through his mind. He found himself sprawling on the tiles and rolled over to see the Chief Architect looking at him.

'Fuck you and all your people,' Alan said. A foot – the Commander's foot – rose as if to stamp on his face, but a wave from the Chief Architect stopped it. 'Your people are killing us. They come out into the Discard and do it with blades and fire, or they stay in here and do it with their . . . their fucking *Stations*.'

'My people are just trying to do the right thing,' murmured the Chief Architect. 'They're just trying to do the right thing, they're just trying to do the right thing for the Pyramid. Without the Pyramid' – he smiled a slow, lipless smile – 'they're no better than *you*.'

'The Pyramid won't fucking collapse if they all stop.'

'They don't know that. Anyway' – the Chief Architect gestured to the Commander, and spoke to Alan as the Commander hauled him back to his feet – 'you have something I need.'

'Benedictions,' Alan mumbled through a bloody mouth. His front teeth were loose. Must've been from hitting the floor.

The man laughed. 'I don't need *that*,' he said. 'If there's one thing I don't need, it's that. No, I'm talking about the fungus developed in the Discard as an antidote to this . . .' He paused and gently touched one of his horns, then went on, 'this parasitic disease. You're the one who was supplying them, yes?'

'They were for you?' Alan looked around. 'Is Tromo here? Troemius? Where is he?'

'He failed me. Your last encounter went badly wrong, as I understand it, so no, he is not here. Now, you brought the fungus in to cure your son, so please, give it to me. Give it to me and you can go.'

'How do you still function?'

'Personal fortitude.' The Chief Architect sounded bored. 'Now, have you got the fungus? Give it to me.'

'I don't have it on me.'

'Where is it? Is it with your wife? Your son? Have you already given it to him?'

'No, but—'

'If you have not given it to him, give it to me, or tell me where it is.' The man's eyes darted around. 'We can recover it. Tell me, or you will die.'

'Chief Architect,' said the Commander from behind Alan, his voice halting, 'we Discarded the wife and child on our way here. It's possible that the mushrooms were on their persons . . . I apologise sincerely. I did not understand the nature of your interest in this man.'

'We can recover them from the Discard,' the Chief Architect said. 'Tell us where they are and live, or do not, and die.'

Alan closed his eyes. Marion probably hadn't given the Benedictions to Billy yet. He wasn't even sure she would. But Billy *needed* them, so his choice was simple: Billy's life, or his own. And as long as Marion was with Billy, his son would be okay. He would be safer with her and without his father than he would be if Alan tried to find his son and wife again.

An unexpected peace came over him. He'd done it, almost. Billy was out, and there was hope for his life. Marion was out. And the Chief Architect was ill, maybe even dying. If Alan denied him what he needed, then the Pyramid might be in trouble.

All it would take to ensure this new status quo was his

own death. All things considered, that was a price worth paying . . .

. . . although there was Bloody Nora to think about. Not that he was *protecting* her; it was more the other way around. But if by any chance she did live through this, it would be beneficial for her to have more information than they currently had.

So he would play for time, and for knowledge.

'I will tell you where we hid the mushrooms,' he said, 'if you will tell me more about the affliction that you share with my son.'

The Chief Architect closed his eyes. 'Are they *close*?'

'Yes, they're close.'

'Chief Architect, I would not trust this man,' the Commander said. 'He is murdering Discard scum.'

'The very same murdering Discard scum who's been keeping me alive these past few months,' said the Chief Architect. 'I will indulge him.' He turned back to Alan. 'Three questions.'

Alan considered. 'How do you still function, in truth?' he asked.

'There are different strains of the disease, some more aggressive, some less so. Some are designed for instant destructive effect and some for more subtle, less traceable long-term placement. I contracted a strain of the latter: the organism spreads primarily through the channels and pathways of the mind, not the body, and it does not reduce its host to a bloody-minded husk.' The Chief

Architect smiled. His teeth were sharp. 'The bloody-mindedness comes, of course, amongst other things, but the body remains . . . *functional*, as you put it. The magic corrupts you on another level.'

Alan had decided on his three questions, but now that first answer had raised many more. He would have to think this through carefully.

'What effects do Green's Benedictions have?' he asked after a moment, adding quickly, 'The fungus, I mean.'

'Ah, I see – you were not offering me *benediction*, not in the true sense of the word.' The Chief Architect laughed then, and Alan shrank from the awful, grim sound. 'Green's Benedictions? How sweet. Of course, we have records somewhere of the creature that gave birth to the legend of Old Green and the idea of such a thing being worshipped as a god is hysterical – well, both hysterical, and hysterically funny. Had the Discard not already been lost and falling away from us, I should have liked to spend some time there, studying you people.' He shook his head, and then returned to Alan's question. 'The effects of the fungus, though?' He clenched his fist. 'Addiction, the like of which you cannot begin to imagine. A terrible burning thirst that only the fungus can sate. The second quality has to do with the origins of the mushroom: the fungus grows from a great old book, and the book is made damp using juices from one of your Discard vermin – a toad that you believe gives visions of the future, if prepared properly.'

'The Omentoad.'

'I should have known you'd have some ridiculous name for it. There's more to creating the . . . Benedictions than that, of course, but that's the detail that pertains to this particular conversation. This intoxicant, harvested from the toad, filtered through the paper and ink and grown through the structure of the fungus – it causes *visions* of places that you have never seen or even dreamed of. You . . .' He faltered, then gathered himself. 'You see these places, *wonderful* places, fantastical places, and you think that they might be real: great rolling plains of grass, snow-capped peaks joined by vast bridges, so high as to be set against the stars. There are oceans of clean water, shallow enough for nomadic tribes to wade across – they seem *real*.

'And the fungus has been conjured into being, yes, by trained and faithful practitioners, so who knows what powers it grants, really? Why wouldn't you be looking through windows into far places, or even other worlds? But then you remember that for the very same reasons, these places might not be real at all.' He sighed.

After a moment, he went on, 'What else? Hellish nightmares: that is another of the effects, and glimpses of the future, too, as you'd expect given that the toad itself has gained its reputation as a precognitive aid. But I wonder if you know, you out there, that it is not the *toad* that grants the visions but a parasite that only that toad can host? Vermin, parasites and fungus: it's a sick world.' He stopped again, before saying, 'And there is the key effect, of course: the mushrooms burn the Idle Hands parasite out of its runnels, for a time at least. They keep it at bay.'

'They *only* keep it at bay?'

'Well, it depends on how far gone the host is when they are administered.' The Chief Architect put his hands behind his back. 'And so. That was your third question.'

'No, I—'

'That was your third question.'

There had been so many more Alan wanted to ask: *Is there a permanent cure for certain strains? How had the Chief Architect caught it? Who created it, and who were the targets? And when? How did the Chief Architect know everything that he knew?*

'Now you will tell me: where are these mushrooms?'

Alan looked at Nora. He knew that this was probably it for both of them; for her to reveal herself as a Map-maker by fighting with her customary prowess would be catastrophic; it would mean war. And there was no way he could defeat all of those Arbitrators on his own. He probably couldn't even defeat one.

Nora returned his gaze evenly. 'I'm sorry,' he said.

Nora looked down.

'We fed them to my son. They are gone, and you can kill me.'

Even though he had resigned himself to death – quite nobly, in his opinion – the look of fury the Chief Architect brought to bear upon him in that moment almost stopped his heart in his chest. The Chief Architect raised his hand and stepped forward as if to rake his long, sharp nails through Alan's feeble flesh, and almost before he had decided what he would do Alan had crouched, then leaped up and rolled to the side. He felt the Commander's sword come down from behind him, catching the sleeve of his shirt as he dodged away. He forced himself up, ignoring his protesting legs, and ran around to the other side of the desk.

As soon as he had moved, Nora had bounded the other way and now they met behind the great desk, which was piled high with rolls of paper and pens with worn or snapped nibs. Many sheaves of loose paper were held down by a large cloudy crystal. A small metal claw held a working pen, which was scratching out tiny words on a roll that was being extruded from a slot in the wooden surface. There was so much more to look at, but no time for Alan to take it all in.

The Commanders were approaching them, one from each side, swords out and ready.

'Get behind me, Nora,' Alan whispered. 'Don't fight them – don't let them know what you are.'

'We will die if I do not fight,' she started, but he was shaking his head. 'No – look: there's a trapdoor. I'll hold them off while you get it open. Then you go.'

'We could both go.'

'Maybe – if there's time.' *If I don't die holding them off.* 'But just – try to open it, okay? The rest will happen as it may.'

Nora fell to the floor and started running her fingers around the edges of the trapdoor Alan had noticed: a tile lipped in gold. There was no obvious handle – maybe it wasn't even a trapdoor.

The Chief Architect remained in front of the desk, his hollow eyes not leaving Alan, his mouth fixed in a furious scowl. The Commanders were moving slowly, poised, prepared. The Superior was grinning as Nora scrabbled ineffectually at the tiles. Alan quickly switched his knife to the other hand, grabbed the paperweight and lobbed the lump of crystal hard at the Chief Architect. The crystal connected solidly with a baleful eye, and the Chief Architect yowled like an injured cat as he fell backwards. The Deputy Commander turned and tried to catch him; Alan darted forwards and sank the knife deep into the Deputy's suddenly exposed armpit. The Deputy screamed and spun back to face his attacker. His sword sliced through the air, but he faltered and sank to one knee, blood pouring down his side. Alan was able to dance backwards, out of his reach.

He stared at the Deputy Commander: this was his chance; he could kill the man, right now. He was down, he was prone, he was incapable with pain. Alan felt the handle of the knife slip in his sweaty palm and tightened his grip. He took a deep breath—

—the door through which they'd entered swung open and the troop of Arbitrators from the corridor stormed through and across the chequered floor. Alan watched his death bearing down on him and it struck him how curiously silent everyone suddenly was. Thanks to their ingrained discipline, there was no shouting at all. Their sandals had soft leather soles which made not a sound on the tiled floor; all he could hear was the Chief Architect panting, the Deputy Commander scrabbling as he tried to stand, the tapping of Nora's pale green fingernails seeking purchase against the trapdoor's edge and the pen scratching away interminably at the roll of paper on the desk.

Alan regretted throwing the crystal at the Chief Architect; he could have used it to break the glass behind them — but he didn't dare try to turn and smash his way out now or he'd get a blade in the back. He shouted over at the Commander, 'Can't take us on your own, then?'

The Commander grinned: a mad grin, his face pale and shining. 'I could,' he said, 'but I don't have to. I have nothing to prove, dog.'

'Alan,' Nora said, 'I cannot open the trapdoor. It is locked.'

'Nora, I'm sorry.'

'Do not be sorry. I have my own reasons for being here.'

'Had, perhaps.'

'No. I have decided. Alan, you have been a friend to me.' Nora smiled at him. 'It will be okay. I am going to fight.'

'But—'

'If I adhered to my training and my instincts and my concern for the consequences, then yes, I would go, and I would let you die. But I don't want to – I don't want you to die. So I will stay here with you and betray myself, and fight.'

'But—'

'It is not your choice.'

Then the wave broke and the Arbitrators were spilling round the sides of the desk. Nora took up position in front of Alan and made claws of her hands. As the first few attacked, she jumped and pirouetted—

—and started ripping into flesh. Whenever an Arbitrator tried to land a retaliatory blow, she dematerialised and appeared somewhere else. Alan heard her laughing as the blood sprayed out. The cry '*A Mapmaker!*' echoed around the chamber as Nora went bounding from shoulder to shoulder, peeling off faces and throwing these vile masks at her oncoming foes, just as Alan had first seen her doing in the Cavern Tavern. The skinned Arbitrators fell backwards, twitching and screaming, as the attackers started recoiling in terror, tripping over each other to get away from her: a demon from the depths of their worst nightmares. Alan defended himself against the foolhardy few who had not retreated from the Mapmaker's onslaught, but they were scared and distracted.

The Arbitrators had been so confident – they had a huge advantage in numbers, they were all fit and well armed and had trained intensively – but few of them had any real experience in true combat; they mostly policed minor crimes in the Pyramid. Maybe a few of them had been involved in Discard raids or tax expeditions, and no doubt some of them had encountered one or two of the Discard's tougher denizens – but it was clear none of them had ever encountered a Mapmaker before. After all, *the Mapmakers did not get involved*.

Alan watched as Bloody Nora got very involved indeed. Not for the first time, he wondered if he was wise in the company he kept. Her tactics were brutal and monstrous, calculated to debilitate her enemies with fear and horror. Alan did not think she was sadistic; in all the time they had spent together she had never hurt anybody outside of combat; he had never seen her cause pain for her own enjoyment. But the violence obviously didn't repulse her as it did him, as it did most people – indeed, he had the feeling she almost *relished* it, when it came.

The familiar humming sound that accompanied Nora's fighting filled the room as viscera laced the air. The Arbitrators were retreating – the Chief Architect had already gone, Alan realised, and so had the Commander. He swayed for an instant, feeling horribly weak, but they'd done it. He'd achieved what he'd set out to do: Billy had the Benedictions and he and Marion were out of the Pyramid. Nothing would prevent Nora finding what she wanted, not now. There would be consequences, but he couldn't work them out yet. He couldn't see beyond smashing the glass and escaping down the side of the Pyramid. His body was on the verge of collapse.

Then he felt sudden agony as something entered into his back. The pain deepened and he screamed and screamed as it spread. Everything went white, then black. The pain burned a path through his core until he felt something scraping against the bones of his spine. He felt it slide out again, whatever it was, but the pain only intensified.

Some dim part of his mind warned him to brace himself against a second stabbing, but his thoughts and actions would not connect. He slid down until he was lying on the ground, and he managed to turn his head – and found himself looking up at a familiar face: Tromo was standing over him, his sword red, wet. Alan turned his head to the other side: the trapdoor had been opened. He watched his own blood slithering down the length of Tromo's sword and dripping from the end of it. He felt it pitter-pattering onto his forehead.

And then Nora was there, snarling like a dog as she grabbed Tromo's face with her bare hands. Everything was happening so very slowly, and though Alan was sure there must be a lot of noise, he couldn't hear a thing.

PART THREE

HOUSE

Skeffington Lutwidge surveyed the Goatherds roaring across the Courtyards below him. He stood between two gigantic stone birds, statues that had lost their detail but none of their hunched, glowering menace. The sky was red, the light was red, the metal of the bikes shone red. The stone of the vast labyrinth Skeffington's bikers navigated looked black in the night.

Round up, round up. Gather in the milk and the meat. Gather in the hair and the blood. He'd slit the bellies, spilled the guts, read the signs. He'd sucked the marrow from their bones and worn their horns on his head and he knew their animal minds. The goats spoke to Skeffington: they spoke through their blood of the winds and whims of Gleam. They told him of the coming violence.

The Courtyards were form with no purpose. Vast squares of stone, paved in geometric patterns, bounded by rows of titanic broken pillars. Skeffington inhaled: grass, goat, oil, hot stone, and the night so hot and so red. There had been very many hot, red nights. He'd found the Carcase long ago and the Carcase had carried him throughout the deep places, high places and distant places of Gleam. Skeffington had spent nights in Forge Country, in the Far Reaches, in the Forests of Liss, the Wide Castle, the Winding Wall, and everywhere the heat crept in and the red crept in.

The Carcase! Skeffington turned away from the vantage point and the carven raptors to approach his trike. The Carcase had screamed through the Discard, splitting the air in two with the roar of its engine. It had torn its way beneath desolate chimneys and smoke-blackened ruins, trailing fire beneath starry skies. The Carcase had a glamour that had wound its way into Skeffington's heart and soul and it spoke of speed and space, of energy and freedom, of combustion and magic.

He'd cut the goats, and also the Omentoads, which had bled their fluids into Skeffington's cup as he'd crisped their skin and broken their skulls and dined upon their potent flesh, and he'd dreamed fever-dreams of shining seas, fields of rippling grass and tall trees heavy with blossom. He'd also seen fire, murder, and disease: crumbling brick and twisting metal, the screaming living and the broken dead.

He'd seen the violence that was coming. And he'd seen the Mapmaker dancing through it. The beasts and the blood and the visions and the signs had shown him her power and her reach. The Mapmaker would show him *the way – but she was not one to press into service; not one to make an enemy of. He would have to play the game.*

Skeffington climbed into the trike's cradle and lowered his goggles. He fired the engine, said the words and hit the pedal. The Carcase leaped, and roared away.

13

An Old Haunt

Alan's perception of time changed. No longer was it a river carrying him along but instead he was moving through a great dark space, although he didn't know where he was going or what surrounded him. The only illumination was the occasional shard of pain that flared suddenly, like a flame catching dry leaves, although it told him nothing; its light blinded him and left him cowering.

But both mind and body kept stumbling on. He was conscious of time parting for him, though his awareness could not grab hold of anything else. He didn't understand why nobody was trying to hurt him; he was expecting another blade in his back at any moment. He looked out for green eyes as his ears strained for the wail of a crying baby, the sound of his son's voice. At every moment he expected arrows to come whistling from the void to pierce his weak flesh.

At some point he wondered if he was living through

an extended hallucinatory experience brought on by fungus he didn't remember eating.

After a long passage through this darkness, Alan saw a different light; for the first time this was not the white heat of pain but something else. He headed towards it as it flickered in the distance, until, when he grew closer, it resolved itself into a small square, like a window – no, it *was* a window . . . It was a window looking out, lit by the rising moons. The window was familiar to him.

The moonlight allowed him to examine his surroundings. The room was small, with a high wooden bed, a soft mattress, a basin, a chest of drawers and that window. He knew the room, he was sure of it, but he couldn't quite place it. He looked out at that glorious sky. He'd thought he was walking towards the window but instead he was lying in the bed. He wanted to throw the window open and commune with the moons that were illuminating the room with their pink light. He pulled the covers back and sat up, and his back *screamed* at him – yet more pain, but it would fade, it always did. He was used to living with pain by now. He wore a loose white nightshirt and nothing else. But when he tried to swing his legs over the side of the bed and stand up, they didn't move. He peered at them: they were definitely there, attached to his body. He stared at them, willing them to move, but they didn't. They *wouldn't*. He commanded them, speaking out loud as if he were telling another person to do something: 'Move. *Move* . . .' But his legs steadfastly refused to obey.

He wondered if he'd forgotten how to control his body. Had his brain been damaged? He cast his mind back to the last thing he could remember: the fight in the Pyramid, Tromo stabbing him with his sword, Nora killing Tromo. He remembered getting that wound, the feel of the blade sliding into his back, scraping his spine: it had been like nothing he'd felt before. He recalled the sensation of slicing and grinding, razor-sharp metal through flesh, metal on bone. He reached around to where the blade had entered. The skin felt ridged, whorled, scabby, and his touch awoke a whole new kind of pain. He looked at his legs again. Again, he willed them to move. *There!* His left leg twitched.

He slid himself out of the bed, tried to stand and hit the floor gasping. He hauled himself across the rough wooden floorboards, ignoring the splinters that punctured his flesh. His arms were still strong, but agony tore along his spine. He saw his boots had been placed against the white-plastered wall, next to the chair under the glassless window. He reached the chair and tried to haul himself up onto it, but the pain flared again, his sweaty palms slipped and he fell to his elbows. His vision faded to black.

He could hear voices, familiar ones, and he opened his eyes to see two figures standing over him, but he couldn't make out their faces. He realised, slowly, that they were carrying him back to the bed. But he didn't feel present, not really; it was as if he were lying in a pool, looking up at people above the water.

'He's to *stay in the bed*,' a woman was saying. 'Is he an idiot? No, don't answer that.'

'It means he woke up, though. And that is good, yes?' That was Nora.

'It's positive, yeah.'

'What's his condition?'

'The blade damaged his spine. It went in low – the lumbar region – and chipped the bone, nicked the cord.' This was Loon speaking, Alan realised; Loon was the House medic. Loon was the one who'd invented the ointment Eyes used to keep his eyes free from infection. 'There's a cord that runs from the brain—'

'The spinal cord. Yes. We Mapmakers are taught anatomy from a very young age. My father had me able to name and number all of the vertebrae by the time I was nine. I was able to remove the spinal cord from a fresh corpse by the age of twelve. I—'

'Okay! That's quite enough. So you know that if it's damaged the consequences can be severe.'

'Of course.' They fell into silence as they pulled the sheets back over Alan, who was struggling not to slip back into unconsciousness. He wanted to speak, but couldn't. 'What I am asking,' Nora pressed, 'is, what are the consequences in this particular case?'

'I opened him up two days ago. I have seen worse; the cord is not severed. There was some slight displacement of the vertebrae, and swelling and bruising of the cord, thanks to the impact of the blade upon the bone. I have stabilised the vertebrae, but we don't know how much control of his legs he will regain. Maybe all, maybe none. Swelling and bruising can itself be very dangerous. But I have tested his involuntary reflexes, and I would not be surprised if his left leg at least comes back to him. And of course it's not just his legs; he's lost bowel and bladder control, too. But with rest and care, the swelling and bruising should diminish.' Alan felt a cool, dry hand on his forehead. 'We'll just have to wait and see what comes back.'

Pain came in waves, chasing consciousness away. He knew where he was now, but he still had no handle on the passage of time. The words he'd heard went around in his head like a song: *Maybe all, maybe none . . . We'll just have to see what comes back.* If he couldn't walk, then he would die in the Discard. It was no place for the crippled, or the old, or the very young. He'd rage against the bed, punching it as hard as he could, trying to rip the sheets and tear the blankets. He'd jerk awake, clutching for Snapper, only to remember that he'd abandoned Snapper to the Pyramid. He was aware of Loon cleaning him, changing him, feeding him water and soup; he'd realise she was there and that he was crying, and try to dry his eyes, try to hide his upset. She was a tall woman with short white hair and a severe face that could have been considered grim, had it not been for her lively eyes. She was part mechanic, part healer and part witch, and she was as good at medicinal brewing as she was with nuts and bolts.

As Alan's consciousness steadied, her visits grew longer and she started encouraging him to try to move. 'Been moving them from the hips? Lying flat, try to open out your hips. Coming back? Yes? No? This one? Good. Bend the knee? No? Nothing? Okay, the other one. Nothing? Try again. *Try again*. There was a twitch there – yes, there was. Yes *there was*. I'm not bloody fighting with you. I saw it, and that's that. Toes now. *Toes*. Come on, Alan.'

She brought him two heavy metal globes, each with a rough, stippled surface. 'For lifting. Get your arms good and strong again.'

Alan took them, and grimaced. 'Heavy,' he said. And, '*Ouch*. What are they covered in? Got any smooth ones?'

'No!' Loon said, pointedly, 'I coated them in that sharp sand and varnish just for you. And they're meant to be heavy, damn it. Well – they're meant to *feel* heavy. Your arms are weak now. You build your strength up with these, get those hands good and callused, and you'll take to the crutches like a toad to muck.'

'I'm a guitarist. I've got calluses already.'

'Let's see? Oh, yes. Your fingertips? You go ahead and hold the crutches with just your fingertips, see how you get on.'

'Okay, okay,' Alan grumbled. He examined his hands himself. They *were* relatively soft; that's what living in the Pyramid and then in the House of a Thousand Hollows did, he supposed.

Alan thanked Loon for her help, and for washing him

and changing him while he'd been out of it. He had no bedsores and had not been lying in his own filth. His fingernails and toenails had been kept clean and short. Sometimes he asked her to stay and chat, but she couldn't, and she wouldn't answer his questions. *How did I get here? Where are Marion and Billy? Who picked them up? Where's Nora? Did anybody find Byron?* And he wondered what arrangements had been made with Maggie the Red to grant him convalescence in the House; she'd been explicit in her exile of him after the Cavern Tavern massacre and she wasn't one to go back on her word.

'You're not my only ward, Alan,' Loon said on one such occasion. 'I can't stay and while away the hours chatting like a drunk. You'll be ready for guests soon. Them's the ones who'll know the answers to your questions. But I want to make sure you're okay in your head before we throw that door open.' She pursed her lips. 'I would've expected more anger, to be honest. A little more rage, a little more fire. I've seen some tears from you but to be frank, I haven't seen enough.'

'I'm okay, though. I'm going to walk again.'

'You don't know that.'

Alan maintained his facial expression. He managed a shrug. 'I'm going to try.'

'You *should* try. But trying might not be enough. That's the hard part, Alan. It's out of your control. You've got to try, and trying will hurt, but at the end of it you might be exactly where you are now.'

'You've got a weird way of helping.'

'There's more than one way to help. There's more than one kind of help you need.'

'So, what? You're trying to upset me? Break through my . . . my *carapace* of denial? Fix my head like you're fixing my body?' Alan tried to keep the anger from his voice.

'I'm *not* fixing your body. That's the point. I want to, I *hope* to, but despite everything I do, despite everything *you* do, your body might go unfixed. And as long as you don't see that, you're primed for a fall.'

'Really? I haven't already fallen?' He was shaking now. 'Tell me Loon, have you ever been hurt like this?'

'No.'

'Then *fuck off*!' Alan yelled.

Loon opened her mouth as if to reply, but then closed it again and nodded. She pointed to a lever on the wall by his bed, and then another by the chair and window. There was one on each wall. 'These bells are connected to my quarters. Ring one if you need any help. Y'know. Or cleaning up.'

And then she left.

When Alan was on his own he punched his thighs, hoping to break through the numbness, and cried and cried. His hands reached for a guitar that wasn't there. Spiders drifted through the air outside to land on the windowsill. He watched them crawl down the wall and across the floor, watched them crawl into a pile of clean clothes that somebody must have left there optimistically. He noted the lack of a belt. Sometimes he caught himself talking to nobody. 'No, not beer! Whisky! And make it a bottle!' Or, 'Bring me my boots. Help me out of this damned bed and I'll be on my way.' Or, 'Cut them off. Cut them off. Just fucking cut the fucking—' Or, 'The Discard's not kind to cripples.' He'd catch himself listing names: 'Marion. Billy. Byron. Eyes . . .' Sometimes he realised he'd been talking but could not remember what he'd been saying.

But on her next visit, Loon was pleased at the progress he'd made with his left leg. 'Good, good. Yes. Very good. Hip *and* knee? See, Alan?'

'What are you talking about? It's a tremor. It's a fucking tremble. It's not control. It's not . . . it's not *walking*, is it?'

'You want to have a go at walking?'

'I can't walk.'

'No, I know. But let's start working on the strength in that left leg there. I'll help. I'll get you over to the chair.'

'Loon, I wanted to ask: what did you do to my back?'

'I put a little rod in it. Just a little rod.'

'You did what?' Alan laughed, and then grimaced at the pain.

'Just screwed it in there, to connect a couple of your spine bones, so they can't slip again. So you've got a little bit of metal in there now. Shouldn't notice it—'

'Good.'

'—unless there are any problems. I'm looking out for fever, any signs of infection. Nothing yet though. Come on now. I'll hold your legs. Use your arms to swivel yourself about. That's it. Now put your right arm around my shoulder. Good job you're as tall as me, makes it easier. Okay now. This is going to hurt.'

'You said you *screwed it in*?' Alan said, trying to distract himself from the pain of moving.

'Yeah, but don't worry. That's not all. I go belt and braces. Mechanics are fine but I back it all up with incantations and a couple of . . . *substances,* of my own devising. Now. Ready?'

'I think so.'

'Let's stand.'

Alan tensed himself. The pain was searing, but he found that the muscles in his left leg responded, and together with Loon's support he was able to put a little weight on it. His right leg hung uselessly between them. That was what it felt like: as if it was a separate thing.

'Can you bend the knee?' Loon asked. 'As if you're going to take a step?'

Alan tried. 'No,' he said. Just the effort of taking his weight – his *partial* weight – suddenly felt unbearable. Pain blossomed and sweat sprang from his brow. 'Quick,' he said.

'Just try to drag your foot a little. Kind of swing it. That's it. Good. Good.'

Once he'd got into the chair, he didn't want to get out of it. 'Loon,' he said, 'thank you. But if I could be on my own for a bit . . .'

Loon had obliged, but pointed at the bell. 'You ring me if you need any help, right? To move from the chair, or to the chair. Sitting will hurt after too long. And don't you bloody dare try to stand up on your own, you hear me? Not yet. Soon yes, but not yet.'

Alan tried to take stock. He was back in the House of a Thousand Hollows. He sat still in the chair, watching Corval slowly descend. He tried to imagine not being able to walk any more. What if he really couldn't use his legs again? He was clenching at his thigh. His mind kept skidding away from the reality. *I'll walk. I will, I'll walk.* The Discard was as much a vertical landscape as horizontal. He'd be limited, very limited – perhaps somebody could permanently affix him to one of Skeffington's machines. He smiled grimly to himself. He was still ducking the question; even in his own head, even when the questioner was himself, he was doing his damnedest to duck the question. And besides, where was Skeffington now? *Where was Byron?* He circled round to those earlier questions. *Where were Billy and Marion?*

On her next visit, Loon brought him some crutches and helped him to practise with them. 'Just to the chair and back. Don't rush. And you need to start exercising your arms again. I'm going to show you. Now. From lying down. Like this.' And when she left, she took the crutches away again.

Alan sat in the chair by the window and looked out over Gleam. Loon's exercises were helping: and he could make it to the chair now, and Loon had entrusted the crutches to him again. Spiders were drifting through the air, trailing their silken threads. There was a flat rooftop down and across from the window, in the middle of which was a bucket-fire surrounded by transients swigging from bottles and toasting snails on the radiating coals. A silver-barked tree grew from out of one of the other windows overlooking the rooftop. Beyond the immediate view, more and more rooftops spread out, clusters of buildings built atop huge round towers joined by bridges, and further away there were white domes, rushing channel rivers and bizarre architectural follies that looked as if they'd been designed by builders lost deep in the chasms of a toadthrone trance. Alan hadn't sampled the Toadthrone fungus for a while; now he looked at the view, at the transients, and ached to just be able to get up and join them.

He looked down at his legs and concentrated. He flexed his left leg and felt the muscles move. He could do it. He raised his heel from the floor, lifted his knee into the air. His left leg could even take a little weight now; it really was coming back, he felt. He flexed his right. *Nothing*. He tried again, and again, and again. Nothing, and nothing, and nothing. He tried some more. His eyelids grew heavy and he let his eyes close.

'Alan.'

Alan shook himself awake. His head was lolling on his chest. He'd dozed off in the Gleam heat, his hands wrapped around his right leg. Spiders scuttled away as he moved his hands; he brushed a load of them off, but more were landing all the time; they were all over his arms, sparks of green and yellow and red shining from their black bodies.

'Alan,' the voice said again, and Maggie the Red sat on the bed, one hand on his back. 'Hello again, Alan,' she said. She passed him a chipped old cup full of water.

Alan took a sip. 'Hello, Maggie.'

'Oh, Alan. What have you done?' Her voice was calm, not quite affectionate.

Alan blinked and cleared his eyes and then started; he hadn't realised that Birdface was there too, standing in the shadows by the closed door. 'Hello to you too,' he said. 'Why have you let me back in, Maggie?' He gritted his teeth. 'Wait – you might need to help me get back into the bed. It hurts so much. So much.'

Maggie beckoned Birdface. Alan made an effort not to recoil. Maggie's bodyguard reeked – it was probably the cloak, a black mass of dusty, matted feathers. And the mask was creepy: a great black beak protruding from a wrinkled, pale leather face. Mesh covered the eye holes so no eyes were visible. Alan would have felt better if he could see the eyes. Alan wasn't even sure it *was* a mask: the leather had been surgically attached, and there had always been rumours that the beak was real and the leather plate was designed to make it just *look* like the whole thing was a mask.

Birdface grabbed Alan under one arm and Maggie took

the other. Birdface's hands, hidden within long leather gloves, felt like iron.

Maggie answered his question once he was lying back down. 'You're here because of your Mapmaker friend: she offered me her protection, as long as we took you in. These are uncertain times, and it would have been foolish for me to decline her.' She bit her lip. 'Increasingly, it appears that anybody not protecting me is protecting some other body. The Discard is anticipating strife, Alan: all the signs point to fracture.' She stroked his hair. 'You need to know you are convalescing here, no more. You *will* have to leave. Nobody from the House but Birdface, Loon and I know that you're here, and it must stay that way. Many still blame you – understandably – for the deaths of their families, lovers, friends. People have not recovered from that night the Arbitrators came to the Cavern Tavern, so you cannot stay. And Green forbid Daunt should learn you're here. Bloody Nora is watching the House for as long as you're here, and when you go, then she will leave too.'

'So you know there's a price on my head, Maggie. I can't fight Daunt. I . . . I can't walk. I mean I will, I *will*, but—'

'Not yet. Loon does hope that with the crutches, you will walk again. I know, I know. It is but hope. But also, we've taken your measurements and Loon is building something for you – a wheeled contraption. Of course you'll be limited: no stairs.' She cocked her head. 'Don't try to fight Daunt, Alan. It's time to stop fighting. Now you need to hide. There's no end to Gleam. Go – head out to the reaches, far from the Pyramid, far from here, far from Daunt, far from the central regions.'

She was watching Alan's face somewhat dispassionately, almost as if she was studying him, and not for the first time, Alan wondered at the emotional distance she was able to maintain. Maggie the Red was the Lady of the House of a Thousand Hollows; she put the House before any one person, before any of her own relationships. She never got too close to any person in case she had to exile them, or worse.

'You have friends still,' she said. 'The bikers, I believe. And Nora, and . . . Churr, is it?'

'Churr! Did she——?' His words deserted him and his eyes filled up.

'Yes,' Maggie said, 'Marion and Billy are here.'

'Oh thank fuck,' Alan said, suddenly dissolving into sobs. 'Thank fuck – thank Green – thank the fucking Builders – no, thank *you*, Maggie, thank you.' Then he paused. Suddenly scared, he whispered, 'So you *have* taken them in, yes?'

'Yes, that at least I can do for you. Marion will be a boon. And Billy is just a child. There are far too few children out here – the Discard is not kind to children, and I will always take them in. I hope that you know me well enough to be certain of *that*.'

'Yes, of course – well . . . I had hoped.'

Maggie looked around. 'Where's your guitar?'

299

Alan had to think. 'Back in the Pyramid, right down at the very bottom, in the Machine Rooms . . . I miss it, but . . .' He trailed off, and then, with a catch in his throat, he asked, 'Will Marion see me? Will she let me see Billy?'

'Your boy is still recovering. He'll be okay in here. The illness has ravaged him, and so has the treatment, but once he is up and about – and Loon is confident he will be – he will come and see you, I'm sure.' She hesitated and then said, 'As for Marion – well, I don't know . . .'

'Tell her where I am, if you would.'

'I will. And also, now that you're a little more with it, maybe Nora can drop in? She's been keen to see you. And no doubt you've some questions for her.' She paused. 'You *are* doing your exercises?'

'Yes. Loon comes in and moves my legs around. Yes.'

'What about your arms? Your hands?'

Suddenly Alan snapped. '*Yes*, Maggie, I'm doing all of my fucking exercises, all right? I'll be out of your hair in no time. Though I'm sure when you've had enough of me, I'll be gone, whether I'm ready or not. Not far, though. If Marion and Billy are here, then I'm not going far.'

Maggie raised an eyebrow. 'I've given you my advice, Alan. You would do well to heed it. But the decision is yours to make. You can of course ignore me and carry on doing things your way, if you think that's working out for you.' She stood up and brushed down her skirts. 'I think it's time I took my leave.' She gazed quizzically at

Alan for a moment longer, and then swept from the room. Birdface followed, the cloak rustling.

Nora came in through the window, squeezing through like a cat. She had a satchel slung over one shoulder and carried a parcel of waxed paper tied up with string. She brushed off the spiders, put the parcel down on the chair and carefully withdrew a bottle of Dog Moon from the satchel, followed by two glasses.

'Good to see you again, Wild Alan,' she said, uncork-ing the bottle. 'You have been gone from yourself for a long time.' She sloshed the whisky into the glasses and passed one over. 'To your health.'

'My health?' Alan said, bitterly. 'Give me that.'

They both downed their drinks. Alan passed his glass back and Nora refilled it.

'And to yours,' Alan said. 'To your health, too.'

Nora smiled wryly, held up her glass, and they drank.

'What does that mean, anyway?' Alan spat. 'Does it mean that the more I drink, the healthier I'll get?'

'I'm sorry about your legs, Alan. I'm sorry I was not there in time to stop him.'

'Troemius?' Alan paused, the glass halfway to his lips. 'You saved my life, Nora.'

'And not for the first time.'

'No. Thank you.'

'In my time I have met many people who have hurt themselves in such a way – being unable to walk, or to move an arm, or being frozen in some other way. Some of them do not cope; they do not wish to live in this way. Will you be such a one?'

'No,' Alan said quickly. Then he amended his answer. 'Well, I don't think so. Maybe I will never walk again – but if I die, if I end my life, then . . . then I'll never do *anything* again.'

'Wise words. You will go down in history as the Discard's Great Sage.'

'You're mocking me.'

Nora began unwrapping the parcel, revealing bread, butter, goat's cheese, ham and pickles.

'Getting a taste for Safe House food, I see,' Alan observed.

'Take what you can get while you can get it.' Nora tore open the bread, slathered it in butter and piled the ham on. 'Aren't you going to ask me how I am?'

'How are you?'

'I am well, thank you. My wounds are healing. No bones broken, no bleeding on the inside.'

'Nora, did anybody pick Byron up? Maggie was here, and I meant to ask her, but . . . the conversation didn't go that way.'

'The Goatherds found him, yes. He's okay. He's riding with them again.'

'Oh, thank Green,' Alan said, shakily. 'Thank Green.'

'Don't expect a visit, though. He can't get in to see you. Maggie's keeping a tight grip on all things Alan-related.'

'As long as he's okay.' Alan laughed; he felt better than he had in days. Or was it weeks? 'What happened, Nora?'

'Well, I will tell you, but you must eat.' She waited until he had filled his mouth, then started, 'From the beginning, then. Troemius came up from out of that trapdoor – he must have been waiting there, I think – maybe waiting for the screaming to stop? And you know what he did when he finally did come up: he stabbed you in the back with his sword! Those who had survived were escaping from the Chief Architect's chamber by then – I had gone after them, but was turning back from the cloud of spores when he got you – I turned back just in time to see him do it. I'm sorry that I was not by your side, Alan, but that is the way it went.'

She looked him firmly in the eye and continued, 'So I came back and I tried to kill him. I jumped onto his shoulders and got my fingers in his mouth, my thumbs in his eyes, and I was pulling, I was pushing. But he ran and he jumped down into the trapdoor hole, with me on his back. I could not let him take me, so I kicked away and spun back to the Architect's office. I saw him fall, but I do not know where he went. Maybe he discarded himself. I had his flesh beneath my fingernails though, Alan, so do not worry; he did not go unscathed.'

Alan shook his head slightly. 'You don't have to reassure me. I'm not after vengeance for its own sake. I don't care whether he's dead or alive or hurt or not, as long as he's no threat. Do you think he'll be dangerous?'

'Outside of the Pyramid? I don't know. Does the malice in these people come from the Pyramid, or does the malice in the Pyramid come from the people?'

Alan thought back to the time they'd spent within those cold black walls, and further back, to his dislocated childhood. 'They're not all bad,' he said. '*We* weren't bad. I don't think we were. Troemius . . .'

'You had been his contact; you had been providing him with Green's Benedictions – but they were not for him, they were for the Chief Architect, to slow the progress of the Idle Hands that had infected him. Maybe he was just loyal to the Architect and the Pyramid and so remains loyal. Or maybe he had been under threat all that time: if he did not acquire the mushrooms, then . . . well, what? He would be Discarded, or something, killed, maybe – or his family would suffer, if he had one: the same way that he forced you to do his bidding. Threat begets threat. That maybe was why he was desperate for you to get the Benedictions. In which case, maybe now he is free to be a good man. Anyway, I interrupted his attack on you. I did not know how long we had before the Arbitrators returned in greater numbers or with greater weapons, but I decided that I had to explore the space below; if the information I needed was anywhere, I thought it would be there. I buried you beneath a pile of the dead Arbitrators—'

'You did *what*? Nora, I was *dying*—!'

'I treated the wound first, of course,' she said, her voice still very matter-of-fact, 'and I bandaged you. But it was not safe to move you too much, not when I did not yet know the nature or the extent of the damage. And . . . well, if the sword had pierced anything vital, then you were going to die whether or not I left with you straight away. So I built up a pile of bodies over you in case they returned while I was gone, then I went down through the trapdoor.' She handed Alan another chunk of bread. 'There was a small spiral staircase, made of some dark stone, with white veins: the reverse of everywhere else. I found a number of rooms including living quarters of some extravagance, as well as a private network of hot pools and channels, strange instruments the purpose of which I could not discern, and art – drawings, paintings, sculpture . . .'

'Stolen,' Alan said, 'must be. There are no artists in the Pyramid. Even the mechanical birds and big sculptures in the plazas were originally taken from the Discard, apparently. We learned about them at school. It was something for us to be proud of: ancient artefacts rescued from the heathens.'

'The Architect's quarters were like a . . . like a little bubble, hidden within the centre of the highest levels of the Pyramid: a closed system of stairwells and chambers and mezzanines. Probably disorientating for a normal person. I didn't see any entrances or exits apart from the trapdoor, but there must have been some. I cannot imagine that old demon hauling himself up out of the floor each time he wanted to attend his desk. But maybe he did, I don't know – these people are a mystery to me. Anyway, I went deeper down and found chambers full of old scrolls. Some of them were like the one that came out of the desk – which, by the way, the Chief Architect was reciting from, into a kind of mouth-tube thing – and some of a more traditional nature, but they looked to be completely undisturbed. Alan, I don't think the Chief Architect really *did* anything; his role was merely to recite. His job is just a Station like any other, except maybe more symbolic than most. But I digress. I read all the scrolls I could, and I found a small chest full of gems. I emptied it so that I could fill it with scrolls.' At the expression on his face she added, 'No, don't worry, the gems had no particularly interesting properties – but oh, Alan, I found *maps*—'

The excitement in her voice was almost palpable.

She took a breath and said, 'Maps, Alan! They were general, and lacking in detail, but they are the largest maps I know of, and they cover a wider area than any I have seen. They will advance the work of the Map-makers by decades, if not generations. And *I* found them!'

She paused to tear a chunk from the loaf for herself and Alan followed suit. After a moment she said, 'Gleam is ancient, we know that – so ancient that even the stone of it remains intact only thanks to some manner of enchantment. The same is true of the maps. I found many scrolls and papers that were crumbling to dust, but the maps were preserved. The builders – by which I mean the people who actually *built* the place, not the mythical god-folk invoked by so many – must have wanted the maps to exist for as long as Gleam itself did. So anyway, I took what I could carry and returned upstairs.'

'When I asked "what happened", what I meant was, what happened with *me*? How did you get *me* out?' Alan gestured ineffectually at his side. 'With the injury, and all. Any more whisky? Pass it here.'

'Oh, I took a mattress from one of the beds in the Chief Architect's quarters and I tied you to it. You are heavier than you look! Well, perhaps no longer. I smashed the glass of the window behind the desk, dragged you over and pushed you through and we escaped down the outside of the Pyramid.'

Shaking his head, he poured himself yet another glass. 'I mean, obviously it worked, but . . . *bloody hell*, Nora!'

Nora frowned. 'You must understand' – she took the bottle back – 'I weigh it up, I make the choice, I commit to the choice. That is the way I am. It *might* have killed you, but not doing it *would* have killed you, no *might* about it.'

'I get the logic. I . . . just . . . not everybody is good at making that kind of decision.'

'Well, yes, and inevitably they face the consequences!'

'You're *very* good at making that kind of decision though, and sometimes it creeps me out.'

'I am willing to creep you out, or anybody else for that matter,' she said firmly. 'So, as I was saying, there are many apertures and extrusions on the Pyramid's exterior, but between them all there are many branching routes smooth enough to slide a mattress down . . . of course I held on to you; I did not simply let you go, not in your condition.'

'Thanks!'

'When we were about halfway down, I noticed some signs of pursuit, but the Arbitrators are obviously not as adept as I am at traversing such environments – and besides,' she admitted, 'I do not think their hearts were in it. They had other problems to deal with – spore containment primary amongst them, I imagine. They did fire arrows at us, lots of them, but we were moving too fast and they never really had a clear shot.' She stopped to drink.

'So . . . did we crash at the bottom?' Alan asked. He realised he was kneading his dead thigh and stopped. For a moment or two he didn't know what to do with his hands; wherever he put them, they felt out of place. He settled for picking up the bottle and glass once more.

'Stop interrupting,' Nora said. 'I am trying to tell you.' She hesitated, and Alan looked up at her. At last she said, 'Alan, those lands around the Black Pyramid, knee-deep in that ash? They are amongst the most barren and desolate that I have ever experienced. Even though the sky was bright, it felt like the fires at the end of the world. The Discard looked like a vast, twisted black ruin. There were strange things writhing in the ground there. Like in the Swamp, a corruption in the spirit of Gleam was entering into me through my connection with it and corrupting me in turn. And the ash was eating away at the mattress and our clothes as the atmosphere ate away at my mind. Whatever is concentrated in the Swamp is there too, in that ash.'

'So whatever the Pyramid . . . *exudes* into the Sump, whatever is leaking from the Sump into the Swamp, it was also released when the Pyramid destroyed Modest Mills?'

'How did they destroy Modest Mills, Alan?'

'Fire and knives.'

'But how? The buildings were stone and yet there's hardly a thing left of them. Just normal fires with torches couldn't have done that. It wasn't a long, long time ago; it was within your memory. There has not been time for the ruins to turn into dust.'

'No,' Alan agreed. He looked at her. 'No, you're right.' He remembered the silver cylinder he'd accidentally loosed upon the Pyramid as a child. 'The things that the Pyramid manufactures? They're weapons, and they're magic.' He told her the story, how a Glasstowner had given him the cylinder, how he'd opened it, his hands shaking as he spoke, and the fresh whisky in his glass slopped over the edge. He recounted how he'd read out loud the words WHO DO YOU HATE, how he'd answered the question, how the cylinder had shot from his hands, burning through the air, and blasted a crater in the side of the Pyramid, killing people, and how the Pyramid had then come for Modest Mills – and how Eyes McAlkie had taken responsibility for the attack. 'He wouldn't go with them unless they spared my life – not just spared my life, but took me in. He hated the Pyramid then, but not as much. He knew it oppressed the Discard; he didn't know it oppressed its own citizens. That was before they tortured him, before they ripped off his eyelids.'

And then he told Nora how Eyes had stabbed Billy in the end, and how he had then throttled Eyes in the very ash that had once been their home village.

He fell silent, and Nora reached out and took his hand. 'You think they used magic weapons when they destroyed Modest Mills?'

Alan nodded.

'You think the magic causes the corruption in the Swamp, and caused the corruption in the Modest Mills ash?'

'Yes.'

'Do you think the corruption is why Eyes did what he did?' Nora squeezed his hand. 'Why you did what you did to him?'

For the first time, Alan let the tears run freely. At last he said, 'Maybe. I don't know.' He wiped his face with his sleeve. 'I don't know.'

Nora kept hold of Alan's hand. He was grateful when she returned to her story. 'Well. At any rate, we landed safely enough, with the mattress underneath us. I tried to drag the mattress through Modest Mills, but I could not. That place emanates its own peculiar despair. The ash was getting into our eyes and mouths – I kept stopping to brush it away from you in case you started choking, but every time I stood still the mattress started sinking into the stuff. I knew that I couldn't carry you, not without bending your back.'

Nora offered Alan some of the goat's cheese and they both took a moment to eat.

'Alan, if I had been thinking straight, I do not think I would have done what I did next, but I don't remember actually making a decision . . . I just . . . I just left you. I left you there and came here, to the House of a Thousand Hollows. When I arrived here, I told the guards exactly who I was and demanded an audience with Maggie. She agreed to help us in return for my protection during your convalescence, and she sent out her people to pick you up – I led them back to you, although I did not go all the way with them. I showed them your position from a vantage point and then stayed back from the wastes. The protection provided by the rotted flesh of the Giving Beast has diminished, evidently, judging by the way the place was eating at my mind.'

'Who was it?' Alan asked. 'Who came to get me?'

'Birdface and Loon – Loon was companionable enough, but Birdface . . . well, I don't think Birdface likes me. So they know you're here, but they are the only ones, I am assured. They have no families, and no friends except for Maggie, so they do what she tells them. And if she tells them to stay quiet about you, then they will. I am confident of that.' Nora waved her hands. 'So you can probably work out the rest. You're here now. Loon is building you a kind of chair with wheels. And that's about it. That's about where we are.'

'Nora—'

'I should return to my post. If you'd like to see them, I'll bring you the scrolls and—'

'Nora, I need the toilet.' He tried to keep his voice calm, but it broke.

'Okay. Using the commode?'

'Yes,' Alan said. 'Now. Quick. *Now.*'

Nora lifted the lid and then came back to the bed and got her hands under his shoulders.

'Quickly,' Alan said. 'Quick.' His desperation was overwhelming his embarrassment; he was suddenly drenched in sweat.

Holding Alan firmly around his chest and under his arms, Nora helped him from the bed and onto the seat. 'There,' she said. 'Is there—?'

'Go now. *Please.*' He hadn't intended to sound so curt, but he didn't apologise. He put a hand over his face and repeated, 'Please. *Now.*'

'Yes – of course. Of course.'

Alan lifted his hips as the door closed, but it was too late: the urine flooded out. He could not hold it as once he would have. He cried out in shock, staring down at the spreading darkness, and the tears came, and, with them, shame. He struggled out of his nightshirt, then didn't move again for hours, just sat and stared, and thought.

14

Origins

Nora brought Alan the documents she'd stolen from the Pyramid. He started with the scrolls she'd identified as particularly interesting and pored over them for hours and hours – after all, he had plenty of time to kill; the chair was going to take some days yet.

The scrolls were very old. The first ones he examined looked like orders.

Two hundredd cannon as per pryor specifica-tions. Four thousand cannon-ball, to fitt. Please calculate the correct measures of your new pow-der. All metalls must be charmed. The crates to be varnished appropriately, so as to prevent charm leakage. Please include full instructionall scrolls, certificates to confirm the qualifications of your enchanter, and records of origins of all materiall.

5000 trgtd exp. dvcs (of the previous type)

5000 crssbws
50000 crssbw blts, enchntd (see attached spec)
5000 enchntd swrds (see attached spec)
Twenty large bombes
Fourty lyttle bombes
One single bombe-thrower
One suit of armour for a man of average hyte,
with a very nycely décor'd helmyt
How much?

There were many like this, some so densely packed with inventory that the scribes had used both sides and then turned the paper sideways to fill the margins. More orders had been scribbled onto scraps. Some had obviously been written by people who knew what they were doing for they were comprehensive and well thought-out. Others were clearly the work of the inexperienced, the semi-literate or fools. Most of the documents were covered in grey smudges and brown spots.

But where had they come from? Had Gleam once been at war, with the Pyramid supplying arms? And if so, at war with whom?

Another scroll detailed a problem with a manufacturing facility:

. . . the original designs omitted the distillation
facilities required for the creation of turpentine,
as well as sufficient land for the requisite pine

trees; when the manufacturing processes were mapped, turpentine was identified as an essential ingredient for the creation of the various varnishes, but the subsequent sub-process for the manufacturing of turpentine itself was never mapped. Given that the Factory design was intended to ensure complete self-sufficiency, this is an unforgiveable oversight. I advise immediate causal analysis. Perhaps a Ritualist could complete the Five Hundred Whys, which is a new Ritual currently in search of a compelling and complex test case, such as a problem with the Factory project. I can source such an individual, if necessary.

But let us also look forward: the oversight needs rectifying; the enchantments require containment, and the containment method decided on was the creation, enchantment and application of the appropriate varnishes. As such, we must expand. The expansion is not disproportionately large – less than a hundredth of the existing structure – but as a consequence of the faultlessly precise project calibrations, there is no available resource. Further resourcing will be required. The resource will require further accommodation. The accommodation will require construction. You can see how such an oversight leads to a spiralling-out. And this is before we

consider the turpentine production processes
and the quality assurance. The turpentine production will need to be monitored to the highest
degree if it is to be suitable for enchantment; this
will require Monitors, and their particular mag-
ickal instruments. Some of the functions of these
instruments can be performed by the instruments used in sampling and assessing the varnish
itself, but some can not. And so further facilities
will be required for the production of these
further instruments. These instruments will
themselves require calibrating. You can see how
it goes on. Forgive me if you feel that I am labour-
ing the point. To be clear, my point is this; in a
project as ambitious and as tightly controlled as
this, any oversight – even those that appear to be
inconsequentially tiny – have enormously complex and costly ramifications. I have expounded
with a couple of minor examples, but the full
consequences will have to be thought out –
and mapped out, properly, by a fully qualified
and competent Overseer – and then, unfortu-
nately, costed and acted upon. My expectation
is an ad-hoc and unplanned growth; a carbuncle,
of sorts, marring the beautiful structure that
we have succeeded in building thus far. And, forgive me for saying so, but given the frailties
and foibles of various Quorum individuals, I do

not expect it to be the last. There is one - a
particular . . .

And with that, the letter degenerated into a thinly
veneered character attack. Alan put it aside and pondered
what he had learned: the Pyramid had been a factory –
or, potentially, the whole of what Nora had called the
Original Structure had been a factory. Alan considered
the wide passages of the Discard, the tunnels, the plains
and the bridges, the great cavernous spaces inside, the
strange bubble-room complexes: all part of one vast factory? The scale of the whole thing was fantastical. And it
had grown a little more with each mistake: a catalogue of
errors made solid. *Sounds about right.*

The Original Structure was all quite wheel-friendly,
from what he'd seen, meaning that much of the Discard
would be traversable – if he stayed low enough – when
he was in the—

His thoughts deserted him. He couldn't focus too
much on the wheeled chair; he found himself simultaneously excited by the freedom it represented, especially
compared to his current situation, and horrified by the
restrictions compared to his previous life. The scrolls
were a welcome distraction; they turned his thoughts
outwards, away from himself.

So the factory hadn't been just any factory: it had been
an *arms* factory – but if it had incorporated all of the
Original Structure, then that meant there'd been no

divide between Pyramid and Discard – in fact, there might not have been a Discard at all, just the factory. Just Gleam. So who had provided the demand? And where had they been?

Outside?

Alan turned his gaze to the window. Skeffington Lutwidge had talked of an 'outside', hadn't he? A 'beyond' . . . He wondered how Skeffington and the Goatherds were doing. They wouldn't be able to get in to visit him, if they even wanted to; there was no guarantee that they would. Skeffington had wanted Nora's help; that's why he'd allowed Byron to help him – and why he'd not handed Alan over to Daunt – but Nora was here, watching the House. He wondered what kind of arrangement they'd come to. And Nora had yet to return to the Mapmakers and tell them what she'd found – and do whatever it was she'd planned to do. Alan had intended to go with her, but now he didn't think he'd be able to. So much had changed . . .

He picked up a scroll from a different time, made of a different material and written in a very different hand:

The trick is to pass it off as intentional. Growth is Good. More people means more construction, more construction means more jobs, more jobs means more construction. More people also means more children, which means more schools, more food, more clothes, more of everything. Encourage this. Tertiary industries and populations justify the continued existence of the Factory, should its primary function expire. Let growth become synonymous with success: Growth for Gleam, and Gleam for Growth. Encourage the people to work towards Growth itself, as opposed to anything more physical, personally rewarding or actually finite. They will forever chase it and in doing so, occupy themselves. Idleness is bad for the individual, and it is bad for the Order in which they exist.

Relatedly, there is no reason for the non-core personnel to be exempted from Core Values and Customer Satisfaction training. The training can and should be introduced in schools. Even though the majority of children are no longer being trained for Manufacturing roles necessarily, the Factory's founding ethos is relevant to all. Customer Satisfaction is a noble aim for any worker, regardless of the nature of their role, their Station or the customer, and Core Val—

The rest of the words were obscured by water damage.

Nora had picked up some very informative documents, Alan decided, piecing together the history of Gleam. He knew it was speculative and incomplete, and he was pretty sure that it barely scratched the surface of the truth, but it was more than he'd ever had before. Although he tried not to focus on it, he wondered how long Nora had searched for them – how long she'd left him buried beneath the pile of dead Arbitrators. She was the closest friend he had now, but she scared him, and he didn't truly know how much she valued him. She'd defended him against the Arbitrators, but had that *really* been for his sake, or just to enable her continued exploration?

So the factory – no, *the Factory* – had produced weapons and armour, and on a vast scale. He'd seen invoices for swords, knives, bows, arrows, cannon, siege-weapons, plate-mail, chainmail, magical powders, mind-altering fungi, dangerous parasites . . . the list went on and on. And they weren't just ordinary weapons; the Factory worked with magic, enchanting what they'd made or creating items that were purely magical – he'd found multiple orders for 'Eaters', but nothing to explain what they were.

And it looked like the Pyramid had always been referred to as the Pyramid, and the same for the Central Keep, the Black Offices and the Palace.

Due to various oversights and mistakes, the Factory had constantly expanded, resulting in many disparate additions to the Original Structure. Dormitory units had spilled out into settlements, for example, until, over time, the Factory had become more of a city. A good many of the scrolls were concerned with the Factory function, though, as were the maps, which looked sparse at first – lots of white space interrupted only by a few thin dark lines, with some spidery text saying things like 'Routes to Market', 'Throughput Channels', 'Station Assembly Points', 'Cart Slopes' and 'Sewer Spirals'. But on further study, those lines turned out to be more interesting: when Alan focused, he could see more and more lines appearing before his eyes – a bit like looking at the night sky on those rare occasions when both moons were down, trying to find a dark spot between two stars only to discover yet more stars in between them, and on and on, until all you could see were stars. So it was with the maps: where at first he'd thought there was only white space, there were in fact densely packed lines of near-invisible thinness. When he lost focus, the white space returned. He couldn't understand it; he felt as if the white space should have been dark with pencil, given the detail crammed in. But there it was.

The lines depicted the Original Structure. When viewed in just that way it was bewilderingly complex and beautiful. Obviously it had been designed initially as a functional factory, but Alan could recognise the work of an aesthetic sensibility when he saw it. He hadn't yet found a map that covered the whole of it, but there was no repetition to the fluid design within the collection he had. There were contours, curved and flowing, gathering in whorls and bottlenecks or coming apart to depict vast domes and concavities that Alan thought were probably

too large to be perceived from ground level. And sometimes they broke and split into crazed geometries, looking
almost like cross-sections of impossible buildings full
of stairs. Alan had to remind himself again and again
that he was looking at the structure from above. Sometimes the lines came close to forming geometric patterns
that nearly – but not quite, never quite – repeated. The
maps reminded Alan of something – doodles, he thought,
the kind of thing he used to draw in the back of his
schoolbooks as a kid, before he'd discovered his cock.
That was one of the reasons Eyes had given Alan the guitar. *Something* else *to do with your hands*, he'd said. *Get good,
maybe one of them girls you dream about might actually notice
yer.* Eyes had never truly understood how relationships
worked in the Pyramid. But the guitar had captivated
Alan; he'd never seen anything like it before. And he'd
never gone back to his doodling. But the doodling hadn't
ever been an occupation; it hadn't been like *proper* drawing. It was just a way of turning his mind off, forgetting
about his parents, about the fire, about the blood. Trying
to teach himself to play the guitar helped in the same
way, except there'd been the added reward of tangible
improvement.

But there was something else that the maps reminded
him of, though he didn't get it until he opened the window, when a big fat spider immediately ran in across the
windowsill. He brought his fist down on it and crushed
it – which was when he remembered Spider's designs, the

huge, intricate things he drew that often hadn't become tattoos because they were too big to condense down into something that would fit onto a human body. He'd drawn them in the depths of his mushroom trances – or perhaps his mushroom *trance*, because thinking back on it, he'd been more or less constantly under the influence.

Does it mean anything? Alan tried to work it out, but his eyes kept drifting back to the squashed remains of the dead arachnid on his windowsill, and his thoughts kept drifting back to his dead friend.

Nora kept him in supplies and the occasional bottle of Dog Moon. He asked for a new knife too, which she also acquired: a wide, wicked blade with a worn and shining hilt.

Billy didn't come to see him, and nor did Marion. He dreamed of Marion, and in his dreams Marion and he were friends. Sometimes in his dreams they would make love, but he would wake to find himself flaccid; he tried to rouse his cock just to prove to himself that he could – but he couldn't; the numbness was not just in his legs.

He continued with the leg and arm exercises Loon had shown him, and practised walking around the room with his crutches. Sometimes he got to the commode in time; sometimes he didn't.

He waited for the promised chair with wheels. As the moons moved across the sky he lit candles and ate mushrooms, washing them down with whisky, then closed his eyes and lost himself in the dances of strange faces and impossible shapes.

Alan came to, hearing a knocking at the door. His eyes were bleary, his head was pounding and his teeth felt misplaced in his head. The room would not stay still; he was as drunk as when he'd passed out.

'Come in,' he growled, only to be answered by silence, and then another knock at the door, more urgent this time.

'Come in!' he yelled. 'I can't bloody come and open it for you, can I?'

The knob turned and the door opened a little way, and then a little more. A small head popped through the gap.

'Dad?' Billy said.

Alan tried to speak, but he couldn't. He started coughing, and at last he managed, 'Billy—' He pulled himself together and croaked, 'Billy! Come in!'

Billy came into the room and Alan caught his breath. His boy had lost such a lot of weight. He had purple circles around his eyes, and his Pyramid-pale skin was even whiter now. His hair looked lank – they had better soap in the Pyramid, of course – but his shirt and plain cotton trousers were clean.

Billy looked around the room. There was nothing really in it apart from the crutches and an empty Dog Moon bottle. He wrinkled his nose. 'Smells bad,' he said.

Alan couldn't remember if anybody had emptied the

commode since he'd last used it. Probably not. And he wasn't entirely sure he hadn't wet himself in his sleep; he always woke up drenched these days. His dreams were either lewd or terrifying, and either way he woke up sweating like a toad.

He wanted to grab his son, hold him close and sob with relief and despair, but he couldn't reach him, not from the bed, and besides, to break down like that would be a horribly selfish act; even in his hung-over state he recognised that. He still felt the tears begin to prick at his eyelids. He pulled himself up, his hips aching like a rusty hinge, and used his hands to pivot himself around until he was sitting upright, his legs flopped over the edge of the bed.

Billy's gaze followed his movements. 'I'm sorry, Dad,' he said. He limped across the room and sat next to Alan.

'*You're* sorry?' Alan laughed, and immediately flinched at the bitterness in his own voice. He put his arm around Billy's shoulders, and Billy leaned in to him. 'What have you got to be sorry for?'

'Your legs – you lost your legs for me and Mum.'

Alan shook his head and said firmly, 'No, Billy, this is on me. I brought myself here.' He hugged Billy to him then. He'd been so desperate to see his son for so long that now they were together, it almost didn't feel real. It felt like one of his daydreams.

'I'm so sorry I hurt you and your mum on the way. I am so, *so* sorry, Billy, for what I've done to you.' Alan meant every word, but it was the whisky enabling the flow. 'It was because of me that Eyes hurt you – it was because of me the Alchemists changed your blood, that you had to eat the Benedictions—' He stopped suddenly and turned awkwardly to look at Billy. 'Did you? You did, didn't you? Eat the mushrooms? Your mother did give them to you—?'

Billy looked down at his hands and Alan noticed for the first time that they were shaking. 'Yes,' Billy whispered, 'Mum gave me the . . . the Benedictions. I saw everything on fire – I felt like I was burning. It was like being in . . . in a nightmare, or another world, not this one . . .' He reached up and took Alan's hand in his own. 'I still have nightmares. I shake now – look, you can feel it. Loon says I will probably always shake – because of the fungus. The Idle Hands, I mean, not the Benedictions. And I limp too. And my words are slow . . . I guess . . . you can hear it. And . . . yeah. And that's it.'

'The burning, the nightmares,' Alan said, 'those things might come and go, for a short while. And your mind will tell you that having some more Benedictions would make them go away for ever. You'll feel sad and angry that you can't have any – but it will pass. And soon, the nightmares will stop and the feeling of burning will stop.' He hoped it was true. 'I'm sorry.'

Billy looked up at him, obviously confused. 'No, *you* didn't do it. That man with the red beard and red eyes did it – I *saw* him! He stabbed my foot and it hurt, a *lot*. It was him, not you.' He stopped, and then confided, 'Everybody said you were bad too, Dad, so I didn't like you, but then Maggie told me, and Nora did too, that that man, the Arbitrator, he would have killed me if you hadn't come to the Pyramid with Eyes that time. And Mum knows that too.'

Alan squeezed Billy tight.

'Dad, I don't like your room.'

'Billy,' Alan said. He looked around, saw the bottles, the unemptied chamber pot, the dirty sheets, and realised how deeply unpleasant the room had become. He saw himself through his son's eyes and he was ashamed.

He breathed deeply. 'You won't see me like this again,' he promised Billy. 'I am . . . I guess I was scared that you wouldn't come.'

'I wanted to see you, but I was sick.' Billy wiped his eyes. 'Me and Mum, we're going to stay here, and she says I can keep seeing you, but she says you're not going to stay here . . . Will you come and see me, Dad? Can I come and see you, wherever you go?'

Alan nodded, because he really couldn't speak. He kept hugging Billy, his face buried in his son's hair, his teeth set as he cried, all the while trying not to make a sound. He didn't know why he was trying to keep it from Billy, because *of course* Billy knew he was crying. But still.

'It's okay, Dad,' Billy was saying, 'it's okay. Hey – I brought something for you.' He got up from the bed and walked slowly to the door, and this time Alan noticed his uneven gait. A moment later he came back into the room, and he was pushing a wheeled chair: the chair that Loon had built.

It had four wheels with metal spokes, and the rims had been coated in the rubber Loon made from the tree sap harvested by transients somewhere out past Forge Country. The two front wheels were smaller than the back ones. A thick red velvet cushion softened the wooden panelled seat. There were various handles and levers protruding from the arms.

Alan stared. It looked quite similar to a normal fucking chair, except it had wheels instead of legs. Anywhere he went, it would go too now. It would be his truest companion. Like all of Loon's creations, it was a bit ramshackle – and no doubt, also like all of Loon's creations, it would be fully functional: it was practicable and serviceable, and he hated it on sight. It was *ugly*.

'It's very nice,' he said. 'I mean, I'm going to be walking again soon – I've got these crutches, and I'm practising. But it's very nice.'

'Look,' Billy said, opening a small hatch inside the right-hand arm, and Alan held his breath. Maybe it had a crossbow built into it, or something else exciting – hidden compartments for smuggling stuff, or spring-loaded knives. Billy uncoiled a long tube.

Alan examined it. 'For drinking?' he suggested, but Billy frowned.

'No, Dad,' he said, 'for going to the toilet! Here's a –
look! – here's a funnel.'

Alan's gut roiled. 'A piss tube.'

Billy shook. 'That's a bad word,' he said.

'What about when I need to take a shite?' Alan
muttered.

'There's this handle at the front,' Billy explained help-
fully, 'see? You pull it out, and it makes a hole in the seat.
You just need to move the cushion and . . . take your
trousers down.' He looked down. 'You can . . . you can
do that?'

'Yes, son. I can do that.' Alan reached out for his hand.
'I'm sorry – I'm sorry, Billy. It's just that I'm not feeling
very well, that's all. You can see that I've been drinking
too much, can't you? Well, it's not an excuse, I know.
Forgive me, will you?' And as Billy nodded hesitantly, he
said, 'Help me into it – into the chair. Come on, let's do
it.' He forced a smile. 'I need to make the best of it, right?
So help me in.'

Billy kicked the debris out of the way and pushed the
chair over to the bed. When Alan felt his son try to lift
him, he nearly broke down again. There was no strength
in the boy; his arms were wasted. 'A fine pair we make,'
he said, after recovering himself.

'What?' Billy looked puzzled.

'Nothing.' Alan got himself into the chair. It was sur-
prisingly comfortable.

'I can push you around,' Billy said.

'I'm not sure,' Alan said.

'Let me.'

'I—'

The sudden motion as Billy wheeled the chair around sent the room spinning; Alan's stomach clenched and saliva flooded his mouth. 'No—' he said, but it was too late. He managed to get his head over the edge of the chair just as he started vomiting. His stomach was heaving, again and again. The acid burned in his throat and he felt the sick running through his beard.

The smell filled the air and the silence grew uncomfortable.

'Sorry, Dad,' Billy said. 'Sorry. Sorry—' He threw himself down onto the floor and started trying to clean up the mess.

'Stop,' Alan said.

'Sorry—' Billy's movements were frantic and repetitive. He kept trying to mop up the vomit but his actions were achieving nothing.

'Son,' Alan said, 'please, leave it.'

'Sorry. Sorry.'

'For fuck's sake, stop saying sorry!'

Now Billy was kneeling, his fists clenched, rocking backwards and forwards. 'Sorry,' he repeated. His body was tense.

'Billy?'

Billy fell onto his side and now Alan could see that his

movements were not panicked repetition but completely uncontrolled. His son was shaking and drool was dribbling from his mouth. 'S-s-s-s-sorry,' Billy said, but his eyes were blank and his limbs were jerking forwards and backwards, like one of the meat creatures taken live from the vats in the Pyramid and dropped onto the floor.

Finally Alan realised Billy was having a seizure and he started howling, 'Help!' He picked up a bottle from the floor and hammered on the wall with it. 'Help! Somebody! Help— Help, Green damn it—! Green be fucked!'

He wheeled the chair to the door and swung it open. 'Get Loon!' he screamed. 'Get Loon!'

Somebody at the far end of the corridor who'd been running towards him turned around and started running in the other direction and Alan returned to Billy's side. He tried to haul himself out of the chair and fell to the floor. He lifted Billy's head so that he didn't drown in his own saliva – he was just guessing, because he didn't know what the right thing was. But then, he never had.

15

Milktree

Loon pulled a large wad of some kind of bark from one of the pockets of her dungarees and placed it between Billy's teeth, then retrieved what looked like a cold compress from another and placed it across his forehead.

'He should have milktree bark on him,' Loon said. 'You could have done this – why didn't you do this?'

'I didn't know,' Alan said, feeling wretched.

'He didn't tell you, I bet. Your boy has fits now. He should be telling whoever he's with: if this happens, do such-and-such.'

'He has fits?' Alan swallowed.

'Yep. Not all the time, but frequently enough. Usually brought on by stress. They're not dangerous, as long as he's not alone and is properly looked after, but they're painful, and embarrassing for a young lad.' She gestured at his wet trousers. 'Point is, he has to be open about it. I'll come running if I can, Green knows I will. But if I can't . . .' She patted his head. 'He'll be out for a short while now.' She picked Billy up and lifted him onto Alan's bed, raising an eyebrow at the state of it. 'Seeing how well you look after yourself, mind, I won't be getting my hopes up for him.'

'I should be able to pick him up,' Alan said, 'but I can't even get off the floor myself.'

'Here.' Loon helped Alan to his feet. 'Let's do some standing exercises. Take this crutch.'

'How am I doing?' Alan asked. 'Honestly?'

'Well, pretty good. But I'm still making no promises. The body's a mystery to me, really. It's not like a machine, where I can see all the parts and take them out and swap them around and check what works and what doesn't. All I know is, your kind of immobility is sometimes permanent and sometimes not. One thing's certain, though: you won't find out if you don't keep trying. Those crutches there? They're pretty nice, if I say so myself. Good padding, nice smooth handles inside those leather cups. Be a shame if you didn't make good use of them.'

'Thanks, Loon,' Alan said. 'And thank you for the chair.'

'That's all right.' She helped Alan into the chair and then returned to the bed and stroked Billy's hair gently. 'I've never known you very well, but I heard all about you from Eyes. Eyes would tell me all about you when he was picking up his lotion. When I heard that he was dead, I . . . Well, my heart goes out to you, lad. I know you were good friends – and more than that, right? Eyes, he

was like a daddy to you, I know that. Those Pyramid bastards got my mammy and daddy, and they got your
mammy and daddy, and then they got him too. He always
talked about you like you were his own, so I feel like I
know you. You're a friend of my gone friend, so you're a
friend of mine. I thought making you something would
be a good way of honouring him, and helping you . . .
Well, making is what I do. It's all I can do.'

'Thank you,' Alan said. His mouth was dry. Where
Loon had heard that the Pyramidders had killed Eyes, he
wasn't sure – Nora must have been putting the rumour
about.

'I know you've got to go. Don't worry about Billy.
Like I say, I'm not a bloody nurse, but I'll watch him,
keep him on track. For you, and for Eyes.'

'Thank you,' Alan said again.

'You know that you're going to have to go now, yes?
Now the chair's done.'

'Now?'

'Yes. Your friend Nora knows it's done and she's readying herself to leave. And Maggie won't have you here
without the protection of your Mapmaker friend. Besides,
you can't use the chair in this stinking little midden of a
chamber – you'd need to take it out into the corridors.
And your name's mud round these parts, lad, as you
might expect. I wouldn't fancy your chances. You want
to make a go of it, you need to be out in the Discard,
Wild Alan.'

'You know you've fucked up when you're safer in the Wild than in one of the Safe Houses,' he said, trying to make a joke of it.

'Aye, well, seems like you've got a gift for fucking up, Alan. Although – there are other Safe Houses, you know. You haven't fucked up in their vicinities recently, have you?'

He laughed. 'Not that I remember.'

'And while we're on the subject.' Loon pulled a tarnished old hipflask partway out of one of the many pockets she'd stitched onto her dungarees and then let it drop back in. 'Now, I like a drink myself, but the truth is, the more you drink, the higher the chance of a fuck-up is, okay? Statistically speaking. I know you know that, Alan. What I'm saying is, perhaps it's time to start acting on that knowledge.'

'I feel worse when I don't drink,' he started, trying to explain himself, but she was already shaking her head.

'Well you look like you feel pretty rotten right now: sweaty, unwashed, sick in your beard . . .'

'I feel ill when I drink, but when I don't drink, I feel angry and sad – so angry and sad it scares me, Loon.' He didn't think he was actually explaining it very well at all. 'My thinking paralyses me – drinking lets me carry on.'

'I've heard similar before,' she said firmly, 'and it's not true. You feel that way *because* of the drink. It's a demon, and given enough influence, it tricks you into thinking it's a friend. It's *not* a friend. The more you indulge it, the more you'll need it.'

'You're saying stop drinking.'

Loon nodded.

'But it's too late – I already need it.'

'With this kind of problem it's always too late. But you've got to do it – for Billy, if not for you.' She pursed her lips. 'He's never going to be a well boy, Alan. He's going to need help. He's going to need *family*. You fuck up just one time too many and you're no help to anyone. You understand me? You need to think of your son, not yourself.'

Loon had gone by the time Billy came round. Alan was practising with his crutches, but all he could do was raise himself up for a couple of seconds, and even that left the muscles in his arms crying out in pain and twitching wildly. Balancing on them was impossible. He tried lowering himself onto his feet, but the joints bent in odd directions; they couldn't take any weight at all.

'You look like a bug,' Billy murmured, behind him. 'A big leggy bug.'

'A mantis?' Alan lowered himself back into the chair and slowly turned it around to face the bed. 'Hello, son. I'm sorry about before. I'm a mess and I'm disgusting. I'm going to change.'

'Don't say sorry.'

'No, it's way past the time for apologies. But it is time

for me to say goodbye, Billy – but just for now. I'll be back . . .'

'Where are you going to go, Dad?'

'Well, son, I know a place . . .' He put a hand on each of the two back wheels and moved himself over to the window. 'If you get up to that rooftop, the one you can see from here' – he pointed into the distance, although he knew Billy wouldn't be able to make anything out, not from where he was – 'that one there with the bucket-fire? You climb into the building with the silver tree growing out of it and then out the other side. You'll have to drop down onto the big round chimney pot, the one that's got a bird's nest in it, then follow the spine of those rooftops all the way to the end. Go around the Dome of the Toad and you'll see a grassy field filling a space between lots of old buildings all made of grey stone. It was once a roof-top courtyard, I think, maybe even with a garden.' He could see Billy was listening intently. 'So, at the far side of that field, there are some little wooden houses. I'll be in the one in the corner.'

'But Dad – you can't get there in that chair . . .'

'Not that way I can't, no. But that was Eyes' house, and he used to bring wheelbarrows of vegetables from his garden to Market Top. I'd help him sometimes. Anyway, you don't need to worry about where I am, because you're not coming to see me, you hear? You're not going out there on your own, not without company.' Before Billy could start protesting he added quickly, 'I'm going to be coming here to see you, right? We'll meet on the Favoured Bridge and go for drinks in Market Top.' He looked around him, at the empty bottles. 'Drinks of tea, I mean. Normal tea.'

'I just wanted to know where you'll be.'

'I understand.' Alan sighed. 'You know,' he said, 'you should have told me about your seizures – then I could have helped you. You do keep the milktree bark on you, yes?'

'Yes,' Billy said, looking sheepish. 'I just . . . I just didn't want you to know. It's *embarrassing*.'

'You *never* ever need to be embarrassed around me,' Alan said. 'Now, why don't you come with me to the Bridge and we'll say goodbye.'

'I'm only coming with you if you wash that sick out of your beard.'

'There's an idea,' Alan said, 'but I'm not going to wash the damned thing. I'm going to shave it off.'

'I need some clean clothes,' Billy said. 'I'll go and find some for both of us, and then we'll go to the Bridge together.'

'Loon said you shouldn't be on your own,' Alan started, but Billy rolled his eyes.

'Me and Mum live just upstairs. If I'm not back in . . . ten minutes, tell people. I don't want somebody *always* with me. I *don't*.'

Alan smiled, and gave in. 'Say goodbye to your mother from me,' he said.

'I will,' Billy said, and left the room, closing the door behind him.

Alan wheeled himself over to the washbasin. He pushed himself up to look into the mirror. His beard was thicker than he'd realised. He turned his head. He couldn't shave it off, he saw, not with Daunt and her goons still on the hunt. It obscured some of his neck tattoos. He'd have to find ways to cover up the rest. *High collars. Long-sleeved shirts.* He looked down at his hands. *Gloves.*

His arms started shaking and he lowered himself back into the chair, took a deep breath and exhaled.

16

News at the Red Cat

Alan nudged open the door of the Market Top tavern. The Red Cat wasn't too busy; the day was only half-done. The barman was a lean, bald fellow with a moustache and a black waistcoat. He looked up from the tankard he was polishing and stared openly as Alan wheeled his way into the barroom. Alan tried to ignore the attention, but as he searched for a table that the arms of his chair would fit beneath he drew more curious glances and a couple of outright hostile ones. A silence fell.

'Barkeep,' Alan said, loudly, sweating profusely beneath his buttoned-up collar, 'a beer, and a lemon tea, if you could. Thank you.' Then he turned to address his on-lookers. 'I understand that the chair may be a curiosity. You are welcome to observe it. But there are those amongst you whose gaze is directed at me. Trust me; I myself am *not* a curiosity; nor have I any meaning to you. You do not know me. So I would appreciate it if you could stop your damned goggling, return to your business and leave me to mine.'

'You want to watch yourself,' growled a big man with a white beard and ponytail. 'Weak enough to require a device such as that and yet wealthy enough to afford one? Some might see you as an easy target. Especially with that mouth on you.'

'My mouth makes me a target to you, does it? You find it attractive? Well, you wouldn't be the first. But you must earn my affections, sir. I do not surrender them to just anybody.' Alan wheeled over to the man, who was scowling and getting to his feet, bottle in hand. 'And I am not *weak*.' He lifted a crutch, already loosened, from the chair and drove the end of it into the man's stomach, hard. The man fell back into his seat, wheezing.

After a moment, he spoke. 'My Connie didn't get no damned magic chair when she lost her legs to a shudder-snake bite. We don't get none of that out here in the Wild. She couldn't carry on – she couldn't bear it. It's all right for you House folk.' He sighed. 'Anyways, I'm too old for brawling. You win. Enjoy your victory, and your damned chair. Drink in peace.'

'I'm sorry,' Alan said. He struggled for words. 'I'm not House folk any more.'

'Aye, but looks like you were for long enough.' He waved Alan away irritably. 'Be on with you.'

Alan spoke quietly. 'Well, we'll see how I do out here now, won't we?'

'You, sir,' the barman said, once Alan was close enough for them to speak quietly, 'a beer and a lemon tea. There's a table in the corner that should accommodate your chair. I apologise for the reception. Some of my regulars spend so much time here – and pay so little for their fare – that they begin to mistake it for their own home.'

'No,' Alan said, 'it's okay. Get the man a drink on me.'

Alan wheeled around to the other side of the suggested table, keeping his back to the wall and his face to the entrance before him. There he remained, growing increasingly desperate for a proper drink. But no, no whisky. He was trying. He listened to the conversations around him. He was too hot in his high collar and long sleeves, and his moustache felt sticky with beer. He hadn't found any gloves yet, but the corner was dark enough for him to hold the tankard without feeling like his hand tattoos were too conspicuous.

He quickly became thankful for his uncomfortable get-up, though. A couple of women arrived, tense and nervy, with a beer delivery, and told the barman of an encounter they'd just witnessed as they rolled the kegs through.

'They were stopping everyone on the bridge, showing them pictures of him. Aye! Asking if they'd seen him. And this one fool punk ripped it out their hands like, told them to go piss up a rope. Told them this Wild Alan was just a singer. Well, they just – they just—'

Alan shrank back into his chair as the other woman took

up the story. 'One of them, a proper brute she was, Daunt's mushroom on her forehead and a big one on her back, she picked this guy up by the hair and threw him from the bridge is what she did. He landed hard on the edge of a roof, smack on the shoulder. Screamed like – you ever heard a Liss Owl making off with a kill? Nope? Well, it's not a good sound. Whole bridge went quiet and listened to him shriek. Everyone answered their questions after that.'

'They're everywhere,' the first woman said. 'We've been travelling four days and we seen 'em . . . at least once a day, I think. They're on all the trade routes. Someone was saying Daunt lost Dok so she's pulled a lot of her traders and gatherers back up topside now. They're real scary – and they've all got their weapons out. Feels like they're waiting for something.'

'Wouldn't want to get on the wrong side of the Mushroom Queen, I know that much,' the barman said. 'She'll be heading back down into the Swamp before too long, and Green help any unfortunates in her way. Especially this Wild Alan chappie. What'd he do?'

'Dunno. They're tough enough not to bother explaining themselves. But they're putting the screws on. Somebody'll have seen him, and when they find him . . .'

Alan chewed his lip and nursed his pint until the sound of a motorbike engine became audible. It grew louder and louder until it finally came to a stop directly outside the establishment.

★

Byron and Nora both drank tea, and Alan was grateful for that, as it made it easier for him to resist the whisky. He succumbed to a smoke or two, though. The three of them raised steaming glasses to each other and as they drank and smoked, Byron told them about his injury.

'Advantage of being meaty,' he laughed. 'Bolt hit nothing but arm flesh — an' that's healin'. up now. Me bones are as good as they ever were.' But to Alan the laughter sounded hollow. Byron's eyes had a troubled, confused look that hadn't been there before their escapade in the Pyramid. It was no wonder; the man had had the sad fates of his parents laid unfairly at his door. His bones might have been as good as they ever were, but . . .

'You know you can't believe a word that Commander said in there,' Alan said suddenly, urgently, leaning forward. 'You *can't* believe it — you can't even think about it.'

'I wasn't.'

'I know you were: you haven't stopped thinking about it. I know what it's like to be haunted.'

'Well if you stop bleedin' goin' on about it, it might be a bit easier, Alan.'

'Yep. Done.' Alan changed the subject to himself, and found himself crying a little as he told them about Billy's recovery. He focused on the fact that the Idle Hands had been halted in its tracks, that Billy wasn't dead . . .

. . . and the barkeep lit the braziers, and lavender smouldered, and they ate bread and cheese, and Nora told them about the perch she'd had right at the very top of the House, and how you could almost see the shape of the Original Structure as depicted in the maps if you got high enough.

'Somethin' interestin' I heard,' Byron said, later, waving at the barkeep. 'Another pot, please, sir. You remember Skeffington's discussion with the Mother, Alan? And you heard the report of a great reptile causing collapse? Well, since then there's been talk that the Hinning House has dispatched its Beasthunters for the first time in livin' memory.'

'I don't know much about the Hinning House,' Alan said. 'They're a long way away, right?'

'Very far away from us,' Nora said, 'both geographically and spiritually. They wear nothing but crocodile skins and they eat a lot of raw meat. I have heard that they are not without wisdom, but I do not see how that can be, because they only allow men into the House. Of course, it was a man who told me that they are not without wisdom. We are entering into a time of change and I feel as if news from afar should be considered as carefully as news from nearby. Closer to home, Daunt is preparing to take Dok from Churr. Churr is shoring up her defences.'

'Daunt will destroy her,' Alan said, a little sadly. 'Daunt is the Lady Redcapper – the Pale Sadist. She's a force like no other.' He paused and then added, 'Except perhaps the Mapmakers.'

'Churr is putting great faith in the magic of Dok.'

'There is no magic of Dok. There's just . . . *poison*. Broken magic leaching out of broken weapons.'

'Churr thinks she's on to something, although I don't know what. I haven't been down to see her recently.'

'Nora, what's the real deal with you two?'

'What do you mean?'

'She called, and you came – back when she allied herself with us? She said she could secure a Mapmaker, which was you – so how did she do that?'

'She doesn't have anything over me. No favour was owed, there was no debt to repay. We are lovers – no, we are more than that. We are in love.'

'You and . . . Churr? But she's . . . she's not . . . she's not like you.' Of course that sounded stupid, but Alan couldn't really say what he wanted to say. *She's not good, like you.*

Nora had taken his meaning anyway, and her expression was icy. 'When I love a person, I love their core,' she said, 'and their root. And I will love them howsoever their branches grow. I will not stop loving them when they grow twisted in the wind, or when they are cut by men with axes, or when a drought comes and they wither. I will not stop loving them when they grow too big for the world around them and break down walls. I will not stop loving them when they are rent asunder by a storm and crush all those around. *I will not.* If I love a person, then it does not matter what that person does. If I would stop loving them, then it is not love that I feel. Love is terrible, it is terrifying. Do you understand?'

'Yes,' Alan said, after a moment.

'I do not pretend it is not a scary thing,' Nora said, 'but I love Churr, and she loves me. And no, Alan, it means nothing that she slept with you. She can sleep with whomsoever she likes. And she likes a man sometimes. It is not a desire I ever feel myself, but there we are.'

The drinks arrived. Nora waited until the barkeep had gone and then resumed her delivery of the news. 'So there will be a conflict.'

A shadow fell across the table; Alan and Nora twisted to see who had joined them and Byron stood up and gave a small salute.

Skeffington nodded to the group and joined in as if he'd been there all along, 'I have arrived at much the same conclusion, as you know, and so I intend to leave Gleam. According to one of the maps Nora uncovered, there is definitely an outside edge to it, as I have always believed.'

'On the conclusion of my business with my people, I am committed to showing Skeffington the way,' said Nora. 'He understands this.'

'And so I'm going to take Nora to the Mapmaker Council,' Skeffington said.

Nora inclined her head. 'You're going to take me *close* to where the Council *meets* – a meaning different enough to warrant clarification, I think. It is Lutwidge's belief that he will get me there more quickly than I would get there on my own; I think that he is correct in that belief. With his help, I should be able to catch up with the Pyramid envoy.'

'What?' Alan was lost.

'My presence there was seen as an act of war. The Pyramid has dispatched an envoy to notify the Mapmaker Council. I trailed them for a short time as they passed through the area – they are hopeless and they don't know the way, so despite their head start, I should be able to catch up with them easily.'

'And kill them?' Alan asked. 'Not that I think it's the right thing to do, but, y'know, it doesn't bother you so much.'

'No; the envoy means only that my people can prepare. I don't want the Pyramid's moves against them to be a surprise. And besides, I don't mind the Mapmakers knowing I was in the Pyramid,' Nora said. 'In truth, I *want* them to know. I wanted to tell them what I'd found, and that would always have meant telling them where I found it. But it has to come from me. It *has* to.'

'Fuck me,' Alan said. 'I felt like *I* was at the middle of everything, but clearly not. Nora, aren't you worried about Churr? Given how you feel about her? I mean – with this thing with Daunt, and with you having to leave soon? And having to go on such a long journey?'

'Yes, I am, but I have to trust to her strength and her intelligence.' Nora drummed her fingers on the table. 'I have asked her to come with me, but she won't. I wish she would.'

'What are your plans, Alan?' Skeffington asked.

'If I could be of much help to either of you – or to Churr – then I would help. But I'm pretty sure you're both better fighters than I could ever be. I haven't done a hundredth of the exploring that you have. I'm going to stay at Eyes' house – I always loved it there. And I miss him, despite what he did. I like what you said about love, Nora: I think it clarifies feelings of my own that I've been struggling with. I want to take what Eyes had, what he made, and look after it. I want to be close to Billy, and to Marion, should she ever want or need me again. My plan is just to live – to live *well*, to live within reach of those I love. And I'm going to exercise and practise with my crutches.' He sipped from his glass. 'I'm going to stop drinking whisky. I think that's about it.'

'They sound like good plans,' Nora said. 'Do you think the world will let you keep them?'

Alan grinned. 'Green help the world if it comes knocking,' he said. 'When do you leave?'

'Not yet,' she said. 'I still need to recover a little myself.'

17

Haunt

Eyes' house was much as Alan remembered it, except dustier, and the bundles of herbs that had been fresh when he'd helped Eyes hang them were now desiccated and crumbling. A pile of bird muck had accumulated at the end of the table; when he looked up, he caught sight of a nest in the rafters. The corners were thick with webs, and spiders scuttled away as he wheeled through the single room. The bed was behind a curtain; there was a toilet out the back. And most importantly, there were no stairs. First things first, he would have to gather fuel for the stove, and food, of course. And he'd have to clean. He'd had this idea that he could take on Eyes' garden, although he didn't know how he'd considered that might be possible . . . but Loon had said that if he practised . . .

So he'd have to practise with his crutches. That was something else to add to the list. And modifying the crutches – he could tie a feather duster to the end of one of them, for instance. His wheels crunched over a broken pot, knocked off the side by a rodent, perhaps.

He'd been looking forward to getting here; he'd felt as if he'd made some meaningful and important decisions. But now he had arrived, all of the things that he'd been planning – the cleaning, the maintenance, the getting-in-order – felt meaningless. It wasn't that he *wanted* to live in a tumbledown mess; of course he didn't. But . . .

I feel lonely. It was a cold realisation. He thought he'd been looking forward to some time alone – and besides, there was nobody else he could really live with: all of his friends and family were either dead, endangered by his presence or somewhere that he couldn't go. And the thought of making new friends was intolerable.

So he couldn't afford to get lonely, he decided, because there was no solution to it.

He sat still for a long time, and then he reached for the feather duster.

He tried to see Billy every couple of days – he didn't want to bother the boy, but at the same time it was difficult to stay away. It sounded as if Marion was thriving; she'd got herself a job already, managing the House's protection contracts. And Billy was doing well too: he was starting to put some weight back on and his hair had recovered its shine. He still limped and he still spoke slowly, but the colour had come back into his cheeks and a spark had returned to his eyes. In fact, 'returned' might be the wrong word; Billy was looking happier in the House of a Thousand Hollows than Alan had ever seen him.

But Billy was increasingly in a rush to get home. He'd made friends with the few children who also lived in the House, and of course he wanted to play with them. He had lessons to attend, abandoned attics to explore. He had never known freedom like this before, and he was making the most of it. Alan was glad to see him settled, but it was beginning to pain him to think that he was keeping his son from things he'd rather be doing.

'I know you're busy now, son,' Alan said over tea, one afternoon in the Cat, 'so how about we just meet every three or four days instead?'

'How about just once a week?' Billy suggested, brightly.

'Yeah.' Alan laughed because he didn't know what else to do. 'Yeah, of course. Once a week it is.' That evening he took a bottle of Dog Moon back home with him, but it didn't block the pain like it once had; it just made it worse. He finished the whisky and ransacked the house, rooting through all of Eyes' cabinets looking for anything that might be even a little alcoholic, something to take him through and out the other side of the state the Dog Moon had put him in. He found a bottle of *something*, but when he downed a great mouthful it turned out to be some kind of oil and it made him very sick. After waking from a broken, drunken sleep, he laughed at himself and his thumping headache. So Billy had friends — wasn't that exactly what he'd been fighting for all this time, and all the while never daring to hope for it? These were the normal problems he'd feared would always be denied his family — but now Billy could grow up.

Alan was in bed, but not asleep — sleep was still difficult, even though he was beginning to come to terms with his new condition — when, from far away, beyond the rooftop field and the crevasses between ancient buildings, through shattered windows and cracked archways, across all of the wild and strangely shaped spaces that lay between the stones of Gleam and the stars and moons of the sky above, there came the high, thin wail of a crying baby.

Alan slowly froze as he listened to it.

There are babies in the Discard, he told himself at last. *It's nothing to be scared of.*

Eventually the crying faded into nothing. But sleep was gone.

Somehow, shaking, Alan got himself out of bed and got into the chair. He'd been practising hard and was able to transfer himself a little more quickly now. He grabbed the crossbow that he kept loaded and wound by the bed — a gift, delivered to him by Billy, with a note tied around the stock: *Against bandits, given your condition. L & M.* It was a real piece of work, ugly but powerful, with a croc-bone trigger and croc-sinew string and bindings.

He wheeled himself round the long dining table. Embers still glowed orange in the stove; he stirred them into life and added another log before putting the kettle on to boil. He crushed some dried chamomile from Eyes' stock into a strainer, which reminded him of a chore left undone the previous day, and while he waited for the kettle to boil, he went over to check the row of pots that he'd planted up himself. Early shoots were just showing now: chamomile, mint, frogfoot, lemon-leaf. He checked the soil and watered them all.

He sat at the long table and drank his tea by the light of a candle. His hands would not rest. Normally, he would have occupied them by playing Snapper, but Snapper, like Spider, like Eyes, was gone. He'd left the guitar in the stillroom in the Pyramid; it had probably been destroyed by now. At first, the loss had felt trivial compared to everything else – the after-effects of Billy's treatment, the use of his legs . . . But Alan did miss the guitar, though not for the potential career it represented – there was no band any more, hadn't been for a long time now, and he wasn't sure where he would perform on his own, or if he even wanted to. But it had offered distraction during moments like this. For want of something else to do with his hands, he picked up the crossbow from the table. It was a nice machine, but he could hardly play with it.

All things considered, he could have lost more. Billy and Marion were both alive and well, and he was actually allowed to see his son. Nora was alive. And *he* was alive, thanks to his friends. And without friends, the loss of the use of his legs would have proved fatal in the Discard. The chair was a compromise that he could accept; it enabled him to live with a degree of autonomy, to see his son, to get to Market Top, where he could barter for goods, although he was running low on herbs to trade. If Nora hadn't got him to the House, if Maggie hadn't let him in, if Loon had not built the chair . . .

Opportunities for death had been plenty, but he had survived where others had not, and their deaths were . . . *Well*, he thought, *what are they?* To say that those deaths had taken chunks from his own soul felt disrespectful; to suggest that their phantoms haunted him was to play the victim; even to say that he was burdened with guilt implied somehow that his guilt was undeserved. *Perhaps*, he decided, *the simplest way to express it is also the best: I feel guilty, because I am guilty.* He finished the tea and slammed the cup back onto the table. *I feel guilty, because I am guilty.*

The words were too small, too easy. They didn't smother the glimmers of contentment that had been shining deep within him this past week and they should have. He did not *deserve* to be happy. He *did* deserve to be broken, haunted, burdened.

He was pouring another cup of tea from the pot when the baby's cry came again, closer, this time. Alan wheeled to the bed and grabbed a blanket, threw it over his lap and rolled across to the front door and outside. The night sky was clear, but Satis and Corval were only just peeking over the horizon so it was still very dark, though the stars shone bright. The crying had stopped again. Alan watched from just outside his doorway.

Long grass swayed in the warm breeze and fireflies danced. All across the Discard plants were growing greener and insects were growing fatter. The spiders were eating each other, thinning themselves out. It was time for the rains to come, but they hadn't arrived yet. The air was warm and smelled sweet.

There, rising up from the shadows at the far side of the field was a huge dark shape: metal glinting in the starlight, two green glowing eyes. Nora had cut its head off back in the Sanctuary, but obviously it had grown – or otherwise acquired – a new one. Alan braced himself for the cry, but instead the creature itself came racing through the grass towards him.

So this was how it was going to end, after everything he'd been through. Now that he had survived the Pyramid and his family were well, Death had regained its horror. He didn't want to die, but die he would, and painfully, at the claws of this weird, unstoppable beast.

'Where have you been?' he asked, as it drew close.

'Looking for you.'

Alan shuddered at its muddy, grinding voice.

'I lost you in the Swamp, and I have been looking for you since. I have been here several times before, but you . . . you were elsewhere. Not so this time.'

'And what do you want with me?'

It slowed. 'We have had this conversation before, Wild Alan. I want to take your life, as you took mine.'

'But I never took your life,' Alan pointed out, gesturing at it, 'for look, here you are, *here in front of me*, right now!'

'You killed me when you communed with our shared ancestors in the name of Hate. You damned me with the words "*Damned Pyramidders*". You launched an attack and you killed my parents. I was a baby, and you killed me. You were but a child, and you killed me. The killing was in you even then. But there was a warp in the magic, there were elements of me that kept on growing. I took the dust and the debris of the explosion and despite the stasis of my lifeless body, my soul expanded. With hate you killed me and in hate I grew and still grow. I took the hate you killed me with and swaddled myself in it, and it bound to me my cloak of dust.'

'So what are you?' Alan asked. Despite his fear, he genuinely wanted to know.

'I am a suckling babe grown vast and twisted outside of its own body. Something warped into a parody of life by the weapon you used. I absorbed the spirit in which you attacked, and now that spirit powers my haunt.'

'You were just a baby.' Alan thought about Billy as a baby: his big-eyed, red-cheeked boy, soft blond curls at the back of his neck; he thought of his son, gurgling and laughing in his sleep.

'Are you crying, Wild Alan? Are your cheeks wet?' The Clawbaby got closer.

'How old were you?' Alan's voice was muffled by his sleeve.

'Four months.' The Clawbaby's voice was as abrasive as it was in Alan's nightmares; it was like the crumbling of wet stone. 'I was four months old.'

'Green's teeth.' Alan shook his head, trying to clear it. He struggled to get his words out. He had done to families in the Pyramid exactly what the Pyramid had done to his, except that *his* act of violence had come first. It was something he'd long been conscious of, but had shied away from really thinking about it. Yes, it was an accident. And yes, he knew now that the Pyramid had not required the pretext of such an accident to attack Discarders. But knowing those things didn't shake the horror of the consequences.

'I'm sorry,' he said at last.

'Good. I'm glad you are sorry. I am glad you feel guilt. I am here to hurt you, to cause you pain before I kill you. And guilt is pain.'

'It is a mercy that I can't see your true face,' Alan said, 'for that would be the greatest pain.' He wondered if he did really want to see it on some deep, masochistic level; if he wanted to throw oil on the smouldering coals of his remorse.

The Clawbaby let loose a vile gurgling laughter that mutated into a series of short cries and then changed back again into unholy laughter. 'My true face would cause you the greatest pain?' it said. 'Then *look upon it.*'

And as Alan watched, its layers of black dust rags frayed and opened out into a cloud of smoky tendrils that moved indistinctly in the night. The stars behind and above the beast dimmed and then went out as its form thinned and expanded. Something small and white became visible inside the splitting chest cavity. Alan choked, unable to catch his breath at all. Tears streamed down his face as the baby started waving its arms and legs, as if trying to break free of the dust that bound it. As the rags cleared from its face it opened its mouth and screamed. Its reddened eyes were panicked as it howled its fear and thrashed about.

Alan stared. His chest hurt. *He'd* done this – he had put that child in its hell. He shifted the blanket, sighted, squeezed the crossbow trigger and closed his eyes.

The howling stopped.

18

Rainy Season

He couldn't look at what he'd done, but nor could he ignore it. He sat in his chair with his eyes closed until dawn, shaking as the hours passed.

He was awakened by something landing on his face. He opened his eyes and found himself on his back, looking up at the sky. He could still see scraps of bright blue between the black clouds that were roiling in from the west, but he knew they wouldn't last long, not now. The air itself felt wet. The raindrops were fat and warm. There would be thunder and lightning before night fell again. Alan lay there on his back as the rain grew heavier. Soon it was torrential, roaring around him, splashing up from the rooftop on which he lay and turning the ancient loam to mud. The sky was now just a swirling mass of black and grey.

Alan opened his mouth to let the water in.

After a while he pulled himself over, reached out to the chair and managed to get it back onto its wheels. He made sure the brakes were fully engaged, then spent a long time trying to manoeuvre himself off the ground so he could haul his body back into the contraption.

He knew there was nothing for it. He had to look.

He wheeled himself over towards the black mound that had been the Clawbaby, lying just at the edge of the long grass, thanking Green that it hadn't been further away, in the longer grass, where he'd have struggled to push the chair through, or get it close enough to see anything.

Mercifully, the baby was hidden from view by the pile of debris that had made up most of the Clawbaby's being: dust and ash and splintered stone. A claw was splayed out to one side, like the broken wing of a dead bird; close to, Alan realised it was a bundle of wicked, rusty, mismatched blades, some notched, but all long and sharp. They were connected at one end by some kind of spongy tissue; Alan bent down and prodded it gingerly, wondering if it was some kind of rubber or glue – but no, it was organic. Suddenly he realised what it was – a tight web of veins, or something like veins – and he hurriedly dropped the big spongy mass of blood vessels. He remembered how the Clawbaby had killed Spider, the way it had impaled him and then held him over its head, and how he'd watched as the blood had coursed down those blades. It had put him in mind of the Pyramid Bleedings, but it hadn't occurred to him that the Clawbaby would have *used* the blood in any way . . .

The device he'd sent to the Pyramid as a child had

blown a smoking hole in the structure's side and had killed many people. Somehow, via the corruption in its magic, it had created the Clawbaby. He'd learned that much – but he'd never realised that the beast had been created in such a way as to *require* blood.

Obvious questions started filling Alan's head as he followed his own line of reasoning: how many people had this thing killed in order to sustain itself as it looked for him? And if the Clawbaby required blood for its magic, then what was the Pyramid collecting blood for? Its own magic? Or maybe a *different* magic? Perhaps the Pyramid itself was full of great veins and arteries locked away inside the stone, coursing with the mixed blood of all its inhabitants, and all of it rushing . . . *where*?

Of course the blood must be used in the creation of its weapons; that was suddenly obvious. The Alchemists harvested the Pyramidders' blood and used it in their work. They might not – probably didn't – know what they were doing with it, but originally, Alan was quite sure, it would have been used in the Factory's manufacturing, in its enchantments, its powders, its varnishes, in its explosives – like the one he himself had used – and perhaps even in the fungal weapons.

Alan was feeling sick just at the thought of it, but he couldn't let himself dwell on the revelation because there was a death to honour – not the Clawbaby's, but that of the poor young life that had *become* it. The rain was beating away the ash and dust and soon all of that peripheral material which had been animated by hate, as the thing itself had said, would be carried away by the water. The baby's body was still sitting on a mound of detritus and Alan positioned the chair so he could reach down and gather it up from the dirt. He held it in his arms as the storm pounded down around him. He felt like it echoed his grief, spilling out from the confines of his body, which was no longer big enough to hold it. He took the small corpse round to the garden at the back of the house, where Eyes had grown onions, potatoes and carrots in the raised beds he'd built to hold the soil. The earth was turning to mud, which made it easy to dig, but he started working increasingly feverishly until the mud was slopping into his hair, down his arms, into his lap as the rain grew heavier still and the first faint rumbling of thunder came in from far away.

He stopped when he'd excavated a grave deep enough to survive the coming rainy season. Eyes' veg patches had survived a good few seasons, after all . . .

His mind was drifting, but that was okay.

He took off his shirt, wrapped the baby in it and lowered it down into the ground by the sleeves. He tried to think of something to say, but after a bit he decided that anything he might say would be an insult.

He dug the soil back in.

Alan could not settle. He left the house once more, before night had truly fallen and wheeled through the worsening rain. He ignored the pain deep in his muscles, across his back and shoulders. He was getting as good at ignoring physical pain as he had been at ignoring every other type.

He gave a message to the House guard, asking if Billy would come down and see him, but it wasn't his son who appeared; Marion came instead. Alan sat in his chair at the end of the Favoured Bridge, hair plastered flat, watching the distant lightning crack against the nameless metal towers that bestrode the far landscape. Despite the rain, the air was still hot and he hadn't bothered putting a shirt on. The rainwater pouring down either side of the bridge in curtains flashed white every time lightning lit up the sky. Below the falling water nothing could be seen; no light illuminated the great green darkness.

'What do you want now?' Marion said.

'Marion,' Alan replied, turning to see her framed by the archway. It was strange to see her without a robe. She wore leather trousers and a pale shirt, though he couldn't determine the exact colour in the stormlight. 'I was – I'd asked for Billy. I mean, it's good to see—'

'Billy isn't coming to see you, and nor will he any more.'

'What—?'

'I want you to leave him alone, Alan. Oh, I know he seems okay when you see him, but you have no idea of the effort it takes – the energy! – to wear that mask!'

'What—?'

'What you've done to him — those *damned* mushrooms . . . you say they saved his life, but we don't *know* that . . . The fits he has, Alan, the terrible words he screams in the night, the vile things he sees — the *fear* in him. It's an unnatural fear.' Marion came out into the rain. 'I hate you,' she said, 'and that Billy loves you so much makes me hate you all the more. It's so wrong that he bears all that love for a man who's done so much damage to him.'

Alan couldn't say anything.

'If you knew what he goes through *every single day* — if he didn't pretend he was okay for you — you would remove your own self from his life,' she spat. She gestured as she said, 'I'd push you off this bridge right now if it wouldn't get me kicked out of the House. And Billy *needs* me — he's *always* going to need me, thanks to you. But you come back here again and I might not be able to help myself.'

Alan stared after her as she returned through the archway and rounded the corner, out of sight. He wheeled himself right out to the edge of the bridge and looked over it.

19

The Challenger

Alan was drinking chamomile tea in the doorway, watching the streams of water running down from the roof, when he heard a woman's voice. At first he thought he was imagining it; that it was the constant sound of rainfall playing tricks with him, but no, it was definitely there: a female voice. Alan sighed, pinched the bridge of his nose and took the crossbow from the table. He'd been expecting Daunt's people to catch up with him sooner or later. He longed for a drink – or for something stronger; he wanted the kind of unthinking oblivion that he had escaped into so easily in the past. He inserted a bolt into the weapon and wound it up, then rolled over to the door and pulled it open.

Rainwater was cascading down across the open doorway and he got soaked to the skin as he pushed himself forward through it, but he didn't care.

Like the previous night, like every Rainy Season night, it was black out there. The clouds blocked any illumination from the moons and stars completely. He could see small lights across Gleam, but they could only be lit windows; no outdoor fire could survive a night like this. But there was a swaying storm lantern, held by somebody heading towards him. And there was not one voice, but two. That made more sense; people talking to each other. He frowned. He thought he recognised the voices, but it might have just been wishful thinking.

Whoever it was, let them come. He backed inside, lit his own lanterns and let the light spill out the door.

Two figures came to the doorway, both wearing heavy waxed cloaks, big hoods almost covering their faces. 'Come in,' Alan said.

They entered the house and lowered their hoods.

'Alan,' Churr said. 'Can we sit down?'

'You two,' Alan said, laughing with relief. 'By Green, it's good to see you. I half thought you were Daunt's people. Thought maybe my time was finally up.' He pointed at the other chairs with the crossbow, then he put the weapon down. 'Let me pour you some tea.'

'Fucking tea?' Churr laughed. 'You, drinking tea—?'

'I told you,' Nora said.

'Nothing stronger?'

'Not unless you brought anything.' He paused, the pot suspended over the second cup. 'Did you? I could use something stronger.'

Churr shook her head. 'We brought nothing,' she said. 'Well. Nothing to drink.' She looked Alan up and down.

'Got you a present.' She shrugged off the waxed cloak and turned to show Alan what she had strapped to her back.

'Snapper!' Alan yelped, almost jumping forward. 'How the fuck—? Churr, *thank you!*'

'The Arbitrators must have discarded it after finding their comrades bound and gagged,' Nora said, as Churr slung Snapper over to Alan. Alan let his hands fall on the strings, felt a calm descend.

'I found it in the dust when we were circling, looking for Marion and Billy,' Churr continued. 'And Nasha re-stringed it, patched it up a little. You met Nasha, I think, when we broke the Seal; she's a fierce fiddler, knows her instruments.'

'She did a good job. Green knows, Snapper hasn't looked this good in . . . well, ever.' Nasha had replaced the strings, replaced a panel on the body with gutwood and filled and smoothed the crack in Snapper's neck.

'You're not looking so great, though,' Churr observed, sitting down.

'I live.'

'No mean feat, given everything.'

'No.' Alan suddenly looked up from admiring Nasha's handiwork. 'What are you two doing here? I mean, I'm pleased to see you both – *really* pleased; I've been . . . I've been lonely – but don't you both have places to be? You didn't come just to bring me Snapper back.'

'Churr first,' Nora said.

'I . . . I'm glad you made it back out of the Pyramid,

Alan,' Churr started. 'I'm glad Nora made it. You did well. And I'm sorry about your leg.'

'Thank you,' Alan said, then looked at her. 'But you didn't come all this way to tell me that – so what's happening? What's going on with Dok, and Daunt?'

'Fucking hell, Alan! I've come as a friend, but—' She grimaced. 'I'm really fucking *angry* with you. I'm angry, and I'm fucking *terrified*.'

'You know I thought it was mad to start a feud with Daunt – and not just a feud, a full-on *turf war*. She *is* terrifying. You're right to be terrified—'

But Churr was shaking her head. 'I'm not scared of *her*.' She shivered. 'Green's teeth, but it's cold in here – colder than outside. What's going on? Can you get that stove lit? Oh, no, it is lit – so bank it up. Have you been sitting here in the dark and cold all day?'

Alan did as Churr bid, but he didn't answer her questions; he didn't want to talk about the past few days' grim business. 'If you're not scared of Daunt, what are you scared of?' he asked at last. If it was something scarier than Daunt, he didn't really want to know – but presumably this was why Churr was here, and so there was no way round; he'd have to go through it.

'Alan, that night in the room, with the ink? The night we met—?'

'Yes?' He had no idea where she was going with this.

'I think I'm with child.' Churr laughed again, a short sharp bark. '*I think*.'

He froze and then asked carefully, 'Are you sure?'

She muttered, 'Sure enough to tell you.'

Alan turned back to her and realised there was a guarded look on her face. She was waiting to see how he would react before she'd let her own true feelings be known.

'I'm sorry,' he said.

'You're not pleased?'

'I . . . No.' Alan shook his head. His heart was kicking. 'No, I'm not going to lie to you, Churr, much as I suspect it might be wise to. I'm very confused – I really wasn't expecting this. I am not a good father. I mean, I try.' He rubbed his face, took a deep breath, and smiled – 'I'm rambling. The truth is, I'm delighted. I know we didn't intend this, but—'

Churr rose to her feet and slapped him hard across the face. 'It will *kill* me, you fucking idiot!' she yelled. 'You with your fucking Pyramid life, your Safe House life – where you've got people who can *help* you if the child breaks your bones or rips you open on the way out! You're not living in diseased sludge and eating snail and rat for your daily meal, and—'

'And I'm not launching a war with one of the most powerful and sadistic Discard rulers.'

'Yeah! Yeah! Fucking *exactly*!' Churr slumped back into her seat. 'People try not to have kids in the Discard Wild – you *know* that. And yet you stuck your fucking dick in me anyway.'

'You don't want the child, then?' Alan asked carefully.

'I do,' Churr said. She interlocked her fingers across her belly. 'I really do. But trust me to end up making a child *now*, with *you*.'

'Yeah,' Alan said, 'typical.' He ran a hand through his hair. 'I want to be there for you – and for the child,' he said. 'However you want me to be. And you, Nora.'

'We don't need you,' Nora said. 'There is nothing you can do that we cannot. But we thought you should know.'

'No, there is something that Alan can do,' Churr said. 'I need to finish what we started in Dok.'

'What *we* started?' Alan said.

'Yeah. Fucking *yes*. Don't fight with me, Alan. I am not in the fucking mood. It needs finishing, because if I don't finish it, Daunt will kill us all.'

'She probably intends to kill me anyway. If she hadn't been preparing to attack you, she would still have been chasing me down.'

And she'd go for Billy too, probably, now he was out here. And Marion. Why hadn't he realised that before—?

'So what is it you want me to do?' he asked.

'*You* – you can go with Nora.'

'Does Nora . . . want me to go with her?'

'If it makes Churr happy,' Nora said. 'We will worry about each other, but Churr has her people, whereas my people could be a danger to me. On balance, you could probably be more help to me.'

'And you owe her more,' Churr added.

'I vowed not to run away from my family again,' Alan said, 'but I . . . after last night—' He fell silent. Nora's words from the Red Cat came back to him. *If I love a person, then it does not matter what that person does. If I would stop loving them, then it is not love that I feel. Love is terrible, it is terrifying.* He loved Billy and Marion, he knew that. And he understood Marion's anger. She was right to be angry; she was right to tell him to stay away. He would do as she demanded. 'When?'

'Now,' Nora said. 'We will go now. We are to meet Skeffington on an Original Structure road. He has a side-car for you.'

Alan nodded, but then he said urgently, 'Churr, let's just give Daunt what she wants. There is a war coming and we need to build bridges where we can. We need her on our side.'

'*Our* side? If Daunt's on our side, who's on the other?'

'The Pyramid.'

'But you've been in already – you and Nora have been in and got out, and Nora's killed loads of the fuckers, and . . . yeah, maybe they will march against the Map-makers. But if Nora can do all of what she did on her own, then what match will the Pyramid be for the Mapmakers?'

'The Pyramid knows what I can do,' Nora pointed out, 'and they're declaring war anyway. So they must know something we don't.'

'Gleam was built as a weapons factory,' Alan said. 'They created magic weapons, in *vast* quantities — weapons, and explosives and diseases and all sorts of really vicious crap.'

'Who for?'

'That's the question.' Alan drank deeply from his cooling tea. 'And the second question is: do they still have any left?'

Churr looked sceptical. 'If they did, wouldn't they have used them against you?'

'They didn't know Nora was a Mapmaker when they attacked us. They weren't *at war*. I mean, I don't even know if the Pyramidders know what the place is — they could have weapons stored and be completely ignorant of what they can be used for. Or they might not have any left at all. But Churr, Nora searched the Chief Architect's chambers and she stole a lot of records and maps from them — *he* had those documents, and so he must know something . . .'

'So you think we need to roll over for Daunt and ally with her, and then ally with the Mapmakers . . . just in case?'

'Yes,' he said firmly. 'And listen, if the Pyramid really is no match for the Mapmakers, then so much the better; and at least we'll still have prevented a little bloodshed.'

Churr smiled incredulously at Alan. 'You think Daunt will *forgive* us, just because we give back what we took? She'll want *revenge*, Alan — after all, she has her reputation to maintain, doesn't she? I think you've taken one too many blows to the head on your adventures!'

He laughed. 'Maybe,' he said. 'Maybe I have.'

Lightning flashed, making bright white squares of the windows, and the after-images started dancing in front of Alan's eyes. The thunder rolled and for a moment he was back in the Chief Architect's chamber with the black and white tiles stretching out in all directions, all of the white tiles dyed red by the light of the moons coming in through the layers of tinted glass. Babies cried and sun-obscuring pillars of black smoke rose up from the shells of cracked eggs. He opened his eyes and looked at his hands, which were shaking. A horned man sat behind a desk. A young boy twitched on the floor as horns erupted from his head too. A silver-skinned tree thrust its way through an ancient window.

'Let's take peace where we can find it, Churr,' he said.

'All right. I will fight Daunt only if our lives depend on it,' Churr said. 'But I'm pretty fucking sure they will.'

The Chief Architect let Troemius support him as he walked. Larissium, the Chief Alchemist, strode beside them, her footsteps silent. And there was a fourth member of the group, a Ritualist, red cloth wound around her head.

The Architect had lost an eye to that Discard worm's lucky throw, and the sight in the other was not good. The Physic said it would improve, but occasional red flowers still bloomed across his vision and trembled there a while before withering. His headaches were getting worse too, although whether or not that was a consequence of the head injury or a worsening symptom of Idle Hands, he was not sure. His sleep was nothing but lurid dreams; being awake meant pain.

There was grit in his mouth. He spat it out. This kept happening; he was grinding his teeth away. His body and mind were both crumbling.

They were deep down in the Pyramid's core, navigating the most hidden, most convoluted of the black *corridors. Glowstones released their sunlight from the low ceilings and white and pink veins glimmered within the smooth black stone of the walls. The Chief Architect could barely see, and only the Ritualist knew the way. And the Ritualist would not speak! They had to follow her slow, swaying walk, breathing in the smoke from the censer she swung. The Architect felt as if he bore a lightless ocean within himself that was surging ever more violently; he was seething with frustration.*

'There's nobody down here,' whispered Troemius. 'She hasn't come.'

'She will be here, one way or another,' the Chief Architect said. 'Do not doubt her, Troemius.'

But even he was troubled by the silence as they approached their destination. There had been no echoing footsteps, no sweep of robes, no sounds of activity or impatience from within the Sanctum as they stood outside it.

The Ritualist knelt at the Sanctum's magnificent solid brass door and placed the censer on the floor. Then she stood and pressed her sceptre against the patterned metal of the great brass disc. The Chief Architect realised that what he had thought was a distant machine activating was the Ritualist beginning her low chant, a bone-deep hum. She swept the sceptre along the whorls of the pattern on the door, keeping it pressed tight against the metal, her hum breaking out into words that the Chief Architect didn't recognise and could not understand.

The air grew thick and his skin prickled. The light from the glowstones wavered. The heavy incense smoke roiled across the floor as the door started to respond. Certain panels and details started to depress, circles began to rotate, wheels turned. There were mechanisms in everything. The Chief Architect was suddenly nauseous at all the motion in his field of vision; was nothing fixed? Everything moving away from everything else. He felt unsteady.

The door to the Sanctum slowly stripped itself back, layer by layer sliding or rolling or slotting away tidily into the deep wall.

The Ritualist remained outside the Sanctum, her back to the corridor wall at the side of the door. The others entered.

The Sanctum was small, shaped like the bottom half of an hourglass. In its centre was a large, unworked chunk of black stone that looked like an altar. Thick and thin metal pipes rose up out of it and vanished into the ceiling. The curved walls were full of square brass panels with handles set into them: drawers. Between the drawers filigree of many different metals was set into the wall: gold, silver and copper wire tracery that in places thickened into strange platework. Larissium walked around the room, running her long fingers along the winding metal. 'What is this?' she asked. 'What is in this wall?'

'It's—' The Chief Architect's response was interrupted

by a jagged bolt of pain lancing through his head. His knees buckled and he grasped at Troemius. Images of bloodletting flashed through his head. 'Larissium,' he gasped, 'blood – give it to me . . .'

The tall, shaven-headed Alchemist drifted across the room and produced a glass flask from within her robes. She eyed the Architect with faint distaste as he snatched the flask from her hand. Her fingernails were long, red and sharp.

Just looking at the vessel made him feel better; the motion of the blood within calmed him. Anticipating the taste of it banished the white burn from his vision. He twisted the wax seal from the flask and drank greedily. The blood was neither warm nor cold, and it tasted bitter. 'Don't look at me like that,' he hissed at Larissium, feeling strength return to his limbs. 'It's either this, or I drink it directly from one of your bodies.'

'You want it more and more,' Larissium said. 'It is concerning.'

'I do want it more and more,' the Architect agreed, grinning. He wiped blood from his chin and took another swig. 'And yes, it is concerning – more concerning for those around me, perhaps. I have come to accept that my time left in this realm is limited. Speaking of which—'

'Speaking of which,' said a female voice, 'welcome.' It sounded metallic, distorted. It came from above. The Chief Architect smiled grimly as Troemius jumped in shock. He was gratified to see a flicker of surprise cross

Larissium's face, too. 'Thank you for joining me,' the voice said.

'Always a pleasure,' the Chief Architect replied. 'Where are you?'

'I am up at the Apparatus. Move closer to a mouthpiece, please.'

The Chief Architect moved behind the altar and saw there a horn, protruding from one of the metal pipes. 'Here?' he said.

'Much better.'

'Where is she?' Troemius whispered. 'How is she talking to us?'

'Troemius wants to know how this works,' the Chief Architect said into the horn.

'Ancient knowledge,' the voice said, 'and precision craftsmanship. I am up here at the very peak of our Pyramid, speaking into a mouthpiece much like that one. And our Pyramid home takes my voice and carries it tenderly through its body, through its bones, through its winding metal vessels, and delivers it to you. And then it returns your small voice to me. Whisper. Go on, Arbitrator. Just give me a little whisper and I'll tell you what you said.'

Troemius looked at the Chief Architect, frowning, and shook his head. 'I believe her,' he whispered, away from the horn.

'Good,' said the woman. 'You know, I can see you too.'

'What?'

The Chief Architect laughed. 'Our Chief Astronomer looks not only to the stars, Troemius.'

Some of the metal plates on the wall behind Larissium suddenly started shifting to reveal what at first looked like a large, flat glowstone recessed into the wall. Then for a moment it looked like a window; he could clearly see long, thin dark clouds ribboned across a bloody sky. His brain processed the image before he realised it was impossible. Troemius' mouth hung open.

'Every glowstone is a window for me,' said the woman. 'I can see through each and every one. And in the Sanctum, through that lens, you can see back. Here.'

The view transmitted to the lens wheeled across the sky, and then settled on a part of the Apparatus. Even the Chief Architect could not make sense of everything he could see there: frames and machines that hung together in ways difficult to discern, lenses and mirrors and scopes and meters shining and measuring and spinning and reflecting and magnifying each other, cogs and wheels, pistons and weather vanes . . . and a cradle? The Chief Architect peered closer. Yes, the Astronomer herself was part of the Apparatus, nestled deep within it: a small figure with spotless white robes billowing back from her in the high wind, a thousand levers at her fingertips, a cloud of spectacles and small telescopes suspended in front of her face. She waved directly at the Chief Architect and Troemius. 'Mirrors, light and glass,' she said. 'Glass and light and mirrors.'

'So.' The Chief Architect gathered himself. 'I have to tell you, the pain in my head grows ever more debilitating. I long for nothing more than to simply give in; to acquiesce to the urges shuddering through me, and descend into a cannibalistic frenzy. I know it is coming – I know it will happen. But there is something else I need to achieve first.'

'Your condition is not the only factor,' said the Astronomer.

'Indeed not. How long do you think we have left?'

'It's time to go. Perhaps the ideal time has already passed.'

'Go where?' Troemius asked.

'Quiet,' the Chief Architect snapped.

'We don't have enough blood,' Larissium said.

'Our Arbitrator needs to acquire it for us,' the Astronomer replied. 'Is that not his role?'

'Yes,' the Architect said, nodding at Troemius. 'It is his role. So what have you seen?'

'The tipping point may be here sooner than we thought. Something has emerged. See.' The Astronomer's voice was weirdly dissonant, and did not fit with the woman visible in the lens. But then the woman was gone and the view was wheeling again, as the Astronomer manipulated the Apparatus, pointing the telescope somewhere else.

The Chief Architect, Larissium and Troemius gazed into the lens at a view of the black, jagged skyline of

Gleam. Something slid across the field and the view was instantly magnified; the same thing happened again, and again, each time the view jumping dizzyingly forward across leagues of space.

They were looking at a pale tower with turrets sprouting from it like the branches of a tree growing out from the trunk. The tower was red in the light of the sunset.

'What is it?' said the Chief Architect. 'I don't have time for guessing. What about the tower?'

'Behind it. The darkness.'

The Chief Architect stared. The darkness was moving: a cloud of black smoke? Or – no, something solid was moving past the tower. The Chief Architect's eyes widened as the tower started to tilt. The whole scene was silent, and so difficult to read; but yes, the tower was being pushed aside as if it were nothing. The great black shape was not smoke, not a shadow, not just an empty space between ruins, but . . . what?

It looked like a building – like a black pointed roof with chimneys protruding from it . . . but no, they weren't chimneys, and it wasn't a roof: it was a ridged back.

The Chief Architect frowned. 'It's happening,' he said. 'What was buried is returning.'

'Yes. So, we need to go.'

'Troemius,' the Chief Architect said, turning to the Arbitrator. 'The war that the Mapmaker has triggered will not be simply a killing exercise – who can kill more, who is stronger . . . It would be that, but for the fact that

our time here is coming to an end. I am not the only one who must depart for another realm. All us Pyramidders have to leave now. We have unleashed something, and there will be yet more to come, and our Pyramid walls will no longer be enough to keep us safe. But for us to leave, we need magic. And for the magic, we need blood. So we must use this war as an opportunity to harvest: for the Pyramid. For all of us.'

Troemius hesitated. 'We've already stepped up the frequency. We're now at—'

'No, we're no longer talking about taxation. We're talking about a war.'

'We don't have enough harvesters. We can all go out and kill, but we can't all go out and exsanguinate. We don't have the—'

'Yes, we do: we have the tools and we have the weapons. It was our purpose, long ago, to make weapons — we just haven't been able to use them, because of the magic in them, for fear of reaching the tipping point that it turns out we may already have reached. And because . . . they're overtly unpleasant.'

The Ritualist entered the room and placed her sceptre on the altar. All of the locked drawers sprang open. Troemius jumped.

'What's wrong, Troemius?' the Architect asked. 'You seem uncomfortable. Are you reluctant? Do you want your people to die?'

'No!'

'Good. Because they will, if you do not do as I now command. That great reptile the Astronomer showed us is only the beginning. There is a magic in the Swamp that will erupt and consume all of us, Discarder and Pyramidder alike, as if we were equal. All I want is to save our people from that fate before it's too late. And before I myself have to die. And I want you to help me. Do not balk now, Troemius.'

'No.' Troemius composed himself. 'I will do as you bid. I always will.'

'The war will be nasty, brutish, and short. For them, at least. It has to be. I don't deny it: the weapons are cruel. But there's no longer anything to lose.'

'To die for us is the most they're good for anyway,' Larissium added. 'To give up their weak blood for us – for their betters – is as noble an act as they're capable of. And besides, they brought it upon themselves. They invaded us. That Mapmaker broke the pact.'

'That she did,' the Chief Architect agreed. He swirled the last of the blood in the flask. He put the flask to his lips and shivered as the blood spilled over his tongue. He swallowed the last drop and grinned at the room. 'That she did.'

Epilogue

Alan changed and packed a bag, though he did not have much to take — Snapper, his few clothes, the crossbow, some bolts. He loaded up his chair up with the last of the root vegetables from Eyes' storage room, then packed in tea, herbs to cook with and smokes. He rolled up a bunch of knives in a cloth and slipped an extra one into his boot, just as he had when he'd set off for Dok the first time. Churr produced a waxed cloak like the ones she and Nora were wearing and he put it on.

Nora and Churr took turns pushing the chair to where Skeffington awaited them in the empty premises of The Cup and Skull. The Carcase shone dimly in the green light. Another bike stood next to it, its rider mountainous and unidentifiable in layers of leather and cloth. The standing water in the long concrete trough looked as if it were boiling, so hard was the rain hammering down into it. Skeffington leaned against his bike. He was wearing leathers, goggles and cap. Alan wheeled himself over to the bike, giving Churr and Nora some time to themselves to say goodbye.

'We'll need to fold up the chair,' Skeffington said. 'There are straps, look. Nora will sit behind me. We've got plenty of storage.' He gestured at the many and varied panniers. 'We're going somewhere unusual, it appears.'

'I . . . I don't know anything about where we're going,' Alan said, realising it for the first time. 'I just don't want to be here any more.'

Skeffington laughed. 'We're going a long way out,' he said, moving around the bike to help Alan out of the chair and into the sidecar. 'There are *creatures* out there – it gets really very strange. It might be too easy to lose yourself, if that's what you're looking to do.' He lifted Alan onto the edge of the car.

Alan hoisted first one leg and then the other, swinging them over until he could slide into the seat. It was almost ludicrously comfortable.

The second biker lifted goggles, pulled down the scarf and waved.

'Byron!' Alan exclaimed, delighted. 'You're here!'

''course I'm bleedin' here,' Byron shouted. 'I'm a bleedin' fool, it appears!'

'Are we ready?' Nora said, appearing beside the bike.

'We are,' Skeffington replied as the chair collapsed down and he strapped it to the sidecar. Then he busied himself strapping Snapper down too. Alan watched closely, satisfying himself that the guitar was secure.

When Alan turned around to say goodbye to Churr she was already gone. Skeffington lowered himself onto the bike and Nora jumped on behind him. As Alan placed the crossbow in front of him, pointing forwards, he wondered if he was doing the right thing, but then Skeffington ignited the engine, it turned over and the Carcase leaped forward and the thunderous sound of the machine in that long dark concrete canyon blasted all thought from Alan's head.

The water on the ground erupted into spray and obscured the world from view.

Alan held the crossbow very, very tightly.

THE END

Wild Alan's story concludes in

The Pyramid Wish